I Can See You

(Emma Willis 1)

A Novel
by

Joss Landry

Book Beatles LLC
1201 N Orange St Suite 700 #7417
Wilmington DE 19801-1186

Book cover design: Ida Jansson of Amygdala Design
ISBN: 978-0-9960441-9-6 :Print
ISBN: 978-0-9960441-5-8 :E-book.

Publisher's Cataloging-In-Publication Data
(Prepared by The Donohue Group, Inc.)

Names: Landry, Joss.
Title: I can see you : a novel / Joss Landry.
Description: Wilmington DE : Book Beatles LLC, [2014] | Series: Emma Willis ; book 1
Identifiers: ISBN 978-0-9960441-9-6 | ISBN 978-0-9960441-5-8 (ebook)
Subjects: LCSH: Children--Psychic ability--Fiction. | Clairvoyance--Fiction. | Only child--New Jersey--Newark--Fiction. | Kidnapping--New Jersey--Newark--Fiction. | Serial murderers--New Jersey--Newark--Fiction. |
  LCGFT: Detective and mystery fiction. | Thrillers (Fiction)
Classification: LCC PR9199.4.A54 I33 2014 (print) | LCC PR9199.4.A54 (ebook) | DDC 813/.6--dc23

VERY SPECIAL MENTION

I am grateful for my husband Gilles' devotion. He is steadfast
a powerful motivator and believes in my stories. In short,
he has slowly become the voice that drives me.

My children and grandchildren also drive me onward to
improve,
and not merely to do more, but to become more than I am.
My personal cloud of angels.
Thank you to Ida Janssen for making this beautiful cover.

Thank you to all the prolific authors, beta readers and editors
who spent time on this book polishing away the cobwebs.
Last, but most important, thank you, Rhabbouni for walking
beside me.

Joss Landry is also the author of :
Mirror Deep
Exhale and Reboot
Ava Moss, coming soon.
And the author of Emma Willis Book II also coming soon.

If you enjoyed this book, please be so kind as to leave a review.
A review is the greatest praise an author can receive. Thank you!

REVIEWS:

FIVE STAR REVIEWS:

<u>Winner of New Apple Book Award for Best Fiction 2015.</u>

I love mixed genres, and this paranormal thriller offered the best of two worlds: it was fast-paced, tension filled and impossible to put down. (Amazon reader)

A gripping, paranormal suspense novel. One of those books that once you get started you just can't put them down. (A. Safer)

I read the description and the reviews so I decided to take a chance on the book. I'm glad I did. (J. Rosone)

I Can See You is a suspenseful and beautiful haunting detective novel and kept me on the edge of my seat with all the twists and excitement right down till the end. (C. Walsh)

Joss Landry, author of the book "I Can See You," writes a compelling novel. The writing is impeccable. (M. Pro)

I really enjoyed this book. To begin with I wondered if it was going to be a YA novel and I wasn't expecting that from the description which tempted me to buy it. (Books are Best)

One

Nightmare

*E*mma twisted her head side to side. She moaned, powerless to change her fate as an unfriendly force dragged her and pulled her along in spite of her protests. Her silent pleas weren't caused by anything she found. Empty haze surrounded her until the long corridor began to take shape and revulsion beat a warning throb inside her head, the pounding in tune with her frightened heart.

Recognition heightened her fear. The lone light bulb dangling on its rope swinging left to right reminded her not to come any further as did the stench of rotting wood. An unseen force yanked her all the way inside this time, making the moans and whimpers drifting toward her appear childlike. She wondered if the cries echoing around her came from the room itself.

She struggled to turn around, to return from where she'd come. By now she realized this trip was a mind trap, her body uninvited to the usual nightmare. Yet she could not shake the weight of doom keeping her prisoner while it moved her forward. She peeked through tear stained eyelids and glimpsed a door which creaked as it opened slowly, revealing nothing more than a black hole she had seen before and from which she might never emerge.

In the doorway, familiar grunts and a ghoulish sound wafted toward her and at once she sensed the painful memory of the sight sprawled before her.

Previously she'd refused to go beyond this point, closing her eyes and screaming to make the visions stop. Now with the timbre of her voice imprisoned in fear little choice remained but to weather a mounting fever as she entered the wicked void.

Inside she stared at a gray-haired man down on all fours like a rabid dog hunched over a small child her eyes wide and dry with terror. Emma attempted to scream, but anger had taken hold of her, anchoring her to the one-room hell as though she couldn't leave without expending outrage.

With all the strength she could muster from the depths of her young soul, Emma yelled for the man to stop and leave the room. She closed her eyes and prayed to be allowed to leave. Yet by some strange occurrence, the madman turned and spotted her.

She wondered how the man was able to see her. She inventoried a round nose broad face with an eyebrow higher than the other as though he wore some grotesque mask. "Who are you?" he muttered. "How did you get in here?"

She lost her words. Emma could not believe he was actually talking to her. When he stared at her legs without feet, his eyes grew as big as her friend Tommy's oxblood marbles the white streaked with red threatening to rip out of his head and hunt her down.

He took a deep breath and reached for her yelling, "Witch— You're a witch. You wretched, filthy little bitch. I'll show you." His voice trembled with menace. "Guess who's next?" His laugh shut her eyes tight, and the scream rose out of her with the faint breath she had left.

She was still screaming when she sat up in bed, in her own room. The old elm branches swayed against her window soothing her to a makeshift calm. A knock on the door and her mother came in, smiling as she did. "Bad dream again, Emma?"

She nodded, her voice tied up in knots inside her throat and her body still trembling.

Eloise sat on the bed and draped her arm around Emma's shoulders. "Want to talk about it?"

Emma shook her head her eyes slowly adjusting to the comfort of her room. The light from the hall poured in to cast a glow of pink on the armoire where she stored her favorite books and keepsakes. "I don't remember anymore," she whispered.

"That's the thing about nightmares when you're ten years old. They fade quickly and don't leave a trace." Her mother kissed her brow sorting through the tangled damp meshes clinging to her forehead. "Get some rest, sweetie."

"Good night, Mom."

The door closed again, and darkness returned. Emma sank into the pillows her heart bouncing back and forth inside her chest as though the slippery organ didn't want to be there. She yanked the blanket up to her nose even though June nights were warm and humid. She doubted she'd go back to the awful dungeon tonight. Yet, she still worried about the vile man personally addressing her. Then again in dreams, anything was likely to happen. Didn't mean he'd actually seen her, or knew who she was. Didn't mean he was real either.

***

Early morning three days later, Hank Apple enjoyed a moment's peace as he stood in the small office he shared with his partner, their two desks facing each other. Door closed he stood by the glass partition on the south wall. A view of the precinct slowly filling up with the morning crew held his attention.

He'd concocted a herb mixture he readied to gulp down when Matthew Logan rammed through the place as though mowing a lawn, the intrusion prodding Hank to turn abruptly and spill green goo all over his white shirt.

"What the hell are you doing?" Hank shouted. "Sorry, Hank. Didn't know anyone was in here."

"This will never wash out." Hank grabbed a paper towel to blot the stain on his shirt.

"I'm just so fricking upset." Matt slammed the door closed and began pacing, rubbing his bald head as nerves took over. "What is that goop anyway?"

"Plants … never mind. What the hell is wrong with you?"

Matt stopped pacing. He seemed to hesitate. Fists at his side he announced, "Another orange bag was found—in a construction site dumpster."

"Fuck!" Detective Apple's yell bounced off the walls and smacked him in the face unanswered and trailing a loaded silence. "Frickin piece of shit." Hank slammed his fist into a filing cabinet and dropped into the first chair he found. Taking a deep breath, he covered his face with his large hands his six-foot-three frame unable to prevent a shudder confronted with another child's death.

He cursed the weakness of being trapped under the weight of one more body bag dropped on his doorstep. "How long ago?"

"An hour."

"Estimated time of death?"

"None yet. Maintenance said dumpster was likely emptied last week. One thing they do know for sure. Dumpster was clean then. We'll have to wait for the Coroner to say." Matt polished the top of his head with a shaky hand. "We may be getting close to the bastard."

"A week or more behind the prick," Hank muttered. "Might as well be a lifetime, one more life." He stared up at the ceiling formulating a vow "Third little girl in three months. This is where we nail the pig." He turned toward Matthew. "Let's put all we've got on this."

Two

The Ride Home

*E*mma Willis blinked at Forest Hill's affluent stone mansions going by as she remembered the essay on Newark she handed in class a couple of weeks ago.

Unconsciously, she pressed on her right arm to ease the soreness from a red welt the size of a bee sting, a little lower than her shoulder. Emma glanced at the bandage around her right tibia just inches below the knee. A little cleaning and a few stitches had eased the throbbing.

She caught her breath drawing an oddly shaped blotch in the car window and couldn't prevent her thoughts from straying to another pain that gnawed at her, one the size of ten tetanus shots and painful enough to drown out all other concerns in her life. Of course, no vaccine or needle would prevent or protect her against this specific ache as though the symptoms might be contagious … or dangerous, she being the only person the curse would hurt. For now, she couldn't even complain about the problem. The mystery needed to remain a secret.

Her long brown hair, yellow these days from the sun's harsh glare, appeared darker in the car window, and she wondered if her eyes might not be better served by her natural brown hair. They'd certainly be less dark, not seem so big which she found gave her face one of those lost worried expressions. Sometimes she thought the contrast of her eye color might be too much for the rest of her pale complexion.

The large, luxurious looking properties all but disappeared as they traveled north. Emma spotted rickety lopsided sidewalks preceding her own neighborhood in the older and more unkempt section of Forest Hill. Through the walkways' weather-beaten cracks, blades of grass and dandelions had sprouted making the pavement threadbare like an old carpet worn from too many years of wear and tear.

"Emma, you're kind of quiet back there. Are you all right, sweetie?"

Emma nodded without looking at her mother as always amazed by the differences in her parents.

A soft sigh escaped her as she stifled a moan. They were headed North-East toward Heller Parkway, and the large homes fast became eyesores while some appeared ready to topple from lack of repair which rendered them drafty in winter and hot and humid in summer, all facts she was well aware of.

Maybe houses were like families she thought. They needed maintenance and constant upkeep. She didn't want to think about her father's words that their house would cost more to tear down than the money a sale might bring. What would this say about their family?

She began to recognize her neighborhood, not that she had permission to bike this far—ten years old and her parents still treated her as though she were seven, unlike her best friend Amelia allowed to bike all the way to Branch Brook Park on her own. She sighed reminded of her latest physical torment.

"The nurse said you should move your arm, sweetie, get the blood flowing to the muscle. Are you doing that?"

Tetanus shot hurt more than the scrape she thought. What did this say about the medical system? Besides, the car didn't leave her much room to stretch. "I'm rubbing it, Mom. It's working."

"Don't be so gloomy, honey. You can show Amelia your spelling trophy tomorrow."

She smiled not wanting to worry her mother. "I miss her, Mom. It's not the same when she's gone." Amelia and her twin sister went to private school. They came home early every Friday, and first thing after class, Amelia would be at her school to walk her home when they caught up on all the gossip.

The car made a sudden stop at one of the busier intersections. Traffic had turned frantic now. School buses invaded the surrounding streets as did parents picking up their children. Strangely, an overwhelming amount of police cars parked everywhere seemed to be creating more traffic.

Her mother turned up the car radio's volume, seemingly interested in the commentator's story.

"This just in on the earlier kidnapping, Ted. They've managed to stabilize the mother after pulling her out of the car."

"That's something, Jane. Any news of the little girl?" "Police are still combing the area. No names have been released."

"For those of you just tuning in, a little girl barely out of school was dragged into a stranger's car while her mother waited to take her home. The mother called 911 and barreled down the street after the speeding vehicle. We can only guess she tried to keep up with the assailant when another driver struck the passenger side of her car, sending her vehicle into a violent tailspin ..."

Her hands pressed against her ears to block out the story, Emma tried to stop the visions from coming. They terrified her at times, much worse than those horror movies her parents forbade her to watch. Only this time, pictures didn't roll out as the gory images she feared—just terribly sad. She wiped a tear rolling down her cheek, and as she caught the cars honking behind them, she witnessed her mother lift both hands in a show of helplessness. The light had turned green, but cars weren't moving.

Emma peeked at the driver directly aligned with her window. She spotted the round nose, the wavy shoulder-length gray hair and a round hairline above a sloping forehead.

When he turned her way, she couldn't wipe the terrified glare off her face. She undid her seat belt and ducked in the bottom of the car. The effigy of the dream she'd had just a few short days ago zigzagged through her mind—as in blood dripping from dirty fingernails. Emma stifled a moan and jabbed her fists in front of her eyes to block the pictures. They just kept coming, screams, a hit in the face, and flash images of horrifying shades of darkness.

"Good afternoon, Officer. Is anything wrong?" Her mother's voice broke the spell. Emma remained crouched on the car's floor, her legs weak and her heart beating fast.

"Looking for someone. I guess you haven't heard."

"Actually, I have. Do you think this man might still be around here?"

"What we're attempting to find out, ma'am. License and registration, please." He took them from her. "You alone?"

"Just me and my daughter," she turned as she said this. When she peered through the space between the seats, Emma observed her mother's eyes round with surprise.

"Emma, where are you?" Emma chose to remain hidden. She didn't want to give the man in the next car reason to recognize her or know her name. She detected panic in her mother's voice, so she owned up.

"I'm here," she said rising a little hesitantly when encountering the policeman's frown. The badge on the police officer's chest caught her eye as it gleamed brightly in the afternoon sun.

She stared into his eyes and felt the cold sensation of utter emptiness as though she stood on the verge of a precipice staring down into a deep hole. She was acquainted with the odd sensation, the same she'd experienced a couple of weeks before Granny Dottie's soul had left for greener pastures, as her grandmother was fond of saying whenever she talked of dying. Was this policeman getting ready for the flight?

"What were you doing in the bottom of the car?"

Emma stared into the police officer's strange, questioning eyes and forced a smile. "Picking up my lucky penny. I dropped it on the floor." Slowly she opened the palm of her right hand and nestled in the center appeared a bright and shiny new penny.

He nodded. Emma sensed him relax somewhat. Emma regained her seat. She buckled her belt and glanced at the car next to theirs also being searched. After the policewoman searched the back seat, she even checked the trunk of his vehicle before she slammed it shut.

"You can go, ma'am," Emma heard the policewoman say. Glancing at the driver a little more, she found he did resemble a woman. Maybe she'd imagined the whole thing.

Nevertheless, when the driver turned to stare directly at her, she turned her face quickly and murmured a little gratitude when her mother promptly drove away.

"Emma, what were you thinking, hiding in the back? I bet that policeman thought I had kidnapped you or something. All those questions." She sighed visibly distraught.

Emma hoisted her shoulders hoping the discussion would end. She had no way of explaining the aversion she'd had of the other driver. The curse again which Granny Dottie had warned her not to mention to anyone, no matter what the consequences, not if she didn't want to spend the rest of her life ridiculed and alone.

Good thing she hadn't made a fuss about the man—or woman. She would have ended up the fool again which happened to be one of the reasons she and her father did not get along. Her mother had once told her she'd cried wolf too many times. Oh, she'd been right more than her share. In fact, what actually angered her father was the curse of sight she'd inherited from his mother, Granny Dottie.

"Goddamn it, Eloise. She's not going to turn into my mother. I won't let that happen. The only way to stop this is to nip the craziness in the bud before insanity takes over her whole life—our whole lives. I'll whop the damn thing out of her if I have to."

How hard would the whopping be if he discovered she held the power to do a little more than sense situations? A secret even Granny Dottie had never realized.

Her father's harsh words had scared the truth out of her for good. Besides, Granny Dottie was gone two years now. And it was no fun practicing since she'd passed away. Being alone, the secret terrified her.

"Emma will you please answer me. I'm talking to you, and

you're ignoring me."

"Sorry, Mom. I didn't mean to cause trouble. Just tired of sitting … and my arm is sore."

"Poor baby. How's your leg?"

"Better." She hated lying to her mother, but if she didn't come up with some explanation she'd tell her dad about the incident.

The sound of her mother cooing comforting words reassured her. A long sigh escaped her when she realized her mother wasn't angry.

She stared at their house appearing in the distance. Her dad called it a big mess. Well, the siding might need paint and the windows a little cleaning, but she loved the big corner lot, and the giant elm as the tree brushed its branches across her bedroom window. The towering presence comforted her on stormy nights. Her father had hung a tire from its strongest bough, and she would swing on it for hours during summer afternoons, the shade of the branches encircling her as Emma imagined the limbs to be those of a guardian's loving arms.

"We're home, sweetie."

Her mom's voice appeared a little shaky, but the warm smile she spotted in the rear view mirror told her she was in a good mood.

"Hey, Mom. Grandma Abby's car is here. I hope Aunt Franka is with her." She loved her mother's sister. She was a chic and together career woman who never talked down to her.

"I doubt Aunt Franka is here, sweetie. She's in class this time of day."

<u>Three</u>

Emma's Family

*A*bigail Tichy had let herself in with the key she'd insisted Patrick Willis give her. Emma had caught her grandmother say that Eloise being her daughter she wasn't about to ring any bell or knock on the front door to wait like a stranger for someone to answer.

Emma enjoyed this about her grandma Abby, the fact she didn't need to hide or withhold anything about herself. She admired her freedom to take charge of her destiny more than anything especially since she'd led a colorful life, and while some whispered behind her back she ought to be more discreet about all the skeletons in her closet, she would say, "Life is grand, my darlings. Love it and live it. Regrets about all the things you didn't do are going to plague you when you're old and gray."

She'd married a man twice her age, a Czechoslovakian business person who had long passed away and left her a hefty nest egg liable to last her the rest of her life—an accomplishment for which she was most proud.

Eloise hung up her bag on a hook inside the hall entrance. Emma followed locking the door behind her.

"Where's my granddaughter? Where is she?" echoed throughout the house. "Come here, my darling."

The tall, lithe woman came toward her and soon, two slim, strong arms encircled her. A stab of pain traveled through Emma's arm when her grandmother accidentally squeezed the swell from her shot. Then one of her eyes went blind the whole side of her face smothered against her grandma's round bosom. She took in the faint intoxicating smell of Giorgio and gave into the effusion hugging her back.

"My sweet darling," Abigail cooed. "How are these folks treating you?" She pushed her away to catch a better look. "My God she's beautiful, El."

However, her mother had gone to the kitchen without Abigail realizing this.

"Eloise, where are you?" She smiled and winked at Emma.

Wrist bangles clinking against her waist and her grandmother's arm firmly wrapped around her ribs, and Emma had no choice but to follow.

They didn't go far. Eloise came roaring back. "You brought supper again, Mom? Patrick's going to flip."

"He wouldn't dare. You've been downtown at that awful clinic waiting for hours. Then stuck in traffic. Of course, you had no time to prepare anything nutritious. I ask you. What's more delicious than Paella Valenciana?" She turned toward Emma with a smile. "A delicious combination of seafood, rice, chicken, and yummy vegetables in a yummy sauce." She hugged Emma saying so.

Gripping Emma's chin, she shook her face. "Look at this beauty. I told you, El. You should send her photos to Wilhelmina's. I can put in a word. My friend Sheila sits on the board of their New York office. Did you ever see such symmetrical features, such huge, deep oval eyes?"

Her mother smiled at her and nodded. She flicked her hair. "I prefer the ale tone of her eyes, at least when her hair doesn't get bleached so much by the sun."

So that's where the thought came from Emma pondered. She wondered how many of her ideas were original. Did kids go around unknowingly adopting statements mentioned left and right until they fashioned a personality of their own? Which would be the reason why one would have a mother's taste or another a father's character? And if children didn't do this, where did they get their impressions?

The sound of a key scratching the latch got everyone's attention.

"He's home," her mother announced somewhat dramatically. "It's the second time you've brought food in as many weeks, Mother. He's going to have a fit."

"Let him. I don't care."

Emma stared up at her grandmother. Of course, she didn't care. Her grandma would exchange words with her father. He would struggle to remain polite—well as polite as his nature allowed— then Grandma Abby would go home, and she and her mom would bear the brunt of it.

"Abigail." Her father nodded. He walked over to Eloise and kissed her on the cheek. "Hard day?" He stared at Emma as he said this.

"No. Everything is fine." Eloise held Emma's hand. "Emma was a real trooper. Didn't even blink from the shot."

He nodded while mussing up her hair. He bent to check the bandage on her leg and the bruise on her arm. "This had to hurt.

Does it still burn?"

She pinched her lips and shook her head.

"Well," Patrick added. "You're being brave about this. I hope you've learned your lesson. No more riding in the old quarry."

"I have." She gave him the emphatic nod she thought would please him.

"Good." He put his briefcase down by the door, walked past them and grabbed the mail Eloise had plopped on the coffee table.

A quick glance later he mumbled. "Bills." He dropped the stack on the table to rub the back of his neck. "Lunch with a client was canceled. I'm so hungry. Got hunger pains on the drive home." A flaming redhead, any part of her father's body not covered from the sun would always look like cooked lobster. Emma detected the freckles on the back of his neck appeared green.

"Mother brought dinner," Eloise said, and Emma sensed how tightly her mother braced herself.

His lips thinned and his eyes narrowed. He turned toward Abigail, who stuck out her chin in defiance.

"Well." He seemed to hesitate. "I guess this time is okay." He stared at Eloise and walked over to her putting an arm around her shoulders. "I had visions of coming home and you having to open cans of something."

"Of course, I—we just got home ourselves. Luckily Mother was here when we arrived."

Emma saw her mom bite her bottom lip regretting the last sentence—another delicate subject with her father—relatives traipsing about his home when he wasn't there.

But he said nothing and marched her off to the kitchen. "Something I like, I hope?" He added his tone gruff.

"Your favorite, actually," Eloise added. Then she gasped with surprise, shock on her face. "Franka what are you doing here?" Eloise turned toward her mother and questioned her with raised eyebrows.

Abigail hesitated to raise her arms to free Emma. Franka was laying out the dishes and the food on the table. The aroma was delicious. Emma sprang to give her a hand. "Aunt Franka," she squeaked with pleasure. "I'm so glad you're here."

"Hey, munchkin." She flashed her best smile.

"Franka wasn't feeling well today. She had a doctor's appointment." Abigail added.

All eyes were on Franka. "True. I've been in your bathroom all this time," she said with a smile. "I think I ate something that didn't agree with me. Anyway, they can do without me for one day over there."

Patrick thundered. "You should have left well enough alone. Your college year finished in April, for God's sake. End of June and you're still at it."

Franka dispensed the silverware. "A little extra cash never hurts, Pat. I'm the only earner in my family. Besides, I enjoy the annex and teaching remedial math. It's more personal and so much more rewarding than addressing Pythagorean's theorem with an auditorium filled with students I never get close to."

Patrick didn't add anything. For some reason, Aunt Franka often had the last word with her father, something else Emma liked about her.

Silence fell around the table as everyone savored the delicacies. Emma watched as they dug in with gusto. She loved it when people came together to pay tribute to some function they all enjoyed. She found gazing at the family portrait more filling than eating, filling her with a sense of peace and with the notion that for a moment in time, right here was where she most wanted to be.

"Emma, why are you picking at your food?" Patrick asked. "Eat. It's delicious."

"I am, Daddy. Chicken is tender and tasty. Thanks, Grandma."

They all turned and thanked Abigail again.

Eloise put her fork down to gather more rice from the bowl. "Emma and I were stopped by a policeman today," she announced.

The message dropped like a bomb numbing the others.

Emma threw pleading eyes at her mother, and Eloise winked her way with a surreptitious nod. "He was searching the cars for the little girl who disappeared."

"Not another one?" Abigail scoffed. "What is this world coming to?" She reached to squeeze her granddaughter's hand.

"I heard about it," Patrick grunted. "Crazy. If you ask me, soon we're going to have to keep our children under lock and key. Homeschool them if we have to."

Eloise put her fork down to address her husband. "I was thinking, maybe I should arrange transportation with the Kramer's. Melanie is in her class and Michelle drives by here every day on their way home."

"What good would that do, sis?" Franka wiped her mouth with her napkin. "News mentioned the little girl was dragged into a car, not far from where her mother waited. Apparently, mother sits in her car day after day and never misses to pick her up."

"You heard about this, Franka?" Abigail asked. "Hum, hum."

"Well, I say you let me pay for Emma's tuition so she can attend the private school her friend Amelia goes to—the only viable solution." Abigail seemed angry.

"Mom, this is not the time." Eloise showed signs of biting the inside of her lip when Emma eyed the smoke stack billowing over her father's head.

"Abigail. I've told you before, and I'll tell you again. Your generosity is noted. But I can take care of my family." Patrick dropped his fork on his plate to drum his fingers on the table.

Abigail's mouth formed an epithet or two then she spotted Emma's pleading eyes and smiled instead. Turning toward Eloise, she added, "This is not the end of the discussion."

Emma noticed her father taking a couple of deep breaths. Then silence befell the group.

"No one has anything to drink," Franka said.

Emma loved her for trying to break the tension. Franka scraped her chair away from the table, got up and asked, "What would you all like?"

"I'll help you, Aunt Franka." Emma edged her lanky body between the wall and the table and bounced up to take the glasses she distributed all around.

"Thanks, Munchkin." Franka smiled. "Hey, I didn't get a hug from you today."

You didn't have to tell her twice. Aunt Franka wanted a hug she would get a hug and a half as Emma wrapped her arms around her aunt's waist in a tight squeeze. At this moment, Emma sensed the wild, erratic beat of a third heart between them, one belonging to the vision of deep blue eyes, blond curls, and pudgy little arms.

Pulling away, Emma ran her hand against Franka's flat stomach. "A beautiful little girl," she whispered. Then looking up at her aunt she added, "You're carrying a baby, a baby girl."

The tension Franka had eased suddenly drew to a pitch as all eyes veered on Emma. Lips pinched, Emma's eyes remained shut tightly. The sentence she'd been unable to prevent had poured out of her unchecked. Now, she feared her father's anger.

Gently, Franka raised her chin to stare into her eyes. At least, she was smiling Emma thought. "How do you know that?"

Checking the others around the table, Emma realized all eyes were now on Franka. Relieved, she said. "I had a dream last week about a little cousin with cute blond curls."

Eloise dropped her fork and covered her mouth with her hands her eyes wide with disbelief. "Oh," she got up and walked toward Franka. "My baby sister's going to have a baby," she cried shedding a few tears. She hugged Franka and cradled her in her arms for a few seconds. Then she turned toward Emma. "You're going to have the cousin you dreamt about."

Emma nodded thrilled her mother was corroborating her story.

She didn't dare look her father's way. Yet she suspected his angry brown eyes were shooting daggers at her. He knew too much about her to accept the dream explanation.

"Congratulations, Franka," Patrick said. "Although you don't know the sex of the baby yet, do you?"

"No, of course not." She turned toward Emma. "I would love if the baby was a girl.

"Did you know about this Mom?" Eloise asked her arm still around Franka.

Abigail nodded her expression aloof.

"How did this happen?" Eloise laughed as she added, "I mean, who is the father?"

"Does it matter?" Franka said regaining her seat.

"No. Of course not. Today a woman can have a child and raise it on her own if she wishes. Are you having the child?"

Franka nodded.

Once the drinks were served, they all sat down again Emma and Eloise still smiling.

"You didn't go to one of them sperm banks, did you?" Patrick asked.

All eyes turned toward him his wife and mother in law's expressions outraged.

Franka started to shake her head then stopped. "You wouldn't judge me if I had, would you, Pat?"

Emma pinched her lips not to laugh.

"Nah. It's your life. These are modern times. Nobody cares anymore."

"He's one of those dreamy muscle men your sister met at a party. Very intense. Irrevocably smitten with Franka," Abigail supplied nonchalantly rolling her eyes.

"Mother." Franka used her teacher's tone. "This is nobody's business but my own."

Eloise touched her sister's hand. "You are planning to tell the father, aren't you?"

"El, it's complicated."

Abigail continued. "Go ahead. Tell her what he does. She'll understand why you're not with him."

Franka gave her mother the evil eye. She took a deep breath and said. "He's a … sanitation worker."

"Oh, oh." Patrick chuckled. Then he turned round eyes on Eloise's stern expression. "What? He'll be out of a job before he knows it. Mayor Booker's thinking of privatizing the whole sector."

"Well, one of the companies they're thinking of outsourcing to, approached Jim and offered him his own truck." Franka stared at the food in her plate. "Besides, he doesn't have to handle refuse anymore. It's all automated."

"Of course, it is, Franka," Eloise added stroking her arm. "Does he know?"

Franka shook her head.

Abigail leered at Franka. "I can just imagine the conversation at the Dean's house. "So, Jim what do you do?"

And Emma felt a sad surprise invade her when discovering how little romance figured in her grandma's life. She grabbed her aunt's hand. "Doesn't matter," she whispered. "He loves you."

"Thanks, Emma." She gave her hand a little tug. "You love him too. I know you do," Emma added.

Franka shook her head from side to side. "I'm not sure, Emma. I can't tell yet."

"Franka," Abigail added. "You're a college professor with tenure. What would you two ever have to discuss?"

"What surprises me," Patrick added taking a gulp of his beer, "is that you're still having this baby with all the crazies running around. Doesn't make much sense."

"It wasn't a crazy man who took that little girl, Daddy." Emma was so angry everyone was picking on her aunt, trying to influence her love life, and now suggesting she get rid of her baby the words just slipped out.

Emma withstood all gazes veered toward her. Her father's menacing glare, she could not. She lowered her eyes praying the moment would wash.

"What do you mean, Emma?" Abigail asked.

Emma opened her mouth to say something, but Patrick stood banging his fist on the table. "Go to your room—now."

"Patrick, she hasn't finished her dinner," Abigail intervened.

"Abigail this is my house, and you'll abide by my wishes."

Emma had already walked to the kitchen archway, abandoning the lovely meal she'd hardly touched. She slid into the dark hallway and ducked behind the dish cabinet so she could stay and listen.

"What has the child done now? Eloise, say something," Abigail thundered.

Patrick answered for her. "She deludes herself into thinking she knows everything. I don't want her talking crazy. First thing you know the entire neighborhood will be throwing rocks at our house. If she keeps this up, our whole lives will be disrupted."

"She's a child with a child's imagination. Weren't you ever young, Pat?" Franka asked. "Besides, she was right about my pregnancy."

"Of course. The child could very well be intuitive," Abigail replied in a huff. "There's nothing wrong with that. It's well received in our day and age. You said it yourself. These are modern times, and Salem is dead and buried, thank God."

Emma didn't hear her father's answer. She left and climbed the stairs two by two to her room. She didn't care that her mother didn't jump in to come to her rescue. She'd stopped waiting for the moment a whole year now, ever since she realized if her mom were to place herself between her and her dad, she'd lose them both. He would begin to resent her mother, much more than he did her, and slowly her mother would be miserable and secretly blame her for the rift between them.

She pushed through the third door on the left and walked into a sparsely furnished room. Of course, this meant she could never really confide in her mother. So, both would go on pretending Emma's curse didn't exist. Meanwhile, the tacit agreement unchecked between her and her mother would continue. Eloise would do her best to calm Patrick whenever she could by extolling Emma's virtues as often as necessary. She, on the other hand, would continue to get all the comfort hugs she could muster out of a happy mother.

She opened her window and sat on the little bench granny Dottie had made especially for her. Granny Dottie had worked with her hands all her life. She had even shown Emma how to smooth the wood into a soft and polished finish. She was good with mending little girls' hearts too.

She smiled at the tree graying against the backdrop of a pink sky. The elm's limbs stretched out to meet her, so she did her best to touch them, approaching the window's ledge and enjoying the summer breeze on her flushed face. With a tight fist, she held on to the tips of the closest branch.

It would be liberating she thought if the elm could understand what she said. Perhaps it did. The enormous branches had rustled many good answers back when Emma had poured her heart out to the leafy friend. After all, plants and trees weren't inanimate objects. They were alive and full of energy, and they took care of their own. Her teacher had read them an article about trees producing special chemicals, a little like aspirin, to protect themselves against natural disasters and warn other trees of impending dangers.

She looked down at the ground, and for a moment, felt suspended in time almost as though she were flying. But nausea suddenly overtook her. Dizzy she anchored her feet underneath the bench to pull herself back into the room.

She took a deep breath and walked over to her bed. She sat on the fluffy comforter and hugged her arms around her. The visions she had seen while poised in midair terrified her. She eyed her comfy pillows, four of them, and doubted the lovely white lace, embroidered with her favorite pink primroses, would help her sleep tonight.

<u>Four</u>

Christina Tyler

One week or so later, on a Friday morning before first bell even rang, buses had lined up in the school court-yard their drivers waiting to take the three classes of fifth graders to Branch Brook Park for their lesson in aerodynamics. At this time in June, the dwindling school curriculum had prompted their teacher, Christina Tyler to suggest that all fifth-grade students build a kite out of their own materials following specific patterns she had handed out.

Emma had fashioned hers out of an old sheet her mother had given her and tightened the contraption with bits of wood she'd gathered from granny Dottie's shed and knotted ribbons and bows into two long tails that dangled at the back. She couldn't wait to fly her crafty design in a big open space. Might even win one of the ten dollar prizes.

Anxiously she scoured the area nearby, her eyes combing through the children pushing and shoving to board the bus. She needed to talk to Tommy before they left. After lunch, Amelia would demand most of her time and after school, Tommy's dad would pick him up, and they'd leave straight away for his aunt's place in Connecticut. Tommy Carson lived with his father and kept telling her how lucky she was to have both her parents. His mother had left them to pursue a career in Hollywood then remarried some young actor.

Emma trusted Tommy implicitly even though his father worked for the same insurance company as hers and both shared a ride to work and back. Tommy kept her secret. Nevertheless, she'd put off until the last minute warning him about the dangers he faced.

"Tommy, come here," she called out and signaled to him.

In the midst of talking to a friend, he looked up. "What?" He tucked the kite rope in his pocket and ran toward her. "We got to get on the bus."

"I have to talk to you." She searched for somewhere private, grabbed his shirt sleeve and began running toward the recessed area behind the gym wall occupied with a neat row of basketball nets.

"What's going on?"

Emma took a deep breath. She eyed Tommy's ear length tuff of chestnut hair, his deep blue eyes and full lips, and sort of understood why all the girls found him such a catch. He happened to be tall too especially since he had a whole year and a half on everyone else. Tommy had doubled grade three. Not due to stupidity. Repeating his grade had occurred because he'd missed so much school due to the trouble with his mom.

Christina Tyler called out their names. Both turned toward the sound, and both ignored her.

"Listen, I … I don't think you should do the pit bike competition this weekend."

"Huh? Not do it—I'm going to win—first prize, fifty dollars."

She shook her head in frustration. "You can't. I have a feeling something awful is going to happen."

"What are you talking about? I wear a helmet. My bike is small, and I've been riding for four years."

"I …" The bus tooted its horn warning the stragglers.

"Seeing things again?"

She nodded, ignoring the tongue in cheek remark glad his joke helped her get the words out. "I caught a glimpse of the wood fixture breaking and you falling. Don't think you made it."

"Don't worry. Turns out you're wrong half the time. I'll be fine."

"Not this time. I'm not wrong. You've got to promise me you won't jump."

"Why would you be right about this?"

"My visions are getting stronger. I can separate truth from imagination now—at least, better than I did before."

He gave her an ironic half-smile. "Come on—getting stronger. How can you tell if you're right? I mean—unless someone does something you told him not to, and whatever you said would happen happens. Did something happen?"

"Kind of. Only if I say, you have to swear you won't tell anyone, and you have to promise me you won't ride."

He rolled his eyes and shook his head. "This had better be good."

She bobbed her head fidgeting with her kite.

"Dad's going to want an explanation as to why I'm not riding."

"Can't you tell him your knee still hurts from last time?"

"Yeah. First, let's hear what you have to say, and hurry. The bus is going to leave without us."

"The girl who was kidnapped?" She nodded nervously. "Not

a kidnapping."

"What?" He kicked a small stone away near his foot. "Her mother's boyfriend—or ex-boyfriend, I'm not sure. He wanted to pick up the little girl and drive her home." She shrugged.

"This doesn't make sense. Why haven't the authorities found him yet?"

"He's scared. He's hiding. He's afraid he'll be charged. The woman he loves is in hospital thanks to him."

"Dad said she's out of the coma. She is recovering."

"She is?"

"Yeah. Story was in the papers yesterday. Some seer you are."

"Thank God. Now, maybe he'll turn himself in." Emma ignored his jibe.

"What about the car chase?"

"No car chase. He took off faster than she did, made the lights when she didn't, and she sped to catch up."

"How do you know this for sure? You didn't even know she was out of the coma?"

"Don't ask me how or why, I do. I just do."

"What about the other kidnappings?"

She hoisted her shoulders and gave him a rueful look. "Can't be sure. Sometimes I get weird flashes—then they're gone." She couldn't tell him the visions terrified her, and that she did all she could so as not to experience any of them.

He nodded. "All right." He grunted dejectedly. I won't tell anyone. And I won't ride."

She smiled and almost gave him a peck on the cheek when out of the shadows, not twenty feet away, there came Christina Tyler slowly walking toward them.

Emma's eyes rounded, and her heart hammered in her chest as she wondered how much had Miss Tyler overheard?

Tommy lowered his eyes a sheepish look on his face. "Sorry, Miss Tyler. Just checking on Emma's kite." He raised his shoulders at Emma, turned and ran in the other direction.

"Sorry, Miss Tyler." Emma prepared to do the same, but Christina stopped her.

"Emma is everything all right?"

She stopped and veered toward her teacher. She had always admired the way she wore her brown hair in a gentle bob encircling a lovely cream complexion. The soulful brown eyes, which made her teacher so beautiful, stared at her and unnerved Emma. "Of course, everything is fine."

Emma searched those eyes and tried to read through her teacher's sudden curiosity. She detected nothing out of the ordinary, so she smiled. "Can I go now?"

"Yes. Hurry."

She felt Christina Tyler's eyes branded on the back of her neck as she ran to the row of buses, holding her kite in her right hand and raising it as though she were about to fly it. She had tried flying her contraption at home in her yard, but the long tail had gotten tangled in the tree. She'd needed a lot of cooperation from her elm to set it free.

Emma sighed a little relieved. She wasn't even the last one to board she consoled herself trying to forget her teacher might have overheard her confession to Tommy.

She climbed the first step and stopped. She found her eyes pulled to the car pool on the other side of the lot. A strange pinkish tan colored roof drew her attention. She smiled shaking her head.

Had to be hundreds of tan colored cars in the vicinity—thousands. They couldn't all be the one she'd seen Thursday before last with the awful driver inside.

She had a difficult time getting through the aisle with people's kites strewn every which way. Most had folded them into neat little packages. Some students, their contraption beyond folding, hung them in the walkway or over the person's head in front of them. Then she spotted Tommy sitting alone and realized he held a seat for her.

He shoved his legs perpendicular to the aisle for her to squeeze in and take the window seat which was the one she normally chose.

"I'd rather sit next to the aisle today, Tommy."

Their traveling arrangement usually suited him. She knew Tommy hated being trapped against the window. "What's wrong now? Afraid you're going to be sucked out?" He threw the words at her as he scooched over.

Emma tried not to let his tone affect her, but couldn't stop her lip from trembling. If Tommy was going to make fun of her, there weren't any safe places left. She didn't want to explain how she avoided the window seat in case some faded tan car followed the bus while a creepy driver tried to find her.

"Hey, cheer up. Bad joke. I'm no comic." Tommy poked her with his elbow.

"I know," she answered mechanically.

"How's your leg? Better yet, how bad was it with your dad? I asked, but you never said."

"The usual. Yelled at me for riding my bike late at night. For going through the old quarry. Said that's what I deserved for disobeying."

"Harsh. You should have blamed me. I was the one in a hurry, remember?"

She didn't answer.

"So why are you so uptight about your kite?"

"It's just that I put a lot of thought into my design, and I don't want it to be squished."

Tommy's eyebrows rose as he eyed the pink and red contraption she'd taken great care to fold. He shook his head rolling his eyes as he turned his attention toward the street.

Emma breathed a little better. She was proud and grateful Tommy Carson was on her side. Nothing romantic between them although she knew many of the girls in school admired their closeness. Joan Tibbs always popped her bubble gum at him, licking her lips when she was done. Franny, allowed to wear eyeliner and pink colored lip gloss, regularly repainted her mouth while she gawked at him. Franny would pucker and smack her lips to even out the silky balm. Others dressed cutely for his benefit, but she didn't care. Theirs was a true friendship she hoped would last for years. "I hate all those cheeky girls," he would say. "One day, they're going to turn into my mother. Run off with the latest Hollywood hunk. They have no substance, no heart."

She glanced over at Tommy and wondered if his mother's departure had not freed him in some way, prevented him from making the same mistake his father had—choosing the wrong person to be his life partner. He was hurting now. But weren't they all at their age? There was just so much to understand and so little time to mull over the incongruities of their young lives. She loved that word, incongruity. Knowing how to spell it had secured the win in the spelling bee over all fifth graders.

They both jumped at the sound of tires screeching and some-one sitting on his car horn.

"Wow," Tommy commented. "A stupid driver just cut Miss Tyler off. I think she's showing him the finger." He laughed.

"Where?" Emma bent over him and searched the area in time to glimpse an offbeat tan colored car racing down one of the side streets. "You're crazy, Tommy. Miss Tyler would never show any-one the finger." She laughed too as a little relief ran through her—yes, so many of those cars.

Then a flash came to her. She remembered. There was a large peanut-shaped rust spot on the driver's side of the roof, on top of the door. Too late to spot anything on that car. It was long gone.

***

Christina Tyler watched the bus mosey along ahead of her as she stopped by the side of the road her heart still beating unevenly from the close call. She remembered the eyes of the motorist and doubted his intentions were honorable. She had no doubt he'd cut her off on purpose.

She stared at her cell phone and hesitated. Her senses in full alert ran goosebumps up and down her arms. She took a deep breath and closed her eyes, trying to reestablish calm within her before she opted to do anything as drastic as place a call to Hank.

Contacting Hank Apple was the last thing she ever thought she'd do in this lifetime. Three years they had lived together she hoping he would grow up and finally commit to their relationship. Until she had walked in on him mussing the sheets with some wild redhead—the picture still anchored in her mind and too well defined even two years later. She might never be able to pry the image from her thoughts.

At first, she had defended him telling her friends and family he was the apple of her eye. Of course, he had sworn to her sleeping with the other woman had all been in the line of duty. He was a detective out to prove something, so attempting to go beyond the job curriculum was his way of becoming an even better detective.

When she'd reminded him he could have moonlighted on his own time, in a motel, he had apologized. Had promised it would never happen again.

Of course, at the time there were friends with their own version of Hank sleeping around, sorry facts weighing in the balance. So, she called it quits, kicked him out of her house and went on with the daily chore of living without him. Besides, she couldn't tell if his promise meant he would never sleep with anyone else, or he would never get caught again. She'd been too embarrassed to ask.

The trouble was, he'd turned out to be one of the best and most celebrated detectives in New Jersey—if not on the whole Eastern Seaboard, so forgetting about him was not in the cards. She'd followed his rise to fame and somewhat understood the crazy career choices he'd made along the way. Understood, yes. Forgave?

She fingered the phone pad on her cell. The children would reach the park soon, and she needed to be with them to help with supervision. Putting her grievances aside, she dialed a number she knew well.

"I'd like to speak to detective Apple, please." She prayed he was there while hoping he wasn't.

"May I tell him who is calling?"

She bit her lip as a slight blush warmed her cheeks. She hadn't foreseen this question. Hank would know who was calling beforehand. Of course, playing with fire meant she was bound to get licked by the occasional flame. "Christina Tyler."

"One moment please."

The wait turned her legs to mush and made her palms moist. In fact, the pause lasted so long she thought Hank might not want to talk to her. After all, since their separation she hadn't returned any of his calls.

Just when she had made up her mind to hang up, she heard a sarcastic drawl.

"Well, well, well. If it isn't the Duchess herself, Christina Tyler. To what do I owe the honor?"

Strangely, the brashness of his tone brought tears to her eyes, and she took deep breaths so her voice would not tremble. Why did he have to be bitter? She found herself uselessly wondering what her sister—Hanks' most loyal ally—would say about his attitude now.

"Hello, Hank." She waited for some reply. There was none. "I need to see you—as soon as possible. Would this afternoon be okay?" She could get Craig Norman to watch her class. He would jump at the opportunity of doing something for her.

"I must warn you. I am in a committed, loving relationship," Hank jeered. "But, if you ask me pleasantly, in that sexy way of yours, I might drop everything and run over to see you … perhaps assist you in a little afternoon delight?"

Mocking her. The arguments they'd had over commitment, loyalty, and all their trust issues. She recognized the taunt and perhaps she even deserved a little of his rancor, but she shrunk with pain at the thought of him being in a loving relationship. She should have been happy for him, and she was in a way. Didn't stop the heart from turning in her chest.

"Hank, I need you to be serious. A car just cut me off. I think it's because the driver didn't want me taking the license number off his back plate."

"Go on."

She tried to ignore the listless tone of his voice but failed. She had the impression she sounded defensive and awkward. "I was following one of the school buses. We have an outing this morning. I spotted this car trailing closely beside it. The driver was checking each window as though scanning for children's faces."

"Could be an anxious parent checking on his kid. We've had a bunch of them call the precinct lately."

"I can imagine, but not this driver. I watched this man stalk the bus. When he saw me taking down his license number, he bolted and cut me off deliberately, enough that I had to stop writing the license number to avoid running into the car next to me. Then he barreled down Degraw. Hank, I caught his eyes before he fled. No good intentions there."

"Well, stop by sometime this afternoon. Give Pete your deposition and maybe try to give him your guy's description. Did you get the license number?"

"I did." She let out a deep breath. "I still need to talk to you, Hank. It's important."

"Work related?"

She thought she heard him hold his breath. "Absolutely."

<u>Five</u>

Hank Apple

The second precinct's halls resembled a thriving beehive in the midst of honey production. Aside from being abuzz with activity and brimming with people of all shapes and sizes with their drone as loud and incomprehensible as that of bee subjects, all workers seemed to fly toward a particular task. Each understood the specifics of what was expected of him or her as they promptly attended their duties, which made Christina Tyler slightly uncomfortable.

For the last half hour, she'd watched through the waiting room's glass the thrust of energy building and receding along the corridors as people came and went about their business totally oblivious to her and her mounting paranoia. Normal she thought since she was usually the one with the ready agenda penned with all the answers. Even faced with a classroom of know-it-all fifth graders she rarely found herself this inadequate.

Of course, there was the fact she was going to meet and talk to Hank again after enforcing two years of deliberate abstinence of the man. She had not returned any of his calls, listened to any of his pleas to understand. She'd ignored his many apologies no matter what they were.

Admittedly the treatment had been a harsh one, at least by her standards, even disregarding the rest of the world—friends stating Hank had gotten off easy which contributed to her thinking herself the heel he no doubt deemed her to be.

In truth, once the anger and shame had subsided, she would have given anything to forgive and forget. By then, Hank had moved on—at least she had stopped hearing from him, and now she knew why. He was in a loving, committed relationship.

The next footsteps coming down the hall triggered her heart to skip beats—not that Hank had a heavy step or even a memorable stride, just a lover's instinct buried deep inside that twitched, still alive and virulent enough to detect her other self even in unfamiliar surroundings. A quick peek at the glass around her as the steps got closer confirmed her suspicions. A few seconds later, the scent of him jumbled her thoughts and colored her cheeks red.

She lowered her eyes and concentrated on smoothing the few wrinkles out of her yellow cotton skirt. She had topped the thinly strapped dress with a yellow-trimmed white bodice. All at once she wished she had dressed a little less frivolously in darker shades, perhaps in navy and worn pants.

He stood in the doorway. "Sorry, I took so long."

She sensed his eyes sweep her up and down, and when venturing her own eyes to glance at him, she encountered his smile. "You haven't changed a bit," he added smoothly.

She smiled, having to stare at him squarely and grateful for the compliment. "Thank you." He was still the same too—tall, square shoulders, hair swept back featuring little curly tendrils in his neck, deep-set hazel eyes. New small lines stretched around those probing eyes and he seemed a little heavier. But he was still the hunk she remembered.

"Is here okay?" he asked.

She rose, unhappy to sense him a little dismissive. "Here is fish bowl central," she whispered her eyes sweeping the windows on all sides while gently indicating the slew of people all waiting their turn to meet someone. "I think we need a little privacy."

"Fine. We'll go to my office." He walked out expecting her to follow.

She thought he'd be wearing a holstered gun around that bulging arm, tight jeans and a washed out sweatshirt. Instead, she stared at tightly flexed muscles, visible through a thin cotton white shirt neatly tucked in at the waist of navy gabardine pants.

He'd changed she pondered. Maybe she'd stopped seeing him during the last year before their breakup, when she'd been working overtime and taking classes at the University to finish her Master's degree in early childhood education.

Sometimes, in the dead heat of sleepless nights, she would bump up against a harrowing thought. Perhaps had she been more present during the last year they shared, they might still be together.

He stopped in front of an opened door. He turned toward her with a sweep of his arm indicating she go ahead of him, and she spotted the blue tie she hadn't noticed. The knot was skewed to the right as though he had tugged on the tie to breathe, but the folds were secured down the middle with a silver clasp, and the finishing touch made his appearance neat and irreproachable.

Inside she tried to spot familiar mementos, in fact, searching for telltale photos of a loved one he might have displayed amongst his personal things.

"Coast is clear—for now." He closed the door once he entered.

"Coast is clear?"

"Matt will be back," he admitted. "He's gone to the evidence locker."

Christina glanced at the door. "I forgot you shared an office."

"Don't worry. Door closed means no interruptions. Should be okay for the next twenty minutes." He crossed his fingers as he raised his eyebrows.

She glanced at the two small desks abutting each other and memories of evenings she'd spent waiting for Hank to finish his shift stirred a smile from her. She even recalled the anticipation she'd held of being enveloped in his arms, his big hands gently caressing her back. Christina found no personal photos anywhere. She gathered no space existed on either desk.

"I thought they might have offered you your office by now," she said a little hesitantly thinking about all the exploits he'd accomplished."

"I'm never here. Don't need one. But Ken did offer me his job." He smiled.

"You? Captain?"

He nodded. "He remarried a couple of years ago. She has family money, and she's been after him to retire. Wants to travel, start a family."

"Doesn't he already have a daughter?"

"Yes, he does—an every-other-weekend father."

He ignored his high back chairs and showed her to a two seater sofa and walked over to a credenza. "Coffee?"

"I'd love some. Black … I take my coffee black now," she admitted as an afterthought. "I figure you turned him down?"

"I hope you like it strong," he said conveniently ignoring her question she thought. He handed her a mug, took one himself, and sat down beside her his long legs twisted in her direction. He made himself comfortable while she talked about what was ailing her.

She certainly wasn't going to repeat the question. Still, she eyed Hank thinking a big part of him was still unchanged.

"Of course, I turned him down. What do you think? He twisted my arm and even admitted Director Larkin approved his choice. Still not ready to stop chasing bad guys."

As she raised her mug to her lips, to hide her disappointment for what she considered was Hank's lack of maturity, she caught his warning.

"Careful, just made this batch. Coffee's hot."

The situation in which she stewed at the moment was hot enough. "Wow, you make coffee now?" She remembered he never used to handle anything in the kitchen.

He smiled. "Yeah. I even dabble with meals every now and again." He rubbed his stomach. "Beats scoffing down greasy cafeteria chicken."

He put down his mug on the corner of a small table and reached for his jacket draped on a chair pulling a hand sized recorder from the side pocket. "Can I tape?"

She hesitated. "This is confidential stuff, Hank."

"I understand. I'll treat the matter as such. Scribbling is just for my benefit anyway—in case I should get lost in your eyes remembering how it used to be. Could be I won't understand a word you say."

He gave her a mocking grin, and this was when she realized he used flirting as an attempt to make her more at ease. His half smirk was funny, so she laughed. Despite tingling nerves, she found herself relaxing.

She admitted. "There's nothing I'd enjoy more right now than to have a real discussion about us." Faced with the probing questions in his eyes, she took a deep breath. "But I'm worried about two of my kids."

He nodded giving her the go.

Christina tried to make her discussion concise and believable. So she began by describing Emma Willis as well as she could. She also talked a little about Tommy Carson and their relationship. "I think Tommy likes her a lot. She has a lot of presence, quite beautiful. Although she is totally unaware of it, unusually naïve about her looks—about life in general, I think."

She related the conversation she had overheard between them that morning. When she finished, Hank rubbed his face with his hands. He had taken a few notes even while the recorder was working, and he hadn't interrupted her once, except to have her repeat the tan car's license number.

Christina appreciated the cup of coffee as the big white mug warmed her hands. Aside from the seesaw of emotions she still harbored for Hank, running chills up and down her arms, she found they kept the place rather cold. "Listen, I don't expect you to believe all of this…"

"You're lying?" His raised eyebrows told her this was a real question.

"No, of course not. I meant believing in a child's—anyone's—special gift of seeing is difficult."

"Hum, hum." He got up and stretched. He walked toward a

phone. "And I made detective by being a close-minded idiot." He turned his back on her as he made a call.

Christina bit her lip and realized she was going to have to forget about the old Hank and treat him as the new and changed person he appeared to be.

"Hey, Cin. Can you drop whatever you're doing and come to the office? I'd appreciate it."

He hung up the phone and walked over to the credenza. "Refill?" He picked up the coffee pot to add brew to his mug.

"No, thank you." She hesitated. "I'm sorry. I didn't mean to imply…"

"Forget about it. Common mistake."

"No. I have a hard time with extra senses people have or claim to have. So, I understand others who do."

"Don't worry about it. No law says you have to believe everything you hear, right?"

His pointed glare told her he referred to one of the reasons their relationship had come to a head, how she'd put too much faith in gossip about him. She thought it best to ignore the taunt.

There was a knock on the door and a young policewoman dressed in a blue uniform walked in. Christina spotted short, curly blond hair that crowned attractive features. She smiled at Hank in a familiar, friendly manner. Christina couldn't help thinking they were close.

"Cindy Revere, meet Christina Tyler."

"Wow!" Cindy gushed as she scrambled over to shake Christina's hand. "It's you." She turned toward Hank. "Now I understand what all the fuss is about."

Hank's menacing glare as he sat on the edge of the table almost made Christina laugh outright. Instead, she fought to remain calm. Hank had talked about her. Flattering. Although, often a new lover might ask a man to confide about his ex.

She greeted Cindy with the best smile she could muster.

"Tell Christina about your aunt."

Cindy's puzzled look went from Hank to Christina back to Hank. "Which one?"

"Do we employ more than one?"

"Ah. I get it." Cindy approached to sit on the sofa. "Well."

"The short version." Hank interrupted her.

"Testy this afternoon aren't we?" She brushed him with a mocking pair of contemptuous eyes but remained standing. "My aunt Val is a clairvoyant. The department hires her sometimes to get better clues on some of our cases—at least on the ones so cold, and we need to wear gloves to handle the files."

"Thanks, Cin."

"That's all?" She smiled her eyes round and provocative.

"Yes," he admonished, his own eyes sending her the message to behave. Christina knew the expression well.

"Oh," he remembered as she opened the door. He rose and retrieved the pad he'd left on the sofa's armrest. "Ask Matt to track these down. Top priority."

Cindy perused the note. "First place we searched, Hank—the woman's ex-boyfriends."

"Seems we missed one." He glanced at Christina.

"We did?" Cindy gave him a puzzled look. "And this isn't the runaway car's plate number."

"No. It isn't."

She hesitated, eyeing Christina as though she wasn't sure she should add anything.

"Speak," Hank bellowed.

"We found the plate the woman called into 911."

Hank shoved his face toward her his eyes round and waited.

"Belongs to a Jaguar. The owner is the manager of a used car lot who swears his Jag never went missing." She made a face. "Matt seems to think she might've gotten the number wrong."

"Doesn't seem likely somehow."

"What do you mean?"

"If you were chasing some lunatic who'd just kidnapped little Janey. Would you get the number wrong?"

Cindy drew a crooked smile. "Think we should go back and talk to him? Strong arm him a little?"

Hank shook his head while rubbing the back of his neck.

"Nah." He checked his watch. "I'm going to the hospital to visit the mother. I'll try to find out what else she hasn't told us."

"What does this last item on the list have to do with anything?"

"Never mind how it ties in. It's also a priority." Hank reached for the suit jacket he'd draped on the back of a chair and slipped it on. "Can you make sure this gets done?"

"Will do, boss." A little bounce to her step she waved a hand salute toward Christina before closing the door behind her.

Christina got up and put her coffee mug down on the credenza. She had done her bit, and now she could leave.

"Want to come?"

She stepped back, wide-eyed and open-mouthed genuinely shocked. "Me?" She looked down at what she was wearing. "I'm not dressed for this."

"That's okay." He chuckled. "No one cares how about what

you wear."

"What I mean is I don't look the part." She slipped him an acerbic smile.

"Just as well. Sometimes victims respond better to women than they do to men, especially to women who don't look the part."

He was laughing at her. That much was evident. But she was touched he insisted she tag along. "Well, if you think I can help."

He gave her a long, poignant look, one that had her cheeks blush and her eyes staring into his—pleading for mercy.

"Come on," he whispered gruffly. Deftly he raced along the halls leading the way to the parking lot. He did not glance back once, not even to check if she followed. Christina had to run to keep up, and twice he let a heavy door recoil on its hinges so that she had to push with all her strength to slip through. He unlocked the vehicle remotely and didn't stride to her side to open the door.

She got it. The message could not be any clearer she rued as she sat in the passenger's seat. Their meeting was not a date, and he wasn't about to be any form of gallant.

Still, in proximity to Hank, a load of fresh memories washed over her when she remembered how tender and attentive he used to be. The recall made the last few minutes much harder to live down.

She rubbed her bare arms to get the circulation going. "I suppose you've spoken to this woman before?" She carefully kept her tone neutral.

He shook his head. "You cold?" He reached to turn down the air conditioning a notch. "I forgot how you sometimes get cold when it's eighty degrees outside." He pulled his window down halfway. "We snooped around her old haunts and old boyfriends while she was unconscious. My partner went to see her yesterday morning. He said she seemed calm and alert which surprised the hell out of me."

"You think she's not worried enough about her missing daughter?"

"Well, something doesn't fit. Mother risks her life and just recovers in hospital with slight concern over the events that put her there in the first place?" He turned to glance at her. "Here you come along with a different story, one that suits and suits too damn well."

"If Emma's version is right, she and her boyfriend must be terrified."

His answer was a long drawn out breath. "So many wrong turns people take in life. It's a wonder this crazy globe is still spinning."

She nodded realizing he being a detective meant season tickets to ringside seats depicting life's worst travesties.

"What's the best way to contact Emma Willis?"

There it was, the question she knew would be coming, the one she dreaded so much it almost kept her from calling him. "There's something I didn't tell you about Emma. She has a bulldog for a father. He is overprotective and very hard on her. I almost called children services on him once."

"When?"

"I had her in grade three. She was small, always scared, and the essay I asked my kids to do on their family gave no evidence of a father in the three pages Emma wrote."

"I remember this, vaguely."

Yes, of course. We were still ..." She bit her lip and didn't continue.

"Together? Don't blame you for being afraid to say the word. You promised we'd be together forever."

"Yes, I did." She eyed him unafraid. "I also remember you made no such promise."

He smiled. "A missing father in an essay isn't grounds to call social services." He snickered.

"There were other indications, Hank—comportment, a few heated discussions with friends."

"Why didn't you call them?"

"Grandmother came to see me. Imbued with her powers—a real piece of work."

"She talked about unique gifts?"

"Not the term she used. She didn't say much. Rambled on about her son, Emma's father, and how he was strict with Emma because he worried about her having inherited the curse—yeah," she said as an afterthought. "Yes, a curse is the word she used. But what threw me was when I realized she knew what I was about to do." She stared at Hank until he had the liberty of doing the same. "I hadn't spoken to anyone about my intentions."

"So, little girl inherits grandmother's seeing powers."

"Father's mother, whom he spent his life calling, crazy."

"How do you know?"

"People talk—about the crazy lady who left her house to an ungrateful son—and they can judge."

"She passed away?"

"A few months after coming to see me. I remember relief washing over me thinking now Emma had a chance at a normal life." She gave Hank a rueful look.

"Tell you what. You arrange a little conversation between

Emma and me, in your presence, of course, any way you feel will not alert the family—at least for now."

She nodded. "I'll try. You might have to allow Tommy Carson to be present. She trusts him implicitly. In fact, I think he is the only one she does trust."

<u>*Six*</u>

Amelia

Emma was in her room hanging with Amelia. They'd caught up on school gossip, and Amelia was curious about the new developments with Emma's aunt Franka.

"Can't believe your aunt's going to have a baby. She must be scared, all alone," Amelia said taking a bite of her apple. "Aren't you a tiny bit curious about the father?" she asked Emma, who lay stretched on the bed flat on her stomach busily circling a word puzzle.

Emma rubbed her feet together. Amelia's words came out all slurred and juicy. She tore herself away from her crossword and spotted her sitting on Granny Dottie's little bench her back to the window. Smaller than she was, the green-eyed freckled brunette packed quite a punch. A real personality. Emma enjoyed her company.

Of course, she'd never told her friend about the curse, so to abbreviate she shook her head. "Aunt Franka likes him which means he is terrific. She's smart. She would never go for anyone who wasn't worthy."

"Not so smart if she forgot to use protection." Amelia rolled her eyes from side to side with a knowing smile on her face.

Emma stopped scribbling. "Did you learn about sex in school?"

Amelia nodded with round eyes. "You should have seen some of the girls. They acted all silly and ditzy."

"Who would have thought private school would teach you about sex so early."

"Yeah." Another big crunch into her apple interrupted her next sentence. "Sacred Heart nuns are cool."

"Okay. I'm sure the nuns also taught you that sometimes, you might do everything you're supposed to do and accidents still happen," Emma said getting back to her puzzle.

"Who told you about sex?"

"Aunt Franka." Emma and Amelia glanced at each other and laughed.

"Guess she does know," Amelia conceded with a chuckle. She twisted on the bench and turned toward the street. "Your grandma's late."

"She'll be here. What's the hurry? Aunt Franka teaches a class until seven on Friday nights."

"Which means dinner and a movie is going to be late."

"So? We're sleeping over, and she lives in a respectable neighborhood. Besides, I like coming home at eleven o'clock at night when the evening is warm, and the street lights cast romantic shadows over everything. I even like the little night critters that fly around your head and tickle your face."

"You are weird." Amelia got up to wrap what remained of her apple in a tissue before she dunked the small core in the basket. "Speaking of weird, where is Tommy tonight?"

"With his dad. Away for the weekend."

Amelia wiped her hands on her jeans and sat on the bed beside

Emma. She leaned back against the pillows. "Good looking weird, though. He's the one boy who'd make me want to go to public school." A little pause later, she asked, "You mean he won't be at your party tomorrow night?"

Emma pushed her crossword away and sat on the other side of Amelia. She nodded. "Father drives him in. Once the party is over, they go back to his aunt's place until Monday morning." She turned toward Amelia with curiosity. "Do you like Tommy?"

"The word like is a bit strong. I just think Tommy's hunky looking. I wonder how much he knows about sex."

"I'm not sure. We never talk about that. I would imagine he does on account of the way his mom left."

"Yeah, must have been rough." Amelia passed a hand through her wavy curls wrapping the ends around her fingers.

"I thought you hated him." Emma snipped one of her toenails with a pair of clippers.

"Hate is a bit of a strong word. I don't like the way he towers over you, all proprietorial." Amelia rolled disgusted eyes. "Like he's carrying around the owner's manual, and I'm the weekend friend."

Emma stared at Amelia wondering if the comment initiated a roundabout way of asking her who she liked best. Or did she have Tommy on the brain like the other girls in her class did? "All I know is every fifth and sixth grader in school wants to date him. Anyway, he doesn't like any of them. He thinks they're all airheads."

"Do you like him?" Amelia looked at Emma squarely.

"I do, a lot. He's my best friend—after you of course." Emma caught the sound of a car pull up.

"Well, I hope so." Amelia laughed as she jumped up to check out the new arrival.

Emma sensed her answer had seemed to smooth Amelia's ruffles.

"Not your grandma. Just your dad. So, when is she going to get here?"

***

Hospitals always made Christina Tyler uncomfortable. She still remembered the gray walls closing in on her the day her grandmother died on the surgeon's table from a routine appendix operation. She was twelve, and the preteen memories made her surroundings seem alien.

She jogged to keep up with Hank, and the square heels of her shoes clacking against the cement floors seemed to laugh at her naiveté.

"Walking too fast for you?"

She rued Hank's chuckle. Of course, he was. What a question. He practically ran—on purpose, she suspected to keep her unbalanced. "Don't worry. The faster we get this done, the faster we can each go home."

Sure enough, he slowed his pace. Christina stared at him and wondered what the gesture meant which was when she encountered the stern, stubborn profile she once loved. His chiseled face could still get her heart beating faster.

Inside the patient's room, the curtains were drawn. The solid poplin managed to block the remainder of daylight and render the room dim enough for sleeping.

Hank walked in without hesitation. A nurse was checking the IV bag. "Can I help you, sir?"

Hank showed his badge. "I've already cleared the visit with Doctor Harris."

The nurse smiled at Christina. "I'm afraid Ms. Castle is sleeping."

"Sedative?"

"No. Patient is only dozing in and out. You might want to tell her you're here."

The nurse left, closing the door behind her.

Christina wasn't quite sure what Hank expected of her, so she stayed behind waiting for instructions.

Hank took a couple of minutes to draw the patient's attention. She opened big eyes when she spotted Hank's badge. He signaled to Christina to come closer, join him on the other side of the bed.

"Don't be frightened, Julia—may I call you Julia?"

She nodded.

"I just need to ask you a few questions. My partner here is a school teacher working with us on the case."

Julia threw wild eyes in Christina's direction and bobbed her head as a gesture of greeting.

Christina smiled at her noticing her lips were tight and her eyes loaded with fear. How Hank's partner could have deemed this woman to be calm was beyond her.

"I need to ask you, Julia. Where is your daughter? Where is Caitlin?"

Christina could not believe he blurted this out. She was as shocked as Julia, evidenced by a grimace of pain on her face. Her lips, eyes, and her whole expression were poised to demonstrate outrage.

"Please, before you protest let me remind you. The truth will save us all a lot of trouble. The city has put in considerable time and money on this case already. You're the only one who can put a stop to it. No one needs to get hurt."

Christina witnessed Julia cover her face and break down in tears. Soon, her whole body was racked with sobs. Christina came forward and laid a hand on her head. "Don't cry. Everything is going to work out."

"Where is your daughter, Ms. Castle?"

"She's at my sister's. She's fine." She uttered between sobs. Once the tears subsided, she blew her nose in the tissue Christina handed to her and admitted. "I didn't realize I was chasing Jeff. He missed Caitlin so much. We hadn't seen each other in months. His father didn't approve of his only son dating a single mother. Jeff came by to tell me he wanted to spend the rest of his life with me, regardless of his father's wishes."

"What's his full name, Julia?"

She hesitated. "I think I should wait to talk to Jeff first," she added in a childlike voice. "He was here when I came to. Told me what happened. Said his father had a complete change of heart. Probably understands now how much we love each other."

Hank glanced at Christina with a stern expression. "His name? We'll find out sooner or later."

"Jeff," she made one last attempt at silence then gave in faced with Christina's warm smile. "Jeff Hannigan."

Hank's eyes rounded. He stared at Christina. He paused seemingly waiting for her to make the connection.

She shrugged, utterly clueless.

"Hannigan? As in William Derrick Hannigan? New-Jersey's Governor?"

Julia nodded as she lowered her eyes.

Hank raised both arms to let them fall by his side as though distraught and beaten. He took a deep breath he let trail in a monotone voice. "Talk to Jeff. Please advise him there'll be someone from our office who will contact him to take his deposition, first thing Monday morning. I'm sure he'll want to have legal representation."

He moved away from the bed, still shaking his head. "What's wrong?" asked Christina.

"Wrong?" he whispered. "You can bet on Hannigan's people calling a press conference, at the crack of dawn Monday morning. There'll be a sincerely felt apology, a plea to gain the public's sympathy for two star-crossed lovers. In short, Hannigan is going to turn this into a three ring circus, milk the cow for his reelection campaign and meanwhile, the DA is going to let him do it. Hell, he'll probably lend his support."

"You didn't actually think the DA would prosecute in a case like this, did you?"

Hank stomped out of there taking giant leaps down the hallway. After a little salute toward Julia, Christina ran to catch up only to be subdued by his angry rumbles unsure as to how her presence had served any purpose.

"All the man-hours we put on this." He shook his head. "Our department is going to be the butt of endless jokes. Perfect example of money talks, bullshit walks. Of course, had the boyfriend been some unknown, there would have been heavy sanctions handed out. You can bet on it."

Christina didn't see how this was possible but refrained from arguing.

Halfway down the hall, Hank came to a full stop. He pivoted toward her with a deeply etched brow indicating grave concern. "You know what this means don't you?"

Busy catching her breath, Christina waited for him to say.

"Emma Willis was dead on—acutely aware of the whole god-damn fiasco. And she was right. Damn it, she was right," he mumbled more to himself.

Turning to stare squarely into Christina's face, he added. "How fast can you arrange a meeting?"

The idea had presented itself earlier. Now, Christina wasn't sure she could trust Hank's dogged determination anymore.

"Not you too?" He rubbed his eyes with a tired hand. "Christina, you came to me, remember? And I was there for you. Now, it's your turn to help me."

She wore her stone expression the one she knew would only prod him to argue.

"Don't cave on me now. Now's not the time. Besides," Hank added as an afterthought. "You'll also be helping Emma."

She sighed giving into his wishes as she knew she might. "Her grandmother—mother's mother—throws a party each year for the kids in her class … and the teacher," she designated herself. "The invitation is for tomorrow night. I'm sure Abigail wouldn't mind me bringing a friend."

"Where?"

"At Emma's house. So both her parents will be there."

He nodded. He understood. "We'll have to rehearse it."

<u>*Seven*</u>

Out with Aunt Franka

*A*bigail drove into the annex parking lot a few minutes before seven. Emma smiled, giddy with thoughts of seeing her aunt Franka. Food did not figure in her mind, although she hadn't eaten since the apple she had snacked on after school. She knew Amelia was starving, though the main draw to this outing being they would spend quality time in a quality restaurant.

"Now little girls, stay close to your grandma Abby." Abigail locked the car remotely encircling each girl with a tight grip. "The annex is like an exotic menagerie filled with unusual people." Emma caught her mumbling, "Perfect place to elicit a child's disappearance."

She had overheard her grandmother's protest at bringing them to what she referred to as a public zoo. Franka had insisted since both Amelia and Emma wanted to eat at nearby Casa Dante, reservations would be easier to make with time to spare.

Franka had promised to leave her class early and take good care of them before heading off to South Manhattan for a movie and a stay-over.

"Your aunt is so cool," Amelia said opening big eyes for Emma's benefit.

"Ahem." Abigail cleared her throat.

"You're cool too, Mrs. Tichy."

"How many times have I told you?" Abigail said to Amelia dragging them both at a jogging pace. "You call me Grandma Abby. I insist, or I shall call you Miss Swift."

"Sorry, Grandma Abby." She turned toward Emma. "Weird." Turning to Abigail, she added. "I find Franka's so lucky to live in New York City. I'm going to live in Manhattan when I grow up."

"Young lady, when you grow up you'll discover that where you live is not as important as how you live."

Amelia answered, "Doesn't where you live influence how you live—a little?" Emma recognized the tone. Amelia was sassing her grandmother.

Abigail produced a loud sigh as she waited for others to open the door to the red brick building. "To be ten again," she said shaking her head while walking them inside.

A guard met them a few feet down the corridor asking Abigail where she was headed.

Abigail scrambled in her purse to find the number of the class-room Franka had given her and mumbled that the three of them did not warrant an interrogation. "The corridor is full of ques-tion-raising characters."

"Merely trying to help, ma'am."

Emma, free at last, peeked inside one of the classrooms the open door ajar enough to draw her attention. Men and women with lost expressions on their faces stared at a blackboard where a professor underlined a bunch of Xs and Ys. She picked up on her grandmother's argument with the guard telling him her daughter taught in a classroom at the end of the corridor. She spotted the back of the teacher's head, wavy long brown hair held together at the nape with a clip, and something oddly familiar about the person's square slim shoulders. Man or woman she thought feverishly as the image brought back what she'd seen before. The man in the car, the one the policewoman had called ma'am.

The professor turned around to face Emma, and she focused on the prominent nose and the green pallor to the oddly shaped face.

She turned around quickly, nausea threatening to overtake her.

"Emma, come along, dear. You're going to make us late."

She carefully put one foot in front of the other as the space around her seemed to shift. She extended her arms to steady her stance and wobbled toward her grandmother.

"Sweetie, are you all right? You're so pale." Abigail bent to her height and checked her forehead. Stroking her hair, she added. "You're dizzy. How long since you've eaten?"

"We're starving Mrs. ... Grandma Abby. Both of us. We ate nothing else since grabbing an apple two hours before we left," Amelia answered pointing to her and Emma.

"Well, this is inexcusable," Abigail roared as she stood to grab both girls by the hand and to resume her walk toward her daughter's classroom. "What goes on in that house of yours? I swear, this time, I'm putting my foot down. You'll be spending a lot more time at my house this summer. I'm going to fatten you up."

Emma started to protest, but Amelia stopped her with keen eyes. "Emma your grandmother has a heated pool and a game room." She eyed Abigail. "Can I come too?"

"Of course, you can."

Emma gave one last look at the room behind her, happy to let her grandmother drag her along by the hand. Did the awful man she'd seen teach a class here or did she imagine things again?

They entered Franka's classroom, and Emma considered the room appeared filled with little wiggle room to spare except for the last row by the door, where there stood four wooden chairs with half-moon tables attached to their right arm. She wondered how anyone could write or keep books on such a small space—not even a cover to lift where a person might stash paper and pen.

Standing at her desk, Franka spotted them and smiled. She motioned for them to come inside.

Amelia raised lopsided eyebrows. "This is worlds from Rutgers University. Your aunt's regular classroom is so much bigger and cleaner."

"Sh. You little girls are disrupting the class," Abigail told them. "Sit down and be quiet." Certainly unusual for her grandmother to be terse. Emma figured she was in a bad mood when she glimpsed her trying to squeeze to sit into the small space. "She promised me she would leave early—fine thing," she mumbled. "You're going to lose your reservation. This child has no sense of time, no sense at all."

"It's okay, Grandma." Emma smiled at her. "I'm sure our reservation is fine."

"You're such a sweet girl—and you being as hungry as you are." She played affectionately with Emma's long hair.

The three of them breathed a little easier when Franka dismissed the class. "An early night of it today. Nevertheless, you've got lots of homework." She smiled and picked up her books making her way through the early risers to get to her mother and the girls.

"I'm sorry, Mom."

"You promised you would finish early." Abigail lamented.

"Had you dropped off the girls in front, as I had suggested, I would have met them at reception, but since you told me you were walking them to class, I figured I had a few more minutes." She checked the time. "Here you walk in seven minutes before the end."

"The damn security guard," Abigail began.

Franka raised a shoulder and leaned over to give her mother a kiss on the cheek. "Don't be mad, Mom. Frowning promotes wrinkles." She laughed at her mother's softening expression.

"So does laughing," Abigail countered.

Like an unstoppable wave rushing through a dam, the throng of two hundred and fifty students shoved and pushed to get out.

Franka scooped both girls up gave them each a hug then urged,"Let's get out of here or we'll be trampled. Don't worry," she added as she turned toward her mother. "I called the restaurant. They're keeping our reservation an extra fifteen minutes."

Squeezed between her aunt and the crowd, Emma bumped into a strange looking person. She looked up and stared at the back of sloping shoulders and mid length gray hair. The man turned toward her, but Emma couldn't apologize. She couldn't utter a single word. The man she'd been glimpsing everywhere stood right in front of her staring at her with faded blue eyes over a big round nose.

In a flash, she was elsewhere on a dark stretch in a strange neighborhood. She spotted the street name on the signpost and the address. No screams, just a whistling wind pushing around dust on the ground. The picture loomed closer and bigger, and she called out someone's name as little hands reached out to her.

Emma's turn to scream only the sound silent and petrifying rippled through her brain.

She opened her eyes and took a few seconds to realize she had fainted because she was lying on the ground with her grandmother and aunt's faces glued to her. She turned and found her head propped up on someone's lap—against the man who'd terrified her. Only looking at him now, his hair was salt and pepper and short while his eyes shone black and his skin appeared swarthy and dark. He wore the same clothes as the man who'd just scared her to death. No mistake. And she worried about confusing such different looking persons.

"Thank God, child." She caught her grandmother's whisper. "Are you all right?"

Emma held out her hand for her aunt to help her up. "One minute I had my arm around you, the next you were on the floor," Franka uttered pulling her up and brushing the dust off her jeans. "You can thank this kind man—Joe is it?" Franka added looking up at the man Emma had bumped into and giving him her best smile.

He nodded.

"He's the reason your head never touched the floor."

"Thank you," Emma muttered shyly.

"S'no trouble. Reckon you got to eat more." He stared at Abigail and Franka. "Girl's too skinny." Lips pinched he flicked a salute and left.

"He's right," Amelia added loudly. "We're starving, Aunt Franka."

"We're going to take care of that," Franka said smoothing

Emma's strands of hair. "In a few minutes, you're going to find more food than you could ever eat in ten meals."

A few hours later riding in the back of Franka's car, they headed toward Manhattan.

Emma found Amelia quiet. Sated, Amelia seemed content to survey street traffic go by as they neared Franka's loft in fashionable Soho.

Her aunt loved her accommodations. Who wouldn't love a one thousand eight hundred square-foot loft in a newly constructed building? White oak floors and rainforest kitchen counter tops, marble tub and all new appliances. The place also featured floor to ceiling windows. They even enjoyed the use of a fitness center downstairs. Still, what Emma and Amelia liked best was the rooftop terrace with awesome views stretching well beyond the Hudson, even to the Empire State Building on a clear day.

Amelia particularly liked that they were close to all the shops and could hop a bus and go any place they wanted.

Except they wouldn't be going anywhere this evening. All three had voted to have an early night—well it was a majority vote. Amelia was still roaring to go. She had quietly conceded to please them which might be the reason for her silence.

"Don't worry, sweeties. Tomorrow morning, I know a new place where we can have breakfast in Greenwich Village. Then we can hop a bus and go to Central Park. Afterward, if you still want to catch that movie, we'll cross 57 Street, the one with the theater on the corner."

Emma had readily agreed, grateful Amelia had glanced at her and opted not to argue. Emma thought Amelia might sense how tired she was, tired and mostly worried—afraid of going crazy.

She was beginning to spot the man's face everywhere. The images surrounding him were increasing in strength. This evidence was no horror movie or bad TV show she could just turn off. Real or imagined, the picture was inside her head and out of control.

Worse, she couldn't talk to anyone about it, unburden herself to make the problem seem smaller or vanish and go back in its cage. Like the monkey who'd gotten loose one morning while her third-grade class visited the zoo. Miss Tyler had been brave she remembered, staring down the animal slowly and motioning the children to leave the premises until guards had come with a net and a tranquilizer gun.

She thought of confiding in Miss Tyler, but she would want to talk to her parents, and she'd be right back where she started. In truth, living with an angry father scared her more than coming face to face with the awful man.

Their arms loaded with leftover restaurant food, they took the elevator to the eighth floor.

"You're lucky to live here, Aunt Franka," Amelia said. "My mother said these lofts are über expensive."

"She does, does she?"

Coming out of the elevator, Emma secured her package before it fell. "Grandma Abby helped her get it."

Franka chuckled. "Grandma Abby talks too much."

"So, your grandma's rich huh?" Amelia's eyes sparkled.

"Not Microsoft rich, but I guess she's got a sizable stash tucked away."

They'd arrived at Franka's door. "Besides," Emma added. "She says she likes giving money to family. She's always trying to give us money, but my father won't even let her get takeout."

"There is someone in the house," Franka said when she didn't need her key to open the door. "Hello?" She called out a little concerned. "You girls stay here. I'm going to check who it is."

She walked a few steps and came face to face with someone she seemed to know.

"What are you doing here?" She glanced at the girls.

Emma and Amelia gave the young man the once over with big eyes.

The stranger took Franka in his arms despite her half-hearted protests. "You give me the news you're pregnant over the internet—in an e-mail?" He pushed her away, and his angry tone of voice carried. "That's how you tell me I'm the father of your child—our child?"

"This is not the time to discuss this. I …didn't know how to tell you. I didn't want you to feel obligated or trapped."

"Obligated? Franka, I love you. And you love me. A guy can sense these things. Don't try to hide this from me."

"Can we please talk about this later? My niece and her friend are here for a visit." Franka gave him the eye.

Jimmy looked at the little girls standing in the hallway as though just noticing them.

"Girls, this is Jimmy, a friend."

"I'm sorry. I rushed right over." He turned toward Emma and Amelia. "Hi, kids. Please, come in. My apologies. I hope I didn't reveal anything I wasn't supposed to."

"It's okay," Emma said, smiling at him. "We already know about the baby. Franka is happy about it." Emma didn't care about her aunt's round eyes on her—not when she saw how happy Jimmy's smile beamed at them.

"She is. Well, well, good to know."

"All right," Franka professed once she'd closed the door behind the girls. "Can we not talk about this anymore?"

Jimmy nodded.

"Good. Jimmy, please go home. We'll have a long chat on Sunday. I promise."

"Okay." He nodded releasing a huge sigh. "I'll go. He looked from Emma to Amelia and parked his eyes on Emma. "But I've got a witness. You heard your aunt, right?" He waited for Emma to nod. She laughed with a shy smile when he winked at her.

"How did you know which one." Franka indicated both girls.

"Easy." He smiled at Emma. "She's a beauty—like her aunt. Oh," he added staring straight at Amelia. "And you're as cute as a button. Don't ever forget that."

Then he grabbed Franka a little roughly and kissed her on the mouth.

Emma noticed Amelia's eyes widening when the lip-locked lovers opened their mouths prolonging the kiss a few more seconds—long enough that Amelia had time to poke her. "They're French kissing," she whispered.

Emma rolled her eyes, though she couldn't help a big smile.

"Goodnight, Jim."

A few minutes later, poised in front of a huge bay window, Emma watched as Jimmy Roth ran outside toward the visitor's parking lot. The area brightly lit allowed her to see the car he unlocked and stepped into—a faded tan bazoo with a peanut shaped rust spot on the roof near the driver's side.

Eight

Waiting For Tommy

*E*mma stared at the dining room crawling with kids from her class. Never failed. Every year, this day in June generated more traffic in her house than Christmas did or her birthday or even New Year's Eve when her mother said the house belonged to family and close friends. Her father would say come January first, her mother would be so exhausted from preparing the holidays she needed a vacation of her own which was why the house stood by welcoming the New-Year in silence.

She glanced at Fran and Lucy eyeing their outfits in the glass cabinet's reflection. Fran applied lip gloss while Lucy scanned her surroundings trying her best to appear bored. A few years ago, the three of them had been good friends, back when she'd enjoyed everyone's company. Now, they had grown apart especially this last year or so.

Sometimes when she was alone with nothing to do, she would wonder if the split between them had been her fault. Could be. She had committed the cardinal sin, as Amelia liked to say, of not keeping up with the trends, clothes wise or otherwise. Personally, Emma didn't care whether she wore the latest fad in shoes or whether she painted her lips to match the color of her sweater.

Maybe she was a late bloomer. Her mother had said this to her grandmother once. Still, she couldn't figure why any girl had to care about such things to be considered on the right road to womanhood. Couldn't she bloom into some other kind of flower? One that didn't snitch on her friends laugh behind their backs to sound interesting, one whose whole world didn't revolve around teasing boys?

She pleaded with her mother to invite only the girls and boys she liked. Her mother countered she couldn't modify the list so late in the game. Such a change would create rifts in the classroom.

Stranger yet Emma wondered why they all came. Surely a girl like Carey Huggins had better things to do than attend her little party. She was cute and fashionable and, except for Tommy Carson, had all the boys clamoring for her particular brand of attention. Peter Lars hung on her arm right this minute. She paraded him around the house like a trophy, getting him to do all her bidding.

As she thought of Tommy, she walked over to the small salon where she would usually find him talking with one of his friends, hiding from the she-devils as he called them.

He wasn't anywhere. Emma checked her watch and worried he wouldn't be able to make the trip from Connecticut. Rain came down in sheets, and she hadn't spoken to him since the morning before, at the Park.

"Hey, how about you put some music on so we can dance?" Amelia sneaked up from behind, scaring her a little.

"Sure. I'm not good with the choice of songs, though. Want to be the DJ?"

"Nope, not me. Doesn't Tommy usually do the job?"

"He's not here yet."

"Let's get your dad to do this. He's hip," Amelia said doing a quick visual search for him around the room. She smiled when she found him talking to one of the parents. "I'll go get him." She winked at Emma.

Emma spotted her dad bend an ear to Amelia and nod, a slanted smile across his face. The gesture clearly meant, go away little girl. I'm working here. He wasn't acquainted with Amelia's determination Emma thought, a smile tugging the corners of her mouth. Presently she was dragging Patrick Willis by the sleeve to encourage him to join them.

At least her father played the attentive host for the occasion. He could be charming when he wanted to be with a bright smile and laughing eyes. Emma had detected his freckles seemed to put people at ease. Of course, many parents being present meant a chance for him to shine and gain their trust. He'd won awards for his salesmanship abilities, selling insurance, and he even took his little family to Bermuda on a trip he'd won when she was five— her memories of the voyage all but gone.

"Emma," he called out. And Emma thanked her lucky stars he was smiling. "I tried to explain to Amelia here that I wouldn't know what kind of music you kids like."

"But Mr. Willis, I have all the mixes you can ever want right here," she said showing him a palm-held device. "In my iPod. All you have to do is supervise the player."

"Where is Tommy?" he asked.

"Did Mr. Carson say anything to you, Dad about not coming?" Emma worried.

"No. Rudy was supposed to call me this morning to give me the assignment for my house client in Boston," he mumbled to himself. For her benefit, he added, "Have no idea."

Emma bit her bottom lip. Had Tommy broken his promise and decided to ride which might explain his delay and why no one had heard from him.

She eyed the door and willed him to arrive recognizing the gesture as futile. Still, she'd never wished for someone to appear on her doorstep as much as she wanted Tommy to do so right now.

"Thanks, Dad. I'll find someone else to do it."

"Good. You girls have fun."

"Give me your iPod," she told Amelia.

"Why don't we do it ourselves?"

"I'll ask Aunt Franka. You and I are not allowed to handle the sound system. Touching my dad's precious stereo is forbidden."

"How come Tommy's allowed?"

"He's not. He brings his own amp. His music. Does his own shuffling."

As she handed her aunt Franka the iPod, the doorbell rang, and Eloise called out for Emma to tend to the guests. Emma prayed the Carson's were at the door. She turned toward Amelia. "You help Aunt Franka. I'll get the door."

"Oh no, you don't. You don't get rid of me that easily, Emma Willis." Amelia gently elbowed her in the ribs. "I'd rather catch who's at the door."

Christina Tyler and a man friend stood in the doorway.

"Hi, Miss Tyler," Emma greeted her. "Please, come in."

Christina smiled. "Thanks, Emma—and who's this?" she added startled as though not expecting to run into someone she didn't recognize.

"My friend Amelia."

"Well hello, Amelia." Christina smiled. "Girls this is Hank Apple. He's a friend of mine."

Amelia gave Christina huge eyes and a knowing smile after which she leaned toward Miss Tyler on her toes to whisper. "Hank's a hunk, Miss Tyler."

Surprised by the bold gesture, Christina glanced at Hank to check if he'd understood. They all had Emma thought. Hank's eyebrows pointing in different directions far above his eyes confirmed this. Emma caught Miss Tyler biting the inside of her lip not to laugh. "Where are your mom and dad, Emma? We'd like to pay our respects."

"Right this way," Emma added sliding Amelia a pair of loaded eyes. Only, she didn't spot any remorse in her friend's playful blue eyes, merely a whole lot of confidence.

When Emma led Miss Tyler and her friend to her mother and father, music blared in the room off the small parlor. Emma thought of Tommy, yet her heart sank as she realized he still had not arrived.

The sound system occupied the center of a large, mostly unfurnished room, and this is where Tommy set up—directly next to the door. A poster congratulating all the students hung in the middle of the area beneath the chandelier, and balloons and streamers decorated the back wall. Below the window stood a large table filled with goodies to eat, but what the kids liked best was the unfurnished room which provided lots of space to mingle and dance.

"Pleased to meet you, Mr. Apple," Patrick Willis said as he shook the man's hand, already eyeing him as a prospective client.

"You seem familiar. Have we met before?"

"I don't think so." Hank's answer was succinct, bordering on terse as he shook Patrick's hand.

"I don't usually forget a face," Patrick added already shrugging off the incident. "I hope you enjoy yourself, Miss Tyler. This party's for you too." He glanced at Eloise and wrapped his arm around her waist. "My wife and I appreciate all the hard work you do with our kids."

Christina smiled. "I'm blessed to teach in this neighborhood. Parents here do a fantastic job raising their children."

"Thank you," Eloise said.

Emma felt her mother was uncomfortable with the compliment.

At that moment, Franka called out. "Pat, I need your help with this thing."

"If you'll excuse me." Pat flew like a bullet his token apology still hanging in the air as he ran to the aid of his precious system being mauled.

Eloise excused herself to cater to other guests. "Girls, can I have a little help with the party favors?"

Amelia followed close behind.

Emma nodded, but a sudden sadness washed over her gluing her to the spot. Tommy and his dad were not there. They were usually the first ones to arrive. The little pinch in the heart vicinity made her want to cry as she realized without Tommy, she had no one. Nobody else mattered. Worse, she'd never noticed before what a big part he played in her life. So she squeezed her lips together and struggled to be strong.

"Is everything all right, Emma?" Christina asked, the warm

concern on her face snapping Emma out of her melancholy.

"Of course, I'm wondering why Tommy and his dad are so late. He usually takes care of the music."

Hank placed a gentle hand on her shoulder. "Don't worry about Tommy, Emma. Thanks to you, he's okay."

It took only seconds for Emma to get the meaning of Hank's gist. As she stared into his eyes, there was no mistaking his words. She turned wild eyes on Christina Tyler and spotted concern on her features—nothing like the fear coursing through her. The eyes Emma directed on her, probing and accusing, coined her teacher with a resentful glare. Emma realized she became angrier with each passing second it took for the betrayal to become real.

She felt as though someone had pried inside her and stripped her of all her thoughts, all her privacy. "You overheard us," she whispered her voice trembling. "You listened in, and you told?" Emma took a deep breath. "You weren't supposed to say. You weren't supposed to listen."

Christina tried to take her arm, but Emma yanked it away. "I trusted you."

"No. You didn't." She spoke quietly, evenly. When Christina searched her surroundings, Emma realized she needed to remain calm. "Had you trusted me, you would have come to me. Told me yourself."

Emma shook her head mutinous to the words.

"Now. Right here, right now is when I show you … you can trust me."

Christina waited her eyes locked into Emma's, the tilt of her head inviting her to take the leap. "I won't disappoint you. I promise."

Emma pinched her lips and stared up at Hank. She wasn't quite sure why, but she read in the slanted eyes that he would do anything to get the information he needed. Glancing back at Christina, she recognized a friend ready to stand guard for her—against Hank Apple or anyone else.

She asked Hank. "How do you know Tommy's all right?"

Hank looked around and nodded to someone waving to him. "Is there somewhere we can talk?"

Emma hoisted her shoulders looking at the floor.

"Emma, why don't you show me your room?" Christina asked nudging her as she did.

She hesitated until she spotted her grandmother coming toward them. "Okay." Emma took the landing and turned toward her grandma. "I'm going to show Miss Tyler my room, Grandma."

"That's fine, sweetheart."

Once inside, Hank closed the door behind them. Christina asked if she could sit on the bed.

Emma agreed and turned toward Hank standing tall beside the door his hand still on the handle. "How do you know about Tommy?" she asked.

"I'm a police detective with the second precinct, Emma."

Emma turned accusatory eyes on her teacher. "He's not your friend, is he?" She'd just made the big speech about trust.

"He is, Emma. We dated for a long time." She eyed Hank. "Two years ago."

"Emma." Hank left the door and came inside the room. He propped up his foot against the small bench near the window, resting his arms on his knee. "We found out where Tommy rides on the weekends. It wasn't hard to do. Tommy has family there. Then we had one of our guys check the jump's frame, thoroughly."

Emma didn't have to look up at him anymore. She stared at his impassive expression and knew he fought to remain calm, not just now, but constantly. She waited.

"You were right, Emma. They found wood rot—a lot of it, a nightmare waiting to collapse. Although," he hesitated looking at Christina. "If it hadn't been Tommy breaking his neck off the ramp, it would have been some other kid with a bike."

She let out a huge sigh of relief. Then she stared at her shoes; the blue pumps her grandma had just bought her to wear with her blue dress. "I didn't think about anyone else getting hurt. I'm sorry."

"Don't apologize," Hank quipped. "It's not your fault. Certainly not your responsibility to take on the whole world's problems. Hell knows there are a lot of those."

She didn't answer, still staring at the ground.

He straightened and walked over to her standing small in the middle of the room. He flicked her chin up to see her eyes. "Emma, a ten-year-old's world should be comprised of friends and family. That's all there is to it."

She was chewing the side of her lip, and she nodded surreptitiously.

He took her by the hand and brought her close to the window. He sat on the small bench to be at eye level. "Taking on the whole world's mess isn't even my problem. It's not Miss Tyler's problem either. My job is to look after this community. Your job is to go to school, enjoy your friends, and build your future one day at a time."

She nodded.

"By being brave, you reached out to a friend. The gesture created a wave that went all the way to me. This was when it became my turn to be brave. I reached out, and the wave helped someone outside my community. This is how we can take on the world, one person at a time."

Emma smiled. She understood what he was trying to say.

"You were also right about Julia Castle, and her daughter Caitlin."

She eyed Miss Tyler, pulled her hand out of Hank's hands and sat on the bed.

"Wait a minute." He rose, mesmerized by Emma's reaction. "You did more than see what happened. You knew their names?" He seemed stunned. "Didn't you? Names aren't going to be released until the press conference, Monday morning."

Emma wished she was a little more worldly, not just a dumb kid anyone could dupe. Hank had tricked her, on purpose or not the result was the same. She couldn't say she didn't know who these people were now, not with the stupid gesture that had given her away.

***

Meanwhile downstairs, Tommy and his dad had just arrived, and Tommy asked about Emma. "She's around here somewhere, Tommy," Patrick answered. "Let me take your coats, Rudy. How was the drive down here?"

"Crazy weather." He handed both their coats to him. "We had to stop by the side of the road a couple of times. Rain was coming down so bad. Couldn't see two feet in front of us."

"Rudolph Carson," they heard from ten feet away. "Where the hell have you been?"

A tall, dark curly haired man holding a glass of fruit punch walked up to them. "Lost touch a couple of years ago," he told Patrick, who took pains to show how much he hated the interruption. "And here our kids hang together at school—same class it seems."

"Bert Huggins," Rudy acknowledged with a broad smile. "Yes, it has been a long time."

Bert turned toward Patrick. "Willis, I didn't know you were hosting a party for celebrities," he chuckled.

"I beg your pardon?" Patrick answered, annoyed.

"Hank Apple. More famous around these parts than Dick Tracy." Again he chuckled. Faced with Patrick's stunned look he added. "You were just talking to him."

Patrick nodded and smiled. "If you'll excuse me, Rudy—Bert, I'll go find Emma."

Patrick's expression changed the minute he was out of view. He located Eloise and asked. "Where's Emma?"

"I don't know." She turned and spotted her mother. "Mom, have you seen Emma?"

"Last I heard she was going upstairs to show Miss Tyler her room."

"Thanks," Patrick muttered. He took the stairs two by two to his daughter's room, anger slowly building inside his head.

Nine

Emma's Room

The door to Emma's room swung open preventing her from explaining anything else to Miss Tyler and detective Apple.

For the first time in a long time, Emma welcomed the sight of her father in her bedroom's doorway like some knight in shining armor. She spotted the anger in his eyes and trembled thinking if a scene didn't arise, she would bear the brunt of his temper later when all the guests had gone home.

"Emma? What's going on here?" Her father stared at one sour face to the next his cheeks on fire with the impatience of a man arriving on the scene after the fact of an evil done deal.

Christina Tyler recovered first. She rose from the bed and quickly explained, "Emma is showing us around displaying for Hank and me her seashell collection."

"That's right, Daddy." Emma picked up a swirling pink shell complete with little decorative holes curled in the bottom. "My father brings them back from his many trips. He knows how much I love the ocean."

Emma measured the slits of her father's eyes—quite narrow as he tried to gauge the mood around the room.

On cue, Hank relaxed and smiled, so did Christina Tyler. Still, Emma spotted hesitation on her dad's expression.

"Wonderful collection," Hank said as his gaze swept the shelves over the desk. He turned his attention to her father. "Say are you Patrick Willis the insurance guy? I say this because my partner, Matt Logan, has a policy from a P. Willis. Is that you?"

Patrick's face toned down a couple of shades, and his eyes lost their unease. "Yeah, Matthew Logan. He's one of my clients."

"Talk about coincidence. Matt told me you gave him a good deal on a term life—made him a whole comprehensive package. I'm looking for something like this."

Emma released the breath she hadn't realized she held. Her dad's face had lost all its animosity. He came inside and shook Hank's hand. "I'm your man." He reached into his pant pocket. "Here, I happen to have one of my cards," he said. "I'm leaving tomorrow night, though. Be back on Friday. I can have my office call you and schedule something for next week?"

"Absolutely. Looking forward to our meeting." Hank turned toward Christina. I think you best give a little attention to some of your other students or they'll call Emma teacher's pet." He smiled stretching out his arm for Christina to join him.

"Are you coming, Emma?" Christina invited her to do so holding out her hand.

Emma nodded, smiling with relief. Apparently, Hank had played the right card with her father. As they followed Patrick downstairs, she wondered if her father's reputation preceded him or if Hank was intuitive? Most likely, being a good detective, he'd studied what her father did for a living beforehand. He revealed himself to be a good psychologist. Emma peered at him from the corner of her eye, good psychologist or not she hoped this would be her last encounter with Hank Apple.

On the landing, she spotted Tommy and waved to him excitedly.

He greeted her with a baked-on half smile. "Hey, they shut down the tournament. How did you know?"

Emma peered around them and hushed him. "You promised me you wouldn't ride."

"Hey, can't a guy watch?"

"You didn't tell your dad, did you?"

"Nah. My father wouldn't believe me anyway. Sometimes, he is as dumb as he looks."

Tommy's comment being so left field, they stared at each other and laughed. Released tensions, calmed apprehensions, both laughed until they were giddy.

After she got him fruit punch, braved the other girls' jealous glares, after Tommy slowed the pace of the music, he asked. "Want to dance this one?"

She nodded a little surprised.

Clumsily he took her in his arms and diligently performed the four corner box step as well as big clunky feet allowed. To execute the preset ritual, he kept her at a comfortable distance, glued his eyes to the floor and remained silent.

Emma recognized the fixed smile on Tommy's face as the one he usually wore when facing Mr. Piccolo, the school principal. Not very flattering she thought, but a show of respect nonetheless.

Emma paid particular attention to avoid Christina Tyler and Hank Apple all evening, although they happened to be the first couple to leave. She even made sure to be unavailable when they said their goodbyes at the door. Hidden in the small room off the hallway, she heard her mother's apology. "I'm sorry. I don't know where Emma is."

"Quite all right. Emma's coming in a morning next week to help me mend some of the books before we put them away for the summer."

"Why? What has she done?" Patrick demanded to know.

"Nothing." Christina's tone sounded surprised yet controlled. "Nothing at all. She volunteered."

Now, the last remaining handful was about to leave—Tommy and Amelia amongst them.

"Amelia, sweetie," Eloise called out. "Your mom's here."

Amelia grabbed her raincoat and bag. "Sure was great seeing you again, Tommy. Thanks for the dance." She gave him her best smile.

Tommy raised his eyebrows and countered through clenched teeth. "You're the one who asked."

Amelia wagged narrow eyes and a sour smile at him, and Emma realized Tommy had hurt her feelings. She turned and gave Emma a hug. "Call me tomorrow, Emma."

Once they had all gone, the house became once more bathed in silence, though the far away sound of music and mingling of people still echoed in her head when Emma took the stairs to her room, and the slow climb accentuated the hour following the party to be anticlimactic. As much as she hated the yearly brouhaha of her parents opening their house to all her classmates, the aftermath drew loneliness in her. The silence drove home the fact she had no sibling, no one with whom she might share the night's events or address the comments people had made to laugh at the quirky moments and amend some of those moments to make them even funnier.

She pushed the door to her room and pondered the area still smelled of Miss Tyler's perfume—a good smell, but a painful memory nonetheless.

She sat on the edge of her bed and worried about Hank Apple. Her restless mind told her he wasn't going to leave well enough alone. He would find a way to contact her again, ask more questions, and maybe even try to trick her purposely now he knew what a dummy she was.

A long sigh escaped her. At least the rain had stopped. She walked over to the window and tugged on it with all her strength to open wide the stiff wooden frame. She glimpsed the tree with its comforting branches laden with water, almost inviting her to cry. She did. Quietly, she wept as she watched the leaves rustle in the breeze. Nature was doing its best to dry the water off the branches, so she picked up a tissue and wiped her own eyes.

She smiled at the tall presence of a friend forever on the outside looking in on her. "I can't cry over my life in front of you," she whispered to the giant elm. "You're always so proud and cheerful. I have to be as brave as you are. The policeman said every day I'm building my future which means I'm going to have to smile today if I want tomorrow to be happy." One thing Hank Apple had said that made sense to her.

Took Emma what seemed like hours to fall asleep. She tossed and turned, and through a bubbling imagination, the day's events cooked in her head and rose like yeast-soaked dough to transform all her thoughts into hot, disturbing images.

Through it all, the face of the stranger she'd glimpsed in the car window the week before, the pale, wide-eyed profile she encountered everywhere loomed largely. The clock ticked on, and the traits became clear. Then his face slowly turned until he was staring directly at her with bulging red eyes, his smile twisted and mean, his whole expression seemingly demented and tortured.

Emma's heart pounded to the pitch of a wild roar—so loud, the startled organ woke her in a stroke of terror. She sat up disoriented, gasping for breath, passing a shaky hand to brush strands of hair out of her eyes.

"A nightmare," she breathed. Merely a bad dream. She checked the horizon. Sleek silver clouds raced against an ink-black sky. The pale moon partially eclipsed meant streetlight glow became the perfect backdrop for her tree coloring the foliage varying shades of gray.

A crackling sound got her attention. Sitting with her back straight against the headboard, she pulled the blanket up to her chin. Her legs went weak, and her hands began to tingle. Someone was outside below her window. It wasn't her imagination. She was wide awake.

She wanted to get up and go see to reassure herself, but she was too scared to move. The Elm would take care of her she thought. Then the idea hit her. All anyone had to do to get inside was climb the tree. It was a relatively easy climb. Tommy had done it many times when she'd needed help with math, and they'd had to study past her curfew. And her window was wide open.

Then her fear took shape. At first a shadow, then a body. Emma realized she was in mortal danger. She could see the outline of a heavy-set silhouette in the tree's branches. Too wide to be Tommy.

She recognized the face her dream had conjured. In the streetlight's soft glow, she could make out some of the man's features. It was him. The one police were trying to find. The man who'd kidnapped those other little girls. She screamed as loud as she could and sustained the cry for help as long as she could. But maybe the piercing noise had just been in her head because the man kept coming. There was no stopping him.

She closed her eyes and envisioned some way to protect herself, defend against the evil staring at her with wide, greedy eyes. That's when she invoked the little phrase Granny Dottie had carried down from her mother, the one Dottie had said was useless because it never procured anything. "Heaven's eye to life beyond, free your love of which I am fond so that my wish may be granted and I not be left stranded. I thank thee for loving me."

She reached under the blankets deep inside the middle and pulled out a small .38 revolver, wrapping her right hand around the rubberized handle.

Slowly, she pulled it out from under the sheet. The light and silvery weapon instantly gave her the confidence she needed to face her attacker. She became angry—deeply resentful that this man, to whom she had never done anything, would want to hurt her.

She stepped out of bed and didn't shake as she stood in front of the open window, prepared to stare him down. She saw him creep over the window sill, put one foot over Granny Dottie's little bench onto the carpet and remain suspended while sitting on the window ledge his other leg hanging in midair. He seemed surprised by the reception.

She could tell he became perturbed by the fact that she faced him unafraid, glaring at him and menacing him with a handgun. "I will use this if I have to," she uttered her voice surprisingly calm.

He smiled, his eyes becoming tight slits. "Toy gun's not going to scare me, lovey."

She remembered Tommy's father, Rudy Carson, showing them how he used his weapon as a decoy only in case of emergency. He'd caught Tommy with the revolver he'd snuck out of the drawer, bragging about the cool gun and waving it around. "Now, children, this is not a toy. Guns need to be handled with care, and only by grownups. In an emergency you squeeze the little button under the handle—a laser you can flare to scare a person into thinking you will shoot if you have to. Always better to scare than shoot."

"This is not a toy." Saying this, she triggered the laser and fixed the light on the man's chest.

There was noise coming down the hall.

The man's turn to glare at her with a hateful, manic calm. "I'm going to get you, witch. I know about you. People will thank me for getting rid of a witch. They'll thank me all right," he muttered before he disappeared into the night. She heard him laugh.

Then her door swung open. The gun fell to the floor just as the ceiling light flooded her room. Both parents ran in. Her mother was the first to reach her.

Eloise yanked her around to face her, to hold her in her arms. "What was the scream about, Emma? You scared me to death. Scared your father too."

"I thought we'd settled the nightmare problem, Emma. You're old enough to work through them," Patrick added.

She twisted in her mother's arms. "It wasn't a bad dream. It was real. Someone was in my room. He climbed the tree and came inside."

"It's just your imagination, Emma," her mom said stroking her hair. She stared at the floor. "What's this?" she asked when she picked up a toy gun beside Emma's foot. What's this doing here?"

Emma looked at the piece of bright orange plastic recently transformed from a Smith & Wesson revolver and shrugged. "I don't know why it's here." She looked at her father thinking she was about to get a lecture on crying wolf again. Instead, he bent to look directly at her, strapping two hands each side of her head. "Are you all right, Emma?"

She nodded. "You guys coming down the hall scared him away."

He bobbed his head. "Good—good," he breathed.

He had turned two shades of dark red and Emma thought he was going to explode.

"Eloise, stay with her. I'm going to have a look outside."

"Patrick," Eloise called out.

Emma sensed her mother's ambivalence as to what to do next, what to think. Perhaps she worried about her husband going out to face a potential threat.

Emma couldn't prevent a bad case of shakes. So Eloise scooped her up in her arms and sat on the bed with her.

Emma hugged her tightly. A cuddle from her mom always felt so warm, even a frightened one dressed in shivers while her mother cooed to her as though she was five years old again.

What surprised Emma the most was how good her father's validation felt. He believed her. He hadn't called her crazy or childish. He worried about her and came to her rescue.

<u>Ten</u>

Patrick To The Rescue

*W*orried about Patrick not returning, Eloise got up and urged Emma to follow. "I'm not leaving you here alone. Come on, sweetie. I'll make you a nice cup of hot cocoa."

About to leave the room, Eloise glanced at the open window. "Just a minute, Emma. I'm going to close the window." Gathering her robe and tugging on her belt, she walked over to the aperture and slung the chassis down. Then she clamped the side bolts shut.

Poised to return, she stopped in her tracks staring at the ground. Mesmerized to the spot, she bent and continued to stare her eyes riveted to the carpet.

"What's wrong, Mom?" Emma couldn't spot what her mother was eyeing the bed frame being in the way. She walked over and glanced at the floor. A muddy footprint had left a giant filthy mark on the beige carpet.

Eloise stared up at her, and Emma bit her bottom lip. Her mother's expression of mild concern turned into a gaze of terror. "Emma," she breathed slowly rising. "Someone was in your room. Did you see him?"

Emma shook her head. "I caught an outline. Room was dark, and I was too scared." She hated lying, but she couldn't implicate her mother, not now. Her father would lose all faith in her story if she mentioned this man was the same she had feared when coming home from the clinic.

"Oh, God." Eloise held her for what seemed like a long time. She was crying. "I'm so sorry I doubted you." She released her daughter and took a tissue out of her robe's pocket. Blowing her nose, she added. "That's what your dad must have seen."

As both flew down the stairs to come to Patrick's aid, the realization her father had believed his own eyes rather than give credence to her word deflated Emma. She supposed his unusual solidarity could be considered a step in the right direction. At least she didn't seem like a fool again, but at what price.

Downstairs, barely lit with night's discreet concoction of street lamps renegade stars and a crescent moon, lay before them fraught with shadows dancing strangely about the walls and furnishings.

"We can check out the tree from the dining room windows," Eloise said. "That's where your father will be." She held on to Emma's hand readying to run, but before they could take the leap the front door opened. Mother and daughter jumped toward each other.

"Patrick," Eloise breathed as she ran toward him. "Did you find anything?"

He stared from one to the other his face grim. Delicately, he removed the goulashes he'd slipped over bare feet.

He eyed the rim of his pajamas soggy and soiled his next words slurred with disgust. "What a mess. Puddles all over the yard, muddy ones." He rolled up the bottoms of his pants to keep them off the floor and away from his skin. Then he tightened the belt to his robe. "I ran across the same prints as the one on the carpet—except a lot deeper and much better defined. The downpour gave the idiot away. No doubt about that."

"What are we going to do?"

Patrick walked into the dining room and opened a small cabinet. He took a shot glass he filled to the brim with Scotch. "What I want to know is why a man is stalking our daughter?"

He turned toward Emma. "Emma honey, did you find anything unusual these past few weeks, anyone following you, some person reappearing a little too often?"

Emma shook her head.

"When you went downtown with your mother, someone staring at you a little longer than necessary at the clinic… listening in perhaps when your mom gave her information to the nurse."

"I don't know, Daddy."

Eloise attempted. "This person might not have realized he was climbing to the room of a ten-year-old girl. He could be a thief seizing an opportunity—the tree being right in front of him."

"Yeah, right. Like we would have something to rob—in this neighborhood." Patrick rolled his eyes. "That doesn't make sense."

Eloise glanced at Emma and smiled her way. She wrapped her arm around her waist. "Well, if as you say he was here to harm Emma," she hesitated. "We have to call the police. He'll be back. Pat, it's just a waiting game." She bit her lip and hugged her daughter.

He began to pace the length of the living room. "We can't call the police at one o'clock in the morning."

"It's only twelve thirty."

"It'll be one by the time they get here. Those patrol cars will disrupt the whole neighborhood. Two years my mother's gone, and they're just starting to warm up to us," he mumbled.

"Patrick we don't have a choice, and you're leaving for the week tomorrow night."

"Not anymore."

"You can't not go. How are you going to pay back the draws?"

"What are draws, Daddy?"

"Weekly advances company makes me against future sales. They pay themselves back when I go out of town to take care of their house accounts."

"Sorry, Daddy."

"Not your fault, honey."

Her father behaved so sweetly. And this was her fault. She bit her bottom lip not to cry. She couldn't risk telling anyone about her problem.

He stopped pacing. He walked over to the small room off the dining room, and Emma and Eloise looked at each other wondering why he was going to his office.

Patrick came back holding a calling card. "There might be something I can do." He picked up the phone on the credenza in the hallway.

"Who are you calling?" Eloise asked.

For a moment, it seemed as though he couldn't get his fingers to push the keys. He put the phone down and turned toward his wife and daughter. "I was thinking of calling that detective, Hank Apple. He seems like a decent man. I think he might be discreet."

"You can't." Emma quickly pleaded.

"Why not? He's done a lot of good for this community." He hesitated. "I guess I could explain our situation and ask him to keep the matter out of the press."

"You might be right, Pat. He's most likely the best candidate to approach right now for us to get some help."

"But he's friends with my teacher. She'll find out, and the whole school will be talking."

Eloise turned to her daughter surprised. "Emma. Your teacher is the best thing to happen to the school in a long time. She is the epitome of discretion and respect. She would never air out our business to other students or their parents for that matter."

Emma lowered her head. Her mother was right. Besides, it was Hank Apple she didn't trust. It would take him seconds to put two and two together before he'd throw hard questions at her. Might even tell her parents what he'd already learned about her.

The words that awful man had muttered rang in her ears. He'd called her a witch. He was going to tell the whole world she was a witch. Of course, she wasn't any such thing. She was just a ten-year-old coward—a liar and a coward. One thing for sure, a witch wouldn't have to hide behind lies.

"I'm sorry, Mom. You're right. Miss Tyler would never tell anyone. I'm sure she wouldn't."

***

A call came into Hank's cell phone, a little past twelve forty-five in the morning.

Christina looked at her watch and realized how late it was. Time had flown by in Hank's presence, and while both of them sat in his car in front of her house, she realized neither one wanted to leave nor was ready to take the next step.

Tuning out what he was saying she stared out of the car

window and had to concede that the rigors of Hank's job he'd once flogged at her as an excuse for avoiding commitment were a force to be acknowledged.

She smiled at her reflection in the window remembering his current admission of a loving and committed relationship being a sham, a lie he'd conjured to make her jealous, to cover his tracks should she be presently involved.

Tacitly she recognized the long and drawn out dinner they'd enjoyed as being another form of cover. A cover which allowed them to enjoy each other's presence without experiencing the awkwardness of a first date or better yet enabled them to avoid the trap of falling into the same old patterns, those vile arguments responsible for separating them two years prior. They both understood the game, although this did not make wanting to spend time in Hank's arms less compelling or the touch of his hands less desirable.

She sensed little tingles going up and down her spine as she imagined the way he used to touch her. Oh, and he remembered how to caress her. How to run his fingers gently around the base of her neck and melt away all her inhibitions—which he was doing now. No wonder her legs had become cotton, and her heart raced wildly. The erotic sensation was no memory. His touch hot and disturbingly real had her poised to beg him to come inside.

She turned, and his face loomed inches away. "What are you doing?"

"What we both wanted to do all evening but kept putting off." He nodded staring into her eyes. "Because we're a pair of chicken shits—you and me," he added more to interrupt the shock of protest on her face.

She gave in and chuckled. "Guess you're right. I'm afraid of getting hurt again, of drifting along in a meaningless relationship."

"Because you're in such a committed one right now?"

She wanted to argue that at least, being alone was her choice and not dictated by someone's selfishness, but she couldn't utter a word. He interrupted her speech, her train of thought, her breathing even as he kissed her lips and pried them open with his tongue.

She'd forgotten. She also gave Hank kudos for kissing. As their embrace grew passionate, as the heat spread to her limbs, she took what strength she had left to clamp her arms around his neck. Relationships be damned, the last coherent thought flooded in and out of her consciousness. She was his to have and to hold and would be for as long as he wanted her. That's why she was stunned and a little winded when he pulled away. She looked at him with concern in her eyes. "I don't care about any of our past issues," she whispered.

"Glad to hear it," he groaned.

Then she wondered if something more urgent called him elsewhere. "Was your phone call business?"

A full ear to ear grin crinkled the corners of his eyes, the smile she loved dearly and hadn't seen in a long time. "Good to find out I can still make you jealous." Then passion leaped back in his body and wiped the smile off his face. "I'm glad you still care."

This time, he pulled away completely and sat behind the wheel. He let out a huge breath as if to steady his nerves. "Call was business." He glanced at her. "Willis."

She laid a delicate hand on his arm, all ears.

"Emma had a visitor."

"God, is she all right?"

"Apparently so. But Willis wants me to go down and take a look."

"Why aren't they calling the police?"

He gave her an eyeful. "This is Patrick Willis we're dealing with. His first words were, 'Don't tell anyone.'"

"He has to know you can't keep this to yourself."

"Well, this is what I'm going to do my best to explain to him and his wife. Mostly, I'm going to try and win their little girl's trust."

"Whatever you do, don't mention Emma's talents in front of her parents."

"Hey," he grabbed a bunch of her hair to run it through his fingers. "You don't give me enough credit you know that?"

"I'm sorry. You're right. I forget what a hot shot psychologist you've become these last few years."

He bent toward her to lean his forehead against hers. "Don't make fun," he stressed each word. Once more he backed off gripping the wheel with both hands.

"Did you ever find the owner of the license plate number I gave you yesterday?"

"Not yet. The car's changed hands so many times." He turned toward her. "Want to come?"

"What? No, no no—not this time. Have them learn we're still together, at this hour? I'm not even sure what you are going to accomplish on site."

"I have some measuring tools trunk of my car ... my camera. I can take pictures and check out the grounds while the place is still fresh."

She shook her head at him. "Tools—in your car?"

"Yeah, pathetic. I know. Matt calls me this often enough. He's always telling me to get a life." He looked at her for what seemed like a long time. "I think … I think I put my life on hold. Now, maybe I'll dust it off, take it out for a spin."

She smiled and reached for the handle to let herself out. Bending to the window, she added. "Not a bad idea. See you."

Eleven

Police On The Premises

*S*unday afternoon, Emma sat in her room watching the beautiful day unfold from her window, mainly to stay out of the police's way. Detective Apple had convinced her father they needed to comb the area for clues.

Hank had stared at her while saying this. He'd said nothing about how she'd helped him solve his last case. She very much appreciated his discretion.

Her father seemed so disheartened, appeared so tired when he agreed to let them trample on his property, Emma felt sorry for him.

On the other hand, Emma was pleased her father's predictions of drawing the neighbors' ridicule had gone the other way. All morning, moms on her street holding on to their children for dear life—and not because they worried they might be sucked up by the house as Amelia said—came to pay their respect, to offer their help and support.

Her mother had let them in, cried a little over their generous contribution of kind words and sympathy and plied them with tea, coffee, and cookies. Of course, they'd discussed the vile incident and added their mix of spices to the facts.

"Most of them came to stick their nose in our business," her father had remonstrated.

Emma didn't care why they came. In a way, their visit managed to shrink her fear to a more manageable size, corralled the ugly beast of terror back in the cage and for this, she silently thanked them all.

Nobody would be against her now she thought, remembering that man's words. He could call her a witch at the top of his lungs for all she cared. No one would listen. No one would believe him. They would arrest him and stop him from doing all those bad things he did.

A knock on the door and she figured Amelia had returned from the dentist. She never just barged in. Amelia prided herself on being extremely polite. Of course, her mouth might be frozen, and her words all stretched and weird like last December when she'd had two cavities filled.

She opened the door and could not stop her face from drooping with disappointment as she stared directly at Hank Apple.

"That's not happiness to see me, Emma." He smiled to ease the tension.

"I thought you were Amelia."

"Can I come in?"

She moved aside.

He closed the door behind him. "I didn't want to mention anything in front of your parents last night."

"Thanks for that by the way."

"My pleasure." He came in a little closer. "I meant to thank you for all the help you gave me."

She afforded him little head bobs recognizing the simple

statement as the preamble to more questions.

"Emma, can you describe the man who entered your room?"

She hesitated for several long minutes even as she realized the long pause had already given her away. "Yes."

He took a deep breath and walked over to the small bench. He sat down, his back to the window. "Want to tell me about him, and what he was doing here?"

Again, her head gave him an affirmative answer. She sat down on the bed. Her eyes glued to the floor she answered, "He's the man who kidnapped those little girls."

She didn't dare look up. She worried shock would cover Hank's face, maybe even revulsion at the silence she'd maintained for so long.

"Emma, look at me." He waited until she did. "You didn't do anything wrong. This situation is not your fault, and certainly not your responsibility. Remember our talk yesterday?"

"Yes."

"Okay. So, what makes you think the man in you room is the madman we've been looking for?"

"I recognized him when my mother and I came back from the clinic Thursday before last. Police were searching all the cars. He drove the car next to ours."

"What do you mean recognized him? Emma, sweetie, you're not making any sense. How do you know he is the kidnapper?"

"He hurt that little girl."

"What little girl?"

Emma put her fists in front of her eyes. "I don't want to remember. I don't want to remember."

"It's okay." He rose and reached for her enfolding her in his arms. He cradled her for a while. Then releasing her, he pulled a tissue out of his pocket for her. "Just describe the man for me."

She moved away to wipe her eyes. "That policewoman called him ma'am. He's a man, though. I'm sure he is."

"The policewoman, who was searching his car?"

She nodded. "She thought this man was a woman because of his hair, long and gray and down to his shoulders with waves. Not his real hair."

"So you're saying he's a man disguised as a woman."

She faced him. "Maybe. His face is pale, and his eyes are sickly blue with red lines in them. His nose is pudgy and round, and his smile is mean."

"How tall is he?"

She shrugged.

"Taller than you? As tall as I am?"

She thought a bit. "Never noticed this man standing. From the length of his legs, he might be a little taller than Miss Tyler. He's big, though and chubby with round sloping shoulders."

"Emma I want you to think. Do you know his name?"

"No. I can't always tell." She hesitated. "He called me a witch. Said he would kill me and that no one would care—because he says I'm a witch."

"No one is going to hurt you. Do you understand? No one," he repeated forcefully.

Lips pinched, she gave him the nod she realized he needed. "Didn't think he'd seen me. I guess this means he knows I can identify him."

"Where? Where did you spot him?"

"In a dream I had." Tears rolled down her cheeks at the memory, and Hank waited patiently.

"Don't worry. We're going to find the creep. Can you remember the car?"

"One of those tan colored jalopies. A big peanut-shaped rust spot hangs from the roof on the driver's side."

He walked toward her. He reached into his jacket pocket. "Here's my card. I'm going to find time to chat with you this week. You're going to class Wednesday morning—to help Miss Tyler?"

She nodded.

"Good. I'm going to bring by someone I want you to meet. Val. She is a seer. Val helps us with some of our difficult cases."

He picked up her hands smiling at her. "I think she can help you, Emma. It must be hell not to be able to talk to anyone about this. Val can help you put it all in perspective, okay?"

She smiled. "Okay."

From the window, Emma watched him walk across the brick path, wave to her father, get into his car and leave. When he did, most of the others followed. They had finished. She could make out the older police officer shouting orders to the others. She couldn't understand the words though on account of her window being shut tight—bolted shut.

She'd pleaded with her parents asking them to reopen the window, at least during the day, but her father forbade her to do so. And Detective Apple agreed wholeheartedly. Both carved out of the same block those two she thought. Even if Hank appeared to be more enlightened, she still found him stiff and rough around the edges.

She supposed no one was perfect, and everyone had flaws. She had more than her share, one of them being she was a wuss—a big fat one. No doubt her troubles began at birth, she thought as she made a face. When she'd inherited none of her daddy's grit. Now, if she wanted to survive in this crazy world, she would have to learn to toughen up and not be wimpy.

Just as she decided to be brave, a loud buzzing sound came from outside below her window. Something about the high pitch whirring terrified Emma. She ran to the window to catch the commotion.

Her father stumbling around the yard tried to control a giant chainsaw from running away with him. Like a wild bronco unwilling to part with his ways, the heavy tool's powerful kick proved difficult to manage. She smiled at the funny picture of ineptness from a man unused to doing any yard work until it dawned on her. He was trying to cut down her tree, one of the few survivors of the Dutch elm disease that had swept parts of Newark a few years prior.

She pounded on the window. Her father couldn't understand her over the noise, and it didn't dawn on her to run outside and yell at him. Shock had her paralyzed to the spot and her legs felt like jelly all of a sudden.

Gathering her thoughts, summoning strength, she ran out of her room and yelled and screamed at him all the way down the stairs. Tears poured down her cheeks. How could he do this? He was a murderer killing one of her best friends.

By the time her mother caught up with her she was sobbing uncontrollably and had stopped thinking. She felt as though someone had reached inside her to tear her heart out. She didn't listen—couldn't reason, and her mother had to yell over and over again for her to calm down.

Eloise shook her daughter, forced her to listen. "Dad's not cutting down the tree. He's just trimming the lower branches, the ones too close to the ground. The ones that make it easy for anyone to climb into your room, Emma." She paused and took her daughter into her arms. She rocked her back and forth, trying to soothe her while urging her to stop crying.

"The tree might die if he cuts too many branches. We learned this in school. They can't always recover when someone removes large major arteries."

"Don't fret. Your father loves that tree. Like you, he grew up with the elm tree. And don't worry, he said he was going to tie your swing on a higher branch and lengthen the cord. I promise."

With a tremulous breath, Emma stopped crying. But until her dad silenced the chainsaw she knew she would not find peace. It was as though someone was cutting off her limbs. She found herself praying the terrible carnage would not bludgeon the tree, and her father would resist the urge to cut away unevenly.

"Come on. I could use your help with supper. Didn't you say Amelia was coming over?"

"She's supposed to. Only she hasn't called me yet." Just as she said this, the phone rang.

"Hello?" Emma picked up her voice still shaking with telltale signs of tears.

"It's me. I won't be able to come for supper."

There was a pause as Emma wondered why Amelia whispered directly into the mouthpiece. Was she trying to tell her something she didn't want others around her to overhear? "What's wrong?"

Amelia's voice lowered even more, so Emma had to strain to understand. "My mother and father don't think it's safe to hang around your house. They don't believe you should be there either."

"Of course, it's safe. Police said it was. They're patrolling the area almost on the hour. For the next few days, this is probably the safest street on the block."

"Got to go. Talk to you tomorrow." Amelia hung up the phone.

"Emma, what was that all about?"

Emma stared at the phone as she hung up the receiver. "Amelia's not allowed to come over. I guess her parents are worried the man is still stalking our house." She stared at her mother's downturned expression. "Do you think this might be true?"

Later that night, Emma was awakened by loud voices downstairs. Her mother and father were arguing. She hadn't witnessed a quarrel of this proportion since Granny Dottie had passed away, her mostly being the source of all their disagreements.

She sat up and rubbed the sleep out of her eyes. No dream. The noise was getting louder now that she was fully awake. She slipped out of bed and tiptoed to the door. Opening it just a crack, she listened to understand the reason behind the commotion.

"I'm not going to ask your mother for money. That's the end of the discussion."

"Keep your voice down. You're going to wake up Emma. And why not ask my mother? She has more than she knows what to do with."

"This is not about how much she has or how little we have. My point is about being independent, about being able to take care of my household. At forty-years-old, I think I've earned the privilege—not to mention that I draw comfort from knowing I can kick her out of my house anytime I want."

"Now, this is your house? What about Emma and me. Don't we have a say in this?"

Emma caught the sound of her mother blowing her nose, a sign she'd been crying through the mess. "You're so dead set on keeping Emma here to prove to a maniac none the less that you can't be scared out of your precious house. You're stubborn, and you're ready to put her life at risk."

"Don't be ridiculous. Even Detective Apple said she is fine here."

"I'll have you know Amelia Swift declined Emma's invitation to supper—probably won't be allowed to come here anytime soon—because her parents worry this man might still be lurking around."

"The Swifts are idiots. If this guy was lurking around, police would have seen him by now. They're patrolling the area day and night."

"What about when all this blows away, in a few days or a few weeks when the trail has gone cold. Do you think they'll still be patrolling the area?"

"Like you said. The whole thing will have blown away, and the jerk will have moved on—after somebody else's kid."

"Meanwhile, I got another e-mail from my mother. She wants to cut her trip short because of what's happened. Angry as hell we didn't tell her about this before she left this morning."

"You tell her to stay where she is."

"I told her. 'Mom, two years you've been talking about taking this cruise.'"

"Exactly. We're okay. We don't need her around telling us what to do."

Emma left the door and walked to the window. She searched the area bathed in the pale light of the lamp post and wondered whether this man was out on her street somewhere, waiting. Police had a good description, the one she had given Hank Apple. Still, this man was resourceful. In no time he had recognized her, done his research and found out about her, who she was and where she lived.

No wonder they hadn't caught him yet. If he had no prior record, Emma overheard one of the officers say this meant he might be difficult to find—like a needle in a haystack.

Detective Apple had mentioned a database of known pedophiles and convicted sex offenders. Once they were caught and sentenced, their names their addresses and the nature of their crime became public which made it difficult for them to repeat their crime or run and hide.

These heavy sanctions also meant this man had a lot to lose if he got caught. And he was apparently prepared to stop at nothing to avoid capture, his little nightly visit to her proof of this.

She grabbed a pillow from the bed and dropped it on the window's ledge in front of her bench. She would sleep here tonight. It wouldn't be as comfortable as the bed, but if she felt the man stir in the yard, she would know.

Her last thoughts were for the Elm her father had mangled. She hoped it would forgive her and still be her friend. A sudden rustling of the leaves made her smile. Emma sat on the carpet and plopped her empty head on the pillow she'd pushed up against the window frame, and fell asleep.

Twelve

The Stalker

*M*onday evening, two streets down at the Kramer residence, a woman had spent an hour under the scrutiny of Michelle and Richard Kramer interviewed for the position of summer nanny.

"I hope you understand our concerns," Michelle was saying to the gray-haired woman whose big behind swelled over the edge of a round rattan chair pinned in the corner. "We've had the same summer nanny for three years. Unfortunately, Nathalie is spending the summer in Europe this year as an exchange student ..."

"Honey." Richard patted his wife's hand. "I'm sure Mrs. Boleslava doesn't need to know all our business." He turned toward the homely dressed Boleslava and apologized. "I realize time's getting late, and you must have your chores to attend. My wife's a little nervous. Trying times we are experiencing. I'm sure you read about what recently happened in our little neighborhood?

"Yes, I overheard two of the young ladies who reside in my building talking about this yesterday. Sordid business," the big-boned woman added in a high pitched voice.

Michelle glanced at her husband. "I hope this terrible situation hasn't deterred you from working in our area. Because I think I can say, out of the many applicants we have met, you are one of the few we've invited to a second interview."

Richard rose all of a sudden. "Excuse us, Mrs. Boleslava. My wife and I would like a word in private if you don't mind."

"Absolutely." She waved them to go ahead with a polite smile.

Once out of earshot, Richard told his wife. "Mich, I don't care for her. Something is odd about that squeaky voice of hers."

"Nonsense. Richard, not everyone fits the sexy young frame all men bestow on nannies." She gave her husband a scathing stare. "Besides, she reminds me of Mrs. Doubtfire. You know the one in that movie.

"What do you say we sleep on this? By the way, the Swifts aren't using their nanny this summer. They're sending their kids off to camp for a couple of weeks, and Marlene said she was taking a month off to spend time with them. Their Marie is the best. You said so yourself."

"Yes, but something about taking Marlene Swift's hand-me-downs rubs me the wrong way."

"All right. You're the boss."

When they came back into the living room, Michelle smiled and invited their potential nanny to stand by extending her hand out to her. Mrs. Boleslava took her time rising, and she shifted her purse under her arm to shake Michelle Kramer's hand.

Michelle hesitated, but glancing up at her husband's mutinous stare, she relented. "We will be in touch, Mrs. Boleslava. Richard reminded me we have two more candidates to see in the morning, and it's too late to postpone them. You understand."

Boleslava nodded already lumping toward the door, corrective shoes clopping against the vestibule tiles. "I'll keep my schedule opened for you a little longer, Mrs. Kramer," she added while grasping the door handle and stepping out into the warm night air.

Inside, Michelle whipped toward her husband the smile gone from her expression. "Are you satisfied? We might lose her."

***

Marley Boleslava sat down in her blue Ford Focus and pulled out of the driveway slowly. She took a left turn and headed South on Highland Avenue. She stopped at one point, turning left on Grafton and pulled into the driveway of a big red brick house. No light in the front walkway. No curtains adorned the windows. The rundown structure appeared abandoned. She adjusted her rear view mirror to stare at the house behind her, or rather at an upstairs window seemingly bolted shut in June's balmy night air.

She removed her shoes and unbuttoned the wrap around skirt she'd slipped over black stockings. She wrested the thick cotton out from underneath her, lifting her behind and banging her head on the ceiling as she did. She shoved the material in the back of the car. From the bag on the seat next to her, she pulled out a huge pair of clown pants and shoved her thickly padded legs in the pants, one foot at a time being careful not to bang her head this time when she hoisted them up to her waist. She reached for the comfortable sneakers she'd hidden under the passenger seat, methodically put them on, and stashed the pair of black clunkers in their place.

She peeled the gray-haired wig clamped around her head a little too tightly and found beads of perspiration had formed underneath the hair's matting. She ran big fingers through long mousy brown hair as dull nails savagely attacked an itchy scalp, the relief over an hour late.

She then tucked her hair underneath a wide floppy brim straw hat more for cover, pinning the hat in place so it would not blow away.

Two police cruisers parked front and back of the house surveyed the premises. Staying in the driveway was out of the question. Police had to know the owners had abandoned this house, and officers were liable to ask what she was doing there.

Gullible idiots, she thought. Then she spotted her eyes in the mirror and held on to her head as though the searing bolt of pain that slashed from one temple to the other might shear it right off.

Once the pain abated, a smile reappeared on Marley's face, slowly stretching from ear to ear. "Morey, you smart, brainiac of a man. Eluding the authorities is becoming too easy. A long time now, and they still can't find a clue. They don't suspect a thing. No one does—except for that witch, and I have numbered her days. You're going to die soon, Missy. Try to show me up, will you? Well, no one tells me what to do. No one," he yelled, uncaring of the officers parked closely. I'm going to kill you," he reiterated in gruff tones. "Something I'm going to enjoy doing."

He laughed and started the motor again. He could do nothing tonight. He would go home and look in on his little sparrow tomorrow. Sooner or later, they would all leave the area, and he'd be free to try again.

Once more, blue eyes fixated on the window behind him, and on the mangled tree that looked worse in the new moon's light. He hurled one last thought in her direction. I'm sure you can hear me, evil one. So listen up. I'm going to kill you with my bare hands, and there is nothing you can do about it. He laughed and rode away.

***

Emma awoke with a start. Crouched in the safe place she'd adopted by the window, she glanced at the big clock on her desk. Only nine thirty. She winced from a serious crick in her neck and marched off to bed holding on to her pillow. She collapsed on top of her comforter looking forward to sleeping a little longer in the morning.

School was out, and even though she loved her classes, it was such a warm feeling to be reminded how she didn't have to gulp down breakfast and run to meet the bell.

Snuggling into her pillows, she considered not running to go anywhere tomorrow, just sleeping in for once. In fact, she wouldn't have to run. She had a car driving her, a dark blue one. Rather, she sat on the roof of the vehicle—strange place to be—streets flying by unfamiliar and dark. Wind mussed her hair, and she held on to her pillow just in case of a tumble or a great fall like Humpty Dumpty. If he'd had a pillow, he wouldn't have broken into thousands of little pieces his fragile body fractured in the fall off that wall—and her surroundings changed to include many walls, unsteady walls surrounding her with bits of bricks eaten away, half torn and ripped to shreds. A commercial complex fitted right in with the rest of the area.

Warning lights flashed around her, neon flares framing a pizzeria, a Chinese restaurant, a purple parlor where girls danced in the window. Without music, they resembled flailing puppets with sickly masks covering their made-up faces.

All at once, Emma recognized the name of the street. She closed her eyes and screamed in an all-out effort to leave this place. This part of town belonged to him, to the man who terrified her.

When she peeked through her eyelids, she'd moved only a couple of feet away, to the top of a broken wall. She hid behind her pillow remaining quite still with her thoughts anchored on home instead of on the man below, lest she drew attention to herself. She might remain invisible if she didn't alert him to her presence. He busily parked his car, and Emma found his hat bizarre used to seeing his weird gray head. The hat was new, and she wondered why he bothered wearing one. She spotted him as he entered a building whose signs on the walls promised it would buy everybody's gold.

She wondered how to get home again and caught the third window in a row of five brighten—a window near a construction site. At first, nothing happened. Then shadows danced against the shade. She spotted her tormentor beaten up with a stick by a much thinner figure with long hair and a pointy nose, over and over until he crumbled into a thousand little pieces, like Humpty Dumpty without the great fall, and he hugged the floor resembling a small ball in the shape of an egg.

A few seconds was all it took to bring Emma back. She sat up in bed gathering her thoughts as she stared at the pillow she still clutched against her torso. A few deep breaths later, she calmly replaced her puffy pink friend where it belonged. Once untangled from the comforter twisted around her legs, she patted bare feet to the window.

The car parked at the abandoned house was gone. A dark blue station wagon—she remembered—had driven up sometime in the afternoon, then again after supper. She closed her eyes and focused, cleared the dream in her mind and recalled her ride sitting on the roof of a dark blue car. She'd read the make of the car when he parked.

I know what you drive now. I won't be surprised by you.

In bed, she wondered if someone had beaten up on the man if the ride in the dream had even happened. Her last thoughts toyed with the odds this man might be some demon or vile magician. How else could he go about his business and police not stir an inch?

Thirteen

Conjuring

Next morning, washed and dressed in her favorite jeans and blue T-shirt, Emma stopped on the landing and listened to the voices coming from the kitchen. Someone was crying. Second night in a row she'd fallen asleep to the drum of her parents fighting, and she wondered if the two had stayed up all night arguing, a marathon even for them.

Distinctly a voice rose. "I can't ask mother for money—not for this." More tears and sniffles followed. "She doesn't even like the guy."

Could this be her Aunt Franka? This early in the morning? And she cursed this sudden need for money everyone seemed to have. Resolutely, she reentered her room and fetched the wooden box her granny Dottie had sculpted and decorated for her. She'd even affixed a keyhole and a little latch to hold the key on the bottom.

She stroked the smooth lid. Closing her eyes, she pictured the eye of heaven looking down at her and the smile of kind souls throughout the ages acknowledging her wish. Softly, she murmured the phrase she had learned by heart. "Heaven's eye to life beyond, free your love of which I am fond so that my wish may be granted and I not be left stranded. I thank thee for loving me."

The third time she used the sentence and the third time she trusted its outcome. Granny Dottie had told her the seeds of doubt planted within us at birth were to blame for our world's loss of magic. Her great-great grandmother and all her other grandmothers had been unable to work the sentence. So far, whenever she performed her visualization, a tingling sensation would trickle down her spine and make her feel warm and airborne as though she were unattached and floating on a cloud. More importantly, the little prayer would always produce results.

Delicately, she removed the little key inside a painted nook shaped like a hook and unlocked it. Nothing stood out inside except for one blue elastic her granny gave her once, a deck of cards she received as a souvenir, an old comb, a few sticks of chewing gum for emergencies, and a small book of poems Amelia had given her for her tenth birthday. She picked up the small leather bound collection of quotes and essays. Right between pages fifteen and sixteen attributed to verses on greed, was the money she had summoned.

She picked up the little bundle and counted up to a hundred one hundred dollar bills, the biggest amount she could think of mustering. She smiled, happy with her accomplishment.

A frown quickly replaced her smile as the concern about another lie she'd use to explain the proper fortune about to befall her little family plagued her conscience. She put the box away and stuffed the half-inch stack of money in one of her jean pockets. She would think of some explanation. She'd had a lot of practice.

When she entered the kitchen, she was surprised to encounter her aunt Franka tissue in hand dabbing at tears pouring out of her.

"Aunt Franka, why are you crying?"

Her aunt hesitated, tossing weary eyes toward her mother.

"The police picked up Jimmy, your aunt's boyfriend for questioning."

"Why?"

"Something about a car he drives. Your aunt didn't have time to get anything else out of him." She hoisted helpless shoulders. "Police aren't talking," Eloise added hesitantly.

"He didn't do anything bad, Emma," Franka told her. "A simple case of being in the wrong place at the wrong time."

"Can't we go down and have a chat with Detective Apple, Mom? I'm sure he would understand."

Eloise glanced at her watch. "I have to be at work in fifteen minutes."

"I'm sorry, sis. I shouldn't be bothering you with all this."

"You're not bothering me. I'd go down to the station with you in a heartbeat, but with Pat as worried as he is…" She eyed Emma and stopped short of continuing her train of thought. "Unable to take care of those house accounts, there'll be a lot less money to make ends meet in a week. Can't afford to miss work, even for a day."

"Where's Dad, Mom?"

"He's at work calling everyone in his Rolodex about their policy, trying to find some money."

Emma hesitated after which she reached into her pocket. "I dug up a little of my own," she said matter-of-factly. She dropped the folded bundle on the table. "Money Granny Dottie left me for a rainy day."

Her mother and aunt stared at her as though she'd landed from another planet. Eloise, first to recover, picked up the cash her expression riddled with disbelief and counted the bills she was holding. Relief replaced the shock on her face followed by tears of joy. "Where did you get this, Emma?"

"Granny said she had left me a few dollars in the box she made me. I never needed any money. I found the money this morning underneath the book of poems Amelia gave me for my birthday. I thought you should have this, Mom. It's way too much money for me."

"No. Sweetie, this is yours, for later."

"I don't need it now. You do. Please use it. I'll be unhappy if you don't."

Eloise hesitated. She nodded and tucked the money away in her shirt pocket. She got to her feet, grabbed Emma and hugged her tightly. "Thank you, sweetie." Releasing her, she added, "Now all I have to do is convince your father we can use this."

"Why do you need money, Aunt Franka?"

"Don't worry about me, kiddo." She gave her tissue the last tug and resolutely put it away. "Should Jimmy need bail." She looked up at Emma, extending a pale smile. "Only if they formally arrest him. Please don't worry about any of this."

Emma nodded. She recognized her aunt trying to lighten the pain for her benefit. Probably thought she had enough problems of her own. "Shouldn't we go down to the precinct and clear this up?" Emma said as she waited for their silent consultation to end. Were they keeping something from her?

She noticed her mother hesitate, heard her fudge with the next sentence. "Your father doesn't think we should leave the house."

"Why not?"

"This man might be lurking nearby, catch us leaving." She

shrugged giving Emma a pinched smile. "Sweetie, police are watching the house. Inside, we're protected."

"But you just said you were on your way to work." Emma dropped in a chair uncomfortable with the innuendo that her father didn't trust her. "You mean Dad doesn't want me to leave the house." She eyed their sheepish expressions while disappointment glared in hers. "Is this why you're here Aunt Franka, to babysit me?"

"To keep you company, honey." Franka pinched Emma's chin as she said it. "This is a big house. Why should you stay here alone? Makes no sense."

Eloise rose, picking up the breakfast dishes on her way to the sink. "Tell you what. Since you've so generously contributed to this family's monetary fund, I'm going to call work and take the day off. Afterward, we'll ask one of the civil police officers in front to give the three of us a ride to the precinct." She walked over to the table and rubbed her sister's shoulders. "I'm sure Pat won't mind if we all stick together. We can help Jimmy's cause. I am positive of this."

Franka agreed, bringing her cup to the sink. "What about you, kiddo. You want to grab some breakfast before we leave?"

Emma shook her head realizing how readily her aunt had jumped at her mother's idea. "I'll grab a juice box. I'm not hungry."

"You sure?" Franka played with her long tresses.

"I'm sure."

Eloise snagged her purse and an extra bag. "I'll pack us some fruit," she said grabbing a couple of apples and a pear from the glass bowl on the credenza. "Just in case we should be there a while."

As they walked out of the house, Emma caught her aunt staring at the little bulge in her mother's shirt pocket. "I wouldn't carry your stack of bills around like that," she whispered. "Put them in your purse, at least until you get to the bank."

Eloise did the switch.

While she did, Emma breathed in the gorgeous day, just now realizing she hadn't been outside for several days. She looked up at the blue vault of the sky and smiled relishing she had the whole summer to enjoy days like these. Then glancing at the tree, Emma saw the damage her dad had done and felt her newfound joy of freedom slip away. The swing lay on the ground, and she knew he would take a long time before getting around to fixing the rope, which curtailed one of her favorite summer pleasures. At least, she'd heard her mother call in a tree expert to mend the ends of the branches' exposed flesh.

"Come on, Emma," her mother called out as she got into a patrol car.

Emma walked toward the car quickly, darting a look in every direction and paying particular attention to their cross street and the red brick house on the corner. No blue car sat in the driveway, and she wondered if she hadn't imagined it all. The man would have to be stupid to lurk nearby, waiting for an opportunity. One more glance through the car window at the shade pooling the front veranda, and she knew this summer would not be like the ones she'd grown to love.

<u>*Fourteen*</u>

Inside The Second Precinct

In front of the second precinct, Emma eyed the massive police sign on the building, and a chill ran through her. Her first instinct was to run and leave this place, but staring down at her ankles she wondered about invisible weights as she toiled to pick up her feet. To line them up and walk up the stairs to cross the threshold became an effort.

"Emma, don't lag. Stay close to your aunt and me." Inside was busy and frantic. She eyed strange people in all sizes and shapes, long hair, pot bellies, stiletto heels, uniforms, and she flinched at the pace they kept. Mentally, she covered her ears to mute the raised voices invading her mind, and she cursed the fast forward button someone had seemed to press which made her dizzy.

Gluing herself to her aunt's backside, she followed like an automaton aware of expressions dressing the faces of police officers and the throng of people waiting for help.

Weird images flashed in her mind, and she put two fingers to each temple which did nothing to check their flow from assaulting her. She needed to avert her eyes, keep them locked onto her shoes. She surveyed the big beige tiles rimmed with brown triangles as her tan loafers shuffled across the floor. She tried not to pay attention to anything around her. But someone whimpered, "I can't believe he's gone. I should have done something."

Emma looked up and encountered a woman with someone's arm around her. "Nothing you could have done. Stop beating yourself up."

Emma shivered as she stared at the woman. She seemed oddly familiar, and the sensation became unsettling to her. She needed to calm down. Of course, police headquarters had to be the worst place in the world for any intuitive to visit—a hellhole where life's tragedies were enhanced tenfold and jumbled her senses like some radar run amok. The same thing had happened when she'd gone to the annex. It will pass she repeated to herself like a mantra.

After her mother identified them to the officer at the desk, they were taken to a waiting room. The door immediately closed behind them. The din diminished. She stared at her mother and aunt's weary faces.

Eloise spoke first. "I left a message for Patrick on his cell to join us here should this last longer than expected."

Beware of explosives, thought Emma. Just what she needed. A tank filled with Hanks and her father—the match to ignite the fire.

Franka wrung her hands together while biting the corner of her bottom lip. "They said the detective would be here promptly."

She'd barely finished her sentence when Hank walked in. A firm grip on the handle his eyes shot straight to her. "Emma?" Emma understood and intercepted the gamut of questions running in his brooding eyes.

"I'm here with my mother and my aunt. They didn't want to leave me alone at home," she added quickly to prevent him from outing her.

He nodded. "I understand. How can I help you, ladies?"

They both rose at the same time. "We need to talk to you about an unrelated matter. It's important," Eloise said.

Emma had never witnessed her mother play the big sister role. It suited she thought.

"It concerns Jimmy Roth." Eloise nodded for Franka to speak.

Franka did. "We believe we can vouch for his whereabouts and his character."

Emma sensed Hank struggled to be polite. She perceived his expression shut down as though he wanted nothing to do with them, almost as though he was about to tell them to leave. But again, he parked his eyes on her and stared long and hard for a few seconds. Surprising her, he nodded. "Very well, follow me." He walked on ahead then turned toward them. "This might not be the ideal place for a ten-year-old," he added, hand on the bulge in his jacket. Then addressing Emma, he added. "How would you like to spend some time with Val, in the outer office? I've told you about Val, right?"

She wasn't ready an inner voice screamed inside her head. The meeting was scheduled for tomorrow, at school with Miss Tyler present. "Is Miss…?" She stopped in her tracks, staring at her mother and aunt not wanting to draw their questions as to why she would inquire about her teacher needing to be on the premises.

"I can arrange for her to be here." On his nod, she couldn't help a smile. Seemed he could read her pretty well which she found comforting right now.

They all followed Hank, who continued down the corridor and stopped in front of an officer's desk. "Cindy, can you take these ladies to Luke in room twelve?"

"Sure." Cindy smiled at her mother and her aunt. "Follow me."

Hank waved them off. "I'll meet you there in a few minutes after I get Emma settled."

Emma gave her mother a little hand wave to reassure her. But Eloise hardly glanced back. Emma realized she and her aunt were too preoccupied with their problems to worry about her thinking she was in good hands.

She wished she felt as confident about her situation experiencing stomach cramps merely thinking about talking to Val.

Back in his office, Hank told Emma to help herself to soda out of the mini fridge. Meanwhile, his back turned he made a couple of phone calls.

Emma curled up on the sofa holding on to one of the small cushions and tried not to listen, but even though Hank talked into the mouthpiece, she did get bits and pieces.

"I need a guardian here, a third party not associated with the police force." Yes, of course, she's agreed to this."

The rest was inaudible, no matter how much she strained to hear, part of it due to the noise in the hallway.

A few more minutes and Hank turned to her. "Val is already here, but she's busy for the next fifteen, twenty minutes which works out well since this is how long it will take Christina Tyler to get here."

Emma took a deep breath and agreed with a smile.

"You're not nervous, are you?" He grabbed one of the chairs and swung it around to straddle as he rolled to the sofa leaning toward her in his seat. "Emma, everything's going to be okay. You'll learn a lot from Val. She's a straight-shooter, a loyal person."

Again she nodded. "Why was that woman crying?"

He seemed taken aback by her question. "Who?"

"She was crying. A man had his arm around her. She seemed familiar."

He nodded as comprehension dawned. "You might have come across Maggie Pearson. She was in here a little earlier. Lost her partner last week."

"How?"

"Drive by shooting. Always hard to lose a partner. Too close to home."

Emma pinched her lips as her head bobbed. She liked that he shared with her as though she were a grown up. "Why the guilt?"

"Par with the territory. Jack wasn't supposed to drive that day, but Maggie had just had an eye exam." He paused and gave her a puzzled look. "Who looked familiar?"

She raised both shoulders. "Not sure anymore. I thought she resembled the policewoman who searched that man's car the day Mom and I came back from the clinic."

All at once she had his full attention.

"Something about her eyes, but then again she's not wearing a uniform."

"Taking time off. And both cars were side by side? Yours and this other man's?"

On her nod, he gave the floor a little kick and rolled to his desk. He rifled through some clippings piled under a blotter and rolled back to her. "Here is a recent picture of Jack. Recognize him?"

She stared at the man her fingers stroking those empty eyes she'd stared into well over two weeks ago. She wanted to shake her head and say no, but when she eyed Hank, she realized she'd taken too long to make up her mind. "He's the one who searched our car. I," *recognized the void in his eyes*. "I'm sorry he's gone," she added.

"Were you aware he was going to die?"

She couldn't sustain his gaze anymore. Emma gave him a slight nod and felt the color drain from her face. She dropped her eyes to her hands wringing the life out of the cushion she held onto for dear life.

Hank rose like a bullet, tripping on the chair, punching the back of it to shove it out of the way. She worried when she caught him make fists high in the air then pull his face into his hands. He had his back to her, and she caught the breath slowly leaving his body. "Are you sure?"

A mere whisper, but she sensed the question rise long before he uttered the words. Now, his thirst for vengeance needed reaffirming, and the query bounced inside her head like a malicious laugh. "Yes." She had to strain to answer.

Minutes had passed before he turned toward her. She spotted his feet moving in her direction while all her strength went to counting the little specs in the pattern of her jeans. She took a deep breath rummaging inside her mind for the courage to stare at him squarely.

When she did, she read another question in his eyes, one he was reluctant to form. She pinched her lips and bobbed her head. "I was unable to tell how or why."

Emma watched as he backed up as though scared of her, of what she might say next.

"There's half a chocolate bar in there, leftover cake." He walked toward the desk and picked up the phone. "Cin, find Maggie Pearson."

"She just left, Hank. Said her goodbyes to everyone."

"Cindy, I don't care how you pull it off. Put a warrant on her if you must. I want her in my office within the hour."

He hung up and walked toward the door.

"Detective Apple?"

"Hank. You can call me Hank," he answered without looking at her.

"Jimmy Roth is not your man."

"Probably not, but Jimmy drove the damn car without registration." He grabbed the door handle.

"Hank?"

He stopped without glancing at her, sidestepping to grab his jacket hanging on the hook behind the door.

"I'm sorry about the officer, Jack. I read in his eyes that he might be about to die, but I couldn't tell how or why I swear."

After a long sigh, he turned to stare at her treating her to a painful grimace. "I'm sure you didn't. Don't blame yourself." He walked up to her and stroked the top of her head with a rough hand. "Sit tight. Cindy will come and get you in a few minutes."

He walked out and closed the door behind him leaving her alone with no other company than the tormented thoughts of a monster and his relentless pursuit. Hank now believed that the faceless man who was out to get her barreled everyone in his path to remain invisible, even becoming a cop-killer to avoid capture, so he could get to her. Up until now, she'd seen the stranger's every move. Emma suddenly worried about not having seen him harm the police officer.

***

Hank leaned against the wall adjacent to his office. He'd stepped out to be alone, to squeeze the moisture out of his eyes—mostly to escape the uneasiness paralyzing him in Emma's presence?

"Hank? Are you all right?" Cindy placed a hand on his arm.

He hardened his jaw as he nodded. "Waiting for someone."

"I'll get Emma and take her to Val."

"Come back in five," he grunted.

She left, disarray painted on her face, glancing back at him once or twice to make sure he was still standing he figured.

He straightened and buttoned his jacket just as Christina Tyler turned the corner as gorgeous as he remembered her, and bringing with her a breath of fresh air.

"Hey." He breathed his voice still shaky.

"Something wrong?" She smiled, tiptoed up to him and pecked his cheek.

"I'll tell you what's wrong. I'm a fraud. A pretentious, lowlife fraud."

Christina's brows shot up her bearing dipped in disbelief.

"I came down on you when you said you had a hard time believing in extra sensory shit. Like an arrogant bastard. I knew it all." He chuckled. "Truth is I never actually believed in it." He shook his head and wiped his eyes again. "I thought I did. I truly did." He hung his head, pain in his eyes. "Deep down, I guess I pictured Val as this brilliant tactician or a master at deducing clues. She'd been around a while and was familiar with the inner workings of the criminal mind. She wanted to call it psychic powers hey, who was I to argue with her? They worked."

Christina stroked his arm staring at his sleeve. She couldn't lay eyes on his face, or she'd break down too. In all the years she'd known Hank, she'd never seen this much vulnerability oozing out of him.

At once, she worried something might have happened to Emma. "Where's Emma?"

He pointed his head toward the door. "In my office, waiting for you."

"What went on in there?"

"She's the real deal, you know? The real deal. For real. She's for real."

"I'm sure I don't know the half of it."

"No," he grunted pointing to himself. "That's my line. I mean every time I'm with Emma, I get dragged deeper and deeper into this quagmire."

Christina gazed at his watery eyes and waited for him to continue. She pulled a tissue out of her purse and handed it to him.

"Thanks." He blew his nose. "She knew Jack was going to die."

"What?" Christina breathed.

"She knew. Oh, she said she didn't know how or when or why. But what if she did? I'm beginning to think she could lead me by the hand to whoever's doing all this."

"Hank, even if she'd told you Jack was going to die and how? Do you believe you could have stopped it?"

He stared into her eyes a few seconds. "I'm beginning to understand why her father treats her the way he does."

"You don't mean that."

"Christina, she just scared the bejesus out of me. That's what her father is, scared to hell of her."

"Well, afraid or not she needs our help. We can't just abandon her. Think how scared she must be?" Christina saw him rub his forehead from side to side with a trembling hand. Sign of nerves in Hank, never a good omen. She'd first seen the lost little boy in him on the night she'd dumped him. He'd remained silent, unable to make coherent sentences. Desperate men came down hard when they fell.

Cindy walked toward them. "Hello, Christina. Ready to go get Emma?"

"Go ahead," Hank told Christina. "I've got to go check on this Jimmy Roth. Tell Val not to leave. I need to talk to her."

Fifteen

Emotions Run High

Hank Apple stormed down the hall his grit restored, and his dark eyes darting left and right as he saluted with polite grunts people he met along the way. Emma Willis occupied his whole mind right now having him chase bullet-riddled discussions inside his brain like some demented fool.

Absent-mindedly he pushed the door to room number twelve. Luke was taking Jimmy's deposition, and Hank remembered Eloise Willis, and her sister sat in the next room leading off the main corridor waiting for the outcome.

Hank eyed Jimmy's head of dark curly hair as he toyed with a ring on his pinky. He took the officer aside. "What have you got?"

"Report's done. Roth's story checks out. His mother and the neighbors filed a complaint with the Passaic County Sheriff about a vehicle parked and abandoned on their street."

Hank walked over to Jimmy and stood close to him. "Why did you take the car? A smart guy like you must have realized the car was trouble."

Jimmy took a deep breath and closed his eyes as though he had answered this same question too many times. "I told you. My mother wanted the damn car off her street. Police weren't doing anything. The keys were in the ignition. I wasn't about to pay to get the thing towed. All I was doing was bringing it to a scrap yard. Then I found out my girlfriend was pregnant, and I just drove to her place in the damn thing. I guess you can say I wasn't thinking." He looked up at Hank, a plea in his eyes. "Listen, the car is a piece of shit. I have an utterly fantastic one-year-old Audi in my driveway. Why would I need to steal a rusted bucket of bolts?"

Hank pulled up a chair. He ran a hand through his hair to sleek some of the strands back. "This is not about car theft, Mr. Roth. The vehicle you are driving is material evidence in a murder investigation.

Jimmy physically backed away all of a sudden. "Whoa. Murder is out of my territory."

"I want you to think. Did you ever spot anyone around the car a glimpse, a shadow?"

"Talk to my mother and the couple of old hags who live on her street. They got nothing better to do than stare out the window all day. I visit with my mother once in a blue moon. But she was riding my case about this car. How the damn thing frightened her. How the clunker shadowed the beauty of her prized Azaleas.

"Why didn't you use your car to go to your girlfriend's?"

"I had to leave mine up in Passaic. I went with a buddy next day to pick it up."

"Yet, the piece of crap was still parked in front of your house."

"Yeah, well I didn't get around to dumping the stupid car."

Hank stood. He nodded toward Luke.

Luke removed his cuffs. "You're free to go, Mr. Roth. But I'm going to ask you to stay at our disposal. No long trips."

Jimmy got up and rotated his shoulders while rubbing his

wrists. "Should I get a lawyer?" he asked Hank.

"We'll be in touch."

Hank walked out with him and witnessed the women's effusion when they encountered Jimmy, worthy of the prodigal son's return he thought. "Mrs. Willis, I'd like a word if you please."

Deep in Jimmy's arms Franka hugged him for dear life as she told Eloise. "We'll wait for you outside, sis."

***

Emma walked hand in hand with Christina Tyler down the wide corridors following Cindy's lead. Relieved to have her teacher's support, she figured she could count on her protection against the many answers this Val person might try to weasel out of her.

"How much farther, Cindy?" Christina asked.

"Second floor, one of the offices on the other side of the building."

When Emma crossed the threshold, she claimed her hand from Christina and decided to wipe them both on her jeans in readiness of shaking Val's hand.

The woman leaned against the edge of an oval table and didn't budge from where she was her only greeting a pale smile. "Valenciana Mezzo," the woman said in a Spanish accent with a pair of weary dark eyes staring at her. "Most people call me Val."

"Pleased to meet you," she answered the woman's polite greeting. Val was not what she had expected. Barely a few inches taller than she was, her small narrow eyes ran circles over Emma's features. A strawberry blond hairdo framed a round face and flowed onto a round body. Mostly she appeared distant and tired.

"This is my teacher, Christina Tyler," Emma introduced Christina smiling at her.

Christina's cautious nod in Val's direction gave Emma a strange boost. Her teacher's solidarity steadied her resolve to go through with the meeting. Determinedly, she took the straight chair at one end of the table and sat down, a few feet from where Christina sat. Val positioned herself at the other end of the table.

From the packsack she slipped off her shoulders and dropped on the floor, Val pulled out notebook and pen. "You don't mind if I write, do you, Emma? My memory is shot."

Emma encountered the weary smile again. She wondered how much the deep ridges permanently etched on Val's brow, just above the nose, were responsible for the tensed expression. "Can't even remember what I had for breakfast."

Emma smiled as a means of reassuring Val realizing her attempt at humor indicated nerves, a sign she wasn't alone at being clumsy and awkward.

Christina interrupted her momentarily. "Excuse me, but the window behind you is not an outside window meaning this leads to another room. Are we being watched or recorded?"

Val turned and looked behind her. "Room leads off the main corridor. I've used the office in back from time to time. I guess police might use the room to spy on people occasionally."

Christina rose as though readying to leave.

"Not now, I can assure you. I have Apple's word. Miss Willis is ten years old. She is a minor. No one is recording anything."

"Okay." Christina sat down again expelling deep relief.

***

Hank closed the door behind Eloise and offered her a chair. He interpreted more than curiosity in her eyes. In fact, he recognized fear-based questions slowly mounting. Before she could direct the conversation, he asked her point blank. "What do you know about Emma's gifts?"

"Her what?"

The only telltale sign of surprise he read on her face was a light pinkish hue coloring her cheeks.

"Surely you're aware of her talents … the gift of sight." With his foot up on a chair and leaning on his knee, he watched Eloise collapse in her chair as her shoulders sagged and her head turned away to stare at a speck on the floor. "How did you find out? Did Emma say anything?"

"A conversation Christina Tyler overheard between Emma and Tommy. Her teacher came to me. She sensed the urgency of the matter. In exchange for Emma's version of the facts, I agreed to keep her secret. I also promised Christina I would keep the information away from public scrutiny."

Hank read embarrassment on Eloise's face. "I'm sorry Emma put you through her crazy notions. She's been dabbling in this since her grandmother put her up to these weird ideas—an old woman's dementia. My husband tried to tell her to stop."

Hank stood to his full height. "Mrs. Willis, your daughter singlehandedly solved one of my cases, a difficult one at that. She not only figured out the outcome, but she was also aware of the names of the people involved."

"How?"

"Details aren't important." He pulled the chair he was leaning on to the other side of the table and flopped into it.

"You don't understand," Eloise added. "She's wrong half the time."

"She also saved Tommy Carson's life, seeing," He stopped and reflected on what he was about to say. "Emma witnessed an accident about to happen in the future." Past and future. Can she also witness something while it's taking place?"

"Patrick said this curse of hers would bring us nothing but bad luck."

Eloise's careless remark pulled Hank out of his thoughts. "Mrs. Willis, the only person to whom this sight is a curse is your daughter. To everyone else, your little girl's craft is a gift, the gift of life." He thought of Jack, the officer who'd died at the hands of a calculating and dangerous sex offender and realized how terrified Emma had to be."

"You don't understand. My husband …"

"Leave your husband to me. Here's what I want from you. I don't want you to alert Emma to our conversation. I want you to go on as though nothing has happened and nothing has changed."

"Then, why are you telling me this?"

He hesitated. "Emma knows who kidnapped and killed those little girls."

Her faced dropped, and her mouth gaped open.

"She has more than a vague idea, although not enough for us to charge anyone which is why we need your help."

"The man in her room?" Eloise held her breath.

Hank nodded.

"Oh my God," she whispered putting her hand in front of her mouth. "But she told my husband and me that she didn't get a good look at the man."

"You've instructed her not to say anything all these years, right?"

An all-out blush covered her cheeks this time. A simple nod was her response.

"Obviously, she will not confide in you. But being aware, as you are now, might be enough to save her life.

"I don't understand?"

"Listen carefully to Emma, pay attention to details. She will give you clues. Should you be anywhere, for instance, and she requests that you leave immediately, don't question her, just do as she says."

Ongoing nervous head bobs made up the gist of Eloise's agreement. "Is this man aware my baby can identify him? Is this why he's after her?"

"If we knew that, Mrs. Willis … I suspect even Emma is not sure of this."

Hank rose, walking to the door. He grasped the handle and added, "Oh, one more thing. Don't tell anyone else we've had this discussion especially not your husband."

"Where's my daughter? I want to take her home."

"I'm not sure where she is. She's with her teacher and a colleague." He hesitated. "They're getting a tour of the place. I will have an officer drive her home."

"You're not holding her, are you?"

"Of course not. As soon as I find Emma I will send her home."

***

Val had stared at the binder in her hand seeming to hesitate on whether to take notes or not. "For what it's worth, I told Hank I was the wrong person to do this—settle any of your fears that is. I'm still learning to cope with my … gift," she spat the word, "and most times, it's a toss between a hit and a miss and a lot of luck." She hesitated. "Hank said you helped him with his last case. He also mentioned you seemed familiar with a lot of the details."

Emma shrugged, glancing at Christina. "Sometimes, I get strong feelings of what's going on around me."

"Other times I imagine it must be difficult to make heads or tails of your impressions." She seemed to hesitate. "Emma, how vivid is the picture you receive?"

Emma hadn't expected such a direct question. She began to reconsider the woman facing her, hoping she wouldn't turn out to be an adversary. "Probably same as you do," she fudged.

Val chuckled. "Don't blame you for not wanting to venture a guess. How can anyone measure sight? We have optometrists for that, and even they get it wrong sometimes."

The tired smile was back on Val's face. However, the eyes were keener now as they narrowed in on her. "Emma I struggle to piece a few vague and blurry images my conscious mind picks up—bits and pieces here and there. From what I gathered, Detective Apple swears you were able to give an incredible amount of details."

Emma looked at Christina with a plea in her eyes. *Make it stop, please.*

Christina smiled warmly at Emma grabbing hold of one of her hands underneath the table.

"Listen, I understand if you're nervous about this, truly I do. I'm in the same boat you are—well, not the same. Little girl, unless you were born with beyond brilliant powers of deduction to supply precise details of the sort you gave Hank means your visions have to be quite clear."

Exhaling a long shaky breath and squeezing Miss Tyler's hand for courage, Emma still could not speak.

"I want to help you, Emma. Only I can't if you don't let me in."

Emma spotted frustration in the older lady as Val rose from the table and began to pace. "How about I start." She eyed Emma trying to coax some response from her.

Emma nodded.

"Last case I helped solve involved a seven-year-old boy who was kidnapped by his father—only we had no idea the kidnapper was the father. He took part in the search."

"Did you find him?"

Val's smile was one of relief. "We did."

"How?"

"My mind kept flashing on the picture of the partial hull of a ship, black with yellow letters only I couldn't make out the letters. Do you know how many ships there are in the harbor?" She smiled. "Then I spotted glimpses of the boy's baseball cap he wore with his initials on the front flap. I got the impression of someone leading him by the hand. I couldn't tell who. That was it."

"How did they find him?"

Val laughed. "Good question." Val pulled up a chair to sit closer to her. "Tell me, Emma. What would you have done with information like this?"

Emma hoisted her slim shoulders. "Ignored it, I guess. I wouldn't have known what to do."

"Well as it happened, a team of detectives took those few little pieces and worked on the whole puzzle. They figured if the child was going willingly, holding someone's hand, the person had to be someone he trusted. They investigated all the ships in the harbor matching my description and went from there. Some of the greatest detectives of our time work with nothing more than logic, reason, and brilliant powers of observation. They never use visions or even vague images to solve their cases."

"Sherlock Holmes," Emma added.

"Si. Fictional character, but yes. There are a lot of Holmes-like detectives out there. I believe Hank Apple is one of them. He's a man who has devoted years to working on his craft honing his particular gift of seeing from actual science."

She looked up at Christina Tyler before directing her attention back to Emma.

"Granny Dottie said that my curse … I mean gift would grow stronger by the time I reached puberty and then increase when I reached my twenties."

"Don't let anyone tell you differently, Emma. What you have is a gift. I begrudged the word earlier because I don't consider my sight strong enough. I'd love to be able to help more."

Emma sensed a surge of energy back into her limbs. Here was someone who knew what she was going through. "I'm getting better now at separating imagination from the pictures that are real." She used her hands to gesture.

"How can you tell?"

"Half the time I would have visions of something about to happen, yet it wouldn't. My imagination just got in the way. My mother says my errors are what angered my father."

Val eyed Christina and asked. "Are Emma's parents not

supportive—at all?"

"Let's just say her father doesn't want her discussing this with anyone. His mother suffered ridicule all her life. I guess silence is the only way he knows to protect his daughter."

Emma smiled at Christina, grateful for the plug about her father.

Val nodded. "How are you now able to tell if your visions are imagination or reality?"

"It's not always the same, but usually, when I imagine something the picture is grainier and less well defined."

"When you told Hank about Julia and her daughter, you could picture it clearly?"

Emma nodded, a frown darkening her eyes. She stared into the distance remembering the impression of flying through the air that she felt the night she was sent to her room when she envisioned Tommy fall to the ground.

"Anything else?"

Emma sensed her head shake from side to side. She didn't want to reveal anything else.

Christina bent toward her. "How was the image when you saw Tommy crashing on his bike?"

Emma bit her lip and lowered her eyes. Then she felt her shoulders rise tentatively depicting ignorance.

"Please, Emma. It's important." Christina insisted.

Emma breathed out her frustration. She didn't want people knowing so much about her life. What would her father say? "The image was slightly grainy. But I knew the picture was real."

Val sat back in her chair staring at Christina. "She sees the future as well as the past. The only explanation."

Christina put an arm around her shoulders. "Makes sense, sweetie. This is why your images of the future, the ones you call imagination, don't always occur. By talking about them, chances are you're changing the future just as you did with Tommy's accident."

<u>Sixteen</u>

Patrick Barges In

At police headquarters, Hank worried about Maggie Pearson. He picked up the phone to talk to Cindy. "Cin, what's taking so long to locate Maggie?"

"Hank she's just one little person in a big city. She's on leave. Her time is her own which means she can be anywhere."

"Find her. Use a few squad cars if you must, talk to people familiar with her whereabouts. She's in danger, Cindy. It is imperative we find her."

"Are you serious?"

Cindy's shocked tone of voice drew impatience from him. "Please. Try harder."

"Of course. We'll find her."

Just as he hung up the phone, Val knocked on his door left ajar. He stared at her his expression dipped in surprise. "What are you doing here? Where's Emma?"

Val shuffled in and closed the door behind her. She raised both shoulders half a smile on her face. "She's gone to the cafeteria across the street with Christina."

"That awful eatery. All sorts of weirdos in there."

"A police officer—not sure which one. Tall, spectacles. He is tagging along.”

Hank rolled his eyes. “Tim Crane.”

“Stop worrying. The kid left home without any breakfast this morning. Quiere comer.”

“So, what do you think?”

Val breathed out shaking her head with a suspicious glint in her eye. She walked over to one of the desks and sat in Matt’s chair. “She’s not talking. You were right, though. She knows a hell of a lot more than she’s letting on.”

Hank slammed the armrests of his chair and leaned his head back, swiveling the chair side to side. His eyes veered toward the ceiling he pondered out loud. “I realize she can see the past. She’s proven this. She can see the future, Tommy’s accident.” He raised his head and rolled his chair right up against the desk. Fidgeting with a little pendulum clock he used as a bookend, he asked, “Wouldn’t it be something if she was able to direct this sight more toward the present, catch him in the act.”

“Nervous are we?” Val chuckled.

He sleeked his hair back. “Yeah. Can you blame me?”

“Don’t get defensive,” she added with an even bigger chuckle. “I asked Emma that question point blank.”

“What did she say?”

“Nothing. More what the child didn’t say.”

“Meaning?”

“Meaning she sat there as though I was suddenly staring at a huge mole on her face.”

“Which is normal, right? Fear—if she witnessed this man in action.”

He rose and stretched his back taking in the traffic outside his window. "What I don't understand is how this man knows who she is?" He turned toward Val admiring her calm. "She said he recognized her. How?"

"Didn't you ask her?"

"She was upset. She said something about a dream. I didn't want to push."

"Maybe there ought to be four victims, not three."

"I thought of that. That's why I didn't pursue the line of questioning on the night of the break-in. Emma could be the one who got away. Maybe she struggled or waited for a moment of inattention before making her escape."

"One loose end your man has to remedy. She's the only one who can identify him."

"Can a ten-year-old go through this sort of ordeal and not breathe a word—to anyone?" He shook his head side to side unwilling to accept this theory. He caught Val's raised eyebrows. "What?"

Val's contorted face with eyes peering somewhere out the window spoke volumes. "Unless, no. That can't be—then again ..."

"What? Say it, goddamn it." He sat on the edge of his desk, facing her.

She snickered. "You just sat on your sandwich."

"Ah, geez Louise." He jumped up to Val's chuckle as he twisted to stare at his butt. "Now I've got mustard on my new pants."

Still giggling she added. "I have a friend who practices OBE."

"OB—what?"

"Out of body experience. Now and then my friend likes to play with my nerves. She appears out of the blue, even talks to me, and disappears just as quickly. Each time, her husband swears she was at home asleep."

"Quite the party trick," he answered wryly trying to blot the worst of the stain with his handkerchief. "This has been a bad wardrobe month." He dumped the handkerchief on the desk. "Again. Can a ten-year-old do this OBE shit? Geez," he added. "I sound like a broken record."

Val didn't seem in any hurry to contain her mirth. "You consider Emma a normal ten-year-old?"

Before he could answer Matt opened the door and waltzed in unannounced. "Sorry, Hank. Didn't realize you had company."

"Come in, come in. You know Val."

"Yeah." Matt came forward and saluted the woman with a head nod. "How are you doing, Mrs. Mezzo."

"Muy bien, thank you for asking." She remained seated her eyes scouring the new arrival.

"Has Ken been here?" Matt towered over Val, jiggling loose change in his pockets.

"Ken's on his way here? Why?"

Overheard Suzy calling SARA."

Val stopped him. "Whoa, what's with all the names? Kenneth Riley is your captain, this much I know." Val stood and invited Matt to take his chair.

"I'm about to go out, Mrs. Mezzo. Don't need the chair."

Val grabbed her bag and moved out of Matt's way ignoring what he'd just told her. "Suzy is Kenneth's right arm, but who the hell is Sara?"

"An acronym, not a person." Hank offered his chair to Val.

She shook her head. "Ah," she added, obviously enjoying herself. "Sexual Assault Rape Analysis unit," she said out loud. "I'd forgotten about Barbara Leclerc and her department. Isn't she Commander in Chief now?"

Hank's bullet proof expression remained blank.

"Hey, how come they're not working on this case and you are?"

"Goddamn it. For your information, this case is foremost a murder investigation," Hank barked. "Because of how the son of a bitch treats his victims we're saddled with SARA as if we didn't have enough to deal with without kowtowing to Barbara Leclerc."

"Because murderers always treat their victims fairly, don't they?" Val poked fun laughing at his expense.

Hank planted his most menacing eyes on her.

She collected her packsack, fluffed out her pink muumuu, and realigned the many bangles dangling on both arms. "I'm going to let you boys have your fun with Barbie and Ken," she said chuckling and giving them each a little wave.

"Well, things just got worse," Matt announced his eyebrows raised an inch off his brow not waiting for Val to be out of earshot.

"Stay in touch, Val," Hank called out.

"You've got my number," she shouted from the hallway before closing the door behind her.

"How can things possibly get worse?"

"Ken wants to contact CIRG. Barb won't let him."

Hank took a step back. "What the hell for?"

"Ken's concerned about our lack of progress on this case, so he's putting the pressure on her. Meanwhile, she says three's a crowd."

Hank expelled tension in a loud, liberating breath. "For once, thank God for Barbara Leclerc." He rubbed the back of his neck at a loss for an argument.

"And Ken found out about all the extra man-hours we've dumped in this case."

"But to call in the big guns. FBI is only going to muddle everything. You don't know the half of it." Hank hadn't had time to brief his partner.

"Is this about the Willis kid?"

"Yeah." Hank collapsed in his chair. "Yeah." He indicated the one facing him. "A meeting is in order." He noticed Matt's temper about to flare. "Relax, no hidden shit. Recent developments that's all."

***

"You were hungry, Emma," Christina said smiling at the way she scarfed down her waffles.

A slight blush crept up Emma's cheeks, and she took more care in chewing and swallowing her next bites. "I didn't have time to eat this morning," she added wiping syrup and butter from the corner of her mouth with her small napkin.

Emma had chosen the last breakfast available. Now the basement cafeteria, part of a commercial building, was filling up fast with the onset of lunch hour diners. Police officer Tim Crane who had brought them there sat at the next table eating a burger and fries.

Christina had long since finished her salad and ice tea. "It's perfectly fine to be hungry, sweetie. Don't worry about it."

Emma realized her teacher had questions for her.

Christina added. "Val was pretty cooperative."

The words seemed a mere preamble to gauge her cooperation Emma suspected. "I like her. She means well."

Christina pulled out a mint from her bag and twirled the ends of the wrapper. "She might be able to help you hone your skills if you confided in her more, don't you think?"

Emma didn't know what to say. She realized she was holding her breath when the vision of a man in the cafeteria doorway forced her to expel a sincere protest. "No." The whisper came while her eyes brimmed with the dismay she couldn't hide.

"What?" Christina turned to catch the cause of Emma's sudden fixation. "What's he doing here?" she mouthed her whole body seemingly tensed for a fight.

"It's okay, Miss Tyler. Please don't get angry. It'll just make things worse." Emma tried to soothe her teacher. The last thing she wanted right now was to make the man explode.

The minute he spotted her, Patrick Willis jogged toward them. As he did, Tim at the next table rose and intercepted him before he could reach her.

"Get away from me, you idiot, this is my daughter. I'm Patrick Willis."

Emma closed her eyes when the slur came out of her father's mouth. He'd gone and done it now.

"Daughter or not, you don't call me an idiot." The officer pushed Patrick away from the table. "We'll see what the sergeant has to say about this."

Patrick tried to shove him away with both hands propped against Tim's chest when a loud rumble across the wood floor was heard a couple of tables away. Two other officers had witnessed the skirmish and busted out of their chairs in their haste to help their comrade.

The taller of the two got there and flung Patrick around. The other came and grabbed his arms, swinging them behind his back. Tim slapped a pair of handcuffs on him. "Now you behave, macho man."

Tim frisked him for weapons. "He's clean."

"Why don't you ask her," Patrick yelled his face a seething red and swollen with anger. She'll tell you. I'm her father." He turned toward Emma. "Emma! tell these men who I am."

Christina stood and wrapped her arm around Emma, who'd backed away from the table. All she could do was nod slightly. No words came out of her throat.

"He is the girl's father," Christina said. "But Emma is due back at the precinct. She has an appointment with Hank Apple," she added so Patrick wouldn't grab his daughter and run.

"Just as I said." Tim sneered. "We'll let the sergeant handle this." He pushed Patrick ahead of him. "Go on. You heard the lady. We're all going across the street."

Emma was grateful for Christina's arm fastened around her waist. The tight grip stopped her shaking from head to toe as they followed Tim and Patrick. Luckily the other two officers had gone back to their lunch.

"Can you at least remove these cuffs? This getup is ridiculous."

"I would, but you can't seem to contain your temper, sir. You showed disrespect to an officer of the law, and you assaulted me."

"Assaulted you?" Patrick shouted. "Don't you think that's a bit much? I merely protected my space. You were all over me."

Her father was good with words Emma realized. But this time, she doubted they would score him points. As good a salesperson as he was Tim was not buying.

Nobody paid attention to their odd little group Emma discovered. Spotting a police officer leading someone by the elbow while their hands were fastened in their back appeared to be commonplace in these hallways.

She blamed herself for the demeaning way Tim treated her father. After all, he couldn't hold his temper any more than she could turn her nose up at a licorice stick. At least the procedure didn't blacken his teeth or make his tongue all slimy and dark blue, although the walk in captivity did paint his face a deep red and detail the freckles on the back of his neck a brighter green than usual.

She shook her head biting her bottom lip and hating the outburst was all her fault. If she hadn't always insisted on retreating from everyone and everything like a coward, her family might not be in this mess. The only sin her father had ever committed was to act out of love with her welfare in mind—even if he didn't realize his way of loving brought her nothing but misery.

Tim had called ahead and so when they reached Hank's office, he opened the door without hesitation.

"What the hell is going on here?" Hank took one look at the situation and with a simple nod, ordered Tim to remove the metal binding Patrick's hands.

"He tried to fight with me when I stopped him from approaching the girl, Sergeant," Tim said as he took his cuffs back.

Hank strapped his hand behind his neck trying to figure what he would tell this man. He recognized how Willis held back his anger—barely. "Tim, can you drive Christina and Emma home?"

"Sure thing."

"Don't let Emma out of your sight until she is home safe and sound."

"No one is at my house. My wife went to her sister's place." Patrick rubbed his hands together.

"Do we have an address for Franka Tichy?" Hank asked.

Patrick stopped rubbing his wrists resentment still sparking from the steel in his blue eyes. He grabbed a pen off Hank's desk and wrote it down. "Here." He shoved the piece of paper in Tim's face. "Take her there. And make sure you call the number to let them know you're coming."

Tim yanked the paper dangling in front of him but stared at Hank for corroboration. When he got the nod, he rounded his arm and motioned to Christina and Emma to walk in front of him.

Emma gave her father one last look. "Are you all right, Daddy?"

"Yeah." He nodded without looking at her.

"Why are you here, Willis?"

Patrick walked up to Hank and made a fist he smashed on the desk. "Do you think you can talk to my wife and gag her so she won't say anything to me?"

<u>Seventeen</u>

Emma's Talents

Hank leaned over his desk both hands flat on the mahogany surface lending support, inches from Patrick's face. "One press of the button over by the side of my desk, and you'll be spending the next couple of weeks in a six by ten cell." Hank threw the words at him in a measured tone.

Patrick backed away turned and acknowledged the other person as though just detecting him. "Logan, happy to see you again. How're you doing?"

Matt smiled and reciprocated. "A lot of work these days."

Hank gauged Patrick's mood as the man closed his eyes, summoned a deep breath, and began wearing a hole in his carpet. He stopped to point the finger at him. "What have you done to Emma?"

"She is a troubled little girl, Patrick."

"She is also in a lot of trouble," Matt added.

"Take a load off," Hank ordered.

"I'd rather stand."

Hank sat down his long legs sprawled in front of him, and Matthew did the same.

Then, Hank wiped his eyes with a weary hand and proceeded

to tell Patrick how he'd become entangled with his daughter's incredible talents, and what Emma and Val had discussed.

"Who is this Val?"

"A psychic we use whenever we can't make heads or tails of a difficult case." He stopped to allow Patrick to say something, and when he didn't, he continued. "Trouble is Emma's not saying much. She's afraid to." He slanted his head Patrick's way.

"She's said too much already," Patrick muttered as he continued to pace up and down in front of Hank's desk.

Hank sensed the man's pain. There was a lot he still hadn't told him. Perhaps Patrick's defense was searching for ways of escaping the truth, imitating a goddamn ostrich by burying his head in the sand while those around him became easy targets.

"What I want you to tell me," Patrick bellowed, "is why Christina Tyler came to you with this story? Why not to her mother and me—her parents for shit's sake."

"I already told you why. Miss Tyler feared for Emma's life—with this man following her." Hank omitted plenty, Christina's speculation about Emma terrified of disappointing her father more than she feared the perpetrator for instance.

Patrick stopped dead and lined up both men in his sight. "Okay, answer me this. How can this man recognize her? Yes, his car was stopped along my wife's car. He might have grabbed the number off her license plate, gotten the information somehow, but how did he find out this little girl can identify him?"

Hank glanced at Matt and let out one long deflated and frustrated breath. "This is what neither of us can figure out. Not even Val. Theories we have. However, the only one who can answer this question is Emma."

"Theories … like …"

Hank hesitated. How could you admit to a protective father his daughter might be caught in the throes of a madman. "Did Emma ever spend time away from home—stayed over at a friend's house?"

Patrick turned toward him, beet red. "If you're trying to say Emma was once this man's victim … Forget it. Never happened," he yelled at the top of his lungs.

"Keep your voice down," Hank spoke in menacing tones. "This is a place of business. How would you like it if I went to your office and started yelling my head off?"

"I'm sorry. I'm sorry," Patrick said to each man.

"In here when people take that tone with me, they're in the slammer five minutes later. People are going to start wondering why you're not."

"I said I was sorry. I'm upset. This … problem we can't demystify has to do with my daughter for shit's sake."

"Val said your daughter seemed able to visualize the past and the future. What if," Hank stopped. He tried to gauge how his assumption might rattle Patrick.

Matt jumped in without thinking. "You mean she might be able to catch this guy in action? In the moment?" As if only realizing what this meant, Matthew didn't finish his sentence. He glanced over at Patrick a worried glare in his eyes.

Matthew's words sank in as Hank watched Patrick's bearing change. All at once, Patrick took huge gulps of air as though unable to breathe. He backed up not stopping until his calves came into contact with the edge of a chair. "Oh my God," he whispered bending in half like a puppet who'd lost his strings. Hank heard him moan and curse—seemingly more in pain than in anger.

Matthew made the motion of calling someone for help, but Hank raised his hand motioning him to be still.

"Oh God, my sweet little girl," Patrick uttered out of breath, on his knees rocking back and forth. "All those bad dreams," he muttered. "She's suffering. She's alone. This guy wants to kill her. No one's there to support her."

Hank caught a couple of the words. "Do you want me to call someone?"

Patrick used the chair to pull himself up and collapsed into it his face in his hands. He was crying, and Hank had never seen another man cry before, not like this.

A few minutes later Patrick pulled a handkerchief from his pocket and wiped his eyes and face. He blew his nose. Glaring at the two officers, he muttered, "She should have been able to come to me. I should have known about her nightmares."

"What nightmares?"

"Emma has had many. Maybe she witnessed one of his attacks. God my little girl. What she's had to live with?"

Hank felt awkward. He didn't know how to deal with Patrick's emotions. He was glad when Matthew changed the subject and managed to cut the tension. "Still even if she has, this doesn't explain how he is aware of her."

"Patrick." Hank waited to give him the chance to rally. When he recognized he would only draw a mitigated interest out of him, he continued, "Val mentioned out of body experience. She said in a trance, you can move out of your body and walk among other people and even draw attention to yourself.

"What?"

Hank repeated what he'd said, patiently.

"You think my Emma can do this?"

"The only explanation," Hank muttered. Hank got up and headed to his favorite spot by the window to stare at the street traffic before him. Gathering his courage he faced his partner. "It's more than just three dead little girls," he told Matt. "He's also a cop killer now."

"What the frick? When did you find out?"

"A couple of hours ago."

Hank admitted to Matthew and Patrick what Emma had admitted about Jack. "When she told me, well scared the hell out of me."

Matt shook his head. "You just said she didn't know how or why?"

"Got to be related."

"My God," Patrick whispered.

"Cindy's scouring the neighborhood to find Maggie Pearson. Her life is in danger, and she doesn't realize it."

"Cop killer," Matt breathed. "FBI would have a field day with this, Hank."

"Hank, you've got to protect my little girl, man. You can't let the FBI badger her or use her. They'll use her. Please, I'll do anything." He began pacing again. "The media will get wind of this and every crook in the country will want her dead." Shakes took over Patrick once more.

"Relax. I have a plan."

"What are you going to do?" Matt asked.

The only people who know about this are her parents, her teacher, and the two of us." He walked toward Patrick. "No one's going to talk."

"And Val," Matt added.

"And Val. I'm counting on Val. In fact, I'm planning to ask Val how famous she would like to become."

***

Richard Kramer had lost the battle. His wife had decided to hire Marley Boleslava as their summer nanny. He knew when she took a shine to someone there wasn't anything anyone could say to make a dent in her decision.

Michelle reached for the phone. It rang just as she was about to pick up the receiver. "Hello? Marlene. What a surprise." She rolled angry eyes at her husband mouthing, "Did you do this?"

He raised his hand as though she pointed a gun at him and shook his head from side to side.

"Yes, Richard mentioned about Marie."

"I'm calling, Michelle cause I'm desperate. I know you need a summer nanny. Richard told Brian. Trouble is I don't need mine this summer. This year is Marie's fourth year with us, and if I let her go, even for the summer, Bert Huggins will romance her right out from under us. He admitted as much, the cad. If I could promise Marie a temporary position with someone we knew well, she would take it. I'm certain of it. Then come September, she'd be back with us and no harm done."

"It's just that I found someone I like."

"Please, I'm begging. You are well acquainted with Marie. You won't be sure about this other person for days maybe weeks."

Michelle Kramer rolled her eyes at her husband. "Well if it

means that much to you, and I do like Marie."

Marlene breathed an enormous sigh of relief. "Great. I'll owe you one, Michelle."

Once she put down the receiver, Michelle stared at her husband. "Guess we're hiring Marie. I never understood why she needed a nanny, anyway, with the girls in private school."

"She has that handicapped stepson at home."

"I suppose. I'll have to call Boleslava to give her the news."

"Let me." He grinned taking his wife in his arms.

***

Morey Boleslaw slammed the receiver, seething. The gall of that man calling him with a delighted tone to tell him he would not be the summer nanny. Well, their little Melanie would be next, after he got rid of the witch. She held the deed to his head, his every waking thought and he couldn't wait to stare at the life receding from those wide, confident eyes.

He stared at the back of his closet door ogling his slim figure in the mirror. He'd tied his long brown hair in a ponytail and donned a technician's pair of beige overalls. Without the mask, his face was slim and angular. Without the body armor, he was skinny. Only the eyes and nose were the same, as was the nasty cut over his right eyebrow. He fingered the last piece of a scab and pressed on the crusty tail end to verify if he could pick at it. He'd be glad when the identifying blister would be gone. Meanwhile, cover up makeup needed to be worn not to attract attention.

He picked up his briefcase and slipped a black satchel onto his shoulders. He owned a heating and air conditioning business, fully staffed with a receptionist, sales persons and five other technicians he'd personally trained. He was proud he'd worked on a mechanical journeyman license right out of high school. It had gotten him out of the house, away from a sex fiend father and crazy brothers.

He cramped from the memory of them dressing him up as a girl and sexually abusing him. He held his head as a searing pain stabbed him from one temple to the other, drawing a cry of agony. He cursed and shouted wanting the pain to leave and free him for good this time. Instead, wooziness overtook him, and he passed out on the floor.

A half hour later, he picked himself up, the shooting throb having at last released its grip.

He rose to his full height and wobbled while rubbing his eyes. He stared at his image in the mirror. As always, his thoughts picked up where they'd left off as though he hadn't just lost thirty minutes of his life. He smiled at his reflection flicking the name tag on his overalls. These days, with ten years of HVAC under his belt, he was proficient in all sectors of the business, commercially and industrially.

Outside he locked the door to his little one thousand two hundred-foot cottage, the smallest home on the block which didn't matter since the place wasn't a home, only a building he came to when he needed to be alone, sleep and watch a little TV. A green thatched roof, beige siding, and white trim made it look like a gingerbread house. He'd even built a white picket fence to ornate the front lawn and walkway. He hung a right to the driveway thinking Hansel would never cross his threshold—neither would his sister. His filthy warehouse would serve as Gretel's last refuge.

He swept the refurbished white Econoline van with a proud

gaze. He'd inscribed the word Con-Air in big black letters on both sides, the name of his business. As he walked around to the driver's side, he opened the door and climbed to get inside. Every winter he put a carport over the van, too big for the doll-size garage attached to his house where he kept his tools and equipment.

He got into the flaming red seat and fingered the black dashboard. Now that he wouldn't play the role of Marley, he had slapped on his belt and would stop by his office to let Corinne know he would not be taking holidays just yet. Not until the witch was dead and buried. Backing out of his driveway, he headed east toward Union Street where he had a storefront concern displaying his equipment in two large bay windows. He needed to warn Corinne about being discreet—not to answer any questions. After going to the office, he would head south toward Forest Hill.

<u>*Eighteen*</u>

Patrick And Emma Chat

*C*hristina and Emma had just arrived at Franka's condo accompanied by Tim, the police officer. He'd walked them up and was standing at the door.

The moment Emma walked in Franka grabbed her crushing the breath out of her as she cried softly. The only thing Emma could imagine was that she worried about Jimmy, and the situation was worse than she'd expected. He didn't seem to be anywhere in the loft.

"Please don't worry, Aunt Franka. No need to be sad." Emma pulled away from her aunt and tried to soothe her. "Jimmy will be released, I'm sure."

Franka bit her lip as she stared at her niece. She pulled out a tissue and wiped her nose already red from too much blowing while her eyes appeared puffy and lined with telltale little veins. Shaking her head she explained. "Your mother told me about your gifts, Emma and the danger they carry."

Emma stared at her teacher just coming through the doorway and threw her a stricken glance. Had Miss Tyler told her mother?

Her teacher shook her head emphatically, and so her eyes swept the room searching for her mother.

Christina addressed Officer Tim. "You can go. We're going to be fine. I can take a cab home. Don't worry about me."

He touched the brim of his cap and left.

"Your mother is resting, Emma," Franka said one hand rubbing Emma's back while the other motioned Christina to enter. Closing and locking the door behind them, Franka added. "Please don't be angry with her. She didn't know who to turn to."

Emma turned toward her aunt. "What about Jimmy?"

"They released Jimmy." She smiled. "Don't worry. We didn't tell him. He's gone to get us something to eat."

Christina cleared her throat. "This may be none of my business, but I believe the fewer people that learn about this, the safer Emma will be."

"I agree. So does Eloise. We also believe her family rallying around her can only help protect her. These measures will allow us to keep our eyes open."

"Yes, of course." Christina moved toward the first chair she found and collapsed into it visibly shaken and drained from her morning experience.

Emma surveyed the familiar surroundings of her aunt's beautiful condo apartment and remembered happier times when she and Amelia would spend the whole night talking about summer and all the things they were going to do. "How long are we going to stay here Aunt Franka?"

"Well, I think you should stay with me for a while. You're safe here. No one can climb a window or even come up the elevator without my permission. Your mother agrees."

"Can I invite Amelia?" Franka nodded. "Absolutely."

Christina rose and mentioned she had to leave.

"Stay," Franka added. "Jimmy's gone to pick up food for everyone and I would very much like for you to share our meal. Please?"

Christina agreed, albeit reluctantly. As she did, Eloise appeared in the doorway and ran to crush her daughter in her arms. "My little girl. I'm so sorry I didn't believe you, Emma. Please say you forgive me?"

Emma felt embarrassed by all this attention as she hugged her mother back. Worse, her throat hurt from being constricted, and her tongue felt tied to the back of her mouth. Even had she been able to utter anything, no words would form inside her jumbled thoughts. All she could do was nod. Surprisingly, tears rolled down Emma's cheeks, and she used her free hand to wipe them her head still resting on her mother's shoulder.

Eloise sleeked her hair back behind her ears and held her tresses looped in a ponytail. Emma let go and moved out of her mother's arms. "Who told you?"

Eloise sniffed tears back and said, "Does it matter?" Upon her daughter's affirmative motion, her mother added, "Someone who is worried about your wellbeing. Detective Apple."

Emma sensed her shoulders sag. She could not prevent disappointment from turning down the corners of her mouth. She stared at the floor keeping her lips tightly pinched so as not to cry.

"Emma." Christina stepped forward. "Hank promised he wouldn't tell anyone, didn't he?"

Emma refused to look at her teacher.

"I think he sensed he had to after speaking to Val and being warned about your lack of collaboration." She eyed the other two women. "Hank and I haven't discussed this, but I understand he was hoping for Emma to confide in Val this … psychic they work with from time to time." She turned toward Emma taking both her hands in hers. "I understand why you're too terrified to say anything. I know Hank, Emma. He's worried your silence might spawn the worst of a terrible situation."

Emma gave Christina a small nod raising her eyes on her mother.

"Your teacher's right, Emma. No more secrets. From now on, I want you to tell me everything."

She caught her aunt's forceful nod, yet she wondered out loud. "What about Dad?"

A loud knock on the door had them jump. "That'll be Jimmy. We'll need to postpone this discussion until later." Franka hurried to answer the door.

Only Jimmy wasn't at the door. Patrick Willis stood before them with a mutinous expression on his face.

He entered the room to silence and bewilderment. "You'll have to train Robocop downstairs to ask permission before he lets anyone up here, even people he recognizes," Patrick said a little peeved. "He chuckled when I told him."

Emma didn't expect her father to show on the premises and from the looks she spotted on the three other women, neither did anyone.

"Pat, what are you doing here?" Franka asked at a loss of anything else to say.

"This is where my wife and daughter are." He looked around at the stunned expressions. "Or is this a private party?"

"Of course not. Come in, please. We just weren't expecting you—thought you were Jimmy."

Patrick entered, and silence prevailed. Emma noticed he appeared tired and beaten as though he'd just weathered terrible news. His eyes seemed swollen. She figured if Hank had told her mother about her he might have also told her father, and when she glanced at her mother as a means to seek shelter, she caught her biting the side of her lip and realized she was the one who'd told him.

He stared at Emma for a few seconds. "I'd like to speak to you, Emma." He glanced at his wife. "Alone, please." Then he eyed Franka his eyebrows raising the question of where.

"You can use my room, end of the corridor to your right." Franka breathed.

Emma could tell the three women were too stunned to speak, at least for now. To prevent any outbursts she agreed quickly. "Sure Daddy."

Patrick led the way, and when they got to her aunt's room, he walked toward the window taking in the view below.

Emma stayed behind and remained close to the door wondering why her father wished to speak to her alone.

"Come in, munchkin, and shut the door behind you." She did, thinking her father hadn't called her by that name since she'd been seven, the time Emma had cried over math homework she didn't understand.

"There's only one chair," he remarked. "Sit on the bed. I'll take the rocker." He pulled the caramel colored piece of furniture close to the bed laid out in tones of cream and yellow. He eyed the pastel almond colored walls shaking his head from side to side. "Seems as though I've walked into a caramel custard dessert. "

Emma didn't say anything. She loved her aunt's room

décor. Warm glows cast by soft lamps wearing ballerina dresses as shades were her favorite.

She sat on the edge of the bed eyeing her father sprawled in the old fashioned rocking chair his long legs stretched in front of him. He was fighting nerves. She had spotted this sort of hesitation from him when he was courting a new client and worried about putting his foot in his mouth.

"I had a long chat with Detective Apple. He … cleared up some things for me."

Emma couldn't find the strength even to nod.

He sat up straight and bent toward her picking up her hands in his. "I never meant to shut you up. Yes, that's what I said, and that's what you understood." He sighed seemingly at a loss for words. He rose to walk to the window and back. And a lion in a cage, a cage with no door and without other bars than the ones in his head struck her fancy. He wanted to roar and escape his mind unable to let loose the words trapped inside but didn't realize how to do so.

"What did Hank tell you, Daddy?" She thought she might help him along and show him the way.

"He told me what you'd done for him. Emma, these bad dreams you've been having. I want you to tell me about them. I want to help you. I don't want you to go through this alone anymore."

She shook her head side to side. "I don't remember them. You know how dreams are."

He kneeled in front of her holding on to her hands. "Please, no more lies. And I won't ask you to keep secrets anymore, deal?

She watched him put a hand over his eyes and she spotted a tear rolling down his cheek. In all her life, she'd never seen her father cry. "I won't tell lies anymore Daddy, I promise." She couldn't bear to see her father cry.

He took in a shaky breath and rising to his feet he reached for the handkerchief in his pant pocket. A few of the bills Emma had given her mother fell to the ground. After blowing his nose and wiping his eyes, Patrick picked them up reaching deep into his pants to get the rest of the bundle.

"I trust you, Emma. I'm just sorry it took me so long to do so."

She stared at the bills wondering how she was going to explain them.

"This money, for instance. Ten thousand dollars here. I know my mother didn't have two dimes to rub together. Honey." He sat down beside her on the bed. "Where did you get this money?"

Any other question but that one she thought. Now she'd gone and promised she wouldn't lie anymore. How was she ever going to get her dad to believe her?

"Emma, please. If we're going to work together to catch a madman, you're going to have to trust me. I know I haven't been the father you deserve until now, but that's all changed. I won't let you down. I promise."

She sensed her head bobbing back and forth. "I conjured it," she whispered.

"You what?"

"Created it, out of thin air." She glimpsed his narrow eyes and the shock on his face and realized he was struggling to understand. "There is a little sentence I use. Heaven's eye to life beyond, free your love of which I am fond ..."

"Don't ... don't continue. I'm familiar with the rotten little phrase."

He was up again pacing and wringing his hands. "My mother—well, she tried hard. My father died when I was five, and she had to raise me." He turned to look at her. "I was a handful always getting into trouble. One day she used the little sentence on me, to scare me. A few of the bullies I hung with heard her and from then on, I lost all my friends and became the butt of everyone's jokes. The worst was I became afraid of my mother. Every time something bad happened to me, I blamed her. It wasn't until years later she told me the little sentence didn't work." He took a deep breath and sat down again, despondent. "I'm not proud of myself, but the day she admitted this, was the day I began to resent her … for all the wrong moves she'd made."

"Maybe she helped you, by hanging around with bullies you might have ended up getting hurt."

"Maybe. Only when I heard you begin to sound like her, I couldn't bear to transfer these feelings to my only daughter. I didn't want to fear you or later learn to resent you."

Emma slipped her hand in his, squeezing to let him know she understood.

"Wait a minute." He brought her hand to his lips and kissed her fingers. "Are you saying this little sentence works?"

She nodded. "The magic words never produced anything for Granny or her mother or her grandmother. But I tried them once, and they did. I never told Granny. I never told anyone."

"And you have to keep it that way. I understand." He intercepted quickly. "I said no more secrets. But it's not a secret if you can tell me, right?"

"Right."

He stared at one of the hundred dollar bills running his thumb over the crisp new paper. "What?" He jumped up and reached for his wallet in the jacket he'd draped on the bed. Opening it quickly, he scanned through the contents discarding papers and money as they fell to the carpet.

"What's the matter, Daddy?"

"How did you conjure these bills?"

"I told you."

"What did you think while you did? I know that to conjure, you need to have an idea of what you are fabricating."

"I didn't want to take anybody else's money accidentally, so I asked for new bills of one hundred dollars—one hundred of them."

"I've got a one hundred dollar bill a client gave me last week." He dumped the content of his wallet on the floor. "Here it is. Thought I'd lost it. He pulled it out. "Just as I thought."

"Money's for real, Daddy. Bills are new."

"They're new all right. Emma, these bills haven't been distributed yet. They were supposed to be released this year. But there were problems with the printing press."

"So?"

"Emma, sweetie we can't use these. If they should turn up anywhere, the bank will want to know where we got them. They haven't been released to the general public. See Ben Franklin's picture, how there are no borders and the yellow one hundred number is on the right—completely different bills." He breathed hard.

"But you and Mom need the money."

"We have to get rid of these bills and not leave a single one behind."

Emma was disappointed. She thought she'd done well for her family. "What are you going to do about money?"

"Bite the bullet. Not be so pig-headed and ask your grand-mother for a loan."

His words and the way he rolled his eyes got a smile out of Emma. She wondered how he would dispose of the stack of one hundred dollar bills without telling his wife.

There was a knock on the door. "Hey you two, the food is here, and it's going to get cold," Franka yelled through the door.

"We're coming," Patrick answered. He gathered the items from his wallet and rounded his arm for Emma to walk beside him. "Would you prefer telling your dreams to Hank Apple?"

"Maybe, for now."

Nineteen

Face Of A Psychopath

ank stared at the small group of people he had convened in the boardroom two doors down the main hall. Matt mostly listened while rubbing his bald head and rounding black eyes on anyone's funny remarks. He appeared to be in a jovial mood.

Maggie Pearson, the plump matron who still frowned on the fact she lived while her partner died, argued with Cindy.

Val sat sedate and unsure—those traits rarely depicted on the seer's features. Pete the police artist who had drawn multiple versions of the perpetrator Val, Hank and Maggie had taken turns to describe until the drawings resembled no one, sat charcoal in hand ready to pencil in any changes people ordered.

They all spoke at the same time, the cacophony loud and boisterous when Hank no longer able to make out a word put two fingers in his mouth and whistled. "Guys, we're not making any progress here." He eyed Maggie Pearson. "So, do you recognize him or not?

Maggie stared at the easel Pete had plastered with too many versions of a weird stranger.

"Val, anything you want to add?" Hank asked her with a slight smile. He'd given her all the information he'd gotten from Emma, and since Hank held the same list in his hands, he realized she'd forgotten an important feature.

She glanced at her notebook. "I jotted down some of the details. I'm sure more will come as I try to recall the madman's picture. Usually, I get these visions at night, when I'm about to fall asleep," she added.

Hank caught Matt's pinched lips as he tried not to laugh. Dark eyes were playful as he pinched the bridge of his nose. He'd keep Emma's secret, but he'd giggle through the process for sure.

Cindy had brought two fresh pots of coffee, and she filled the cups for people who'd asked for refills while she eyed the etching of the man they were desperately trying to find. "Doesn't he remind you of someone?"

"Why? Have you seen him?" Hank asked her. She raised her shoulders.

"I think the man I spotted resembled more a woman," Maggie added. "A big boned, mannish woman."

"Yes," Cindy added. "That's where I've seen him." She faced Hank. "Remember that movie? Can't think of the name. Where this guy becomes a nanny to be with his kids."

"Yeah," Matt nodded. "Yeah. Robin Williams. Mrs. Doubtfire," Matt answered.

Everyone began talking all at once again, and Hank had to intervene.

"Okay. Getting late, people. Val anything about the eyes?"

She hesitated a few seconds. "Si, the eyes are a tired blue, big and round and have ugly red lines running through them."

Maggie took in Pete's adjustment. "Hank," she breathed

excited and angry at the same time. "This is her—or him. Son of a bitch. I can't believe this creep killed Jack."

She turned toward Hank wanting confirmation. "Are you sure? How can you be so sure the sex fiend we are chasing is the cop killer?"

Hank stared at Val with round eyes.

"I can't be sure." She raised her chin at Hank in defiance. "Simply intuition, of course."

Matt frowned. He no longer found the situation amusing.

"No offense, Val," Maggie added. "Ken doesn't believe the kidnapper and the drive-by shooter are one and the same." She turned toward Hank. "I don't either."

Silence descended on the group. Hank considered he'd done all in his power to make sure Maggie would not encounter Jack's fate. Now the rest was up to her. On the other hand, probably was a good thing Ken didn't believe in their perp being the cop killer. Otherwise, the FBI would not only be on the premises they'd be handling the case exclusively.

Hank ignored Maggie's statement and changed the subject, stating an observation. "Of course, you all realize what this means."

All eyes on him, they waited for an explanation. "Means the man wears camouflage. You mentioned Mrs. Doubtfire, and this made me think major disguise. We have no idea what this killer looks like. For all we know, the man might be a skinny, stupid kid with long hair and facial acne."

"Still," Maggie reiterated. "Eyes can't be changed, Hank. This picture represents the man I remember. If he's going around in disguise, perhaps other people have seen him as well."

"Good point. All right, Pete. The session is a wrap. We're going with the picture," Hank said as he fingered the drawing with the colored eyes. Let's spread the poster far and wide. We may get lucky."

"Did you get anything from the car you brought in?" Maggie asked.

"How do you know about the car?"

"Lab guys were talking," Matt answered. "I told them to be discreet."

Hank eyed Maggie. "Nothing. Couldn't have been the car he used to commit the murders—too clean. We couldn't even trace the license plate yet."

"Well, thanks to Val, we've got a picture." Maggie smiled at Val who assembled her notes and tucked them away in her bag— too embarrassed to take the credit Hank thought.

***

Soya sauce chicken, BBQ pork, stir-fried vegetables and stewed beef brisket lined up in tall boxes to form a dominant centerpiece on Franka's dining room table. The aroma wafted by in a delicious scent and the snow peas in ginger sauce happened to be Emma's favorite.

"Wow, this food is good. Haven't had Chinese in a while," Patrick said. "Where did you get this?"

"Pat, New York is all about Chinese takeout at all hours, and these are traditional dishes. Of course, they're delicious," Franka said with a smile.

No one had commented on their talk in the room Emma thought

as she eyed the faces around her. No one had mentioned a word. Nevertheless, Emma sensed a change of attitude toward her father as though she read more respect for him in her aunt and mother's eyes. Even Christina Tyler's expression was kinder when she looked her dad's way. Jimmy was the only one who seemed unaffected, only happy to be seated next to Franka. He wouldn't know that her father's eyes were swollen as though he had cried, and the thought of her father's tears robbed the fight out of Emma. She imagined what this knowledge did to her mother and her aunt, and of course, both recognized his sad demeanor. One thing Patrick Willis did poorly: hide his feelings.

He picked up a carton of rice and dumped a ladle full in his plate. Emma caught his hands shaking.

"I've made a decision," Patrick announced his eyes still riveted to his plate. He looked up to gauge the effect of his words on his audience. When they stopped eating, he added, "I'm not going to touch the money my mother gave Emma." He picked up his fork and began eating, though he seemed to be waiting for the repercussions Emma guessed.

"Pat," Franka was the first to react. "Emma was so pleased to do this for you."

He acknowledged his daughter with kind eyes and patted her hand. "I realize she means well. But my mother did without any luxury most of her life—a bare to the bone life. She managed to save up all this money for Emma, for her education. The money is earmarked for this purpose. Next week, I'm going to find a fund that pays well and put this money away for her."

"Wow, Patrick, that's perfect." Eloise smiled and wiped a tear from the corner of her eyes.

Emma guessed her mother appreciated her father finally embracing his mother's wishes—they had fought about this many times in the past. And even though she'd conjured the stack of hundreds, her education scored high on her grandmother's wishes. Of course, only she realized he was not going to invest any of this money for fear of attracting a whole bunch of questions from the authorities. He would burn the bills somewhere, probably hoping to replace them one day.

"Are we going to be okay?"

"Absolutely. I'm going to ask Abigail for a loan. When is she coming back, by the way?"

Emma bit her lip not to laugh at her aunt and mother's expression which reminded her of the cartoon where Sylvester the cat sticks his finger in an electrical outlet. Glancing at Christina, she spotted her teacher peering at Franka and Eloise her brow furrowed with questions.

Franka said, "Sometime next week." She choked on something she'd swallowed. She tried to cough it up and Jimmy, unaware of the mouthful Patrick had said, patted her back to help whatever she'd eaten go down. "Here, sweetheart," Jimmy added. "Have a sip of water." He handed her his glass while she agreed rolling her eyes as she took a few grateful gulps.

"Thanks," she said able to breathe again. "I think a tiny bone in the mouthful of chicken I ate went down the wrong way."

Or was it her father's news? Emma wondered.

Franka didn't add another word. And Emma spotted her mother rallying a tissue to blow her nose. She wouldn't add anything either, embarrassed by Christina Tyler and Jimmy Roth's presence, but she was shedding tears of joy for the rebirth of her rigid husband.

***

In front of the Willis home, a police car was leaving while another was preparing to go. An officer stuck his head out of the window asking the identity of the man by the curve. "Can I help you, sir?"

The man came forward and smiled. "No. I am waiting for the client two doors down. I'm supposed to fix his air conditioning, but he's not here yet. I was just wondering about the commotion over here."

"I don't see that's any of your business," the officer replied. "Do you have identification?"

"Sure." The uniformed man reached into his pocket and pulled out his wallet. He presented the police officer with his license and registration.

"You're Moey Boleslaw?" The officer asked.

"Yep. The truck is registered to the company I work for, Con-Air." He fidgeted uncomfortably. "Neighbor told me this was an empty house. That true?"

The officer didn't answer. He waited for his partner to make the call.

"I usually go around and give my business cards to the neighbors when I do a job somewhere. Company rules."

After a few minutes, his partner gave him the thumbs up, and the officer handed him his papers. "I wouldn't stay around here if I were you. Get to your client and stay put or else we'll have to bring you in."

"Of course, officer. Thank you." The stranger watched them leave snickering at what he considered their stupidity while he cursed inwardly. "This means she's not coming back," he mumbled. Walking up the street back to his truck, he spotted a kid rounding the walkway of the house he stalked. He witnessed him ring the doorbell. Then he stared at the boy as he left, head down and shuffling his feet. Maybe this punk knew where the witch was Moey thought.

***

Everyone had left, and Hank sat alone, lights off, churning dark thoughts. Leclerc had caved and agreed to bring in the FBI. They would be there by the end of the week which meant he needed to work with Val and have her rehearse her role. No way was he exposing Emma to thieves and bandits out there. If the story got out that a ten-year old could identify them, she wouldn't last a month in this city.

He remembered what she'd said about the madman calling her a witch and hoped he hadn't blabbed to anyone. Who could the maniac tell? If he did, suspicions would rise and with a little luck, someone might even report him.

He picked up the phone wishing it were tomorrow, so the bastard's picture was already blasted in the papers and on billboards and in public places everywhere. One thing was sure, if he ran around town comfortably hidden behind a disguise, he'd no longer be able to wear this one.

"Hey, Christina, it's me. Where are you?"

"I'm at Franka Tichy's condo in Soho. We just finished dinner.

You sound awful. Are you all right?"

"Yeah, just brooding. Could use some cheering up. Going to be there long?"

"I came here courtesy of Officer Tim, remember?"

"Stay put. I'll be there in 30 minutes."

***

Christina wanted to tell him how tired she was and how tonight did not figure as a possibility in her date book. But he hung up before she could say. Just as well she thought. She wasn't free to discuss this where she sat, in Franka's living room, listening to Jimmy make plans for their future. Eloise and Patrick Willis were seated almost next to her, whispering to each other. She was glad Hank had promised to pick her up, but she wasn't in the mood to bear anyone's company this evening, much less nurse a surly detective needing comfort.

"Does anyone know where Emma is?" Christina asked.

Eloise turned toward her an apology written on her face when she detected Christina alone. No one with whom she could share a few words. "I'm so sorry for our rudeness, Christina. We didn't mean to exclude you from our conversation."

"Don't be silly. I'm sure you have lots to discuss. I was just wondering where Emma is." She looked at her watch. "I'm expecting a ride soon. Wanted to say my goodbyes."

"She asked permission to take the phone in Franka's room earlier," Eloise answered.

"I'm sure she won't mind if you check in on her," Patrick added.

"Thank you, I will."

When Christina rounded the room, she overheard Emma's conversation. She smiled thinking she had quite the knack for surprising her in the middle of her discussions.

"I'm sorry I couldn't get back to you earlier, Tommy. I've been with my folks and my Aunt Franka all day.

When Emma noticed Christina standing in the doorway, she signaled for her to enter and close the door. "Just a minute Tommy, Christina Tyler is here too. Can you repeat what you just told me? I want her to listen. I'm going to put you on speaker phone."

"Which part?"

"Start from the beginning."

Christina sat down on the bed beside Emma to listen to what Tommy Carson had to say.

"Hi, Miss Tyler."

"Hey, Tommy. What does Emma want you to repeat?"

"Well, as I was saying, my dad and I came back from Connecticut late last night. On the ride home, he told me what had happened to Emma. I was upset. So this morning I tried to go to her place, but police cars were there. I tried phoning, but there was no answer. So later this afternoon, I rode to Emma's house from the side street. I parked my bike against the house near the tree outback. I figured I'd climb the tree into Emma's room. By the way, Emma. That's quite a job some butt munch did on your tree. Poor thing needs help."

"My father did the best he could under the circumstances. My mother called in a tree expert who is going to mend the ends of the branches—so it can grow again."

"Sorry, Emma."

"Go on with your story, Tommy," Christina added. "Since there was no way up that tree, I waited. Then a police car left. So, I waited for the other one to leave too. But before the last one pulled out, a skinny guy came up to the cop car window and must have asked for directions. I don't know. The officer asked him for identification, and he pulled some out. Then he told him to leave the area, this part I heard."

"Tell Miss Tyler what happened next."

"I'm getting there." A long sigh afterward, he said. "He began to walk up the street to his truck. He wore a beige overall like a mechanic or something. He stared at me hard after I'd rung the bell. When I spotted him jogging in my direction, I grabbed my bike and rode out of there, but not before he ran after me. I got kind of scared he'd hop into his truck and follow me, so I rode through back yards, throwing my bike over fences when I had to."

"Would you recognize him if you saw him again?" Christina asked.

"Don't know. Never saw the jerk up close. His hair tied in a ponytail swung at the back when he ran."

Christina heard the door buzzer, then the intercom. Hank had made it there in record time, and she wondered if he'd raced over using his siren. "I'll make sure to tell Detective Apple about this, Tommy. Thanks."

Christina got up. "I have to go. Hank is waiting for me. Want to say hello?"

Emma nodded. "Tommy, I'll ask my aunt if you can come over tomorrow. I'm sure she'll say yes."

<u>Twenty</u>

Christina And Hank

Hank quickly saluted everyone and nudged Christina to hurry. He glanced at Emma for a few minutes. "Everything all right?"

She smiled. "Super." She sensed he referred to the fact that he'd told her parents about her actions, and she wanted to reassure him.

"I'm glad. Does this mean I can visit tomorrow?"

"You want to come here?"

"I don't want you at the police station anymore. Listen, Emma," he placed an arm around Christina's waist, and this made Emma smile. "Whatever you tell me will be kept in strictest confidence. I'm not sharing with anyone except Val."

"Dad told me Val had stepped in for me. Please thank her. I appreciate her kindness."

"Why not thank her yourself? May I bring her along? To sound credible, she will need to hear this from you. Is that okay?"

Her first instinct was to say no, but she bobbed her head instead. She would get used to Val's ways. After all, tons of efforts from dedicated people poured in to catch a madman who snidely killed everyone in his path.

***

Out in the car, Christina thought Hank appeared quiet. He hadn't said a word since she'd related Tommy's conversation practically word for word. She glanced at him and recognized the gloomy port of his head, the downturn of his mouth. He juggled with dark thoughts all right, negative thoughts she didn't wish to become acquainted with, yet she held an insatiable urge to learn their source.

"You thinking about Tommy?"

He shook his head from side to side.

"Could be the same man who is after Emma," she added more to break the tension between them.

"A lot of weirdos in our fair city. If the officer on duty called in this man's identity, we'll be able to pull the file on him, won't we?" He glanced at her. "How would we even recognize if he is the man we're searching for?" He threw another glance her way. "Camouflage is hard to detect if you don't know what to expect … Even camouflaged relationships can't be trusted."

"Relationships?" She hated to ask since she realized where this conversation was headed.

"You and me for instance."

He paused, and she closed her eyes taking a deep breath. She'd guessed he brooded over their failed affair, like one of her kids during detention. She blamed herself for insisting, he spill his guts and remained quiet while she waited for the other shoe to drop.

"I thought our relationship was the real deal. No disguises, no phony baloney crap. When you walked in on me and that bitch,

I swear. Took six weeks to get the smell of her off me. I realized that day and every day since how I'd done a stupid thing, all in the name of my career. Didn't matter because I remembered. You and I were the real deal. We'd rise above it—together."

Christina thumbed at the tears streaking her cheeks, but they left traces she was sure, little imprints in her conscience but deep gullies in her lonely heart. She'd cried so many of them after they'd gone their separate ways.

"Surprise, surprise. Smoke and mirrors were all our love meant to you. Still, can't believe you dumped us away like a bad costume after the party's over."

"Hank," Christina hesitated. "I don't think this is the time to talk about you and me."

"Of course, this isn't the time, but I need to vent. Got this all trapped inside and seeing you again, working with you on this case brought all the drama back."

She wanted to apologize but wasn't sure why she ought to. However, glimpsing Hank's big hands on the steering wheel and hearing his sad confession, she urgently needed to change the subject. "I'm glad to learn Emma's going to help you. Her assistance should make things easier."

"For Val, yes. The woman can't improvise to save her life. FBI is coming at the end of the week, and she needs to get her act together."

"I understand what you mean. Press would jump all over this story if they discovered how much Emma suspects about the circumstances behind these killings."

"Now she's decided to talk, I get the sense we can jump ahead of the game and catch the son of a bitch."

"Suppose this man who was running after Tommy is the same man who is chasing Emma? He might be trying to get to Tommy to find out where Emma is."

Hank pulled the car up in front of Christina's house. He turned the motor off and stared into the distance. "You might be right. We'll need to find out who he is. Find out what he is up to."

He turned in his seat to stare at her. "You just said a mouthful." She cocked her head.

"He might be trying to find out where Emma is? Trouble is I can't get a rat's ass of what he looks like." He nodded as though coming to a decision. "I think once she's stayed at her aunt's place a couple of weeks we're going to have to move her."

"You can't send her back home."

"Can't afford to. No way can I ask Ken for more money in this case."

All at once he got out of the car and strode to her side. He opened her door and waited for her to exit.

Christina couldn't help a pang of disappointment when she stepped out of the car. Despite all her protests, the thought of spending more time with Hank had spread warmth inside her.

When she lined both feet on the curb, he did not move aside to let her pass. Instead, he blocked her way until she had to stare into his eyes, a question shining in hers.

A frisson ran across her neck when his hand caressed her face, ever so gently, and the memory of his words in the car brought home the fact he had never stopped loving her these past few years.

Tingling from his touch, she closed her eyes to savor the fullness of Hank's delicate brush against her cheek, her chin.

Then staring at him she admitted, "I didn't shed my love for you or lose it. I couldn't. The feeling is too much a part of who I am. I merely buried my love and went on pretending I was okay living without you."

He stroked her lips with the tip of his thumb until she couldn't prevent parting them. She barely resisted the temptation to kiss his thumb, caress it with the tip of her tongue.

"I couldn't live through that again," he said with a surly tone to his voice.

She realized he was fishing for a promise, the avowal she would never leave him. They weren't back together, and he already wanted her declaration of fidelity. What about his missed promises? Rather than argue, she opted to hand him an olive branch. "Would you like to come inside, have a cup of coffee?"

He didn't answer, just moved in closer. Christina sensed his breath on her temple just before he bent his head and nibbled her earlobe. "I can't do that," he whispered as he took her in his arms, applying the span of his big hands on her back to press her against him. "If I go in there, I'm not coming out until morning. Unless this is what you want, please don't invite me in."

She moaned as she moved in his arms, sensing his readiness to fulfill his promise. "Would that be such a bad idea?" She whispered shyly.

He pushed her away to stare into her eyes. "You'd be willing to be mine, all mine again without any promise of forever?"

"Maybe I've realized forever is not what I want from you." She smiled realizing the light in her eyes teased him no end.

"Why does this idea not make me sing like I thought it would? You're a wily one, school teacher. You know that?"

She raised her shoulder brushing her lips against his. "Of course, I do," she whispered. The last thing she remembered was their breath mingling and his forceful hand guiding her toward the front door. Tired or not, Christina would take him on for as long as he wanted her.

***

The night bore diverse aspects for different people: shimmering in multicolored folds of sultry passion for lovers, mystic haze for dreamers, and clouds of hope for those with new tomorrows.

Sometimes, the night's ebony clouds parted and translucence appeared, revealing eyes avidly peering through the mist of a moonlit night. Staring across the void, they lurked to catch a glimpse of a shadow which might be watching.

He is out there Emma thought while lying in her aunt Franka's guest bed. Her head propped up on fat pillows. She turned to reach and grasp with both eyes the glow of a white moon. Though bright and familiar the astral body would not help her. And she sighed as her hand flipped the pillow over her ears to shut out his breathing and his cursing as he slashed the night's veil trying to find her.

She didn't hear the knock on her door until someone gently shook her shoulder. She yelped, jumping back against the headboard in a sitting position. She spotted her mother and began to cry.

"I'm sorry, Emma. I was calling you from the door, but when you didn't answer … I thought you might be sleeping." Eloise took Emma in her arms and rocked her gently smoothing her hair back like when she was a little girl. "I need to talk to you, Emma, and what I have to say can't wait till morning."

Eloise handed her a tissue, and when Emma blew her nose, she noticed her mother's eyes were red also.

Eloise moved in closer sitting on the bed and urged Emma to put her head back down on the pillow. Emma stared up at her mom and swallowed the last hiccup bubbling up inside her throat.

"You do have a magnificent gift, Emma. I needed to tell you. I know I haven't been there for you as I should have." She put a finger to Emma's lips already forming a protest. "I know my duties, and I did not fulfill them the way I should have. Now, your gift has brought this family together." She shook her head for emphasis. "Your dad and I had a long talk … let's just say we aired many past misgivings ."

Emma could well imagine. The long overdue chat could not have been easy for her, for either of them. Especially since her father seemed to be the more emotional of the two.

"You were covering your ears when I came in. Why?" Emma turned her head. She could not face her mother. She couldn't stare at her mom's lovely face, or she would just break down and cry again. Both her parents being so supportive worsened the moment for Emma. Somehow their compassion made her weak, and all she craved was to hide away in her parents' arms and never come out.

"Those nightmares you had," Eloise paused biting her lip and seemingly fighting tears herself. "Nightmares were about him … weren't they?"

Emma nodded without glancing at her mother.

"I have something for you." Saying this, Eloise reached in her blouse's pocket and opened her hand. In her palm, there glowed a strange pendant dangling at the end of a gold chain. Emma sat up in bed gazing at the piece of jewelry her full attention focused on four concentric circles. The first one was biggest and blue. The others, a pink and a gray seemed smaller while inside the gray appeared a black center. "Looks like an eye," Emma whispered the pendant now in her hands.

"You're right. The jewel is the Eye of Horus, an ancient Egyptian symbol of protection. Your grandmother Dottie called it oudjat also symbolizing wisdom and regeneration. She wanted to be buried with the talisman."

"Why wasn't she?"

"She was very ill by the time the ambulance came, weak, stretched out without any strength left whatsoever. Somehow she found the power to tug my sleeve. She put the amulet in my hand and told me I needed to give the talisman to you. She said the oudjat would protect you and keep you grounded. She must have seen something during her last hour."

"Grounded?"

Eloise scooted closer, stretching out her legs on the bed. "I debated lying here with you all night. To comfort you, to protect you—mostly to try and stop you from traveling," she breathed out while biting her bottom lip. "I don't want you to go back there. No child should have to go through what you did, no one, certainly not my little girl." Her mother put her hands around her shoulders and hid her face in her hair, and Emma figured she fought not to let her see how scared she was.

When Eloise regained control, she released Emma and wiped her eyes. "This amulet will keep you here. I never understood what your grandmother meant by grounded. Tonight I remembered."

"You carried this with you all this time?"

"Your dad went to get it, in my jewelry box at home." Hank Apple had asked them not to go back there, in case the madman followed them, Emma remembered. "Detective Apple is counting on me, Mom."

"You have rounded up more than your share of information to give Hank Apple. More than your share. In the morning, tell him everything you already know. It will be enough. Let him do the rest."

Emma sensed her mother was pleading with her, afraid she would have another nightmare. Now that her parents both knew the basis of her night terrors, they were genuinely worried she would head there again. She nodded putting the pendant around her neck. "I'll wear the oudjat, Mom. I promise. And thank you." She released a lungful never realizing how much she'd stopped breathing.

Eloise rose and smiled at her. "I'll be just down the hall."

"Dad too?"

"Dad too. Jimmy's gone and Dad's sleeping on the couch. Franka and I will use her room—just for tonight."

Emma lay back into the pillows. She was alone again, and though the same unfamiliar shadows stretched and danced in the room, she fingered the amulet on her chest and didn't dread them anymore. Even the moon playing hide-and-seek behind silver phosphorescent clouds no longer frightened her. She fell asleep her eyes confidently embracing the ink-black sky.

<u>Twenty-One</u>

Hank Introduces Val

ank opened his eyes and tried to focus on where he'd spent the night. Memory trickled through a fog of shadows in his mind—a haze at least as thick as the one filling the room where he lay. Flowered curtains drawn, windows closed to keep the cool air in, the only sound of what took place outside came carried by light rain tapping against the windowpane.

He rubbed his eyes and felt a long slim arm drawn against his torso. Christina, he thought, a twinge of excitement coursing through him.

He stretched his right arm to grab the clock on the nightstand, but connected to the wall the timepiece didn't go quite far—far enough to show him he would be late if he didn't get up and leave.

With care, he slipped Christina's arm by her side and gently slid out of bed. Thank God he'd taken a shower only a couple hours ago, so dressing in the dark and tiptoeing out the door would be easy. He watched her sleep pangs of guilt assailing him. He grabbed the blanket and the small coverlet she used as a comforter and drew them over her bare back.

She slept on her stomach with face deep in the pillow. She likely wouldn't discover his departure until much later.

Unable to get enough of each other, their passion taking over their senses, he depended on three hours of sleep to get him through the day. They'd talked for hours and pooled a lot of their dreams and thoughts, more so than during the two years they had lived together. Now he was sorry he hadn't told her how much he loved her. She had, more than once. His stupid pride had choked the words out of him, still unable to live down the years she'd forced him to struggle without her.

He slipped his pants on, found his shirt and jacket and slipped on his shoes shoving his socks in his pocket. He'd put them on later.

On his way to the door, he doubled back to take one last peek at the woman he loved. The real reason he hadn't spoken up dealt more with other issues, like the shame of betraying his former avowal of love to her. A bloody miracle she was even back in his arms. She'd certainly held nothing back.

***

Emma stood in her aunt's living room looking down at the street below. To get a better view she'd pushed back the white satin sheer curtains she now rolled between her fingers the sensation tickling her pleasantly. She wondered if the rain was an omen of a gray day ahead of her.

"Coming, Aunt Franka."

Her mother and father had left early to go to work. And after a bout of morning sickness, Franka had resolutely wanted to make her breakfast despite Emma's protests that she was old enough to make her own.

She let go of the curtains to finger the amulet still hanging around her neck, tucked under her t-shirt and swishing smoothly against her skin like a protecting hand. She figured she wouldn't always wear the Eye of Horus. But she'd slept beautifully, staying put the whole night. Or did her environment have something to do with the peace of a dreamless night? She often wondered if Granny Dottie's influence might still be connected to her through the house's familiar surroundings, lending her the possibility to perform the unusual things she did. Then again, she'd conjured the shiny new penny for the officer's benefit while on her way home from the clinic.

"Better get some food inside you, sweetie. Hank Apple will be here soon."

After breakfast, Hank would arrive. He'd bring loaded questions, and she'd work to remember all she'd seen in her dreams while trying not to juggle with the emotional baggage strapped to the memories. She would do as her mom had asked her to do. Dispatch the facts, let Hank connect the dots and forget about the rest.

She pulled the wooden chair away from the table, the scraping sound on the tiles echoing throughout the open concept breakfast nook, and she wondered why her aunt needed such a large apartment living by herself.

Settling in, she bit into a mouthful of pancake dripping with maple syrup. "This is delicious, Aunt Franka. Jimmy's a lucky guy." Emma teased.

"What are you trying to say, munchkin?" Franka grabbed her glass of juice and sat down facing her.

"Just that you're a good cook."

"These pancakes came from a mix. Nothing to them," Franka

added.

Emma thought she seemed self-conscious about the compliment. "You're going to make a good mother too," she smiled nodding for emphasis.

Franka pinched her lips as though tears were close at hand. She stared at the pancakes in her plate seemingly mesmerized with her fork pushing the pieces around to soak up syrup.

"You're not having second thoughts, are you … about the baby?"

"No, no. Nothing like that." Franka put down her fork and wiped her mouth with her napkin. "I guess I better tell you. You'll learn about it soon enough." She toyed with Emma's fingers. "You have lovely shaped nails. They'd look spectacular with a little pink polish."

"What are trying to tell me?"

"Jimmy asked me to marry him." She stuck out her finger and Emma gazed at a small pear shaped diamond. Then she stared into her aunt's eyes. "You're not sure, are you?"

"I'm not. Can't say why. I love Jimmy and all … he's just not the type of man I saw myself ending up with, make sense?" She shook her head, and Emma realized her silence wasn't making it easier for Franka.

"We all dream of prince charming," Emma said. "Of some white knight. We're all guilty of doing that."

"Or of some intellectual equal …"

"He's smart, though, about the day to day things, right?"

Franka was quick to nod which only gave Emma the impression her aunt was covering when she added, "I mean this business about the car. He should have realized an abandoned vehicle is not good news. Should have brought the car straight to police or to the pound, gotten rid of it somehow."

"They might have traced the car back to him anyway. He did a good thing for his mother."

"Not out of kindness, only because she nagged him."

"Maybe you're a little hard on him. Think of my father. Who would have thought he would ever come through for me? And he certainly was not kind to his mother while growing up, but I recently learned that they fought because they were both scared. She feared him hanging with the wrong crowd, and he rebelled because of all the threats she made. Men like Dad and Jimmy, well, strong emotions have them by the neck. They don't always say nor do the smartest thing. But they'll lay down their life for the people they love.

Franka squeezed Emma's chin. "How did you get to be so smart?"

Emma raised a couple of nonchalant shoulders.

"Ahhh," Franka breathed out with despair, her eyes closed. She smiled at her niece. "I'm just not sure this is enough. You'll understand all this someday."

The door intercom had them jump. Emma figured this wasn't the time to ask her aunt why she wore the ring if she hesitated to marry Jimmy.

Once Franka hung up, she said. "Speaking of men who are slaves to their emotions. Got a big one on his way up."

Emma giggled at her aunt's attempt at crossing her eyes as she went to unlock the two bolts to her door. She was right. Hank would be another one of those primates who'd go to war, pound his fists against his chest in a show of triumph only to wrap his arms around the girl adrenalin feeding his frenzy.

Hank came in flanked with Val. He'd picked her up at the subway, two blocks from Franka's condo.

"Howdy, folks. Franka, this is Val."

The two women shook hands. "Pleased to meet you, Val," Franka said. "Please come in. You can use the small parlor to your right. I'll close the French doors to give you privacy."

"Very thoughtful. Thank you." Hank took off his shoes to protect the floors.

"Don't, Hank. My floors need a good scrubbing, and I have excellent help."

"Nah. My big tumblers have been everywhere. They'd only muck up the carpet in your sitting room."

Emma glanced at Hank and wondered what was different about him this morning. He seemed tired, yet not as edgy as usual almost happy if this word could be used to describe the rugged detective.

"I'll bring in a pot of coffee," Franka said. "Anyone want anything else?"

Val smiled and tugged at her backpack fidgeting with the zipper. "I stopped …" She tossed the flap to her big shoulder bag and carefully extracted a bulging box. "I got donuts for everyone," she said as she opened the lid to let them gawk at the treasure she carried. "I got one of every kind. Hope it will do."

"Do?" Franka opened wide eyes. "It's wonderful. Sweets are about the only thing I can keep down these days." She took the box from Val. "Okay, then. So there'll be donuts with your coffee."

Hank laughed, and Emma pondered she'd never heard him

laugh. The rugged tone suited him.

When they finally sat down in front of coffee and donuts, and a tall glass of ice tea for Emma, silence fell like a shroud and Emma found herself wishing for Christina Tyler's presence.

"He drives a blue Ford station wagon." Emma didn't know why she'd blurted the words out. Perhaps a sense of duty since she'd promised her mother or because her secret being out in the open with her father, she needed to unburden what she carried. Whatever the reason, she stared at the shock on Hank's expression hoping he didn't judge her confession too outrageous.

Hank glanced at Val to make sure she was ready to take notes. "Do you mind if I tape, Emma?" Val asked.

"What if someone was to get hold of the tape?"

"No one will, I promise. You have the information in your head. I don't. I'll never remember everything you tell me."

She pinched her lips and lowered her eyes. She did not want Val taping her conversation. She glanced at Hank.

"Never mind the taping, Val. Emma's right. We'll both take notes, and this will suffice."

Hank asked. "How do you know he drives a blue Ford? What kind of blue?"

She gazed at Val whose own eyes had narrowed on her as she waited pen poised in hand.

"I'd rather not say how I know the things I do. I don't want to go to that place if I don't have to. I'm just going to give you the facts. That's what important, right?"

"Of course. The why and the how are just to help Val."

"Don't mind me. I'll make time to weave a credible story. After all, turns out I'm going to be right a lot. They'll have to take my word."

"Car was dark blue, but not new. He parked across from my parent's house two nights in a row, in the driveway of the abandoned Henderson Home."

"He was stalking your place?"

"I saw him."

"How could you see him at that distance?"

"I can tell when he's around. I can sense him." Hank released his breath shaking his head.

"He has a place on North Walnut Street in East Orange."

Hank's arms fell to his side, and Emma could tell he tried not to appear shaken.

"How … Can you describe the place?"

"There's a torn building beside it. A church or synagogue nearby. His building is old and rambling, and there's a big sign on it that says: We buy gold. There are five windows on the second floor. I believe his window is the third one in the row, two away from the demolished construction site—at least this is the window that lit up that night."

She sneaked a peek at Val. The woman had stopped writing, and her hand shook as she took a sip of her coffee.

Hank got up and began pacing. "We've got him. Can't believe we've got him," he muttered.

"No, you don't. This warehouse is not where he lives."

Hank stared at her long and hard. "Do you know where he lives?"

She shook her head from side to side.

"What is this place then?"

"It's where he brings," Emma hesitated. Taking a deep breath, she added, "His victims."

Val bent toward her and for the first time, Emma spotted compassion in her brown eyes. "Emma," Val said. "You've been there?"

"Only in my nightmares. The crazy man brought Ashley there, Ashley Miller." She pinched her lips not to cry and wiped the tear pearling in the corner of her eye.

"Who?"

Emma didn't answer.

Hank grabbed his leather schoolbag and rummaged inside for his files. "We have no victim by that name," he muttered as he poured three folders on the coffee table in front of him. He stared at Emma.

She raised her shoulders in a show of ignorance.

"Last little girl was Anne, Anne Ripley.

"No. Ashley her name is Ashley Miller."

"Geez Louise." Hank bounded up again unable to contain his energy.

"Maybe she was supposed to be number four." Emma stared at her donut having lost her appetite.

"Emma, could this be a snapshot of the future," Val breathed. "Did it seem grainy? At the time, did you recognize you might be looking ahead?"

"No. I didn't realize anything. I just dreaded being back there again. But this time, I made it all the way inside the room past the dirty walls and the lone light bulb. I tried to turn back, but I couldn't. Like there was a magnet drawing me inside against my will. He behaved like a vicious dog, and I yelled to make him stop. That's when he turned and stared right at me. Called me a witch."

Val got up and walked toward the settee Emma occupied alone. She sat down beside her and wrapped an arm around her shoulders. "Poor chica. No one should live through this," she cooed. "To think I envied your talent. Not anymore I don't."

"All this time I thought he'd killed her, and I hadn't been able to stop him.

"Emma you said Ashley was the fourth," Hank said. "What did you mean by that?"

"She's not anymore. The picture has changed. We altered it or rather I did because now he's after me."

Hank sat down on Franka's coffee table to be at eye level with Emma. "He's never going to lay a hand on you. I promise."

Emma smiled to relieve the pain she glimpsed in Hank's eyes. He seemed the more frightened of the two, and she pitied the vulnerability she read in his mind. To a strong man like Hank, helplessness had to be akin to torture.

"One last question, Emma. When you spotted this man with Ashley what did he look like?"

Emma stared from Hank to Val. Her personal space had shrunk to nothing, invaded by two people who meant well but whose fears she could not ease.

She took a deep breath and Val understood to sit further away. As for Hank, he let go of her hands. "He wore his costume. So no, I don't know who he resembles when he removes the wig and the large body shape."

Hank jumped up to pace. "Shrink at the precinct mentioned that since he's wearing a fat woman's disguise, chances are he's slim or skinny in real life."

"Do you think you might recognize him if he were out of

costume?" Val asked.

"Don't know. He'd remember me, though."

Val and Hank threw each other a quick glance.

Hank took a big gulp of his coffee, swishing the hot liquid from cheek to cheek. "You ladies have your coffee tea donuts. I have a couple of calls to make. Going to start the ball rolling."

"You've got his picture circulating this morning." Val reminded him.

"Right. All this is going to help." He left the room to call from his cell but doubled back. "Val, ten minutes? I need to get back as soon as possible."

"I'll be ready."

<u>Twenty-Two</u>

Emma Helps Hank

What Emma had told Hank still echoed in her head. Her mind kept playing the words she'd spoken in fear complete with the sound of her childlike voice echoing between her ears and making her resent her vulnerability. She'd wanted to be more grown up, in better control of her emotions, and she wondered what Hank might think of her now as she bit her lower lip and passed on the third donut her aunt offered.

"Cheer up, Emma. Hank left here all fired up excited about the information you'd given him."

She bobbed her head and flicked a strand of hair behind her ear. She peered down at the street comforted by Soho's commotion. She couldn't sense him below which meant he hadn't followed her to Manhattan. He most likely had no idea where to find her. The thought put a smile back on her face as she stared at her aunt. "I hope they find him soon," Emma said finally agreeing to pick a third donut from the box Franka held in front of her.

"Hank is nothing if not competent. He has quite the reputation."

Emma agreed as she bit into her choice of a deep chocolate delectable covered in a chocolate glaze. Hank had won medals and a lot of press sympathy for all the cases he'd solved.

"While you eat this, I'm going to finish getting dressed. I want to go down to the Deli and pick up something for dinner."

"Don't you want me to come with you?"

"I'd rather you stayed here. I'm expecting a phone call from the Dean. When he calls, I'll need you to get a number where I can reach him, okay?"

Emma agreed, not sure if her aunt didn't want her out and about in case the madman was on the prowl. She did expect to schedule an appointment with Dean Samson, though. "Where's your cell phone, Aunt Franka?"

Franka stepped out of her slippers on the way to the bathroom, and Emma caught the tip of her fingers waving at her as she rounded the corner. "It's dead. Needs to charge."

Don't worry. I'll make sure the Dean gives me a number."

"Good girl," she called loud enough to be heard. Emma jumped when Franka reappeared in the hallway.

"Did you forget something?"

She threw Emma a big smile. "Cheer up, sweetie. Tommy is coming to visit later remember?"

Emma donned a smile in part to ease her aunt's worry in part because she had forgotten about her visitor, and as she pondered on all the cool places where she and Tommy might hang, her smile grew.

***

Hank dropped Val off at the metro station without either of them ever sharing a word, except for the usual goodbye banter. He figured Val struggled with a lot of emotions. Hank certainly did. He still couldn't fathom how a ten-year-old scrap of kid harbored so much information about someone so evil and not collapse or slowly go mad.

The shrink at work had suggested life to be less complicated for children Emma's age, easier to forego real drama in their lives since much of their world involved the immediate present. Of course, the shrink didn't know who he was talking about, and somehow, he didn't believe in the good doctor's suggestions when it came to Emma.

The memory of events she'd recounted from her dreams was vivid, too close at hand to be anywhere else than at the forefront of her day to day life occupying her present. He also wondered if she'd ever experienced what it felt to be truly content, being just a kid without a care in the world. What if the fact that she'd never been happy became the reason she accepted her lot in life with such stoicism, even in the midst of life-threatening danger?

He cursed while sitting on the horn to indicate to the woman who'd cut in front of him how narrowly she'd escaped getting her car rear-ended.

A deep sigh escaped him as he flicked his Bluetooth hooked around his ear. "Hank."

"Hank, where are you?" Cindy sounded out of breath.

"What do you mean? I had my meeting with Val this morning. Where have you been?"

"That's true. I forgot. Just got in and I'm swamped. The one morning I'm late, and people are lined up waiting for me, and the chief …"

"I spoke to him already."

"What did he want?"

"Good news. With the break Val has provided us, he's agreed to postpone the FBI for a week."

"That is good news. More good news. The perp's picture you launched is already getting attention. Two people are here with paper in hand, waiting to talk to you. Meredith Ripley …"

"And Mr. Ripley."

"No. I asked. Meredith said her husband is at work. Something tells me he's fallen off the wagon and is not seeing the family counselor anymore."

"Who's the other person?"

"Some man. Doesn't want to leave his name—also holding the paper, clutching it would be a better word. A flight risk. He walked in at the same time I did, so I've been trying to make him comfortable."

"I'll be there as fast as I can."

"Oh, and Shirley at reception said Christina called." Hank flicked the Bluetooth. Seemed as though the whole world now meddled in his love life. Public eye in the bedroom happened to be Hank's biggest pet peeve about sharing his life with a significant other. The problem weighed heavily on his mind, even measured against his love for Christina and all the years of yearning and lost passion.

Aside from the fact his job consumed him which made it danger-ous for anyone else to be around him, he sometimes compared lov-ing Christina to Superman's Kryptonite. Lost in her arms, he'd often wondered about chucking it all away—taking a desk job and leaving the field to someone else. Perhaps this sense of inadequacy had been the real reason they'd split up. He didn't want to go indoors just yet. He needed to continue to best the bad guys, score more wins.

The ring in his ear indicated another caller. "Hank."

"Hi," he heard Christina's soft voice and for an instant, worried she might have picked up on his thoughts. He snorted at the sheer idea of this. Too many spooks in his life all of a sudden. "Hey, listen. I'm sorry I skipped out like a thief ..."

"Don't worry about it. I realize you had an appointment. How did it go with Emma?"

"Better than expected. I'll fill you in later. I'm on my way to the office to get the ball rolling."

There was silence at the other end, and a painful grimace painted gloom on Hank's face. Another one of his weaknesses—he couldn't do small talk over the phone. "I'm sorry. I don't mean to be abrupt. I just have so much on my mind."

"I understand, Hank. No need to defend yourself. I love Emma, and I can't help her right now. So I can imagine what you're going through."

"Can I take you out to dinner this evening?"

"You need your space right now, Hank. The last thing you want to worry about is taking me out to dinner. I would appreciate you keeping me abreast of what's going on, though."

"I will." He ripped the gizmo from his ear and dropped his Bluetooth on the seat beside him. He shouldn't have taken her call. He wasn't ready. He hoped her offer of space was genuine and not merely some clever means for her to save face. Was this what had kept him from telling her how much he loved her? His damn job?

After he entered the building, he strode down the corridor like a steam roller ignoring everyone in his path. He stopped in front of

Meredith Ripley, the mother of the last little girl they'd found. She sat beside Cindy's desk her eyes swollen and her gaze somewhere beyond the walls.

"Meredith." He stroked her arm when she rose. "Thank you for coming." He indicated the door to his office and followed her in.

"Where's your husband?"

"Stormed out when he laid eyes on this picture." She flicked the folded issue of the Star-Ledger and plopped it on his desk. She reached into her pocket to grab a tissue and blew her nose. "I'm sorry. He didn't want to come. He blames himself, and me."

"Why don't you tell me about the picture?"

Releasing a great sigh, she continued. "Marley Boleslava. We hired her to drive Anne to school and back after the two little girls were kidnapped. She seemed like a frail old lady. Could hardly walk. We both thought she needed the job."

"Go on."

"Things went well for a few weeks. Then Anne started complaining she didn't want to go to school. Wouldn't tell us why. We asked her teacher who swore everything was the same, except for a little more inattention on Anne's part. Ed pressed her and pressed her and then he got angry when she admitted she didn't like Mrs. Boleslava. He thought her sulking was a whim, a kid's inability to handle the physically challenged. Now."

Hank handed her a tissue when Meredith couldn't seem to find another. He could have used one too, but he kept his icy determination instead. "Did she … this person give you any references?"

Meredith nodded. "She did." She handed Hank a folder she pulled out of her bag. "This was her résumé. Not much to it, I'm afraid. I called the Agency she mentions and left my name for someone to call me back."

"Someone took your name and number?"

"A machine. I did get a callback, though. A friendly voice, woman, told me Mrs. Boleslava had been working for them for ten years and came highly recommended."

A knock on the door interrupted Hank's perusal of the file. He looked up as Cindy poked her head inside. "The man's leaving."

Hank was up like a bullet. "Meredith, thank you so much for coming. I'll be in touch." The wide eyes he plopped on Cindy indicated for her to placate Mrs. Ripley while he ran like hell to catch up to the anonymous snitch.

He caught up to him outside the precinct's steps. A hand on his arm he stopped him from running. "I'm Detective Apple. I'm the man you've been waiting to meet."

Hank surveyed the stranger as he hesitated, tall, well dressed in casual clothes. Stranger quickly glanced at the row of parked cars a hundred feet away.

"Please, we need all the help we can get in this case."

A slight nod gave Hank the go, and he followed the man inside leading him to the first space he found. Closing the door behind them, Hank asked. "What about this picture?"

"My wife would kill me if she knew I was here." He stopped, but when Hank said nothing, he continued. "This is undoubtedly Marley Boleslava."

"Please continue."

"We were too late to register our daughter for any day camp. Well, with everything going on, and with my wife's new job we decided to get a summer nanny. I didn't like Mrs. Boleslava. Shifty eyes, a real screwball. My wife thought she reminded her of Mrs. Doubtfire. Anyway, she was as good as hired—Michelle takes care of these things." He shrugged apologetically. "This was when a friend, Marlene Swift begged us to take her nanny for the summer. They weren't going to need her for the next couple of months, but didn't want to lose her to this other parent."

"What happened?"

"My wife caved and agreed to help Marlene and take on Marie for the summer."

"And ..."

"I don't mind telling you. I was relieved. But, when I called Mrs. Boleslava to let her know we wouldn't need her services, her voice went from soft and high pitch to that of a raspy man voice who practically yelled at me. I even wondered if I had the right number."

"You said your wife would kill you if she found out you were here?"

"Figure of speech. Michelle fell in love with the woman. When I pointed out to her that this picture could be our Mrs. Boleslava, she laughed and laughed." He took a deep breath which he released as he added, "Then she called me an idiot."

"Did this woman leave a résumé behind?"

"Yeah she did. Only don't ask me where it is."

"How long ago?"

"A few days now."

"Thanks for coming in." Hank stopped him just as he was about to cross the threshold. "Mind telling me what part of town you're from?"

He hesitated.

"It would help. You came all the way down here."

"Forest Hill, two streets off Highland Avenue."

Hank ran a nervous hand through his hair. "Thanks." When he returned to his office, Meredith Ripley had left. "Said she had a doctor's appointment and couldn't wait," Cindy told him. As Hank made to move, Cindy added, "By the way, I called that Agency's number." She gave Hank an apologetic frown. "No such Agency. No such number."

"You sure? Of course, you are," Hank answered his question.

"How does he do it?"

"Who knows? An accomplice disguises his voice. Apparently, uses trunked numbers." Hank stretched and yawned, fatigue making his eyes droop. "I'll be in my office. Let me know if Matt calls in."

Hank's eyes were drawn to the sofa when he closed the door behind him. He gave up and gave into lying down while his legs hung over the armrest. Three measly hours of sleep were starting to catch up to him. About to doze off, he jumped when his office door swung open.

"This is where you're hiding. Missed you at Jack's funeral this morning," Matt said as he strode in decked in his finest.

"God." Hank sat up rubbing his face with his hands. "I forgot all about it. No wonder Cin was late. "

"I explained to Maggie Pearson you were out catching the guy who did this. She understands."

"Were you able to get close to Jack's widow?"

Matt shook his bald head rubbing the top as if searching for a reason. "She disappeared hidden behind a tight web of friends and family. You know how she felt about his job or this precinct. Her youngest started crying when they launched the three-volley salute. Can't figure why they still do that." He stopped then continued. "I handed Meredith's information to the lab. Maybe they'll find us a lead with those numbers."

Hank lay back down on the couch. "I doubt it. This man's smart. Numbers he used no longer exist." He spotted Matt's face knotted with questions. "Trunked numbers on which he props different voices to validate then disconnects them just as quickly."

"Welcome to the age of technology," Matt breathed. "We'll find him, Hank. We've got people looking for the car Emma described."

"You won't find that either."

"What's up with you? Slept on the wrong side of the bed or something?"

Hank got up to sit with his head in his hands. "Maybe. The fact is, guy buys cars in these old jalopy type garages, pays cash and slaps on any license plate he has on hand. That's why we could never trace the one we confiscated from Jimmy. Had Jimmy not run a red, we might have never found the damn thing."

"Maggie checked his car, remember?"

"Yeah, looking for a body. How many cops make sure the license plate matches the paperwork? Maybe he can do both. Making up the paperwork is not hard to do."

Matt pulled a chair and sat in front of him. "I know what'll cheer you up." He waited before Hank looked up and stared straight at him. "How about you and me go check out that warehouse. Bet you we find lots of clues there."

"How did you know about the warehouse?" He hadn't had time to talk to Matt about this.

"Ken told me. Said information was courtesy of Val." Matt

winked at him.

It's a place to start." Hank got to his feet, stretched and stopped by Cindy's desk on his way out. "I want you to dig up everything you can on the person those two policemen checked out yesterday, the one chasing little Tommy Carson."

"Sure thing, Hank. Oh, I already know a few things," she said after she had remembered research had dropped a file on her desk. She flipped the cover. "I have his name and …"

Hank motioned with his hand her to hurry .

"His name is Morey Boleslaw."

Hank's eyes grew wide and enraged.

"Wait just a minute. Don't go ballistic on me," Matt told him pulling on his arm to get his attention. "Remember that case where the two people had identical initials and you were convinced they were one and the same? Remember how much flack we got? I thought Ken would never let us live it down."

Hank gave his partner a twisted smile. Turning to face Cindy, he added, "Don't tell me. He's young, skinny, five eight or five nine, oh, with long hair."

Cindy glanced at the file and looked up at him. "You've seen this?"

Hank's wry smile disappeared as he grabbed the folder from her hands. After close examination, he tossed it to his partner.

"So, what does this prove?"

"Val and I debated this, so did the shrink in the office by the way. She said odds are his costume is likely to be the opposite of what he looks like in real life which is why he becomes a chubby older woman with short gray hair and round shoulders. The height can't change, unless he wears those corrective shoes with the thick heels which is why I gave him an inch or two, edgewise."

"Want me to find out more about him?" Cindy asked. Hank stared at Matt waiting for his answer.

"May as well," Matt said reluctantly. "You got to promise me, man. You don't go overboard on this one."

Hank raised both his hands. "You got me. Calm and collected."

***

Emma hurried to answer the phone. She worried about her aunt, Franka. She'd been for a couple of hours.

"Hello?"

"Emma sweetie, it's me. I met up with Jimmy and we're having coffee at Dean & Deluca. I lost track of time, honey. I'm sorry. But don't worry about me. I'll be home in half an hour."

"Okay, Aunt Franka."

"Are you and Tommy having fun?"

"He isn't here yet. Thought he would be by now."

"Poor sweetie, you're all alone. Hope Tommy didn't get lost. Did Dean Samson call?"

"Yep, and I have a number for you."

"Terrific job, Emma. Be there in a bit."

Just as she hung up, the phone rang again. Emma smiled thinking her aunt had forgotten something.

"Emma? It's me. I'm at the subway station, and I can't find the street you told me to take."

"Tommy. What subway station?"

"Spring Street."

"You had to get off at Prince, silly. Now you're two blocks

farther south."

"I've got money. I can take a cab if I get tired of walking."

"Don't. I'll meet you half way. Hang a left on Spring Street. Keep going past Green. The next one will be Wooster. My aunt's place is a short walk up Wooster, close to Houston."

"Okay. See ya."

Twenty-Three

Perils And Dead-Ends

*E*mma hurried to power off her aunt's computer. She changed into a pair of jeans and checked her hair in the mirror. It was long and fly away today. She grabbed an elastic she wound twice around her fingers to tie her hair. She smiled grateful she'd no longer have the meshes dangling in her face.

She laced her running shoes and tucked her T-shirt inside her jeans. She grabbed her packsack to rummage for a pen and paper wanting to leave her aunt a note.

Contented with the heart-shaped kisses she drew at the bottom, she left the message by the vestibule credenza where Franka kept last minute items she needed before leaving the house: a hat, keys, a couple of umbrellas pegged near the shoe rack and a wooden board where she pinned reminders and grocery lists.

Once out of the building, she slipped her aunt's condo key inside her jean pocket—proud Franka had given her the only spare she owned.

She cupped her hand in front of her eyes and regretted not grabbing a hat. Sun beat down on her head. Emma hesitated faced with the indecision of which side of the street Tommy might take. She made up her mind to stay on the left. Tommy being right handed she figured he'd opt to stay on his right to walk toward her.

Resolutely she started toward Spring Street walking fast. She didn't care for this narrow end of Wooster, where skyscrapers gave the impression of overpowering stacks glaring down on her—cynical and spinning wild tales the wind carried to one and all.

Almost running, all at once needing to be where more people ambled ahead, she felt a tug on her ponytail sudden and tough, a jab that nearly knocked her down. Tommy she thought. But the tug became insistent and painful. "Ouch," she complained out loud reaching for her hair. A laugh, more like a snicker froze her heart. In seconds, the madman of her nightmares stood behind her, grabbing her waist and pulling her up against him.

"Don't yell. Don't move." He spat in her ear as he uttered the words. No one's around to save you now, are they?" Another laugh.

She sensed the foreign object he ran up and down her back and worried this might be a gun. She tried to gather peace inside her. Her wits were the only weapon she might wield. She conjured her little phrase and threw a small rock at the head of a man as he loaded boxes in a truck a few hundred feet away.

He turned abruptly and yelled. "What's the big idea, Lady?" He came toward them.

"I didn't do anything. It's this kid here. Don't worry. I've got everything under control."

Emma stared at the stranger with pleading eyes.

"Hey, let her go. Kid wants to go. Let her go I said. The stranger grabbed her captor's shoulder to pull him off of her. "Hey, what are you made of, lady? Memory foam? You're nothing but one big lump of fat."

The man keeping her prisoner turned and showed him the rock hard piece he held in her back.

"A gun, you're holding a gun?" The man screamed. "Someone call police.

This crazy woman's got a gun shoved in this kid's back."

While a few people ran for cover, Emma spotted a woman grabbing her cell phone. Emma needed to stay out of harm's way until police arrived.

Two burly men came at them each taking a side. The man fired a shot in their direction, but they kept coming and amidst her fears, Emma couldn't believe how brave they both were. One kicked the guy in the shin while the other one grabbed him from behind. At this moment, Emma stomped on his foot as hard as nerves allowed.

His hold dropped, and this was all the time she needed. Emma ran trying not to think how much faster a bullet flew when compared to the speed of her skinny legs. She cried as she ran away from her temporary home, from her aunt's house.

Franka was due back, and this mad man would not think twice about hurting her too. Stubbornly she ran as fast as the pedestrian-packed sidewalk allowed while refusing to glance back. The commotion behind her had died down. The silence could only mean the madman had resumed his chase. No mistake as with a strident tone he yelled, "Witch."

When she reached the corner of Spring Street, she knew she had to hide. He would catch up to her quickly if she kept a straight line. She couldn't involve more people. She didn't even want to think what he'd done to the men who'd come to her rescue.

She spotted the work area across the street. The enclosure

fenced with sturdy mesh, invited her in while the door stood ajar and the numerous places to hide in there appealed to her. She ran and squeezed by the door. A group of four men was sitting down eating lunch by a window-washing platform in the outdoor compound. She ran and snuck in behind a huge green garbage bin with her back against the fence. She closed her eyes and tried not to make noise as she caught her breath, praying he hadn't seen her go in there.

"Hey, lady looking for something? The fenced area is private property."

"Chasing this kid who took my wallet. All my money was in there."

"Nobody here matching your description, ma'am." Emma lay flat on her stomach to peek under the bin at the shoes of this woman the workers had called ma'am. It was him. She bit her lip not to cry out. She picked herself up quietly, and as tears streamed down her face, she spotted the hole in the back fence two feet away— not so small she couldn't fit through. On her hands and knees, she crawled to the gap in the links and gently slipped through. The path lead to an alley connecting her to the next street.

As she did, police sirens wailed in the distance, and even though they appeared to get closer, she couldn't afford to go back. The perp would spot her for sure. Out in the clear, she began to run.

"Hey, lady there's you kid. Running in the alley," Emma heard one of the construction workers shout.

Unable to stop crying, she continued to run until she came to a dead end. The alley didn't lead to the street. It was fenced off with a massive brick wall she would never be able to climb. She scanned the area and pulled at the few doors she could see. They were locked. She wiped her eyes with the back of her hand and noticed a stack of trash cans in the far corner with a huge mountain of garbage on top of them. Climbing them would provide a way over the wall.

As she approached the mountain of trash, a mongrel and vicious dog sprung out to protect his territory. His eyes were slits, his fangs yellow, and his mouth drooled as he growled at her. She screamed the little yelp blocked by a lump in her throat the size of her fear. She backed up slowly unable to choose which way to go or what terrified her more, the wild dog or the rabid man. She couldn't go back. She overheard the man cussing and harping as he tried to fight his way through the chink in the metal fence.

Even as she continued to back up, the dog began to advance even faster now. She backed up taking bigger steps to match the dog's speed but tripped over empty cans. She lost her balance and fell. At that moment, the dog started to run toward her, and she watched him about to sprint on his hind legs.

Rolled up in a little ball with her arms covering her face and head, she squatted on the ground and closed her eyes, hoping her submissiveness might stop the beast from hurting her. But it didn't. She glimpsed the dog leap toward her, and part of his back foot hit the arm over her head as he jumped even higher soaring through the air behind her.

Ferocious barking and tearing ripped the air around her. She was all right. She picked herself up off the ground and saw her would be attacker struggling with the beast.

She had difficulty shaking the terror from her limbs. A voice inside her yelled to run, and she did. Toward the hole in the fence toward the street and she kept running past the corner, up Wooster ramming into Tommy.

By then she was shaking and crying. She couldn't tell Tommy anything. He must have understood while he stared at her tear-stained face because he grabbed her hand and ran up the street encouraging her to move faster.

When they got to her aunt's condo, Emma doubled over with a cramp in her side, breathing in short spurts. She gave one last look behind her making sure they had not been followed. Police officers interrogated people in the street. An EMC unit's lights were flashing, and she witnessed two paramedics loading two stretchers into the white van. The men were hurt, but giving the officers their version of the facts.

Tommy laid a hand across her waist to help her stand and walk. "Let's get inside."

Once inside, Emma leaned against Tommy's shoulder and could no longer hold back the sobs that shook her, coming out in small hiccups and a torrent of tears. "The man had a gun." She shot this out in little breaths.

"What's she saying?" a neighbor asked.

"Someone had a gun," the other neighbor said. "Did someone hurt you, honey?"

Tommy eyed them and added, "Man out in the street has a gun. Police are outside, making the arrest."

"You don't say." Both ran out the door, leaving the way clear for Tommy and Emma to take the elevator and head to her aunt's apartment.

"Emma," a loud voice startled her. She released Tommy and glanced toward the front door.

"Grandma Abby," she mouthed. Next thing she knew, with a will of their own, her legs had run to her grandmother's side while her arms encircled her in a tight embrace.

"Sweet child what is wrong?" Soothing her as best as she could, Emma sensed her grandmother's worry turn to anger, and she directed her anger toward Tommy.

"Young man, are you responsible for this outpour?"

Emma released her grandmother and glanced at Tommy his eyebrows up in the air with outrage while his head slowly moved from side to side.

The bell to the elevator rang indicating their turn to go up.

"Tommy is my friend, Grandma. He would never do anything to hurt me."

The older woman's arm around her waist, Emma allowed her to lead her to the elevator taking hold of Tommy's hand as they walked past him.

As soon as they walked through the threshold, Franka came to greet them warmly. "Jimmy's gone back to work. It'll just be us." Franka's expression changed to surprise. "Mother? What are you doing here?"

"What do you think I'm doing here? I jumped ship and took a plane off some remote little island two thousand miles away. The first vacation I take in ten years and my family falls apart."

Tommy coaxed Emma inside, and as she stared at her aunt Franka rolling her eyes at her mother's words, she made sure she still held onto Tommy's hand for strength. The instant she was finally able to face her aunt squarely, she whispered, "He was down there, waiting for me."

"Tommy?"

Tommy gave her a negative shake while helping Emma to the sitting area's sofa.

"I'll call Hank."

Emma heard Abigail demanding to know what had happened, and even though her grandmother shouted at the top of her lungs, she only remembered the crazy man's snicker, remembered his awful breath as it snaked its way into her ear.

"Mother, this is not the time. I'll tell you later. I have to call the police."

Twenty-Four

Hank, Matt Dig For Clues

ank and Matt had searched North Walnut Street up and down for over an hour.

"I was beginning to think Emma had made a mistake," Matt said.

"If we hadn't deviated onto Garden Parkway's on ramp, twice, we'd have found this site earlier."

"Yeah. Tricky, a goddamn street that divides into two parts. Let's not tell anyone about this," Matt added.

Both looked up at the dilapidated building and agreed this had to be the one in Emma's dream. Hank took a deep breath, dreading what he'd find up those stairs. "There's the sign, and the torn building Emma mentioned."

"You were right," Matt said. "We won't need a warrant—not to search this empty hole."

"As long as we can get in quickly enough."

The place was open and appeared abandoned.

"No concierge in this dump," Matt spat the words with disgust as he walked around a dusty, grimy room the size of a small one-bedroom apartment. Unfurnished, walls unadorned, floor missing wooden slats in some areas, the afternoon sun streaked through the dirty window creating a dense fog with particles as big as dust bunnies floating in midair. Hank instinctively brushed away at them as he walked around.

"Stinks to high hell," Hank said, putting his hand in front of his nose. "He was here all right." Cuffs to his pants rolled up, shirt sleeves folded above the elbows Hank blew a breath of relief he'd had the good fortune to leave his suit jacket in the car. "He tried to rip out these floor boards but missed a big spot. Stain is blood all right in a pool pattern. Probably killed his victims right here in this room."

"Bastard hadn't counted on us finding this place." Matt stared at Hank's raised eyebrows. "Well, not as fast as we did."

"Not fast enough." Hank wiped his hands together to shake some of the dust. "I'm going to call Cindy and tell her to send forensics up here."

While Hank phoned Cindy, Matt kept on searching the corners of the room trying to locate a weapon or a piece of clothing.

Hank gave the address to Cindy as he filled in his request. "Cindy, can you transfer me to Ken? Thanks."

Hank caught Matt staring his way as he tried to listen to Ken while keeping his eyeballs from rolling out of his head. "What?" He weathered Matt's glare as he walked toward him putting up his hand to prevent him from saying anything.

"Yes, of course, we're on it. This pursuit is all we do these days. Of course, I will keep you posted."

"What's going on?"

Hank's arm momentarily dangled by his side his eyes taking in the dirty room. He needed to expend anger, so he turned on his heels and punched the lone light bulb that squeaked as it swung on its rope. With a loud growl, Hank sent the broken bulb crashing against the wall next to him.

"What did Ken say?"

Hank took a deep breath and put up his index finger as he went through the messages on his cell with his right hand. "And, here's the message."

"What the hell's going on?"

Hank made a face at Matt as he waited for the caller to pick up. "Hi, Hank Apple. I'm on my way."

He clipped his cell back on his belt and without another word he headed for the door. He began running down the rickety set of stairs followed by Matt, who peppered him with questions all the way down.

"Hank? What's the skinny? Talk to me."

Hank got in the car and stretched his arm out the window to plop the siren on the hood. Then he tied his seat belt and veered the car one hundred and eighty degrees toward the parkway they'd tried to avoid all afternoon. "Soho police are on the lookout for a chubby older woman who held a kid at gunpoint and shot two men, one in the foot and one in the leg, to escape with the child."

"God! Did the broad make away with the kid?"

"No. Kid got away."

"Emma?"

"Think so. Had a message from Franka on my phone. Of course, no one is aware who the victim is."

"I'm thinking South Manhattan and a man who's after Emma with a dogged determination. Has to be her."

"Name has to stay between us," Hank added. "If the fact got out this maniac is after one child, the press would ask questions, and they'd go sniffing until they got their answers."

"You think this guy is trying to attract attention to tell the world Emma's a witch?"

"Wouldn't put it past him." Hank slammed his fist into the steering wheel instantly shaking the wounded hand. "Geez Louise, this prick is getting on my nerves. Doesn't care who he mows down."

"How do you suppose he found out where she was?"

"We have no idea who he is which means he could have easily followed us from the precinct to Franka's place. He could be following us now."

"What does Ken say?"

"He connected the dots. He realizes this is related to our case because of the guy's description. He also believes this is a significant breakthrough, and he wants us to locate the kid before Manhattan police do."

"Easy to avoid," Matt added. She slipped between our hands and we don't know who she is."

"Won't be hard to believe. One man apparently thought the boy was a punk with a long ponytail. Said he ran too fast to be a girl."

"Wow." Matt snickered. "Stereotypes don't die."

"Ken asked Cindy to send a squad car to paste the crazy's picture on lampposts and in public places around the area.

"Reaching." Matt let go a huge sigh. "Yeah. There's just so much we can do."

Speeding along the parkway back to Manhattan, Hank knew when his phone rang that he wouldn't be able to take the call. He tossed the Bluetooth to Matt.

Matt barely caught the gizmo midair. He rolled his eyes as he put it up to his ear. "Hanks' phone?"

"Oh. Is Hank close by?"

"He's driving—more like he's racing the Indy 500," Matt said with a snort. "Not the right time. Can I help you?"

"This is Christina."

"Hey, Christina. Matt here. How's it going?"

"I'm okay. I need to talk to Hank about the case he is working on. Can you please have him call me?"

"Absolutely. I'll make sure Hank gets the message."

"What was that all about?"

"Christina," Matt said slowly and deliberately. "Still sounds sexy."

Hank felt his jaw harden. "Did she say what she wanted?"

"Said she needed to talk to you about our case. Didn't seem to want to speak to me, though. Oh no. Got to be Hank."

Hank tossed him a knowing smile. "That can't be jealousy talking? What are you up to?"

"Maybe I ought to tell Christina what a loser you are. Have those huge brown eyes stare in my direction for a change."

"She's off limits to you, buddy." Hank's voice appeared menacing.

"Well, well. I should play the jealousy card more often. Told Cindy my method would work better than nagging—fear of loss never fails."

"You're sick. You know that?"

"I'm sick? You don't have a life. About time you got one."

"This from the man who just dumped his live-in girlfriend of three years."

"Exactly. We were headed in different directions. At least, I'm out there, man, looking for a new one." Matt grabbed hold of the handle above his door to remain in his seat during a particularly sharp turn Hank made to avoid a cement truck in front of them. "Unlike you, married to your job. A word to the wise, my friend. Once your legs give you'll wake up one morning, glance beside you and realize your life is as empty as the cold space between your sheets."

Hank zigzagged through traffic and yanked on his horn. "Touched by your concern." He pronounced each word with an edge. Hank gathered Matt was having a good laugh at his expense. Only, part of what he said made sense. Running into Christina had made him realize how lonely he was.

"Just looking out for you partner," Matt's neck quickly whipped to the right while his bald head rammed the window hard enough to leave an imprint.

"Do you have to be driving this fast, man? We're not chasing some goddamn suspect. No emergency call."

Forty minutes later, Hank pulled into Franka's parking lot at the side of the building and threw Matt a dark glance.

"God I feel as though I ran the whole way."

Matt's tone sounded belligerent. "F.Y.I., man a siren on the roof doesn't give you the right to drive this jalopy as though you're Mario fucking Andretti in broad daylight, in the middle of New York City."

Hank didn't say a word. He kept on brooding, in no hurry to get inside now.

"Don't tell me. You've lost your voice along with the use of your legs."

Hank covered his eyes with his right hand. "Yeah, a woman will do that to you."

"Or exceptionally dangerous driving." Matt took a deep breath letting it rush out in a loud noise of protest. He rubbed his head as he checked the car mirror for a mark. "Feels like a bump the size of an egg growing out of my head," he added. "For the record, I always thought you and Christina made a great couple—thought you'd last forever—until she caught you cheating which gave her the right to dump your sorry ass."

"You think that's why I did it? Subconsciously I mean, cheated on her so she'd be the one to end the relationship?"

Hank stared at Matt who remained silent except for the sour expression screaming on his face. "I can't tell you that, man. I'm no shrink. Although, let me state the obvious and say I've witnessed you pining for her these past few years. If your subconscious did you in, man," he wiggled the fingers from both hands in front of his face. "You got to hold a little meeting with yourself—discuss your priorities."

Hank stared out his car window and expelled all the breath he'd been holding. "Yeah."

"Why are you concerned with this now, anyway? Timing is not the best for you to focus on a relationship with Christina."

"We live a cop's life. Is it ever the right time? Besides, we spent last night together."

"Howl!" Matt imitated the sound of a wolf. "Joyride explained. Next time you want to end a relationship—or your life—give me warning beforehand so I can stay the hell away." Matt snorted.

"Can't you ever be serious?"

"I am." Matt drummed his fingers against the dashboard.

"Don't know why you're so worried. Just give it twenty-four hours and you'll be horny again."

"Watch your mouth," Hank said, giving him the evil eye.

"Who cares about what I say or what I think. I got my own problems. All you want to hear is you two make a cute couple," Matt said with pursed lips from the tip of his tongue. "Already been stated. Handle it."

Hank went to punch the steering wheel but thought twice and pulled up his hand running his fingers through his hair instead. "What if I can't commit? I don't want to hurt her again."

"Don't probe. You make the whole thing sound like an investigation. Hank, you're analyzing the crap out of your feelings and F.Y.I., trying to predict what'll happen tomorrow is not a prerequisite for a healthy relationship. All you need is to take baby steps."

Hank checked his partner's face. You never knew what to think with Matt's outbursts.

"And you can start by returning her call. If I know Christina, she's sitting by the phone waiting." Matt tossed the Bluetooth back in Hank's lap.

"Yeah, I guess you're right." Hank propped the wireless device against his ear and picked up his cell to call Christina. He gave Matt half a smile. "Thanks, man."

"Who instigated last night?" Matt asked.

Hank gave him a sorry ass glare. "Me, all me."

"Hey, Christina. Sorry, I was driving when you called—in pursuit of a suspect," he said casting a sheepish pair of eyes in Matt's direction who was busy rolling his.

"You needed to talk to me about the case?"

"Yes. The picture posted in the morning paper looks nothing

like the man I described to Pete—your police sketch artist."

Hank struggled to understand, to remember. Once the fog began to lift, he dropped back in his seat his arm falling off the arm-rest. As memory of that first day slowly returned, he made more sense of Christina's words.

"Hank?" Christina repeated twice.

Hank couldn't even muster the energy to answer Matt's question-marked expression.

"Sorry. I forgot you gave Pete this man's description." He eyed Matt whose face was bulging with shock. "Did you get a good look at him?"

"I doubt I could pick him out of one of your police line-ups, but I am sure he doesn't look anything like this."

"I'm going to put you on speaker, Christina, for Matt's benefit." Hank still shook his head dreading the fact he'd accidentally let the detail slide.

"How well did you see him?"

"Mostly his profile. Maybe a little more when he turned to stare at the back of the bus."

"Is this when he spotted you?"

"Might have been. I'm not sure. A few minutes later, the man cut me off, so I had to stop, barely had time to get the license plate numbers."

Hank stared at Matt who kept rubbing his hand up and down his head when a thought occurred to him. Hank muttered, "This man didn't give a shit about his damn license plate. Getting caught out of costume was the reason he high-tailed out of there."

"Can't believe we didn't associate the episodes," Matt added staring out his window.

Hank rubbed his eyes with a shaky hand. "Can't imagine telling Ken about this."

Then he rallied to address the problem. "Sorry, Christina. Can we meet in a couple of hours at the precinct? I'd appreciate it."

"Sure. I'll be there."

The phone call ended on stunned silence filling the space between Hank and his partner which neither one of them had the strength to bridge.

Hank cleared his throat. "Pete didn't remember either strangely enough."

Matt uttered, "This is textbook psychology. That's what the shrink at the office would call it."

"What do you mean?"

"She'd call it a clear case of trauma bonding."

"Bonding as in allowing the weird workings of a defective brain to hypnotize us? Enough to subconsciously omit clues?"

"Something like that. It got to a point where I thought this asshole was a genius."

"Well, now he's just a regular asshole. If they didn't slip up now and again, how would we ever catch them?"

Hank opened his door and stepped outside. They'd cleared the street, and traffic had returned to normal. Some people were still assembled and exchanged stories no doubt.

Matt followed, still mumbling. "How could the demented prick fuck up his otherwise flawless plan?"

"You rooting for him?" Hank headed for the elevators.

"You know what I mean. Ahead of us, everywhere and nowhere at the same time? He had me thinking he was diabolically shrewd like one of them savants."

"Nope. Just an ordinary idiot psycho."

Twenty-Five

Identifying A Mad Man

Franka's apartment had returned to normal once Abigail had listened to her daughter's summary of Emma's situation.

Abigail stood in the hallway glancing at Emma and Tommy's interaction with the Wii Console. Fed and rested, Emma attempted to beat Tommy at ping pong.

At this moment, a thought struck Abigail. For her granddaughter's sake, and for the first time in her life, she would not be able to gossip to anyone about what she'd learned.

She wiped a tear rolling down her cheek when the bright trill of her granddaughter's laughter rolled unchecked.

"Don't disturb her, Mom," Franka whispered.

"I won't. Hard to believe this puny child can still enjoy herself after what she endured."

"She's ten years old. She'll bounce back."

"You think so? The worst is still ahead of her. Oh, I don't mean this maniac on the loose, no. My worry is about these gifts she'll have to deal with all her life."

"I spoke with her teacher yesterday, Christina Tyler. I expressed those exact feelings. She recommends we take Emma to a child psychologist, one who can help her deal with the issues which might aggravate with age."

"Not a bad idea, but how do we handle Patrick? He'll be dead set against any intervention."

Franka motioned for her to speak lower. "I wouldn't swear to that. You'll find Patrick a changed man. He's made Emma promise not to keep secrets anymore."

Abigail's expression became one of disbelief. "Patrick? Changed?" She waved a finger at her daughter. "I'll have to experience this miracle with my own eyes."

The sound of the intercom interrupted Franka's response. "Thank God! Hank Apple and his partner," she added on her way to the door. "I want you to promise you'll behave, mother."

"What are they doing here?"

"I called him earlier—left a message." Franka glued her eyes to the peep hole looking out into the hallway. She couldn't wait for Hank to take charge.

"Of course, and you ask me not to interrupt Emma," she grumbled between her teeth.

Franka turned to toss her mother an eye roll. She began to defend her position, but what seemed like seconds later, the knocker on the door had her jump.

She opened and stared at Hank Apple inviting him in. "Thank you for coming, Hank. I realize this is not your jurisdiction, but I didn't want to call the police."

The two men entered, and Franka closed the door behind them.

"This is my partner, Matthew Logan. We rushed here the minute I got your message about what happened this afternoon."

"This is my mother, Abigail Tichy," Franka said inviting Abigail to come closer.

She did, extending her hand to shake Hank's. "I remember you from Emma's party. I'm pleased you're looking after my grand-daughter, Detective Apple. Pleased you both are," she added as she shook Matt's hand. "What now?"

Hank indicated Emma. "How's she doing?"

"She took a while to catch her breath. I think what disturbed her most was that she never sensed the creep coming, no premoni-tion of any kind," Franka said.

Hank glanced at Matt standing awkwardly close to the door as though the frame might protect him. "Can I talk to her? Think she'll mind?"

"Don't believe so. Emma is aware you're coming." Franka walked over to the small living room where Tommy held his arms up in triumph yelling, "I won."

"Emma, sweetie, Hank Apple is here."

Emma's smile disappeared. She took a deep breath with lips stoically pinched. She tugged on Tommy's sleeve the slant of her head inviting him to come with her.

"Think I'm allowed?" He asked his shy eyes peering out at the two officers.

"I'd like to talk to you too, Tommy," Hank said.

Once Hank got the recount of Emma's facts, he interrogated Tommy on the man he'd seen at her house the day before.

Tommy gave him a shrug. "Skinny, wiry. I noticed a ponytail at the back of his head. The thing swung side to side when he ran after me."

"How tall?"

"My height, I guess."

"How long did he pursue you?"

"No idea. He ran to his truck. I had a hunch he might try to catch up to me, so I went through the yards."

"With your bike?"

"Hey, my bike's light. I can pick up the thing and throw it over a fence. Not my first time running."

"Would you recognize him if you met him?"

Raised shoulders and a dah smirk on Tommy's face, his answer resounded emphatically. "No. I was running the other way."

"How would you kids like to ride to the precinct with us? We'll bring you right back."

Emma bit her lip clearly not enthused with the idea. "Christina Tyler will be at the precinct in a little while, and she has a fair picture of this man. Her description might trigger some memory, Tommy."

Emma cheered up at the mention of her teacher. "It's okay, Tommy. They'll drive us back in time for dinner, right?"

"Absolutely," Hank answered with a smile. "Plus you'll get to ride in a squad car," he added when he caught Tommy's hesitation.

***

They drove South on Wooster and Hank asked Emma to point out the construction site she had mentioned.

"On the corner," she said. "The dog attacked the man on the other side of the fence. A small hole in the chain link lets you get through to the back of those buildings, but the yard doesn't lead anywhere."

Matt drove, and Hank kept an eye peeled for anyone apt to follow. "Matt, stop on the corner. I'm going to check the area take a peek at the hole in the fence."

Hank stopped mid sentence his hand on the door handle. "A tan car has been following us since we left Franka's place. Conveniently, driver has decided to stop at the same time we did. Coincidence?"

"Where?"

"Right behind us."

"Might be looking for parking."

Hank closed the door and twisted to stare at Emma in the back seat. "You said you could feel this man's presence whenever he is close. Can you feel him now?"

A head shake from side to side was her only answer.

"You didn't sense his presence this afternoon either." Hank was puzzled, yet his goal was not to spook Emma. Has anything changed with you? Or knowing what you can do, can he be blocking this somehow?"

Raised shoulders and a hesitant twist of her head tugged on Emma's hairs at the back of her nape as they snagged in the chain from the amulet she still wore around her neck. "Maybe," she added tentatively stroking the medallion lying against her chest. After recruiting Tommy's help to untangle the small chain under the curtain of her long tresses, she removed the amulet pulling it over her head. She stared at the pendant wondering if its magic was not more potent than she had anticipated. The Eye of Horus had kept her from traveling. Could her grandmother's oudjat keep her from using all her powers?

"Never mind, Hank. Car's gone," Matt added. "Probably visiting someone who lives in those condos. Parking's a bitch around here."

Emma turned toward Tommy. "Can you take my chain for safekeeping? Remind me later?"

"Sure."

Emma eyed Hank, who was still waiting for an answer. "My grandmother's amulet protects me, keeps me grounded. My mother gave it to me last night."

"And now that you've removed the chain?"

Emma released a long-winded sigh. A few seconds passed before the peace she'd found from life's chatter slowly ebbed. The clutch of the world's problems once again weighed heavy on her slim shoulders. Lips pinched she nodded clasping Tommy's hand for courage. The veil had lifted. "He's out somewhere, not anywhere close. I don't think so."

"Good. I'll be right back." Hank walked through the open gate of the first fenced area. Two men perched on a platform twenty feet above street level faced the building they were working on.

Hank strode to the back of the fence and spotted the carcass of a dog lying in the alley between the buildings, not moving. He couldn't get through the small hole in the wire, so he called his office and spoke to Cindy.

"Found a dog in an alley in Soho. My guess is he was shot by the perp we're after. Better send someone down here before the pound picks up the carcass or Manhattan police gets a hold of the dog. Discretion is necessary."

"I understand, Hank. We will be covert."

"I want the slug that killed him, and I want the lab to run tests for rabies. If he bit our guy, there'll not only be human DNA somewhere on him, but this will give us a clue as to where our guy's headed next."

"Hospital."

"Is Christina there yet?"

"No. But if she's coming, I'll wait for her. I was about to leave."

"Thanks, Cin … oh, and please have Pete stand by."

On his way to the car, Hank joined Matt, who was outside talking to one of the construction workers.

"This man witnessed the commotion earlier," Matt said to Hank.

"Yeah. A big-boned woman ran after this young punk who'd stolen her wallet." The man wiped his hands down his overalls. "For a heavyset woman, she could run."

"What happened next?" Hank asked. "Woman that size couldn't have gotten through the hole in the fence."

"She ran to the wall, grabbed one of our ladders and wheeled it over. And that thing's heavy." He rubbed his face. "My jaw still hurts from dropping so fast—was like one of them cartoons. This broad hauls the ladder against the fence climbs to the top throws her fat leg over and drops to the ground like a bomb. Don't know what was in the wallet. But punk kid's sure going to think twice before robbing an old lady again."

Did you witness the woman get attacked by the dog?"

"What dog?" He hoisted his shoulders and called out to his partner that he was on his way."

"You must have seen her come out," Matt said. "No way out of that yard except through one of those back doors. You just finished telling me they're all locked."

"That whole building should be condemned, crawling with

wood rot. Good stiff shoulder in anyone of those doors will split it right up."

The man looked up and stuck his hand out with his middle finger up in the air. "Coming… I gotta to go. Chump givin' me the look. Luck to yas."

Hank told Matt what he'd found in the alley. "Don't talk about the dog bleeding to death in front of Emma. She's had enough of an ordeal for one day."

"I'll take care to set up the test when we get back," Matt said.

Remind me to look around here in the morning. If that man's right, and our crazy perp went through one of those doors, someone might have seen him, talked to him even.

"I'll get on it, Hank."

Hank took the driver's seat. "Make sure you keep your eyes open," he told Matt.

As they traveled down Wooster, Emma put her arms in front of her eyes and screamed, "No." Then she yelled at Hank to stop the car.

He moved the car in front of a parked van and signaled to the other cars to continue. He turned toward Emma. "What's wrong?"

"I saw him. He's waiting on a side street in a truck. He's planning to ram us before we take the tunnel." She nodded her hand covering her mouth. "I …" she hesitated. "I saw it happen. No one is moving in the car. People are screaming everywhere. Then he grabs me, and there's nothing I can do." She bit her lip and took a deep breath squeezing Tommy's hand. "He runs out of his truck and grabs me."

Matt stared at Hank for a few seconds, his eyes wide with disbelief, although Hank realized Emma was telling the truth.

"Do you know if this is the Holland tunnel?"

"She shrugged to convey ignorance." Hank glanced at Matt. "Any other way?"

"Nope. Best bet is to double back, go north and take Lincoln." He drummed restless fingers on the dashboard in front of him. "Wait a minute." He turned to face Hank and lowering his tone, he added. "This guy's where she says he is we can catch him in the act."

Hank's vehement response was final. "Not with the kids in the back." He straightened in front of the wheel adjusting his GPS. Sensing Matt's reproving eyes on him, he turned and added. "We'll get him, but not when the kids are in the back of the car."

"No way around that whole circle—not that I know of," Matt added peevishly.

Hank turned to talk to Emma. "Do you know what side of the car he strikes?"

"She shook her head."

Hank looked at his GPS. "I think the only street he can hit us from is West Broadway. All the others are one way heading south."

"Suppose he misses us. What's to stop him from following us? For all we know he has a goddamned police scanner in that truck," Matt mumbled under his breath.

"Your first suggestion is the better one," Hank gave him a pair of facetious dark eyes. "We'll head on back and take Lincoln."

"Goddamn waste of time. Why don't we just call Manhattan precinct and have him picked up? We know where he is."

"How will you describe him? On what charges. And when they ask, how are you going to explain that you are aware of who he is and where he is?"

"Goddamn it, Hank …"

"Hey, life's not fair. We play the cards universe deals us." Hank stretched his arm out the window to plop the siren on the hood and quickly began his ritual of zigzagging through traffic. "Just be grateful we didn't end up in whatever violence he'd planned. Can you imagine how many other people might have gotten hurt in a rumble that size?"

***

By the time all four arrived at Hank's office, Cindy and Christina sat face to face, sharing coffee and conversation. Matt went his way, and Hank stared at the woman he couldn't shake from his thoughts. All at once, the urge to be alone with her hit him hard.

"Here they are." Cindy smiled.

"You can go, Cin," Hank said. "Thanks for your help."

If Cindy wondered why he behaved like a bear all of a sudden, she kept it to herself, the only sign of awareness in her narrowing eyes.

"Sure. Pete's in his office, waiting." Cindy turned to approach Hank, whispering for his benefit. "Patrick Willis called here yelling and screaming. Demands that you bring his daughter back immediately."

"What?"

She rolled her eyes. "Says it wasn't Franka's call to make. Aren't you glad you're not in that apartment?"

"Good God. Does anyone else know about this?"

"No. Willis came straight through your private line.

Hank nodded his eyes downcast. "I'll call him."

Before greeting Christina, he turned toward the children and noticed they were holding hands. "This way," he indicated. Then as if just spotting Christina he added, "Thanks for coming. I appreciate it."

She smiled at him and slipped her arm around his while the expression he read in her eyes was undecipherable. She'd never done anything as bold as to latch on to him at work. Rather than remove her hand, the urge possessed him to let his arm dangle while still entwined with hers so he could stroke her thigh gently.

All at once, she became the shy one quickly taking back her arm to rummage in her shoulder bag. An excuse Hank figured. There was nothing she needed in her purse that badly. She was reclaiming her space, or perhaps correcting a mistake she'd made without thinking.

Hank looked up when he heard Cindy doubling back running as she yelled, "Hank—wait." She signaled before they could enter Pete's office. "I almost forgot," she breathed in and out to catch her breath. "Ken's in there."

He turned toward Emma and Tommy. "Follow Christina and wait in my office, Okay?"

They agreed, and Christina gave him a little sign indicating she knew how to get there.

"I'm so sorry, Hank. Completely skipped my mind."

"Go home, Cindy. It's been a big week."

"Night." She stopped mid-flight and called out to him. "The red folder on my desk is about the Boleslaw fellow. It's all typed up. You're welcome to it. Oh, and that's your copy. You don't have to bring it back."

Hank waved to Cindy as he knocked on Peter's door and entered.

<u>Twenty-Six</u>

Relocating Emma

The image of Kenneth Riley pacing the backside of Peter's office did not augur well.

"Apple just the man I want," Ken bellowed.

Hank stepped forward rolling a furtive eye toward Peter. "Anything wrong?"

"Anxious to learn about the disaster on Wooster. What did you find?"

"What do you think I found?" Hank thought he'd gauge how far he might stretch the truth and in which direction.

"Come on. Don't play truth or dare with me."

"Who's playing? I'm not even allowed down there." Hank caught Ken's eyes turning an evil black. "Relax. Matt and I snooped around anyway. We're planning to go back there in the morning. People we spoke to all think the shooter is a woman."

"Any news on the kid?"

"Word on the street kid's a punk who tried to steal this woman's wallet."

"No way." Ken stopped pacing and leaned both palms on the desk in front of him. "Description I got from Manhattan Chief Lang is identical to that of our child killer—the one Val gave us—

the poster circulating all over Newark." He resumed his pacing behind the desk.

"Right—cop killer, let's not forget."

"No. No." Ken stopped, jiggling keys in his jacket's pocket. "First thing Lang sent me. Report on the bullets they took from the people this guy shot."

"Why is he collaborating with you on this?"

"Jack is dead. You know we all pull together when this happens. What's wrong with you?"

"And?"

"Not the same bullet that killed Jack."

Emma was telling the truth when she said she didn't know who had killed Jack or why. "Maggie's going to be relieved."

"Yeah, well this means we're going to hold off bringing in the FBI." He danced on both feet hesitantly. "Barbara's department needs to prove they deserve their funding. You understand."

"Politics." Hank shook his head. He didn't like fancy overpaid liars and cheaters sticking their noses into police matters. Of course, they did this on a recurring basis which in this case relieved him no end as he now had one less agency to avoid.

Ken seemed to hesitate. "Barbara wants to meet with you to discuss the situation as soon as possible, you and Val—oh. Did Val change her number? Cindy can't seem to reach her—her own aunt."

"Val's out a lot. What's this about Barbara?" Hank worked hard to lower his eyebrows inexplicably rising.

"I told Barbara you'd be glad to cooperate with her department."

"I already have a partner."

"She certainly doesn't want to partner with you." Ken's tone was bombastic.

Of course, Barbara Leclerc didn't want to partner with him Hank thought. She wanted to corner him for information and try to beat him to the punch.

Ken added in the measured tone of someone about to erupt, "She only wants to touch base. After all, you're the man with all the tools. Plus Barbara wanting to work with you is flattering. Collaboration can only help your career, Hank."

Ken faced Pete as though the matter was closed, and added, "I'll need that report by Friday. At least an outline so I can work the stats."

"Almost done. A few finishing touches left. Friday for sure," Pete added.

"Hank, keep me posted," Ken threw as he walked out of the office. "Oh," he added as he stuck his head back in. "Don't worry about traipsing through Soho. Lang and I are meeting tomorrow about this. Our perp is in their corner now, and we have more information than they do."

"Is that wise? I mean, for all we know this guy might be back. Somehow, I don't think he's gone for good."

"Hey, no harm in putting together a task force which is how we'll be able to broaden the net and catch the SOB. Lang's sending a group of men tomorrow up and down Wooster to interrogate people about the kid who ran. They're going to ring every doorbell. We'll find her."

"Her?" Hank interjected for good measure.

"Between you and me. Had to be a girl—a feisty one who got lucky." He did a little hand salute and left.

Hank remained fixed to the spot. Ken's revelations had just knocked the wind out of him. His left hand rubbing his forehead and covering his eyes, he took deep breaths to ward off the panic his captain's bravado stirred in him. Then he remembered Pete staring at him with narrowed eyes. "Are you all right?"

"Yeah, of course." Hank let the air out of his lungs. "Just tired." He ran a hand through his hair. "What's this report Ken has you working on?"

"More people came forward today with so-called sightings of the picture we posted everywhere. A lot of phone calls. Ken wants me to scan the files and typecast the people who answered."

"He is using you as a profiler? Might become quite the undertaking." Hank gazed at some of the paperwork Pete had started. "I guess that's what happens when you own a degree in psychology," Hank mumbled as he studied one lady's file more explicit than the others. Only he didn't see words. Hank worried about the children in his office and how they should not be there. How he should have stuck to the promise he'd made to himself not to bring Emma to police headquarters anymore. He also realized he would have to move Emma from her aunt's house early morning.

"Only summarily put together for now. Research will fill in the details."

"Remember that first drawing you did for Christina Tyler?"

"Yeah. When Cindy asked me to standby, I thought you might want to compare the two."

"Can I have a look?"

Pete had already pulled the poster from beside his desk. "What are you hoping to find?"

"Some connection between the man in the costume and this

picture." Hank stared at it, but couldn't find any resemblance.

"Something about the eyes," Pete mentioned, but then he shook his head. "Honestly, I can't find any similarities. Mere supposition. Would never stand up in court."

"You've compared them already?"

Pete nodded. "I remembered him as the man who drove the car we found." Pete shrugged. "I never brought it up—there's no likeness, none whatsoever."

"Can I hold onto this for a couple of days?"

"They're yours." Pete handed the two cardboard frames to Hank.

Hank's first intention had been for Tommy to give Pete a description. Now, he feverishly toyed with the thought of getting the kids out of there anonymously, hoping no one had noticed them when they arrived. Hank walked toward the door.

"Is this the only reason you wanted me to stay behind?" Pete asked.

"Cindy wanted to leave, so I said she could. Hoped I could count on you for this mug." He indicated the posters in his hand.

"I spotted Christina with Cindy earlier. Is she in your office? I'll just drop by and say hello," Pete added rising as he did.

Hank couldn't think of a way to say no.

Pete's phone rang, and he turned to take the call. While he did, Hank ran out of his office and into his own.

"Let's go," he whispered to Christina. "Ken says the hunt is on for the kid the creep attacked this afternoon. Don't want anyone to see Emma and Tommy here."

Christina nodded her pleated forehead showing she'd gotten the whole picture.

"Tommy, Emma. You have to be silent and stick between Christina and me. We're going out through the back."

Hank grabbed the red folder Cindy had plopped on her desk and lead the way out through low traffic areas, down corridors that appeared abandoned, cutting through double-door rooms when he had to. Christina closed the procession and made sure the children filed in strictly between them.

When they reached the alley out back, he unfastened the bolt, pushed the heavy door aside, and told them to hug the wall and look for any suspicious cars. He turned toward Emma. "Is he here?" he asked of the kidnapper.

Emma shook her head. "No." She closed her eyes and took a deep breath. Hank realized he was asking a lot of this young girl, to locate the man who not only gave her nightmares but had tried to kill her earlier today. "He's still in Manhattan," she whispered.

"Figures." Hank breathed loudly, exasperated. He stopped when he felt Emma's hand on his sleeve. "Something wrong?"

She nodded. "Madman spotted me when I screamed earlier when I was in the car going to the police station."

Hank glanced at Christina and realized she'd caught Emma's words by the horrified look in her eyes.

"How can he see you?"

"I told you. When I draw attention to myself, he finds me. If I'm quiet, he doesn't."

Emma's answer did not fit Hank's question. He was asking how this man became aware of her when she wasn't there. "Is he also a seer?"

"Don't think so. I believe he finds me when I travel."

Hank remembered Val's conversation about her friend that

played tricks on her by coming near her and talking to her while still in bed. She'd called it, 'out of body experience.'

"Okay." Hank rubbed her back to stop the tears from pouring out. He checked his immediate surroundings and worried they might attract attention. Gently he put his arm around her shoulders and hurried them to the car standing in the back of both children as they boarded. He turned toward Christina and asked, "Where's your car?"

"I took a cab here. Didn't want to drive."

After closing the passenger door behind her, he dropped the small posters in the trunk along with the red folder and drove in silence through Newark.

"Where are we going?" Christina asked. We missed the turn for the Holland tunnel."

"We're staying Jersey side, going to my place."

Hank glanced over at Christina and studied the worried frown across her forehead. "Don't worry. My home is not a bad place considering."

"Considering?"

"Meaning it doesn't have a woman's touch." He glanced at her and smiled. "Considering you don't live there." He gave her a crooked smile with his eyes on the road.

"You used to live at my house, remember?"

Hank could tell his words made Christina uncomfortable by the way she fidgeted in her seat at the sound of them. He didn't have to worry about the children listening in, they were arguing, comparing the grades they'd received the day before. "How can I forget?

"Hank," Christina put her hand on his arm. "Why not bring

the children home. Emma's parents are there, and she'll be able to have a good night's rest."

Furious with the helplessness invading him, he smacked the steering wheel with the palm of his hand. "Patrick and Eloise are at Franka's condo. He called the precinct earlier." I'm going to call him from my place. I have a plan."

"Emma," Hank glanced in his rearview mirror to ask her. "Are your mom and dad working tomorrow?"

"I think so."

"You can't stay at your aunt Franka's anymore. Miss Tyler thinks I should bring each of you home."

"That's okay by me," Tommy said. "My dad's there and my aunt is picking me up in the morning. I'm starting my weekend early. Dad doesn't want me to be alone at home, not with the man who ended up chasing me last night. He shrugged a pair of help-less shoulders Emma's way. "Sorry."

"Well we certainly can't leave you alone, Emma, not during the day."

"What about her grandmother? I heard she was back," Christi-na added. "Emma could stay with her."

"She is back. She was at Franka's earlier," Hank said.

Emma perked up. "That's true, and Amelia could visit," Emma said with a smile.

Their first stop was the Willis house. Hank parked and looked around. There was no sign of a blue station wagon or any other suspicious cars lurking by the curb. "Are we still good, Emma?" Hank asked.

Emma stared out the window, at the Elm tree looking abandoned and frail now that the sun had begun to plummet slowly. She remembered the terrifying nights she'd spent in that house, in her room along with the loneliness and suddenly she missed her parents—her newfound parents who supported her and hugged her every chance they had. She pictured the kindness in her aunt's wide eyes and the sweet torment in her grandmother's expression. Life wasn't about four walls, her possessions or even the elm tree. It all boiled down to family, and the people she loved. She nodded Hank's way.

Christina grabbed her hand. "I'll go with you. You can take anything you like, whatever you might need, okay?"

"Hey, I'll go too." Tommy slid over to the street side and climbed out.

While they were out, Hank called Patrick.

"Where is she? And who gave you the right to just up and take her, you moron? We're worried sick over here."

Hank let Patrick vent until he couldn't take it anymore. "Goddamn it, Pat will you shut up and listen? She isn't safe there anymore. The maniac knows where she is. He's the one who attacked her, in broad daylight, not one hundred feet away from Franka's building."

The sentence worked like a powerful tranquilizer as he heard Patrick's tremulous breath in the background. "I'm sorry. I don't mean to scare you, but she can't be at Franka's anymore. Besides, Manhattan police will be scouring the neighborhood tomorrow to try and find her. I think she should stay with Abigail. Her place is fenced and well-guarded with alarms, I heard. I, on the other hand, plan to keep the creep preoccupied in other ways."

"What's that supposed to mean?"

"I have a plan to lure him away somehow. Nothing definite. My partner and I will work out the details and let you know, don't worry. We'll get him."

Hank spotted Christina, Emma and Tommy running back to the car. "Can you let Abigail know?" He looked at his watch. "I'll make sure she eats, and then I'll drive her to her grandmother's around nine o'clock."

Twenty-Seven

Emma On The Run

Hank stopped two streets away from Emma's house to drop Tommy home, but the driveway was empty. Hank suggested he eat with them. Tommy stared at the house slowly fading in the shadow of a seven o'clock sun, and Hank realized he was sticking close to company.

"Here we are. Final stop—for now anyway." Hank drove around the high rise apartment building on Mt. Prospect and swiped his keycard to the electronic eye opening the gates to the underground garage. "This is home," he indicated with a little shrug.

Upstairs, he allowed Christina to go first. He surveyed her reaction. Emma walked past him and went straight to the window. Hank's attention was drawn to Emma as she pulled the curtain to gaze below. He didn't want to ask again. He kept the question to himself. *Is he down there?*

"Quite charming." Christina's comment drew his attention. Two bedrooms and two big bathrooms. Roomy."

"A lot better than the dive I lived in when you met me," he added with a smile.

"Yes, almost bigger than my little house. Sixteen hundred

square feet?"

"Close."

"And so tidy. I'm impressed."

"Cleaning lady comes Mondays and Thursdays. I'm hardly ever here."

Christina picked up a few of the knickknacks he had on a shelf. "You'd be here on weekends."

He chuckled at the apparent probe to find how he spent his spare time. "I coach little league on weekends. A group of us get together to make sure the neighborhood kids stay out of trouble, and we take turns manning a youth center not far from here."

Hank turned and realized with a frown Emma was still in front of the window. "Emma, is everything all right?" When she didn't answer, he tilted his head toward Christina silently asking her to talk to Emma. "I'm going to order Chinese—a little of everything." He took his cell phone as Tommy was still on the phone with his dad.

Christina avoided walking into a glass coffee table situated between a flower-patterned sofa and matching chair Hank had propped close together. Cautiously, she approached the large bay window where Emma had her eyes glued to the street below.

She put her arm around Emma's shoulders. "Feel like Chinese?"

Emma turned, surprise in her eyes as though she just remembered where she was. She nodded but then returned her eyes to the street.

"Busy street huh?" Christina searched for any reaction from Emma.

"Yes, compared to the street where I live."

Christina sensed homesickness in Emma and certainly didn't want to bring up the man they were fleeing. "Can you read people from up here?"

Emma's shrug had Christina realize that up until a few days ago, her young student had been ordered to be secretive about such things. She also remembered Emma's granny Dottie, who had visited her at school. A pang of regret filled her for the way she'd dismissed her. The old woman must have had a hard life. No wonder Dottie feared her talent and the fact Emma had inherited those skills. Christina had no time to probe as Tommy came toward them.

"Dad's with a client. Says he'll be home around eight." He settled on the other side of Emma in front of the window. "What are we watching?"

"Food is on the way," Hank called out.

Unable to pry the three from the view, and to make the most of their time together, he retrieved the posters he lugged from the office. "Guys, I need your help here."

Tommy was the first to respond, followed by Christina and Emma.

"Sit down," Hank indicated the sofa. "I need you to tell me what you think of this picture." He propped one up on the chair in front of them. "Take a good look and try to remember if your man looked anything like this, Tommy."

Tommy hesitated. "No ponytail, nose is somewhat the same. I was far."

"Was still light out, right?" Hank asked.

"Getting dark. I'd waited a long time by the side of the house. Didn't want to ring the doorbell with cops lining the drive."

"Then what happened?"

"This guy gets out of his truck and starts talking to them." Tommy stopped as though trying to recall the incident. "One cop shined a light in his face." Tommy got up to take a closer look at the profile picture.

Hank pulled out the smaller side view of the same drawing. "What do you think?"

Tommy bent to be at eye level with the photo. "I remember the man smiling and talking while he pulled out his wallet." He frowned, his eyes turning to tiny slits. "Might be him. Definitely. Sleek the hair back as though tied in a ponytail." He straightened to nod Hank's way. "Yep, could be him."

"Now we're getting somewhere. "Christina?"

"I'm not sure, Hank. I'm trying. Mostly, I remember his eyes or rather his expression. I don't recall any ponytail, although the hawkish nose is familiar, yes. Sorry."

Hank noticed how Emma fixated on the profile pictures. He didn't have to ask her. On cue, she stood and sat on the edge of the chair in front of the sketches. She fingered the eyes all the way up to the narrow sloping forehead.

Hank said nothing, even held his breath so worried the noise might disturb Emma's thoughts.

Emma recalled the annex where her grandmother had taken her and Amelia to meet her aunt, Franka. The teacher she'd mistaken for the vile man. He was skinny and wiry and had long hair. Of course, she hadn't stayed long enough to confirm if the teacher was a woman or a man, just seemed like a man from the square and skinny shoulders. She pictured the villain coming over her windowsill, and the memory of him crouched over a child forced its way through. He was fat and round but now that she was aware he owed his pudginess to a disguise she wondered.

Emma finally glanced in Hank's direction. "Something about the eyes, they're the same. They're the wrong color, and I think whatever mask he wears gives the illusion of a different shape. But they are the same."

"Anything else?"

She stared at Christina Tyler, at Tommy, and parked her eyes on Hank Apple. She took a deep breath and expelled it slowly. Biting her bottom lip, she admitted, "The night I found myself riding on the roof of his car." After an apologetic grimace toward Tommy she continued, "Before I found myself back in bed, weird shadows danced in the window in the dirty shade dangling in front of his window." She bobbed her head faced with Hank's pleated brow. "The man who is after me was being beaten with a stick by a thin skinny man with a bent nose and long hair. He hit him until he fell and crumpled into a little ball."

Hank massaged his scalp for a few seconds. "That doesn't make any sense. Could this have been part of a dream you had afterward?"

"No. I wasn't back yet. Happened at his window at the exact place I told you about."

Christina smiled. "Hank, think about this. Emma's explanation may not make sense, but Emma's vision ties them together."

The door rang, and Hank got up to pay for the food.

***

Hank drove Tommy home making sure his father had arrived before he left. All during dinner, he'd steered the subject on safe topics: school, summer, anything to engage Christina and the children to think more pleasant times. He realized the distraction had pleased Christina, relaxing him as well when he noticed tension ease from her wan expression. Now, the strange picture Emma had drawn pairing the two characters still bothered him.

On his way to drive Emma to Abigail's house, he made another stop on Montclair one block south of Emma's school.

"You're dropping me off first?" Christina seemed surprised and a tad miffed.

"I thought you could use the break."

"You don't know how to get to Englewood Cliffs," she added a little belligerent.

"Oh, and you do?"

"Yes." She seemed to hesitate. "I dated someone for a couple of months. He lived in the area."

"Interesting. Anyone I've met?"

She glared at him, and he figured she was angry with his decision to leave her behind. He reached into the back and handed her the red folder and flicked her chin with his finger.

"Something to remember me by," he chuckled.

Christina grabbed the file from him. "What's this?"

"The folder Cindy compiled on the man who chased Tommy. Might be something between those pages worth checking. Would you mind giving it your undivided attention?"

She picked up her purse, and after saying goodnight to Emma, she left promptly walking up the few steps to her front door without looking back.

Hank turned toward Emma. "Want to sit in the front?"

"Sure." Emma climbed out of the back and buckled up in the front seat, a proud smile on her face.

"And don't worry about us getting lost. The GPS will get us there without a hitch."

Emma sat back into the cushions and relaxed. Just a week ago, she would have been terrified making this little trip alone in the car with Hank. Now, she felt protected and at peace. She recognized Hank was going to excessive lengths to keep her identity a secret, risking his job and his career in the process. She'd heard her mom and dad saying as much just the other night. She wondered if Hank realized how the vile man chasing her was trying to expose her as a witch. He wanted to tell the whole world. Most people wouldn't take the word of a madman, but what if some did, the ones with the fear of being uncovered for something they'd done or planned to do. A small sigh escaped her.

"Listen, Emma. We're going to be at your grandmother's house in about twenty minutes. I want you to get a good night's sleep. Not worry about anything, understand?"

She bit her bottom lip, trying to swallow what worried her most. But the lump was too big to ignore, and she turned her head toward him. "You said they're going to be searching for me all over the neighborhood tomorrow. Some people saw me in the building and talked to me. What if they tell?"

"Did you talk to any of your aunt's neighbors?"

She tried to remember. The only ones she'd seen were a couple of people in the lobby when she and Tommy had come running in after the chase. "A few people spotted Tommy and me and how scared I was after the man chased me."

"Did you tell them why?"

"No. Tommy told them there was a man outside shooting people and they all ran to check it out."

Hank didn't answer, and she wondered what was on his mind.

"I want to thank you, Hank, for everything you're doing for me. Dad said you could lose your job if they found out."

He stretched out a hand and squeezed hers. "Don't you worry about me. Don't ever worry about me. My job is helping people. I'm doing my job the best way I know how."

He grabbed the wheel with both hands to negotiate a turn on the exit ramp. "You're the one who's taking the risks, Emma. And I appreciate what you're doing. I know if Ashley Miller's folks realized that their little girl was safe on account of you," Hank let out a grunt. "They'd appreciate you too."

"You met her?"

"Matt had a team circulating flyers in her neighborhood with the man's picture on it. He spoke to Mrs. Miller while he was there, asking her to be especially careful not to leave Ashley out of her sight, at least until we caught the man. Ashley stood beside her mother with a big smile on her face, apparently a very sweet little girl."

"I'm glad she is okay."

"The OBE that you do, " Hank hesitated. "I mean this out of body experience."

"I know what OBE means. I looked it up on my dad's computer." She moved her head to stare at Hank's chiseled cheekbone and strong chin. She could read some of his thoughts. "They say it's a genuine science that people practice, but no one conceives how to initiate it correctly. There are a lot of theories."

"Anything you can learn to better control this maybe?"

"I'm working on it. I found some passages on the subject in the big book Granny Dottie left me. There are some tricks I can master to control better the way I appear to people, so they don't know I'm out of my body."

Emma could no longer prevent wording what she read in Hank's mind. "If you truly believe this man's trying to dim some of his actions by denouncing me as a witch, well if police arrest him, won't I also be caught?"

She regretted her question instantly when she witnessed how startled Hank was. "Are you picking my brain?" He eyed her squarely. "Please don't do that, young lady," he scolded with a smile, a smile to soften the words she figured.

"I'm sorry. I didn't mean to."

"Leave all that to me, agreed?"

"Agreed."

He slowed to listen to his GPS and check the meandering streets which seemed to run in circles. "Any of these streets seem familiar to you?"

Emma checked the houses and the large properties. "Not yet. My grandmother lives on a big lot with a stone fence that borders the perimeters."

Hank smiled, and Emma wondered why. "Did I say something funny?"

"No. You express yourself like an adult with grown up words. I like that."

"Hum. English is my best subject in school."

A few minutes later, Emma spotted the house and grounds. "There. The one on the corner."

Hank veered the car down the lane, came to a large gate, and pressed the intercom button. He waited. "Hope she's home." He checked his watch. "She should be here by now, almost nine thirty." Then he heard a male voice answer, "Tichy residence."

"Detective Apple and Mrs. Tichy's granddaughter, Emma."

A few seconds later, the gate slowly began to part. "Your grandmother has a huge lot," Hank mentioned as he drove the car down the drive.

"She purchased the lot next to hers to have more space. There are indoor and outdoor swimming pools and a tennis court on that side."

Hank took the key out of the ignition and turned in his seat to look Emma in the eye. "This will be a great vacation for you. Were you able to reach Amelia on Christina's phone?"

"Yes," Emma answered excitedly. "She'll be here tomorrow morning for a whole week."

"Listen, Emma. You should not be reading my thoughts," he remonstrated gently. "You never know what you might encounter in there. Half the time, I don't even know myself."

He saw her lower her eyes. "I don't do it on purpose," she whispered. "Sometimes, when it's quiet, and I have an interest in the person who is with me, they materialize. Sorry."

Flicking her chin to see her eyes, he smiled to reassure her. "I understand. And don't worry about that man. Whatever he says, no one will ever believe him. I'll make sure of that."

He knew the words were flimsy and not favorable to gaining

anyone's trust. But he saw the sweet smile Emma directed toward him reach her eyes, and whether it was a smile of pity or a smile to let him off the hook, her relief calmed him. Even if all he did brought a mere flicker of light in her otherwise dark world, his was worth the effort.

"Come on, I'll help you with your bags," Hank offered as he left the car in front of the main door.

Twenty-Eight

Emma Tests Her Powers

mma felt safer in her Grandma Abby's mansion than she did in her Aunt Franka's condo, out in Soho. She wasn't sure why the vast halls and large rooms with high ceilings gave her a homey sense or inspired confidence. Nevertheless, a gentle peace washed over her. She was glad her Grandma treated her as she normally did.

Although, she suspected her grandma did think of her as more grown up. The tone of her voice had dropped somewhat when she spoke to her, geared more to an equal and not merely to a little girl.

Her room was huge complete with four poster bed, an ornate desk and computer, and a flat screen television in the corner facing the bed, and on the front wall, a communicating door to the bedroom next to hers. Amelia would sleep in that adjoining room as of tomorrow night.

She'd bathed in a big whirlpool tub in the large ensuite bathroom, and was preparing to watch one of her favorite shows before bed. She eyed the wide French doors and thought she should secure them. They opened onto a terrace from which circular stairs brought her down to a small adjoining garden. She twisted the knob to make sure they were locked.

Padding back to bed, she spotted Granny Dottie's book hanging out of one of the bags she'd brought with her—more like a diary she thought, kept through the ages by many different women. She picked up the leather bound book smoothing its soft, well-worn surface. She brought the handwritten book up to her nose breathing in the familiar scents of home. Even from the dedication page, the yellowed sheets featured neat square letters making the text inviting to read.

A different ancestor of a different name had added various sections to the big tome. Granny Dottie had never said who the first woman was that started the three-hundred-page book. All she had mentioned was that the diary went back more than one century evidenced by the beautiful calligraphy in the first fifty pages of the book. Of course, blotches throughout the first few chapters attested to the ink of fountain pens.

Deciding this was more entertaining than watching TV, she began to read on one of her great grandmother's prowess of floating in and out of her body. The chapter described a lot of tips and tricks handed down on how to perfect the craft. The book specified she needed to encourage her body to sleep while keeping her mind alert and awake. But not tonight. She yawned, stretched and closed the book sliding the heavy volume off her lap. She'd had a long, trying day, and now, thanks to her amulet, she'd sleep peacefully. She lay down on the comfy pillows and grasped the familiar pendant in her neck. Instead, she opened her eyes wide with fear.

With a kick, she sat up in bed while little beads of sweat amassed on her forehead. She didn't have her amulet. It was still in Tommy's coat pocket. Unable to fathom how she'd forgotten about her newfound protection, she could almost catch the echo of the crazy man laughing at her. What if as tired as she was she traveled to him, and he found her. He might realize she was no longer in Manhattan.

In a big huff, she threw the blankets to one side and grabbed her jeans and T-shirt. As a precaution, because she planned to do this right, this time, she put on her socks and sneakers.

Nestled on the edge of the bed with her feet tucked in underneath her, she closed her eyes and concentrated on Hank Apple. Maybe if she fixed her thoughts intently, Hank would spot her. She would tell him she is missing her pendant.

She focused on Hank, and after a few minutes of picturing him in her mind, she felt herself lift off. She was moving quickly through the air, and she slapped her arms around herself wondering if she was headed somewhere or aimlessly spinning in any direction.

Just as she feared she might not be able to get back, she spotted her school and recognized Miss Tyler's house. The movement stopped when she stood in front of Hank's car. He was at Christina Tyler's house. Shyness crept up, and remembering Hank's request of not reading his thoughts, she couldn't make herself go inside and risk disturbing their privacy.

She willed herself home and opened her eyes smiling as she took inventory of the room she'd left. There'd been no dizzying motion when she'd returned, only quick conjuring of Grandma Abby's home.

"Conjuring," she whispered. She'd promised her father she wouldn't conjure anymore. After her last failed attempt at materializing money, they'd both agreed the results were too risky. Still, she needed her amulet. She closed her eyes and pictured the little pendant on its chain, pink and gray rim, with the black eye in the center. "Heaven's eye to life beyond, free your love of which I am fond so that my wish may be granted and I not be left stranded. I thank thee for loving me."

Immediately, a little pendant appeared in her hand. She opened her palm and checked the amulet. The pendant was not hers. The piece of jewelry did not resemble the Eye of Horus nor was the color the same and the chain smaller and silver instead of gold. She hoped the item hadn't belonged to another little girl who would wonder why she'd lost her chain. She would be unable to return this unaware of the owner of the pendant. Obviously, her father was right. Conjuring was dangerous since she had not yet learned how to direct her thoughts to what she truly wanted.

She closed her eyes once again and decided to go to Tommy's house. She'd need to be careful not to scare him.

Her mind took a little longer this time before her thoughts carried her away as the rush of lifting off grabbed her without any of the dizzying, twirling motion. She caught sight of Tommy's house and headed for his room. She peered through the window and found him tinkering with his computer. She stepped inside and noticed that all of her was present: pants, shoes, and sweater. No floating parts or missing legs. She looked whole and definitely in the room. "Tommy?"

He jumped and drew a loud breath when he spotted her. "What are you doing here?"

She glimpsed fear in his eyes. "Don't be afraid. I'm here in thought only. I forgot to take my amulet. It's still in your coat pocket."

He'd backed up to the furthest part of his room, still terrified. "You're not … here? How are you doing this?"

"Long story."

He took a deep breath and walked over to the chair beside the bed. He reached for the light jacket and grabbed the pendant from the inside pocket. "How am I going to give this to you if you're not here?"

She eyed the oudjat Tommy dangled in front of her.

She tried to grab the amulet, but couldn't. "There ought to be a way to do this. I just can't figure out how." She let go a frustrated breath. "Can you ask your dad to put my pendant in a cab to be sent to my grandmother's address? She'll pay the bill at the other end."

"Next time, pick up a phone instead of scaring me half to death."

"Sorry. Thought I could just reach for it."

Tommy hesitated. "Not a good idea asking my father. He's in a shitty mood. His meeting with a client didn't go well."

"He's the only one who can help right now."

"What about Hank Apple? He lives ten minutes away from here. He could pick it up and bring it to you."

"He's not home. He's at Miss Tyler's house. I don't want to bother them."

"Who told you?"

She struggled with the words and rolled her eyes. "Never mind. Can you please ask your dad?"

"Okay. Might take forty minutes or so before you get this. How are you going to get home?"

"I'll just close my eyes and think of home again, and I'll be there." She smiled and raised her right hand as a little wave. "Bye."

When Tommy told his dad about the call he'd made to Emma, to inform her about her pendant and chain, Tommy also said she'd asked for a taxi to bring the item to her immediately.

Rudy Carson weighed the chain and the amulet in his hand. "I'm not sending this via taxi. Broach looks like a family heirloom." He walked over to the bright hall light and scrutinized the chain's little tag to try and read its label. "Son, this is 18 karat gold."

"But Dad, she needs it."

"It's a bloody pendant. What is the girl going to do? Sleep with it?" He plopped the piece of jewelry in front of his son's face for him to take it again. "I've had a very shitty night, and I have to be at the office for eight tomorrow morning—drive myself in because Patrick's not going to be there."

"But Dad, Aunt Caroline's picking me up in the morning. How am I going to get this to Emma?"

Rudy raised a pair of hopeless shoulders, giving him the best sorry mug he could muster, but Tommy was not impressed.

He realized his dad was under a lot of strain, but he was usually a lot more helpful than this. He would need to call Emma and tell her he couldn't get the pendant to her.

***

Hank had knocked softly on Christina's door after having seen the light on in her kitchen. He'd gone through the shed at the back not to attract attention from the snoop next door.

"Hank?" Christina's surprised expression couldn't hide the smile in her eyes when she opened the door.

"Hope it's okay. My car's in your driveway," he whispered.

"Sure come on in. Don't worry about Elsie. She's in California for the next two weeks visiting her daughter."

Stepping inside her small kitchen, he let out a tremulous breath. "Lucky lady. That's where I'd like to be."

Christina grabbed a mug from the shelf and offered him coffee.

"Yeah, coffee would hit the spot."

She brought the two mugs and sat down beside him. "You'd like to be in California?" she asked before she took a sip of her coffee.

"Anywhere other than here—New Jersey here, not your house."

"I understand." She rubbed the top of his hand to show she did.

"Job's starting to get to me." He took a big gulp of his coffee feeling the burn scald his mouth the trail of fire speeding down his throat.

"Careful!"

"Hot. Geez Louise." He wiped his mouth with the back of his hand. "You just made this, didn't you?"

"Should have warned you." She snuffed a giggle. "Would you like some cold water?" She made the motion of going to the freezer to fetch some ice.

"No, no. I've had worse burns than this." He rubbed his eyes with a hand he would have preferred a little steadier.

"Anyway, I don't believe you about your job." Christina eyed him with kindness. "You love what you do."

"Not when I need to take my cue from a ten-year-old." He gazed at the runner's flower pattern and remembered the sweet memories they'd shared around this table, the sound of Christina's laughter still filling the room. "I think Val's scared."

"Cindy's aunt?"

He nodded. "Woman's screening all the department's calls. Won't return Ken's calls."

"Why? She's risking they won't take her seriously anymore."

"She obviously put more thought into the situation than the rest of us did. She's scared. I'm starting to understand why."

"She put her hand on his squeezing as she did. "Hey, you're going to catch this man. I am sure you are."

"Absolutely." He picked up her hand and kissed her fingers intently before letting her go. "No doubt about it whatsoever. But then what?"

Christina gestured both palms upward. "They're going to put him behind bars for life. That's what."

"First, there'll be a lengthy, very public trial." He strummed his fingers on the wooden table. "I can't help thinking what's Val going to say under oath?"

He spotted Christina's shoulders sag as she sat back in her chair her brow tightly knitted.

"I know what I'm going to say under oath. And I'm pretty damn sure Matt will say and do anything to put this guy away."

"You don't think Val would crumble, do you?"

"I don't even know if she will be credible. More and more people have learned about this now. Parents, grandmother, aunt, school teacher."

"I certainly would never reveal Emma's name. No matter how many Bibles they make me swear on."

He leaned over and stroked her arm. "I trust you. But can you say the same for the perpetrator?"

Christina's eyes widened as she bit her bottom lip, and the expression did nothing to reassure Hank. Hank added, "The creep is going to make sure he turns his trial into a three-ring circus. And he will not perjure himself to protect Emma. In fact, he's going to go out of his way to accuse her, try to sway public opinion."

"My God. I never considered that he knows who she is. Most victims can't usually point a finger in cases like this."

"Exactly. Emma is the one who got away. The killer may even turn this around and blame her. Say she knew who he was, knew he was sick, but did nothing to stop him."

Christina shook her head from side to side, and Hank knew her well enough to realize she was on the verge of tears. "No one would believe that would they?" she whispered.

Hank stared at Christina slowly rubbing a trembling hand over her forehead. "People will believe anything they read in the papers—even those who don't."

***

Tommy sneaked back to his room with the portable phone. He figured his father wouldn't need it anymore this evening.

He searched the phone's recent list to find Franka's last call. Luckily, Franka didn't find his request strange or out of place and kindly gave him her mother's private number without any fuss.

Tommy then called Abigail Tichy's house and waited a long time for the phone to pick up. "Tichy residence."

"This is Tommy Carson. I'd like to speak to Emma Willis, please."

Again, he waited several minutes before Abigail picked up the phone. "Tommy, what are you doing calling Emma at this hour? You can talk to her in the morning, young man."

"Wait. Emma needs her pendant, and I'm the one who has it. I need to tell her that I have no way of getting it to her. My father won't send it in a taxi, and he certainly won't drive it to your place."

There was silence on the phone, and Tommy hesitated. He didn't know if Abigail knew about the amulet's powers.

"You mean the little oudjat Granny Dottie gave her?"

Maybe she did know. "Yes."

Tommy worried about the troubled sigh at the other end. "Hold on. I'll go knock on her door and ask her to pick up the phone."

Tommy realized Abigail was on a portable phone herself as he could make out her giving orders as she rushed up the stairs. "Henry, get a hold of Detective Hank Apple at the second precinct. His number is on my agenda in the drawing room, by the phone. Tell him Abigail Tichy needs to talk to him."

Then he heard Emma's grandmother knock on her door. "Emma sweetheart, Tommy needs to talk to you. Emma?"

"I think she is already asleep, Tommy. She's not answering."

"That's impossible. Emma stood in my room not ten minutes ago."

"Young man, if you're trying to make me angry you're saying all the right …" Then as though Abigail suddenly understood, she banged on the door this time, and Tommy assumed since no sound arose inside the room she opened the door and barged in.

He listened as she ran around the room frantically calling Emma's name over and over again, rattled the French doors.

"They're locked from the inside," she mumbled to herself. "Which means no one entered the room unexpectedly."

Tommy heard Henry coming up the stairs saying that he couldn't reach Detective Apple. He had gone for the day. "Would you like me to call the station and ask for someone else, ma'am?"

"My God where is she?" Then Tommy began yelling through the phone to get Abigail's attention.

"Tommy," she added. "You'll have to call back later. We can't find Emma," she said with tears in her voice.

"Hank Apple is at Christina Tyler's place. That's where you have to call him, on his cell phone. I have the number."

Twenty-Nine

Trapped

Maurice Boleslaw, branded as Moey to most, had waited on the corner of West Broadway where he thought Detective Apple would show his face. He'd spotted him on the police scanner in his truck when Hank had called the office. Hours later he finally came to terms with the fact Hank wouldn't be there. He figured the witch had silently warned him. She hadn't been quiet either. He'd caught her scream at one point her wild doe eyes extended with fear and clashing with the night. "A little prissy sissy much worse than the others," he muttered to himself, cursing as he packed up his gear.

He'd hooked up the hitch at the front of the truck to ram their car. Now, he would have to go around the streets a little less conspicuously, hide again.

The witch would pay for all the trouble she caused. Once he told this story to the world, they would forget about what he'd done and concentrate on her, the evil one.

He would get her tomorrow. At least, now he'd found out where she stayed. He didn't care how many police officers would be down in Soho in the morning. He would be waiting for her.

He slammed his fists into the hood of his truck, the third time wincing with pain, but nothing compared with the shooting agony in his right temple throbbing nonstop. Then he took a rag out of his pocket to polish away any dent he might have inflicted on his pride and joy, crying as he did. Reinforced with extra layers of sheet metal the cargo van would take more than one of his angry fists to be damaged.

He wanted his world dark and quiet, and the growing number of bobbing lights from passing cars only worsened the pain. He still needed to get home and would have to do so slowly, driving through the torture cramping the right side of his head and blurring his vision.

Behind the wheel again, he focused on finishing the bottle of Johnny Walker he had started a couple of days ago. In the morning, he'd have a different kind of a headache, but one he'd be able to medicate and control.

***

Emma opened her eyes and slowly peered out into the dark. The odor of dirty socks wafted toward her and finished drawing her senses. She jumped up, her heart beating wildly inside her chest. She'd landed in a strange room—she turned about the place surveying the bed, the small bureau, and the window flanked with metal bars and panicked. How had she landed somewhere else? Emma first thought to sit on the bed again and try to think of home. When she did, she steadied herself on the bed with both hands brushing up against a rough woolen blanket.

She jumped up as soon as the realization hit her that her palms could connect with the objects around her. She walked moving one step at a time. She extended her hand toward the small dresser and grabbed a chain lying on top of it. She rolled the bristly link between her fingers grasping the small blue locket. She hadn't been able to do this at Tommy's house, which meant she had to be whole. She had materialized elsewhere.

She bit her lip to stop from crying out. Anyone finding her on the premises would think her crazy or a thief, and they'd call police. She had to get out, discreetly and silently.

First, she had to find out where she was. She listened intently hoping no one else was in the house. Not a sound came through except when a dog barked outside, and fear snaked a path down her back paralyzing all coherent reasoning. Even her feet seemed glued to the spot.

A small moan escaped her, but she realized she didn't have the luxury of breaking down in tears. All her instincts warned her she had to get out of that house fast.

Emma had the sense she walked into an attic because of the sloped ceiling. She tread softly and with carpet underfoot this was not difficult to do. However, when she came to a staircase, and hurried down, every step voiced a complaint or a whine as though they wanted to be elsewhere also.

Appeased by the sound of cars outside, she welcomed the full moon's glow coming through the windows to guide her steps, and she breathed a little better once she spotted the front door just a few feet ahead of her. Indeed a small house, and there didn't seem to be anyone else around.

She aimed for the door but found the only way out locked— one where you needed the key to unlock from the inside. She knew about these locks. Amelia's family had one in their house to prevent the autistic stepbrother from going outside alone.

Dread was back, urging her to find an exit. She noticed the lights of what looked like a truck or a van coming up the driveway. She bolted to the back door which she figured had to be directly opposite her. Crossing through a small kitchen, she found a screen door with a simple metal latch attaching it to the door frame. She stretched to unlatch the hook and peered outside.

She fought to find her bearings, but darkness prevailed. She surveyed the area, and with her eyes getting used to the night, she recognized she would need to run through two yards to get to the busy cross street she eyed with hope. Luckily there were no fences to block her way. The sound of the key in the front door made her bolt outside.

At the last minute she stopped, the front of her sneakers hanging midair as she attempted to balance herself not to fall from the small slab of stone extending from the house, the only outside ledge that kept her from an eight or ten foot fall.

Emma had wondered why no lock on this door. Now she knew. Having no idea what sort of ground waited for her down there, Emma couldn't just jump. She thought of the recently dissolved stitches from the cut on her leg and wondered how long the effect of a tetanus shot lasted. But soon, the person who'd entered would spot her.

She kneeled on the narrow step. Slouching down to her stomach, she crawled backward until she was at the very edge. The sound of footsteps came toward her, so she looked down one more time and let her weight drop as she clamped her fingers onto the ledge hanging on for dear life while trying not to let out a scream. If she fell now, even as a featherweight, the noise would alert whoever stood at the back door that she was on the premises.

"Who the hell unlocked this door?" The voice seemed familiar, yet all she could think about were her fingers beginning to cramp. Thankfully she witnessed the screen door swing shut. At that moment, she glimpsed a pair of big black sneakers stepping out on the small ledge.

She prayed he would not crush her fingers, and she would have the strength to last a few more seconds.

Time seemed to stand still when the door swung open and shut closed again. This time, the stranger was gone.

What were the odds that he would hear her from that small kitchen? Her tired arms assured her she had to take the chance and make a run for safety. All she hoped was the dog wasn't in one of the yards she needed to cross.

Emma let herself drop and hit dirt and rocks underfoot. Though she managed to land on her feet without a scratch, she'd been right to estimate ten feet. Once she allowed her height to bridge the gap, Emma was able to shorten the distance considerably, she thought to wipe her hands on her jeans. As she did, she noticed the little chain she'd held onto without even realizing. She slipped the pendant into her pocket. No way was she returning this now.

She didn't wait for the noise to alert anyone, she began to run through the yards, and as she reached the sidewalk to the main street, a big German Shepherd climbed the fence of the adjoining property and growled at her. She screamed, quickly realizing he wouldn't climb all the way over to where she stood. She ran down the sidewalk, happy that bushes hid her from where she'd been.

She walked into the first store she spotted and asked the small man behind the counter if she could use his phone. "I'm lost." She started to explain, but in vain.

"Payphone," the short Asian clerk yelled indicating the phone at the far end of the store.

She scrounged in her pocket for money and had to invoke her little phrase to get the quarters to make the call. She didn't know how many she'd need.

Angrily wiping at the tears pouring out of her eyes, she dialed a number she'd learned by heart.

"Hank, it's me," she whispered swallowing the lump in her throat happy he'd picked up his phone.

"Thank God, Emma. Where are you? We've been running around worried sick trying to find you."

"I don't know where I am—in a convenience store some-where."

"Where are you calling from?"

"A phone booth inside the store."

"Give me the number on the phone and I'll find you. Whatever you do, stay put and don't move. I'll be there as soon as I can."

Emma felt awkward standing in the aisle waiting for Hank. She didn't like the neighborhood and worried someone might think it odd her loafing around the store without buying anything at this late hour. Most people were in and out in a few minutes. So, she hid in the furthest aisle from the door making herself as small as possible and pretending to read labels on boxes.

***

Hank started to call his dispatch and stopped. Instead of taking the car radio, he used his cell phone. He didn't necessarily want to let people know where he was and why. It took him five minutes to get to the right person, and another ten to obtain the store's location.

"In Belleville, you're sure?"

"Yes, no doubt about it."

He put the siren on his car. It would take him another ten minutes to get there.

Ripping around the corner, he asked his cell phone to call Matt. "Can you please call Abigail Tichy and let her know I'm picking up Emma and bringing her back."

"Please don't tell me what this is about. Sounds long and drawn out by the tone of your voice. Why are you calling me on my cell?"

"Didn't know you were at the office. Besides, I've been thinking about this, and I think you're right. Our man has a police scanner. He's too quick on the draw. Knows our every move. And what are you doing at the office?"

"Came back to hurry the tests on the dog … and there's been a development."

Hank didn't answer, unsure if he wanted more bad news himself. Matt's tone sounded worse than his did.

"Valenciana Mezzo is dead."

Once Hank remembered to breathe, he had to ask, "Foul play?"

"Not established yet. Cindy worried. She said it wasn't like her aunt not to return her calls, so she went over there."

"God! How is Cindy?"

"She's been better. Bawling her eyes out. "Woman had been dead for two days."

"Geez Louise, poor Cin. Val's death will complicate matters."

"For starters, FBI's going to be invited to the party."

"On account of Val? Why? She may have passed from a heart attack."

"Coroner is hinting at a heart attack, so her death is most likely not related to this case or any other case for that matter."

"Why did Ken change is mind?"

"In Ken's head, Val's mind was the only real link we had to this guy. He's scared."

"Oh, please call little Tommy Carson and reassure him. He's pretty worried about Emma."

"Yeah, I'll do that, but don't tell me why. Seriously, I can't take any more bad news tonight." And Hank remembered what a softy he was at times.

Hank also recalled how disoriented Val had been of late and wondered if her lack of attention hadn't been health related. He would miss her. She was a fine human being who'd brought a lot of glory to his team.

As he barreled down the streets, he mentally combed through the files of psychic help the department carried. He would find someone else who'd be pleased to take credit for Emma's prowess, increase their notoriety—one more person to entrust with Emma's secret. The thought struck him perhaps he didn't have to mention where the information came from or who gave it to him. He could say he'd come face to face with his incredible intuitive talent. 'Johnny-come-lately's weren't rare in this kind of business. They'd have to take his word for it.

Hank turned off his siren three streets away and crossed the intersection in time to catch a man walking out of his front door. A ponytail swung at the back of his neck, and his profile depicted a long, crooked nose. The truck sat parked in his driveway.

Hank slowed to a crawl to let the man walk away. Coasting up slowly with lights off he waited for the stranger to turn the corner. He flashed a light on the truck's license number and wrote it down. Then he kept his distance as he caught up with the slight build man entering the store where Emma supposedly waited.

He turned into the driveway next to the convenience store and turned off his lights. Emma was in this area for a reason. His instinct kicked in and dictated he waited until the individual who'd just entered the store was gone before he rescued Emma. If this person turned out to be their poster boy, the last thing he wanted was to give the creep a clue of Emma's whereabouts.

***

The little bell hanging on top of the door told Emma someone had entered. She crouched while browsing at boxes of cereal on the lower shelf, an all too familiar sounding voice drew her attention.

"Give me a pack of Parliaments," the man asked. Emma peeked through the space between the shelves and caught sight of a man with a ponytail and a bent long nose and had to stifle a scream.

"Did any weird punk come in here?" he asked the clerk.

"Nine dollars," was all that the clerk shouted.

"Highway robbery. These cigs were seven fifty yesterday. You got a gun back there or something?"

"You pay and get out or I call the cops," the little man spouted in a strong accent.

"Take it easy, Chink. No one's out to hurt you. I just need a few more things."

Emma eyed the restroom to her right and hoped the door wasn't locked. She crawled to the door on her hands and knees, stretched to turn the handle and slid inside where she hurried to lock the door. Alone in the dark, she sat on the toilet seat and cried silently. Now, Hank would come around and think she was gone.

<u>Thirty</u>

Hank And Emma

Hank spotted the man come out with a cigarette in his mouth and a bag in his hand. He walked with a bounce in his step then he dropped the bag he held and bent from the waist twisting both palms against each side of his head.

"That's right," Hank muttered. "Make sure your head's on tight, fella. Take care you don't lose it."

A few minutes later, the stranger picked up a couple of cola cans and the few more items that had rolled out of the bag and walked toward home his stance considerably slower.

Hank left the car and ran inside the store. "Excuse me." He showed his badge to the clerk behind the counter. "A young girl came in here a while ago, made a call from this phone booth. Do you know where I can find her?"

Wide-eyed and terrified, the clerk backed up a few steps and stuck his chin out to indicate the back of the store.

"Thank you."

Hank found no one in the store. He walked over to the washroom and knocked on the door. "Emma, it's Hank." He waited.

He caught the sound of the door being unlocked and gazed at a tear-stained face and puffy eyed Emma walk toward him. Next thing she clamped her thin arms around him and used his torso to muffle her cries. He held her soothing her as best as big paws allowed while stroking her hair.

"Let's go home," he whispered.

Once in the car, he turned to her before starting the engine. "Want to tell me how this happened?"

Emma blew her nose, wiping her eyes with her sleeve. No words came out.

"Before I forget." Hank handed Emma the amulet. "You should put this around your neck and not take it off for the next little while."

She reached for her pendant her hand trembling and slipped it over her head closing her eyes as she leaned back while Hank caught the tension leaving her body as the Eye of Horus worked its magic. "Thank you," was all she whispered.

Hank waited for Emma to say something. When he realized she wasn't ready to talk, he gripped the steering wheel tighter unable to wrap his mind around what Emma had done.

"Can we get out of here, please?" She asked him earnestly in a small voice she couldn't recognize. "I hate it here."

Emma wondered why Hank didn't flinch. He turned in his seat and put the key in the ignition. He backed up the car and left the area. He kept his eyes on the road, his thoughts to himself. As the car sped, she noticed Hank make a left on Main Street. He wasn't taking the Turnpike as he previously had. Apparently, he was adding to their travel time most likely waiting for her to say something. She still couldn't talk.

Emma stared at her fingers, at the scratches and the red blisters on the inside of her thumbs, and wondered how she'd managed to hold on to that ledge for so long. Mostly, Emma felt ashamed. Twice she'd played with her newfound powers and twice she'd ended up punished. When she conjured the money for her parents, and she created a worse problem for her father. Tonight, when she flaunted her powers in front of Tommy, she ended up putting her life in mortal danger. Turns out Granny Dottie spoke the truth. Powers like hers stirred nothing but trouble. Perhaps her father had been right all these years, forbidding her to acknowledge this curse.

Emma rested her head on the back of the seat and closed her eyes. Today, long and outdrawn, had left her tired and edgy and frightened of her thoughts. While the trip to her grandmother's house was familiar, the second time this evening in Hank's car, and gratitude at heading home filled her with awe, the night's events kept replaying in her mind like a jammed movie real over and over again. She tried not to panic when remembering how close she'd come to being an unwilling prisoner of that evil man. No one knew where she was. No one would have ever suspected him.

As the miles swept by, she didn't even find the thick wall of silence between Hank and her odd or misplaced so lost was she in her troubled world.

Hank visited his own hell. Not only frightened for Emma anymore, he feared they might never catch this man, at least not before he took another victim. If Emma refused to talk to him, he would no longer be able to help her. Reinforcements would be called in. Obtaining more help would mean exposure for Emma and airing out the grave admission he had withheld vital information to this case—eventually having to let go of the secret he'd been sworn to keep.

The train of thought upset him. He hung a left onto North Woodland, and another immediate left onto the winding road that led to Dwight-Englewood School. He parked behind a clump of trees and turned off his lights. He sat there, staring into space, hoping he would not have to be strict with Emma, praying she would realize she needed to tell him exactly what had gone wrong tonight. What sort of crazy turn of events had led her from her grandmother's bedroom in the middle of the night to the hell hole from where he'd picked her up?

"I'm sorry," she said in a small voice.

"I know you are. Unfortunately, that doesn't cut it." He turned to look at her. "I didn't want to tell you this," he hesitated. But then he fingered her chin to turn her face, to stare into her eyes. "They found Val dead this evening. In her house."

"Oh," she breathed. "Not …"

"No. Heart attack looks like—as far as we know."

"Poor Val." She continued to stare at him. "This is going to complicate things isn't it?"

"Afraid so." He made a fist to punch the steering wheel but reneged on the gesture and only brushed past it. "I need your help more than ever.

She lowered her head, and he figured by the sight of her pinched lips she didn't want to cry again. "Does this mean you're going to have to tell my secret?"

"I would lose my job before I did that, but to tell you the truth, I'm concerned. We're going to need all the help we can muster to catch this guy which means you and more people in my department are going to need to help if we're going to tighten the net 'round this maniac."

He took in the tears on her cheek and the deep breath she gathered.

"You're going to have to trust me, Emma." The quick little nods she sent reassured him.

"What happened? How did you end up in a convenience store, in Belleville?"

"I'm not sure." Hank witnessed Emma lower her eyes and put up both hands to cover her cheeks. He figured she was confused and frustrated which might explain the embarrassment coloring her face.

Once more reminded she was a ten-year-old child, he turned away and stared at the tall violet butterfly bushes the flowers a dark purple under the street lamp. Maybe they were called something else. He wasn't good with names of plants.

"First thing I realized, I was thinking of home. That's when I began spinning—more so than I did when I was looking for you. I couldn't get my bearings. I became dizzy almost to the point of throwing up."

"You were looking for me?" Hank couldn't stop the motion that brought him face to face with Emma.

This was when Emma told him what she'd done and why. "I couldn't pick up my amulet at Tommy's house. I wasn't physically there and I hadn't planned that far ahead."

"Okay. Then what?"

"Tommy asked me how I was going to get back. Guess I became overly confident. I told him it was easy. All I had to do was to think of home."

Hank waited. For the first time, he realized Emma might not understand herself what had happened to her.

"I'd read up on out of body experience in the diary my grandmother left me—a big book filled with advice from generations dating back to the mid-eighteen centuries."

"What went wrong?"

She hoisted slim shoulders. "One of my ancestors wrote about projecting versus propelling and outlined the differences between the two. The only explanation is that I confused them. She did say propelling oneself safely required a pure heart and a calm spirit. She said fear rules us and whatever we fear we tend to bring about or gather 'round."

Hank scratched his head and tried to remain patient. "You're not making any sense."

"After I left Tommy's house, seemed a long time before I stopped spinning and when I did, I was in another bedroom, dirty, small."

"Not in the convenience store?"

She shook her head. "I sensed I needed to get out of there. This house was weird, and I worried that if I tried to think mentally of home, I would reach my room but in spirit only leaving my body in a stranger's house."

"Someone else's house?" She had Hank's complete attention.

She recounted what she had done to get out of there, the jump off the gallery, the run through the yards, the hiding at the store.

Hank covered his face with his hands. Imagining what Emma had just gone through overwhelmed him. A deep breath later he felt her tugging at his sleeve. He turned to stare at her.

"The house is his house," she whispered unable to hide the terror in her eyes.

Both Hank's hands turn into fists as he tried to contain his temper realizing exactly who she meant. "Whose house?" he asked very slowly more like a knee-jerk reaction.

"The crazy man who is after me. I stared right at him when he came into the store—that voice. It was him."

"Emma, are you sure? All the reports say he disguises his voice."

She shook her head vigorously. "No. The night he came into my room, the dream I had, today when he grabbed me and whispered in my ear. And tonight when he asked the store clerk for cigarettes. The same voice."

"God help me." This time, Hank did punch his steering wheel in anger. "Ponytail guy with long, crooked nose."

"Yes."

"Fuck! I was two feet away from him." He glanced at Emma. "I'm sorry. I didn't mean to swear."

"Don't worry. My father uses the word often enough."

"What about his house? Where?"

"Fourth down from the corner."

"Smallest house on the street with a truck parked in the driveway?"

Emma nodded.

Hank's blood pressure pounded in his ears. All the hate and the fear he held for this man converged into one loud chatterbox spewing ideas round and round in his head. Like an automaton, he started the car and drove up Woodland in silence, until he came to Abigail's front gate and driveway. He announced himself to the guard and drove through. He could see Abigail running toward the car.

"Can you do me a favor?" Hank asked Emma.

"Sure."

"Call Christina Tyler and let her know you're all right. Tell her. Tell her I had to go back to work."

"It's so late."

"She'll be glad you're safe." He couldn't face talking to Christina right now. She would have a lot of questions, and he didn't have any answers, not a one he could give her. "Do you have the number?"

"I do."

Abigail had her hand on the car door as she waited for Hank to unlock them.

When he did, she yanked the door open and scooped Emma out of the car. Crying softly, she squeezed her granddaughter against her, and Hank could see Emma had difficulty breathing.

"You might want to ease up on the hug, Mrs. Tichy." He prompted stepping out of the car for a few seconds.

Abigail was sobbing. She released Emma to blow her nose before throwing Hank a raised eyebrow. "Thank you, Detective. Thank you for bringing my granddaughter back to me." She stroked Emma's hair.

"Did you tell Patrick and Eloise about this?"

"No. At this hour, they're sleeping. I was going to, but then I got your partner's call."

"Good. Don't. The fewer people know about this, the better."

"Can I go inside, Grandma?"

"Run along, my love," Abigail answered tucking her tissue

away in the sleeve of her blouse. Turning toward Hank, she asked. "What happened?"

"I'm sure Emma will tell you when she's ready. For now, I wouldn't ask too many questions. She needs to forget about this for a while."

"Of course, you're right."

"I wouldn't get too paranoid, but just make sure she's around the house on a regular basis."

"Her friend Amelia is coming tomorrow to spend some time with us. This will help get her mind off of all this."

Thirty-One

Hank Faces His Captain

Christina simply thanked Emma for calling her and letting her know she was home and safe. She was not about to ask for drawn out explanations at this late hour. She wondered why Hank asked Emma to call her.

Sitting in the chair by her bed with the room plunged in darkness, she recalled the kiss they shared before Abigail's phone call—tender and passionate, not the embrace of a man just looking for sex. She was well acquainted with Hank, enough to realize he not only wanted her, but also loved her—his touch so emotionally charged nerve endings in her neck and all the way down her spine still tingled from evoking the memory.

She got up and pushed the curtain back to glance at the street below while her eyes swept past the empty vast expanse of school yard, familiar yet resembling a huge patch of ink at this time of night when the city dimmed the yard's perimeter lights.

Though her heart went out to Emma, the poor little rich girl, rich on talents yet poor on happiness, she prayed Hank would remember the promise he'd made to her between the sheets, to be open and above board with her during a crisis rather than letting the walls close in behind him. She kept her fingers crossed he would call her to confide about the heavy burden obviously weighing on him right now.

She glanced at the portable phone perched in its berth on her night stand and found it impossible to pick up. She'd promised Hank she would not put her pride before her love for him. What welled up inside her was not pride, more like a voice of reason stating Hank needed to make the first step.

***

Hank rolled into police headquarters wondering what all the cars were doing there. He even recognized Kenneth Riley's two door coupe parked in the handicap zone next to the front door.

He reached for his briefcase on the back seat, and recoiled as he came to drop his phone into his coat pocket. He'd acted cowardly having Emma call Christina. Truth was after the conversation he and Christina had shared in her kitchen tonight, on who would be strong enough to keep Emma's secret, he thought himself a coward and a fool when he considered what he was about to do.

Without giving himself time to think he called her number. "Hey, it's me."

"Are you all right?"

All he could do was heave a heavy sigh. He hadn't really thought this through.

"Hank, whatever you do or decide to do, I trust you. No doubt in my mind you'll do the right thing."

Another deep sigh escaped him. "I wish I felt the same way. I just wanted to say goodnight."

"Call me in the morning?"

There was so much he wanted to say to her, but the words

stuck in his craw. "You bet." He hung up, his emotions more in a turmoil than they were before the call. He'd made such a big deal of obtaining Emma's trust, yet he couldn't confide in Christina. Or was it himself he didn't trust, worried he'd fall apart if he admitted what he intended to do?

He walked down the fully lit corridors and bumped into Matt.

"Hank? What are you doing here?"

Hank eyed him a little sheepishly. "I'm going to talk to Ken."

He realized his tone more than his words seemed to alert Matt of what was on his mind.

"What do you mean, talk to Ken?" He caught Matt pale under his dark skin as he shifted his weight. "Wait a minute. You didn't come here to see Ken. No one knows he's here. Did you call him?"

"Actually, I came here to talk to you, but then I saw his car out front …" He raised a shoulder. "I think we should include him in our conversation."

"Talk about what? What's going on? You're not going to do anything crazy are you?"

Hank all at once realized any discussion he'd take up with Matt would run in circles. He sidestepped Matt and took long strides toward Ken's office.

"Hank?"

He detected panic in his partner's voice. No surprise he came waltzing behind him to try and stop him, but he was shaken by the strength Matt exuded when he clamped down on his arm in front of Ken's door.

"You son of a bitch. Think of our roles being reversed. How would you feel? What would you say?"

"I'm not going to implicate you—whatever happens in there."

Hank pulled on Matt's arm and rammed into Ken's office, Matt on his heels.

The two stopped abruptly, interrupting a meeting Ken held with Barbara Leclerc in charge of the Sexual Assault Rape Analysis unit, Newark's police Director and the Deputy Chief in charge of criminal intelligence.

Kenneth Riley stood. "What's this all about, Apple?"

"I'm sorry for the intrusion. I wanted to talk to you, sir. It can wait." He doubled back to leave.

Director Bob Larkin stood at once. "Wait, Hank. We're finished here, Ken. I'm satisfied with your proposal. Keep me posted of any changes you make."

He gathered his briefcase and his hat, and he left followed by Deputy Chief Mark Sanchez.

Larkin shook Hank and Matt's hand before stepping out. "Counting on you two to catch this sicko."

"We're working on it, sir."

"Good luck."

Their departure left an uneasy mood in its wake. Hank spotted the storm cloud brewing over Ken's head. His bold interruption did not sit well with him. Not a good omen to start what he had to say.

Both hands flat on his desk Ken stared at him as though he was about to chew him out, then seemed to give up sitting down with a slump. His eyes fixed on the mahogany cabinet holding all his treasures, medals, official pictures, favorite books, he rubbed his hands together before he began cracking his knuckles, a sound usually coupled with perplexity in his chief's demeanor. The noise of bone on bone always managed to irritate Hank no end as he stood there his own fingers curling into fists.

Barbara rose and came around the table with her right arm outstretched. She wrapped it around Hank's back. "Come and sit down. You look positively haggard. I've never seen you so pale." She turned toward Matt and motioned to him. "You too, Detective."

Hank sat in front of Ken and Barbara and stared at the woman wondering how she managed to always hold it together. Her wiry black curls never out of place, her warm brown eyes staring out of a round face, and her bosom as big as mother earth herself never appeared to be fazed or unnerved by anything.

A huge sigh later, Ken sat down still cracking his knuckles. Mechanically Ken asked. "What have you got?"

A quick glance toward Matt, and Hank swallowed the nausea suddenly creeping up on him. The Moo Goo Gai Pan he'd wolfed down at supper wanted out. "Valenciana Mezzo was not the informant on this case."

Hank held his breath. In front of him, Ken displayed a bad case of slack jaw topped with two beady grey eyes suddenly appearing unattached and more angry than mystified.

Ken leaned across the table. "What?" He tilted his head to the side. "Tell me I'm not hearing correctly. Please tell me you're out there playing goddamned Captain America again." He rose slowly. "I told you I would fire you the next time you did."

Hank rose so quickly his chair went rolling back. "Well fire me. I don't care. I took the initiative to use Val as a tool in order to protect the real collaborator."

"Every goddamned time you do this. You're sorry. You swear you'll never do it again. This time, you've gone too far."

Hank turned his back on him. He withheld mentioning how his gut had been right more times than Ken cared to admit. This was not the time to flaunt his decision-making skills.

Hank once again faced his audience of three. "Well, this time, I'm not sorry."

"You're not sorry? That you withheld police information again? What kind of space do you have between those ears?"

Ken tucked in his shirt and gave his fingers another tug. "Okay. Fair enough. You give Barb and me the name of the informant then pack your stuff and leave."

His boss' slow and deliberate words knocked the wind out of Hank. He glanced at Matt who had a hand over his eyes trying to hide a nervous smile. Barbara seemed deflated, sitting back in her chair with her forehead lined with questions.

Ken turned toward Matt. "Matt, what's the name of the informant?"

Matt showed his face and chuckled as nervous as he was. "Me? I don't know."

"You guys hold farting contests and you are going sit there and feign ignorance?"

This made Matt giggle even more. "Sir, I'd never win that kind of contest with Hank, not with him being the wind bag he is."

Ken turned a brighter shade of red than Hank had ever seen, and though he worried he was far from what he'd set out to accomplish, he couldn't seem to maneuver his way out of this quagmire.

Barbara came to their rescue rising from her chair and walking over to Hank with a heavy foot. "Please, Ken." She held on to Hank's arm. "Hank came here to tell us something obviously, and we're not giving him the chance. We're getting nowhere with you two pushing each other's buttons."

The words seem to calm Ken like a cold shower. After tugging on his chair, he pulled on his jacket to straighten it and button it down. He sat as he continued to nod his head dangling so many times, Hank thought it had become loose. "Right. Right." So, Apple, aside from interrupting my meeting, and throwing your insubordination in my face, why did you come here?"

Hank waited until Barbara had regained her seat, until Matt had wiped the smug look off his face before he sat down and announced. "I know who the perp is."

Hank thought Ken would erupt again. But he let go a huge breath and acknowledged. "Good news, good, good news. Arrested him yet?"

Hank hesitated. "Can't."

His captain's face became the color of overcooked beets and Hank thought he would lose it. Ken turned toward Barb motioning for her to step in.

"Why not, Hank?" Barbara asked with a solicitous smile. "You do have a name?"

Hank reached in his briefcase and dropped the red folder in front of Ken. "Here he is. Name, home address, what he does for a living—all there."

Ken glanced through the file. "I remember. This is the man who ran after the kid on the bike." He handed the file over to Barbara. "This is a far cry from the chubby woman who talks with a squeaky voice and walks with a limp—in corrective shoes—even when we consider the theory of a disguise."

"I know. However, tonight I received positive identification."

"From who? From this informant you don't want us to know

about?" Ken rose and walked around the table to pace. "Obviously, if you've made no arrests, you have no proof. Only this … informant's hearsay."

Hank could not remain seated. As tired as he was, he stood. He had considered leaving the chips fall where they may, or rather, wherever they might be best for Emma. He realized tonight faced with the close call she'd experienced, and learning about the maniac they'd been trying to nail for months, he needed more help on his side if he was going to catch the son of a bitch.

"Why do you feel the need to protect this informant?" Barbara asked earnestly.

Hank sensed this to be the moment of truth. He eyed Matt, who gave him a shoulder shrug and a head toss, and realized the knee-jerk reaction would be the only green light he'd get from his partner.

"The informant is a minor, a ten year old child." Hank breathed.

Ken quit pacing like a lion in a cage, and Hank could sense his eyes burning the side of his face. Meanwhile, he watched Barbara the mother, grandmother and indefatigable defender of children's rights as her eyes welled up with tears. "Oh, my God, a victim who got away?" she whispered a hand shaking in front of her mouth.

"No. Not a victim—exactly." Hank took a deep breath and added. "A talented seer possessing more powers than the twelve or so psychic bozos we have on the payroll times ten."

"Oh, my God. Poor, sweet child," Barbara said.

"A sweet child saddled with a tyrant of a father who would not allow her to tell anyone what she was going through," Matt added as though this made a difference.

"I've had to deal with her teacher her parents her whole family, and God forbid, well, I don't have to tell you what would happen if this leaked out to the media."

Ken flopped in his chair. All the fight seemed to have left him with Hank's avowal. "I take it back, Apple. You did the right thing—keeping it quiet. But you should have trusted me. I'm not an idiot. I have a fourteen year old daughter. And Logan, I would be exactly like that girl's father—fiercely protective."

"You haven't met him, sir."

Barbara massaged her temples. "If the press should get wind of this."

"Every bastard in the county would want her head." Matt hissed.

Ken stared at Hank. "Wait a minute. Is this in any way related to that earlier surveillance on the little girl's house? Where a big chunk of our budget disappeared?"

Hank nodded.

"All those weeks ago," was all Ken added shaking his head in disgust.

"What happened tonight, man? How did Emma recognize him?" Matt wanted to know.

Hank shot him a look and Matt held out his arms, explaining. "You just gave away who she was. Her name is in the file."

"A moment, Hank." Barbara raised her hand preventing him from answering Matt's question. "You're talking about the man trying to get into this young girl's room, the disguised man, the one who attempted the assault inside her Forest Hill home. This is who we are talking about, right?"

"Yes," Hank breathed realizing Barb was doing the math.

"So, our perpetrator is deliberately attempting to attack this young girl. This can only mean he has to know she can identify him. Can't be simple coincidence … can it?" Ken asked.

Hank hesitated eying Ken's dropped jaw again. "No coincidence."

"Son of a bitch," Ken yelled. "Who does he think he is?" He was pacing once more. "And the attack in Soho, today. Please tell me the punk kid wasn't that young girl?" He eyed Hank's raise of eyebrows, and Hank realized no answer was necessary.

"We can't let him get away with this. We have to find some way to protect her or bring him in NOW." Ken was upset and about to wear a hole in his carpet.

"When we do, he's threatened to tell the world Emma is a witch." Hank took in the fear in Barbara's eyes, the helplessness in his chief's cheerless expression and knew he would need to be the one to come up with a solution.

"If you ask me," Matt added, "this man is diabolical, and our only solution is a silver bullet to the heart."

"We can't just murder someone in cold blood, Matt," Ken said without conviction. "Although I pray he doesn't cross my path."

"Can you waylay the FBI?"

"Absolutely." Ken affirmed unbuttoning and tying his jacket in the same motion. "After all, we know who the killer is we just need proof." He stared at Hank, Matt, and then Barbara. "Other than little Emma's testimony. Besides, this information cannot leave this room."

"Will you tell Larkin about this?" Hank asked.

Ken Riley glanced at Barbara. Hank had never expected the woman to be this vulnerable. "No." He stared at each person seated around the table taking a deep breath as he added. "You men realize we're going to have to play this by ear. In other words, we cannot let the media get wind of this."

Hank's eyes narrowed not quite sure he understood Ken's words. "Never thought I'd hear you say something like that." The brief scrutiny of his chief's narrowed eyes and set jaw revealed there was no misinterpretation. "When time comes for an arrest, I doubt I'll be able to do that," Hank admitted.

Matt stood and stretched as he did. "I'll be glad to do it, sir. No problem whatsoever."

"Gentlemen." Ken rose and stared at both of them. "This remains between the four of us." He turned to check on Barbara's reaction, and stared at her until he detected a faint nod. "Our silence will ensure when we do make an arrest, however this plays out, no one will be able to accuse us of wrongdoing. Are we clear on this?"

Hank and Matt glanced at each other and also agreed. Hank asked, "What about Soho in the morning, Chief Lang and the task-force?"

Hank realized his question took Ken by surprise when his chief began cracking his knuckles again. After a particular loud snap, Ken rose and stared at both men in the eye. "We'll go through the motion. I already promised. No harm done. We just need to keep this information to ourselves."

Ken dropped his face in his hands. When he looked up at Hank, he seemed older without being the wiser as though age had taken a ten-year chunk out of his life. "Please tell me you have a plan."

Thirty-Two

Emma Hones Her Powers

Hank admitted to Ken he had not yet formulated a solid plan. Of course, he would be in Soho early morning as he suspected the maniac would be there also to intercept Emma. He maintained the only reason they had not found any new body bags was that the perpetrator was obsessed with catching Emma. "This one little girl consumes him, and he won't rest until he gets her. He's like a rabid dog."

He'd answered Matt's questions while discussing as little of Emma's secret as possible, at least keeping quiet what he deemed unnecessary.

The two had spent the last hour in Hank's car trying to verbalize some plan for the next day. Finally, Matt agreed with Hank's decision to confide in Ken and Barbara.

On his way home, Hank began to have doubts about the confession he'd made to his chief. Emma's life depended on him being discreet. He wondered about the safety of his decision to include two other people in Emma's world, a world he knew so little.

Two a.m., driving around the streets of Newark, lost in thought, he battled nerves which made him wide awake and unable to calm down.

Vulnerability gnawed at his conscience. Of course, having Ken shoulder some of the responsibility gave him the notion power had shifted, and he no longer held the reins to his case. Did the job wear him out to the point of not thinking straight? Was this what was in store for his future—asking for help whenever the case got tough? These doubts had plagued Hank as a newbie detective when he remembered inadequacy and fear of not measuring up. Seemed as though nothing had changed, merely ran in circles all these years.

In circles all right, round Emma's school. He slowed and gazed around him. He'd taken the wrong turn and now found himself in front of Christina's house instead of his own. He looked at the two-story cottage he was well acquainted with and realized he'd come full circle.

These past few years without her, the little boy in him had grown into a man and learned a few valuable lessons, but he suddenly worried this man was full of shit. Perhaps merely a boy who'd simply learned to hide his shortcomings. He borrowed the lingo and the tone he needed to talk the talk in a deeper voice only to get into even deeper trouble.

It made no sense him standing on Christina's front stoop this early in the morning, but before he rang the bell the door opened.

"I saw you drive around the block a couple of times."

"You couldn't sleep either?"

"Come on in." She moved aside for him to enter.

He hesitated. "Listen, Christina." He searched her eyes wanting to gauge what she expected of him. "I'm a little vulnerable right now, and I don't want to pour my shit on you."

"You're going to stand at the door to debate the issue, at this hour?"

"Bottom line, maybe we can talk?"

"Of course."

As soon as he entered the small living area, he regretted having landed on her doorstep. He had no right to annoy Christina with his insecurities—let alone take her in his arms and kiss the hell out of her which was what he ached to do about now.

Honestly, he was all talked out. He didn't know how to put the night's events into any semblance of coherence. She would insist he spill his guts. He would sputter nonsense while gawking at her breasts, her milky skin, her full lips, and she would discover how much he needed her and would believe all he wanted from her was sex.

She was right behind him. He could sense her energy, and he picked up on the fruity peach scent she wore before bed. The aroma drove him mad. Christina ran a hand down his spine, slowly and deliberately, from his tired shoulders down to the small of his back. Unchecked the loud groan drawn from his loins gave away how good her caressing hand was down his back. He guessed the repressed need sprung from all those nights of needing her in his arms, endless nights when his hand had stroked the sheets only to find her side of the bed empty.

He turned and grabbed both her hands. "Don't do this Christina. You'll hate yourself in the morning. Then you'll hate me."

"Why?" she whispered gazing into his eyes.

"You'll remember how all this happened. You'll think me coming here at this hour was nothing but a booty call. I know you." He brought each of her palms to his mouth, sensuously kissing her wrists one after the other.

"I'm not that girl anymore." She took a deep breath. "You're not the only one who's grown and matured. And you don't hold the patent on needing to make it all go away by burrowing inside someone you care about."

As it turned out, Christina's vulnerability showed. She needed him as much as he did her.

When she gave him the nod to emphasize, he ran his hands through her hair and brought her face close to his. Another loud moan escaped him as he felt her pressing her body against his while staring into his eyes.

He sensed more words rising in her throat, but too late. His mouth had sealed hers in a deep longing kiss, his tongue unable to take possession of the sweet breath fast enough.

Lifting her off the ground, he claimed her mouth completely and without mercy, her gesture of utter surrender drawing tears from him.

***

A pale hue of light filtered through Emma's bedroom windows. Inside, strange shadows flitted up and down the pink and yellow daisy wallpaper. While the rest of the household slept, a large mountain shaped cloth had taken over Emma's bed. Tucked inside was Emma, the bed sheet over her head going through her grandmother's diary with a flashlight not to wake everybody—mostly not to worry her grandma by showing how sleep eluded her.

Every couple of minutes, Emma clasped her pendant to keep her thoughts from racing back to where she'd been that evening, to make sure the little stone still dangled around her neck.

The oudjat did help her relax, but still scared of what her sleeping mind might do, she had decided to research the passage on out of body experience to understand her mistake and how to make sure she never did this again. She would need to read more carefully. The English idioms were old, some words strange to her, some words too smudged to make out. The sentence construction was also different—in a more roundabout way which made it easy to confuse.

She hadn't told her grandma anything, and luckily, Abigail had not asked for an explanation. The fact of speaking out loud about her ordeal to Hank had terrified her. The recounting of details had colored and drawn the danger so much bigger than when the episode had just been a picture in her mind.

She pinched her lips and swiped at a renegade tear rolling down her cheek with the back of her hand. She didn't want to cry like a baby. What would Tommy say if he found out what a coward she was? Another tear sneaked its way out. She wiped at it hard. She'd have to dry those tears in time for Amelia's visit. She didn't suspect any of this, and Emma was looking forward to the reprieve of a friend not observing her with a strange mixture of pity and curiosity.

Emma read: The astral body has many endearing properties, Unlike the physical body, it cannot fall prey to injury or harm. At the speed of thought, the mind travels experiencing situations while preventing mistakes and costly errors when the otherwise same situation might occur in the physical realm.

Her great-great grandmother was smart, she thought. She wished she had written down more about the subject. She wrote of projecting as the astral body traveled from one point to another to collect information. She had a couple of pages on how to perform the task.

In the middle of such a passage, she wrote of a predisposition only a handful of humans seemed to possess which was to propel themselves throughout the astral realm with their physical body intact. To land on the Earth plane, they needed to use astral portals which acted as gateways to the physical world.

All at once, darkness spread around Emma making her jump. She could not prevent a little squeal. Emma wiggled the little flashlight to get the light on again and wiped the few tears that streaked her cheeks. She'd never been this wound up before. She was probably just too tired she thought.

Whenever a traveler propels his astral and physical form out into new frontiers, he or she is still guided by thought rather than physical locomotion. Therefore, the traveler needs to be pure of heart and possess a mind devoid of fear. Emma wondered how she would ever be able to accomplish this. Because the physical body is magnetic, the traveler will be more easily attracted to profound thoughts usually engendered by fear-based conditions.

Emma realized until she handled her fear, she would no longer be able to propel herself anywhere. Once more, she clasped the amulet resting against her chest relieved the oudjat would keep her grounded. Just as she was about to close the book, the next paragraph grabbed her attention.

Hold your thoughts on the light. The light that shines brightest—the light which belongs to other astral souls wandering in a state of euphoria, and there to help all travelers. One will find them through love and the gift of self. Confidence in their power will bring the traveler home safely.

Emma thought of her little sentence she used for conjuring and wondered if the power she prayed to was the same one she needed to travel?

She emerged from the sheet and found little beads of sweat on her forehead had made her hair damp. She closed the flashlight and placed the book on the nightstand. Still trembling a little, she laid her head on the pillow. She could spot the stars through the French doors, lighting up the sky. A smile chased her jitters away when she imagined them as a long string she could follow to find her way home.

***

Hank watched Christina's peaceful, contented expression as she slept her head resting against his shoulder. His right arm wrapped underneath her back, he thought of giving her a little squeeze to prod her awake gently. After a short rest, Hank was ready to go again. Exhaustion would crucify him in the morning, but he wanted to forget and take part in the ecstasy of delving inside her once more.

Desire mounted in him. He traced the contour of Christina's breast, the one not cupped against him. When even the caress of her nipple didn't get a reaction, he capitulated deciding to let her sleep. He pulled the sheet over their naked forms and snuggled into her a little closer.

His head tilted toward hers, and he checked out the string of stars out in full force. He thought of Emma and the close call she'd barely escaped alive. The effigy of a plan stood before him, still out of reach, hazy and unstructured. He couldn't wait to bounce ideas off Matt and get feedback on his thoughts.

His eyelids felt heavy all of a sudden nevertheless grateful sleep was about to take him. Christina stirred in his arms stretching against him and wrapping her arm around his stomach. The gesture pulled him out of his sweet torpor, and he glanced her way to make sure she was still asleep.

He caressed her forehead with the brush of his lips. Had it not been for Emma, Christina might not have called him. They might never have gotten together each waylaid in their separate corners held back by stupid pride. Somehow, Emma had stepped in and mended them like some guardian angel. And for the first time in a long while, the offerings of a prayer sprung from him as he closed his eyes and asked the stars above to light Emma's way home.

<u>Thirty-Three</u>

Shots Fired

Hank surveyed the area near Franka's condo, eyes running up and down Wooster trying to catch the profile with the bent nose and the long hair. For once, they were a step ahead of the idiot. They would recognize him out of his disguise.

He called out to Matt, jogging down from Houston. "Did you check the hotdog vendor at the corner of the street?"

Matt nodded catching his breath. "He's clean." A few more intakes of air and he added, "Did you warn Franka not to answer the door—for anyone?" Matt asked.

"She's the first one I spoke to when I got here. She understands she needs to lay low." Hank checked his cell phone ringing. "What else did you find?"

"Not much, and if anyone suspects Emma of being the runaway they're not talking which is good." Matt smiled.

"Hank!" He harped as he answered his phone.

"Detective Apple, this is Jimmy Roth. I'm Franka's boyfriend."

"You can't call me here. I need to keep this line free."

"Franka's in trouble, at least I think she is."

He had Hank's attention. "Spill already."

"We were on the phone, and there was a knock on the door. I told Franka not to answer, and she mentioned you'd already warned her, but when she asked who it was, a man yelled, "Police officer." The man said he had something to hand her from Detective Apple.

"Goddamn it."

"Now when I try to call her, I can't get an answer."

"Trouble?" Matt asked.

"Yes. Matt, find the landlord. Get a key to Franka's apartment."

Matt left to find the landlord.

While Hank ran to the apartment building, Jimmy yelled through the phone. "I got a key. I'm driving up Wooster. I'll be there in thirty seconds."

Jimmy drove up, recklessly double parked and jumped out of his car while the motor still ran. He rushed toward the condo building.

"Wait a minute, fella," Hank ran after him. "You're not going in the building. Give me your key."

"The hell I'm not. She's my girlfriend, and I'm not letting anything happen to her." He swung the door open and ran for the elevator. "You want inside, Apple you'll have to keep up."

Short of shooting him which he held back from doing, Hank took the elevator with him to the eighth floor still trying to talk some sense into him. "You can't merely walk in there, goddamn you. You'll be putting her life in danger."

"Listen, Detective. I got no idea of what's going on or what the whispers are people exchange sometimes when I'm around. I hope Franka is doing what she can to protect herself." He nodded with a smug look on his face. "Here's another one for ya. I may not be aware of all the details or why, but the secrecy revolves around little Emma and keeping her hidden somehow. Now, I like Emma as much as the next guy, but Franka also needs to stay out of harm's way. She's pregnant for shit's sake."

Hank didn't say a word. He gazed at the pain on the man's face and imagined how crazy he'd be if Christina were in this position. He'd tear the walls down and blow the sucker away.

Jimmy ran off the elevator toward Franka's place. He banged on the door. "Franka, open up." No answer came, so he used his key.

"Wait," Hank whispered. "You may be signing her death warrant barging in like this." His back to the wall Hank stood beside the door, his gun cocked and ready. From the corner of his eyes, he gazed at Matt running toward them. He mouthed, "Get reinforcements—at the exits."

Matt hesitated. Then he left to comply.

Jimmy refused to listen to reason and depressed the door handle, so Hank decided to follow him in and stay glued as though he were his shadow.

In Franka's hallway stood a police officer, and he held a gun to Franka's temple. Hank surveyed the man's face—no ponytail no bent nose, altogether different features. Shit! Another mask.

"Back off and walk out of here or I'll kill her. I mean it."

Probing the situation, Hank stood close enough to spot bruises on Franka's face. She was unconscious, a dead weight for this man to carry. The crazy fool would not be able to use her as a hostage. He would have to leave her behind which meant he might not hesitate to kill her to kill all three of them.

Jimmy didn't back off. He took small steps toward the man

slowly, pleading with him as he did. "Please don't hurt her, man. She's all I've got. I love her. You have to take someone, take me. Please. I'll follow you. I won't be trouble."

"Follow me?" The officer laughed. You think I'd bother with hostages—lame bag of shit like you?" He laughed a vile, mean sound that had Hank's tough hide shiver.

"You want me to take you? Sure I'll take you—take you straight to hell," saying this he shot Jimmy, who fell hard.

"You son of a bitch," Hank uttered.

"Detective Apple. We meet at last. Can't shoot you. Need to keep making you look like a fool—gives me so much pleasure." Another ghoulish laugh. "Guess I don't have to tell you what else gives me pleasure."

Again he laughed and Hank cocked his gun ready to plug him. All he had to do was aim accurately and plug him between the eyes. He'd miss Franka entirely.

But the fool poked his gun in Franka's temple ready to shoot. "If you don't want her to go from comatose to dead, you'll throw your gun on the floor.

Hank had no doubt this maniac would shoot Franka if he didn't do as he said.

"That's right," he added as Hank complied. "Now, get over there and stare out the window."

His heart pounding and all his muscles twitching to pulverize this man, Hank faced the window as ordered. When he heard Franka's body slump to the floor, he found himself hoping she wasn't already dead. Fists clenched, tense and on edge, he waited while wondering what the idiot would do next, idiot because he was never getting out of the building alive.

The brush of quick footsteps closing in made Hank turn his head. A fraction of a second later the butt of a gun rammed the back of his neck. He thought his head might spin off.

Hank's vision blurred and he was no longer able to make out any sounds except for what seemed like the high pitch noise of a loud buzz saw.

He fell to his knees, and then allowed himself to slump to the ground. He realized although he did not have all his faculties he wasn't out, merely in excruciating pain. He couldn't figure how long he was down, though he suspected only seconds. When he got up, the buzzing in his ears had subsided to a ringing. Then he realized there was a call on his cell phone.

He answered but couldn't utter a word. He grunted, rubbing the back of his neck, pulling a hand full of blood that trickled down his jacket's sleeve. Bad wardrobe month.

"Are you all right, man?"

Dizzy, trying to put one step in front of another, he tried to force air out of his lungs. "Medic," he managed to fashion the words.

"Where is he?"

"All exits," was all Hank could utter hoping Matt would understand.

Hank wanted to get to Franka. Make sure she was still breathing. She seemed to have contusions and cuts on her arm, a bruise over her left eye.

When he did reach her and kneeled down to check, he found a large size bump at the back of her head, probably from when the creep had let her fall. But she had a pulse. He put a cushion under her head.

On his hands and knees, he crawled to where Jimmy had fallen. He checked his pulse and was surprised to find one. He'd lost a lot of blood, but he was alive.

He pushed the speed dial on his phone, still dangling from his hand. "There is a gunshot victim. Man's lost a lot of blood."

"They're on their way, Hank. Hold on. And don't worry, we've secured all the exits including the garage and the elevator dedicated to it. No way can this guy get out of here without us grabbing him. We even have some of our men on the roof, in case he tries to climb his way up—no more underestimating this prick."

A dish towel hung on the arm of the chair in front of him. He grabbed it, refusing to consider its cleanliness.

A quick inspection from his blurred vision showed the bullet had just missed Jimmy's heart. He found the entry puncture near the shoulder. He tore Jimmy's shirt open. The gesture caused him enough pain Hank thought he might keel over. He applied pressure on the wound with the cloth. He had to stop the bleeding until paramedics got there.

As he applied firm pressure with the heel of his hand, Hank noticed the flow was slowing which might also mean Jimmy's blood pressure had dropped.

At least Matt had called the man a prick Hank thought as he held his position. All this man was a dirty underhanded prick. Now that he'd checked him up close, he realized the crazy had used anonymity to hide from the law. In a city the size of New York or Newark, he recognized how the creep had easily become unseen and silent. Well, no more. He'd caught his stench and Hank could also be a crazed dog with a keen sense of smell.

The bell to the elevator sounded, and Hank prayed this

indicated the paramedics to the rescue. He could feel his mind wander, his strength waver. He didn't know how long he'd be able to keep the pressure on Jimmy's punctured shoulder.

The last words Hank made out, "We'll take over now, sir."

***

Hank opened his eyes and felt like he was on a cross. His feet were barely touching the ground and both his arms were stretched out. He glanced at Matt, who had one of Hank's shoulder hoisted under his arm and a burly police officer had the other. "Where are you guys taking me?"

"Stretchers are gone," Matt said. "We're bringing you to the hospital."

Someone opened the building's front door, and Hank tried to struggle to get free. "Let me go. I can stand." He tried to yell, but the words came out so small.

"Hank, you probably have a concussion—a bad one. You haven't seen the back of your head. It's a miracle you're even up and awake with the injury you have." Matt's tone was adamant.

"Put me down," Hank managed to say a little louder than a whisper. "Please," he begged with a throaty voice.

He caught Matt's nod to the other officer, and when Hank's feet touched the ground, he would have collapsed had Matt not held him up with an arm around his waist.

"Hold steady, Hank. Are you good?"

Hank could only totter without putting his full weight on his legs.

"Somebody, help me here," Matt yelled.

An officer came running just as Ken's car pulled up.

"I want to gawk at the son of a bitch. Take me to him," Hank said.

"Take it easy. Doctor says you can't get riled up. You'll start bleeding again."

"Where is he?" Hank couldn't get anything he said to sound louder than a whisper.

Ken came running up. "Why is this man not on a stretcher?" he barked. "He should be on his way to the hospital."

"Stretchers are gone, sir." Just as he said this, another EMS drove up with lights flashing.

"Make sure he gets on this one," Ken added his arm waving the medical team their way.

"Hank wants to see the creep." Matt told Ken under his breath.

"Can't you do this later?" Ken yelled.

"Where is he?" Hank muttered.

Releasing a tired, impatient breath, Matt held on to Hank's tall frame to keep him from toppling over. The emergency team helped to get Hank on the stretcher.

"Please," he whispered toward Matt.

Matt nodded and spoke to the medic in front. Before carrying Hank to the ambulance, they stopped by one of the police vans out on the street. Hank reached for the strength to turn his head to spot the creep. All he saw was a police hat sitting on top of a uniform with shoes sticking out underneath.

All of Hank's muscles relaxed. They'd pulverized the son of a bitch.

Thirty-Four

Recovery

Hank opened his eyes and spotted the glare of a fixture on top of his head. He squinted at the intruding flash of light and turned his head encountering more pain when he moved his neck a few inches.

The effort had him close his eyes again. Then the scent of Calvin Klein's Obsession brought him out of his lethargy. He recognized the aroma having purchased the perfume on several occasions for Christina. *Christina!*

He opened his eyes to gaze at her, at the lovely expression marred with worry. She appeared drawn as though she hadn't slept in a long time. Then the memory of the night in her arms came back to him, and he smiled at her, not quite sure if he'd be able to express this newfound, king-size need to be hers and only hers as the sensation traveled through him with a warm wash of calm.

"Thank God, Hank. Thank God," she breathed running her hand up and down his arm. "I'm sorry. All this time wasted."

He lifted his arm to catch her hand grateful he could move. Aside from the ache in his head, he didn't seem to have any other problems. "Don't apologize—not for this." He took a long breath admiring her smile wishing he could wipe away her tears. He closed his eyes and took another sharp breath. He had a difficult time stringing sentences together. His breath was short.

Warmth spread through him when she squeezed his hand. He whispered, "You complete me."

Before Christina had a chance to answer, Matt thundered as he entered the room. "How's our friend doing?"

Hank remembered to turn his head slowly this time. He faced Matt. "How long have I been here?"

"A couple of hours. It's four o'clock."

"That's most of the day. Frustration of not being able to get up and get dressed suddenly tackled him. "You didn't get the son of a bitch, did you?"

"Nope. All we got was the little pile of clothes we showed you—left in the elevator as though the fool is laughing at us."

Christina let go of Hank's hand and rose. "I'm going to get coffee. Want anything, Hank?"

He started to nod when the sting of his wound reminded him not to. "Juice, please—any kind. I'm thirsty."

"Matt?"

"No, thanks."

When she'd gone, Hank addressed Matt sternly. "How? How could the son of a bitch get away?"

"Come on, Hank. We're the only ones, you, me and Ken who are looking for a skinny man with long hair and a crooked nose." He pulled up a chair and sat down beside Hank. "Barbara doesn't count. She ain't out in the streets. She certainly hasn't told her team. We've sworn her to secrecy."

"Can't believe this." Hank tried not to shake his head.

"Well believe it. "They're all out combing the grounds for a fat semblance of a woman. All those officers understand is perp's most likely a man."

Hank didn't answer. His thoughts ran back to the morning when the fool had laughed at him.

Matt said, "Now, he's impersonating a police officer—at least he was."

"He had another disguise on." When Hank glimpsed the surprise on Matt's face, he added, "He wore a different mask."

"Well, mystery solved—the missing link." Matt rose and picked up the water pitcher. "Want some?"

"Yeah. What do you mean missing link?"

Matt propped the bent straw in the glass and used his free hand to pull on the lever at the bottom of the bed to help Hank into a sitting position. "Here."

Matt sat down again. "One of the cops manning the garage door said the only person who left the building was an old man in an old bazoo. He wore a straw hat and had a little dog beside him. He checked his license, address—everything fit."

"Had to be him."

"I thought the creep would wait for the commotion to die down, for nightfall to make his getaway. Ken, on the other hand, thought the old man in the straw hat might be him."

"You know what this means? Emma's in trouble." Hank put the glass down on the cabinet beside the bed and tried to slide his legs off the bed.

"Whoa, buddy." Matt stood in his way. "Not for another twenty-four hours or at least until morning. Doctor's orders."

"Get out of my way, Matt. Don't make this harder for me than it is."

"Relax. Ken's brain works the same way yours does—apparently. He also thought Franka might have spilled the beans about Emma's whereabouts. Who can blame her?"

"What did Ken do?"

"He ordered a chopper—airlifted Abigail and Emma off their property."

"Amelia?"

Hadn't arrived yet." Matt went to the door to help Christina with her tray.

"I brought a few more things I thought you might like, Hank. Don't know when they're going to serve dinner. Might be a while."

"Thanks, love." Hank breathed easy now that he knew Emma was safe.

Matt continued as though uninterrupted. "Abigail phoned her alarm company to have the place booby trapped. They're working on it as we speak. Soon as the perp shows up, we'll catch him. Don't worry."

"He's not going to show up at Abigail's." Hank checked out the hot wrap Christina had brought back loaded with vegetables and chili sauce. "This looks delicious. Hadn't realized how hungry I am."

"That's a good sign." Christina smiled at him.

"What do you mean he won't show up there?"

"His mind works like mine. Trust me. He already guessed we'd move Emma."

"I figure Ken thinks the same way, which is the reason why he had them airlifted and not driven out, so no one could follow them."

"Where are they?"

He glanced at Christina, and she motioned putting her hands over her ears. "Don't be silly, Christina," Hank said throwing Matt a pointed stare.

Matt checked the open door and came closer to the bed, "At the Marriott Marquis, Mid-Town Manhattan."

"Why so far from home?"

Abigail is calling the shots. Asked for an executive suite— she's paying for it."

"How is Franka?" Hank asked hoping she'd made it but worried all at once since everyone seemed to be still guessing about what Franka had told the perp.

"She hasn't recovered yet. She had internal bleeding. They had to operate. We're keeping our fingers crossed. Same hospital, just a floor below."

"Well, this explains why Abigail wanted to be in midtown Manhattan. Did she lose the baby?" Hank asked. He turned toward Christina when he heard her quick air intake. He reached to squeeze her hand.

"Don't know. Didn't know Franka was pregnant. No one told me."

"And Jimmy?"

"He's all right. Lost a lot of blood, but there's no internal damage. Bullet went right through him without tearing so much as a muscle, go figure."

Christina got up and retrieved paper napkins she dampened under the faucet in the bathroom. "Here, Hank. You have a chili mustache," she chuckled.

He wiped his mouth and continued to eat. He sensed his strength coming back with food inside his stomach.

The nurse entered and pretended to scold him. "Doctor hasn't cleared you for solid food yet."

"My fault. I brought it up from the cafeteria," Christina said.

"Food has made me feel a whole lot better," Hank added. "The reason I was weak was that I needed something to eat."

"Whatever makes you feel better," the young nurse answered. "What we like to hear."

She checked Hank's IV bag and left.

"Matt." Hank took a deep breath sensing sleep about to overtake him. The food was on his lap and he'd only eaten half of it. He wondered if the nurse had done something to his IV bag to make him sleep. "I need to get out of here. Do what you can to get it done, please."

"Hank!" Christina protested. "Don't you think you should get better first?"

"That idiot isn't stopping for anything. You and I would be crushed if anything happened to Emma. She depends on us."

Christina glanced at Matt with a tearful expression. Hank realized she didn't want him to go back out there, but she also recognized the wisdom of what he'd just said. She nodded toward Matt as if her gesture might make a difference.

"I have a plan," Hank added. "You and I know who the man is under the mask. We have to start bringing him into the picture which is how we're going to catch him and get the media on board once we do."

Matt bowed his head and groaned. "I'll get you out, Hank. But not before morning," Matt said, saluting Christina before he walked out.

***

Later that evening Emma still had the nose in her granny Dottie's diary. Bustled from Abigail's place to the Marriott, circumstances had forced postponement of her much-awaited meeting with Amelia and through it all she'd kept on reading, learning what several generations of women had accomplished already.

She'd cried when she'd witnessed her grandmother's shrieks about Franka, ranting about the place as though pacing and pulling her hair out would change anything. She'd hidden in her room terrified upon learning about Hank's injuries.

The only solace she gathered came from the diary's energy and all the information the teachings brought her. The book's writings had kept her from falling apart. Generations of women that all had one specialty or another and here she seemed to be able to accomplish the lot of them.

Her grandmother was finally asleep. Earlier she'd left Emma with a police officer to see Franka at the hospital. They didn't think it was a good idea for Emma to show herself in public, so she'd stayed in her room.

Upon her return, Abigail had called out to her through the closed bedroom door. "You haven't even touched your delicious meal, Emma." Her meal was still on the credenza in the hallway. Emma hadn't mentioned she didn't like pickled herring and beats, food her grandmother had ordered because she was determined to fatten her up. She wasn't her usual nurturing self, so she'd found it best no to argue. Understandably, she worried about Franka, who had not yet recovered.

"Emma, did you hear me?"

She would have to answer, or Abigail would storm into her room to make sure she was still in the suite. "I'm not hungry, Grandma."

Now, at last, the hotel suite was quiet and dark. She had to do something about her aunt Franka, one of her favorite people in the world.

She got up and tiptoed to the window. She'd tried to open it but hadn't been able to do so. Didn't matter. All she needed was to dress appropriately and carry the piece of paper filled with her notes inside her jacket's pocket in case she forgot the thought and incantation to get home again.

She gazed around the room one last time to imprint its familiarity in her mind. She removed the amulet she wore on a chain. She didn't relish leaving the little oudjat behind, but with the precious stone close to her heart, she would be grounded and unable to lift off.

In her jacket pocket, she had two pieces of paper: the address to New York Downtown Hospital with her aunt's room number and the Marriott address for her return.

She whispered a little prayer, sat on the bed and crossed her arms as she placed a palm on each shoulder. *Lift me away oh Universe lift me away so I may fly to serve a loved one best.* Emma mentally recited the address of the hospital and her aunt's room number praying she would land in the right place.

Emma opened her eyes in a room that was dark and quiet. Street sounds busy and frantic had her hoping she'd landed in the right place. She opened her eyes and stared at the pale white flask of an IV bag perched high on a pole as the phosphorescent glow caught the light of the moon's crescent through the open curtain.

Gently she approached the bed and gazed at her aunt's face. Franka appeared peaceful and asleep, and she reached for her hand lying on top of the blanket.

"Aunt Franka?" Doctors said she'd fallen into a coma, and all they could do was hope she might wake up. She took one of her hands in hers and rubbed it gently. "It's okay, Aunt Franka. The evil man is gone. You're going to be all right now."

After cooing to her aunt for a few more minutes, a soft moan echoed her words. Franka opened her eyes. Immediately she began to cry as she stared right through Emma. "Emma," she whispered. "I didn't tell him where you are."

"He's gone, Aunt Franka. And I'm fine. He doesn't know where I am."

"I didn't tell him." She wept, and Emma grabbed a tissue to wipe her eyes and dry the tears streaming down her cheeks.

"Don't cry. You're okay now."

"No. I'm not," Franka kept on crying. "I lost my baby. They took her away. She died."

Emma stretched out on the edge of the bed against Franka to be close to her, to whisper in her ear. "She's not lost. She will be back, I promise. When it's safe, she will return."

Emma's words softly spoken in Franka's ears finished drawing her from the half sleep in which she hovered. Franka turned her head toward Emma. "Emma? What are you doing here?"

Quickly Emma slid off the bed. She stretched her arm and pulled a straight chair closer to Franka, sat down and held her aunt's hand in hers. "I came to tell you not to worry about your little girl. She'll be back, the little angel with the blond curls and the blue eyes. I promise."

"How do you know this? How is it possible?"

Emma smiled, thrilled her aunt was awake. She would recover quickly now. "Amelia was supposed to come visit me today. Because of that man, we had to postpone our visit. Just a postponement. That's all."

Franka squeezed Emma's hands. "I dreamt Jimmy was shot. He fell. I saw him in my dream—he took a bullet for me. Is he? Is he dead?"

"He's not dead. He's alive and well. He did take a bullet for you. By some miracle, I overheard grandma say the slug had gone right through him without causing any damage."

Franka let go of Emma's hands and seemed to relax. "I wanted a sign," Franka whispered. Her voice was faint. Emma had to strain to listen. "Whether I should spend my life with Jimmy. I wanted to die when I thought I'd lost him."

Emma acknowledged Franka's words with a squeeze of her hand and waited until she fell asleep. She was out of danger. Emma breathed easily again. Her aunt would sleep through the night and in the morning, wake up and be grateful for all the blessings she'd received. She bent and kissed her forehead. It was hot but moist. Fever had broken.

She prepared to leave so no one would see her on the premises. She checked the address to the Marriott committing it to memory and assumed the same position of crossed arms with both palms reaching toward her shoulders.

She invoked the sentence: *Lift me away, oh Universe, lift me away so I may fly home unharmed.* She fixed her mind on the loving souls surrounding the living. She felt herself lift and be carried off in a gentle cloud of weightless warmth.

Seconds later, she landed in her room at the Marriott at the same spot from where she'd left barely twenty minutes earlier.

She stuck her face to the window to watch the rain. Lightning in the background drew a fiery specter in the sky while her eyes traced the water droplets running down the pane like tears. She listened to the city's cries and sorrows, the thunder no match for them. Some people she received louder than others. The one she'd gotten accustomed to, she recognized most of all. He was in agony somewhere in the little house where she'd landed. He was writhing on the floor lamenting as though someone tortured him.

Before she even got undressed, Emma walked to the night-stand and placed the little oudjat around her neck. All the unwanted sights and sounds ceased. She'd be at peace for a little while.

<u>*Thirty-Five*</u>

Etchings Of A Plan

In Hank's hospital room at six a.m. the next morning, commotion overruled the tranquility from the night before.

This morning Matt, Kenneth Riley, Christina, and Emma's dad Patrick Willis clamored for his attention. Meanwhile, Hank wore the brave face of being healthy and fully mobile as he stood on wobbly legs. The sham cost him more pain than Hank had imagined since he'd slept fitfully, nightmares yanking him in and out of sleep. Nevertheless, he had work to do and was in a hurry to put his plan into action.

"Can you please not all talk at the same time?" Hank sat down on the bed with blessed relief. "Matt, please close the door."

He looked at Patrick Willis. "Didn't Abigail call you?"

"Blubbering and crying. Had a hard enough time making out what she said. What's going on? Where's Emma? Where's my daughter?"

"Lower your voice. For what we can tell, this idiot might be standing in the hall listening."

He watched Patrick's lips curl into a menacing smirk and his hands become fists.

"Where?" he breathed.

"She's with Abigail in an undisclosed location." He put up his hand to prevent Patrick from yelling out again. "This maniac is no longer the fat woman every police officer in the city thinks he is. He has other disguises. Yesterday, he made his way into Franka's apartment."

"I know. She told us. My wife is still with her."

"Did she tell you he got into her apartment by claiming to be a police officer? I was there facing another one of his disguises. One we've never seen before."

"In other words, you're saying this prick is uncatchable."

"Not true. We just have to be smarter than him. Start thinking the way he does."

"How are you supposed to do that? And where is Emma? You can't keep her from me."

Ken stepped in. "Mr. Willis, if I may."

"Who are you?"

"Kenneth Riley, captain in charge." Ken dug in his briefcase and threw a cellular phone in Patrick's direction. "This is how you will reach Emma, and how Emma will reach you. There's a private number attached to the phone, and I suggest you don't share it with anyone else but your wife."

Patrick stared at the little phone he'd caught midair and checked out front and back as though searching for a number. He nodded as if only now realizing the seriousness of the situation, a situation Hank realized he would not be able to manhandle with force or a temper tantrum.

"Emma is equipped with the same sort of device. Speed dial of 9 will reach her. She can do the same to call you or your wife.

Number will never register on the phone or anywhere else," Ken finished.

Patrick nodded. "Franka never told the creep where Emma was. I knew she wouldn't."

"Yes, she told me. I was in her room earlier going over the story she is allowed to mention," Ken added. "The fact this guy wore the disguise of a police officer will nullify him as our suspect. More than likely, the man yesterday is believed to be a career criminal who took advantage of the number of cops surrounding the neighborhood by disguising himself as one of them to steal from the tenants in the building."

"What?"

"To corroborate the theory, a handful of tenants reported thefts yesterday. Luckily, they were not at home when the robberies occurred."

Patrick eyed everyone in the room with a raised eyebrow as though Ken treated him like a patsy. Hank recognized the expression too well.

"This is the story we are sticking with, Mr. Willis—a story I advise you to learn," Ken said in menacing tones.

Hank held pride as he eyed his captain. Up until now, he'd doubted the wisdom of his decision to bring Ken in on the conflict. Now he lauded the same decision which meant he would not only receive Ken's help, but someone with Ken's clout would step in with more authority.

Patrick slipped the little phone into his pocket and nodded repeatedly. After all, these precautions were taken to protect his daughter. Head down he saluted everyone and left.

Hank stood and gave Christina a hug, a hug he prolonged

drawing much-needed energy from the embrace. When he withdrew, he caught not merely shyness on her expression, but surprise he'd displayed affection in public. Hank had never done this before. "I'll keep you informed, Christina. I promise."

She reached to peck him on the cheek, big smile lighting up her eyes as she squeezed his hand. Standing in the doorway, she saluted Kenneth Riley and turned toward Matt. "Take care of him, please."

"Easier said than done, Christina," Matt said rubbing the top of his head. "I will try."

Once they'd gone and only Matt, Ken, and Hank remained, Hank was dying to ask. "Is this true? About the tenants calling in with reports of theft?"

Matt laughed. "Five of them called in and reported expensive jewelry missing."

"Can't be true. Can it?"

"Of course, not," Ken breathed. "Oh, they called all right. New-York Chief Lang told me they did. Only the three of us know. Obviously, these people did not have anything stolen."

"What about the little dog?" Hank asked.

"That's what started the phony rash of thefts. One miniature poodle yapping at the door—unlocked, as per victim. Next thing, our man opens the door and makes off with the dog."

"Where is it now?"

"He left it on the street. Someone called the pound. Dog was equipped with a chip. Owner picked up the pooch a couple of hours later," Ken said.

Hank chuckled. "All thieves aren't behind bars. Well, at least the story works in our favor right?"

Ken sobered at the sound of Hank's joke, and Hank read the little twitch of his right eye, his captain was uncomfortable.

Matt also snickered. "Lucky we won't arrest the five of them for insurance fraud."

Hank lowered his voice. "So, Franka didn't tell." He wanted to ask Ken what bothered him but didn't dare.

Ken cracked his knuckles wearing his round beady eyes. "She swears she did not. I'm having them flown back to Abigail's place later today." He took a deep breath and eyed Hank with curiosity. "What's your plan?"

"Still sketchy. One thing I do know. We have to bring this Morey Boleslaw into the picture. He might elude us for months otherwise. Plus, if we don't bring him into the picture soon, no one is liable to believe us when we tell the world he is our man."

"We had better be able to prove he is our man is all I'm saying." Ken walked away from both of them to stare out the window, jiggling some change in his pocket. "Wouldn't want him to get away on a technicality."

Hank figured he hid something and worried about what he might say next.

Ken turned and eyed both the officers up and down—wanting to impart his next trump card Hank thought. "What if this crazy lunatic gets tired of chasing shadows—young Emma— and seizes the next little girl he comes across?"

Hank didn't like the sound of that. "He won't. He's obsessed with Emma Willis."

"Is he now? He told you this?"

Hank perked up to shelve his pain as adrenaline raced through his veins. From the corner of his eye, he could see Matt's own eyes fixed on some spot on the floor. "What are you getting at?"

"Simple. You and I cannot predict what a crazy man will do next. No one can. Yesterday proves that." Ken extended both hands as though weighing something heavy. "This bastard fits no mug shot we can decipher. I've had two of my best psychological profilers on this case, and they can't find zip. Doesn't help the man's a ghost. Nevertheless, this is where we stand."

"Meaning?"

"You've got one week, Hank. If we can't get anything to stick in seven days, I'm turning this over to the FBI."

"You son of a bitch," Hank whispered. He walked over to where Ken stood, fists clenched while itching for a fight.

"I'm going to pretend I didn't hear that. A man with a blow to the head is liable to say crazy things he doesn't mean."

"You promised. All this heartfelt crap about you being a father."

"So why did you come to me?"

Hank eyed Matt, who was flexing both hands, one of his many anger management exercises. He remained silent taking his cue from Matt and controlled his anger.

"You came to me because you'd done all you could on your own, both of you. You needed help. Age-old story: cavalry top of the hill."

"I trusted you. That's why I came to you," Hank muttered surprised he could still stand and possess the strength to argue.

"You trusted me to help and to provide you with muscle, more resources. I repeat. All the bastard has to do is change his mind, forget about Emma, and get his hands on another victim. God help us if this happens."

"He won't," Hank yelled.

"Worst scenario," Ken continued. "Perp tires of the chase, tires of the heat and decides to disappear—go underground. Then what do we do? Wait for the next victim?"

Hank hung his head. Yes, they had the man's identity. Only they had no proof which meant spending all their time watching him except if he disappeared. Pain-killers aside, lucid or not he could not fault his captain's arguments. He also sensed Ken's dilemma. He'd jostled with the same guilt of breaking his promise to Emma the other night on the way to the office.

Matt had long since given up the anger he replaced by a nervous smirk, only now he rubbed his bald head with the frequency he'd use to give it a polished sheen.

Ken raised his right leg to prop his foot on the chair. "Did you ever think what would happen if the media got a whiff of what we know and are keeping secret? What Lang would say if he found out we allowed him and his men to traipse through Soho on a wild goose chase?"

"Seven days," Hank muttered defeated and out of breath.

"I'll be there to help in any way I can. I'm on your side. I say let's get the son of a bitch."

Hank sat down on the edge of the bed his face in his hands. He'd had the wind knocked out of him. Now the bad bruise throbbed at the back of his head, and the imperceptible twitch of a sharp knife cozied up to slit his throat.

"You sure you're up to this?" Matt asked.

"Yeah." Hank realized a slight fever caused his lightheadedness. "Once the nurse changes my dressing, we're off."

Ken walked toward the door. "Keep me advised of all moves,"

he requested. Depressing the handle he added, "Jimmy has been briefed."

"Why?"

"Nothing important, at least for now. Was told Emma can identify the man who's responsible for the rash of killings lately. Wrong place at the wrong time. Man knows she can identify him. That's all." Ken stared from one to the other, and Hank realized his and Matt's stunned faces spoke volumes. "Don't worry. He's sworn to secrecy."

After he'd left, Hank stared at Matt to gauge what he had to say. Matt hoisted a shoulder. "Short of killing the bastard which is what I maintain we do, we had better get the proof we need." He helped Hank to get to his feet. "I say we go eat breakfast somewhere. Get food in your belly. Then you can walk me through your plan."

Hank nodded meekly. "Did you bring the turtleneck I asked you for?"

"Yeah."

The nurse knocked on the door frame before coming into the room. "I see someone's going home today," she said in a large expansive voice softened with a bright smile.

"I'll wait outside," Matt said walking to the door. He turned and gave Hank the nod. "After breakfast, I think our first visit should be to Emma."

Hank refused to answer in front of the nurse.

***

In another room one floor down, curtains were pulled against the bright sunny day shielding Franka and her soft whimpers from the gaiety outside.

"Don't cry, Franka. You did the right thing protecting Emma." Jimmy held her hand while the gloom around him matched his mood. "Doctors said you would have no trouble getting pregnant again. We have all our lives in front of us."

Franka realized Jimmy kept a brave face to boost her morale. Doctor had mentioned they wanted to keep her under observation. Only she figured they worried about how she might react to the trauma more so than they worried about her health.

Jimmy had to be devastated she thought. "I'd like to get out of here, Jimmy. I'm fine, really I am."

"Doctor's coming by in a little while." He grabbed both her hands and rubbed his thumb over the engagement ring he'd given her. "I'm going to get you a better ring," he said. "I promise."

"I don't want a better ring." She brought one of his hands to her wet face and kissed the blistered knuckles. Abigail had told her how he'd slammed his fist into the wall when he'd heard about the baby. "I just want to spend the rest of my life with you, and I want this to start as soon as possible."

He hid his face from her, but she still felt his tears on her hand. "Me too," he grumbled.

Jimmy would never find out about the hesitation she'd felt about marrying him. Luckily out of all this pain and frustration, she'd found her way to love.

Thirty-Six

Visiting Slime

The eggs and toast had gone a long way to restoring Hank's strength if not his morale. Sitting at a sidewalk café, he couldn't help relive the day before. "That son of a bitch. If you'd stared into his eyes and recognized how he took pleasure out of the chaos he inflicted."

"You're going to need to get past this. We need all our wits to get the maniac. If you're stuck on this creep, he's won again because you won't remember anything else about yesterday."

"Yeah, you're right."

"What about the night before last when Emma found herself in his house—of all places? She didn't describe anything to you?"

"A few things. Outside the convenience store, I had a hunch the man was bad news."

"What man?"

"I witnessed our perp walk from his house to the store. I didn't go in because I knew Emma was in there, and for some reason, I didn't want him to spot me. Turns out my hunch paid off."

"Was he running after Emma?"

"No. If he had been, the bastard would have torn the place apart to find Emma. He came out with some cola, cigarettes, and a few other things."

"How do you know what was in the bag?"

"He fell to his knees, a few feet from my car. Dropped the bag he was carrying. Held onto his head as though it might fall off and roll away." Hank took another gulp of his coffee. "I waited until he was gone, then I ran in to fetch Emma. She told me the man was our perp."

"God, this would mean he's crazy and sick in the head." Matt pushed himself away from the table.

"Might only be crazy because he's sick in the head. Either way, he's a live bomb ticking away."

"What's our first stop?"

"This morning, my first stop was to pay a little visit to Boleslaw's place of business. His address and work number are on file. He gave them to us."

"You see, now why would he do this? Doesn't make sense. Puts him on the grid." Matt signaled for the check while the girl was outside.

"Merely wanted to cook up an alibi, a reason to give him an explanation for chasing Tommy—a model citizen."

"I say we talk to Emma." Matt rose to take the bill and plunked money on the table.

Hank checked his watch as he rose from the table slowly. "We will. First, I want to investigate the warehouse business again. Something doesn't jive."

They walked to the unmarked car Matt had taken off the police lot to pick up Hank at the hospital. The car had no radio, and Ken had agreed to handle all communications by cell phone.

Matt stopped at the passenger door where Hank stood. "Hank.

Seven days—seven. Why would you want to waste time on the warehouse? A forensic team went over it. They found traces of blood but none that matched those of the victims."

"A forensic team? Two guys went down to the warehouse," Hank yelled as he got into the car. He reached to close the door pain marring his face. Getting in and out of the car gave him the most trouble. "They had no warrant. They took samples of blood in plain sight."

Once Matt was in the driver's seat, he asked. "What do you hope to find?"

"Emma told us specifically that our man was in the warehouse when he killed his victims. You and I both know their blood is somewhere on the premises."

"Yeah, we'd need to rip the place apart plank by plank to make a more thorough search."

"Exactly. The only reason we can't is that Cindy could not locate an owner. "

"Where to?" Matt droned.

"Essex County Hall of Records."

"Such a waste of time," Matt muttered as he spun the car into a uey to head west toward Newark. "Cindy dealt with the matter. She's very competent."

"Of course, she is, but Cindy is not aware of all the facts is she?"

Matt drove in silence, and Hank lay back on the pillow Matt had brought grateful his neck and head would get to rest for a while. "Thanks for the pillow by the way." He tilted his seat back and closed his eyes.

Next, when Hank opened his eyes, Matt was shaking his arm.

He sat up with a grimace of pain and eyed the tall building of the Hall of Records. "You should park on West Market Street. There is a door at the side."

"That's where we are."

"God we got here fast." They walked toward the building, and Hank suffered from the pounding at the back of his head. He went to rub his neck but thought better and resisted the urge.

"Are you all right? Painkillers get their revenge once they are out of your system." Matt appeared concerned.

"Didn't take any painkillers this morning. Can't afford to."

Once at the desk of one of the clerks, a tall, bespectacled woman with an inane half smile hovering on her expression accosted them with a sigh.

Hank showed his badge. "I'm from the Second precinct, and I need information on a warehouse in East Orange, on North Walnut Street."

She stared at both of them with narrowed eyes her smile never wavering and checked her computer screen for answers. "Ah," she nodded as though pleased with herself. "Thought the request sounded familiar." She turned her screen for him to verify. "Cindy Revere from your precinct, Detective called for information on that particular building. I gave her all I had."

"Are you sure you gave her everything? Building's got an owner."

She slid the screen back to her eyes appearing to search the folder. "Absolutely. I remember telling her building belongs to Karl Schmidt and Sons."

"Got to be more information than this. Listen." Hank stared at the woman's name tag. "Miss Clark this is part of a murder investigation. Imperative we find out who owns this building—not just a name, an address an actual location of an owner."

She released a long, annoyed breath but never lost the unnerving smile. "There is a small annotation here." She sat down on one of the stools and proceeded to dig deeper.

Hank caught the flicking of Miss Clark's computer screen as it scanned through various images. "Says here the warehouse was sold, August 2002."

"To who?"

"No mention of any name. Probably some corporation—could be foreign owners. They purchased the going concern, the name and the storage facility."

"You mean there is a building, and you don't have an owner, who it belongs to?"

"Detective Apple. Around us is a big county. Do you know how many vacant buildings there are in Newark?"

"I understand, but someone has to account for them."

"Of course. In the case of this building, taxes have been paid twice a year. There have been two inspections since the business was purchased." There were more clicks to her computer keyboard. "Last time was in 2009. A request was issued for some repairs, mostly to bring the structure up to code. Says here, all of them were agreed upon and executed."

Hank glanced at Matt. "Who pays the taxes?"

"As far as I can see here, taxes are paid by solicitors." She put her hand up forestalling his next question. "Leventhal and Associates."

Before Hank could voice his next question, she handed him a paper on which she'd scribbled the lawyer's address her smile a permanent fixture.

"Thank you." As irritating as the woman was she had delivered.

They practically ran down the broad corridors back to the car. Hank slowed down a couple of times. Matt waited for him. "Where does this leave us, Hank? How will this prove Morey Boleslaw is our killer?"

"We are one step closer," Hank said as he slid into the passenger's seat. "Think of it," he added once Matt drove. "If we can tie Boleslaw to the ownership of a building where the murders took place, we're one step closer to getting a warrant to search his house."

"But the blood …" Matt didn't repeat the argument. "Did Ken show you the report on the blood findings?"

"Yes. Report said gender was male." He glanced at Matt. "Hey." Hank waited for Matt to stop at the light. "Come to think of it lab did a GCMS test."

"A gas chromatography–mass—whatever?"

"Yeah. Mass-spectrometry. They found large quantities of barbiturates and antidepressants in the blood."

"Like someone needing help with their head about to fall off and roll down the street?"

Hank's face broadened into a wide smile. "You got it. Never put the two together."

"You just spotted him the day before yesterday." Hank sat back unable to wipe the grin off his face. "Might be the creep's blood," Matt said.

"I mean, I lay in bed last night unable to sleep thinking the proof we need has to be in that warehouse. I just know it.

"Well, we'll soon find out." Matt parked by the side of the street indicating, "Leventhal."

"This is a hole," Hank said as he stepped out of the car not impressed with the man's office.

"Yeah, can't be too many associates in the place," Matt chuckled.

They didn't need to ring a bell or speak through an intercom or even knock on the door. A man spotted them walking up to the entrance through the bay window. Hank caught him waddling to the door as fast as his heavy set frame allowed him to move. "Definitely no room for associates," Hank grumbled drawing a chuckle from Matt.

"Can I help you, gentlemen?" The big man asked the exertion having him wheeze through his words.

"Leventhal?" Hank asked.

"Yes, I'm Morgan Leventhal?"

Since the man had not yet invited them in, Hank pulled out his badge. "Detective Apple. My partner and I have a couple of questions we'd like to ask you." The smile hovering on Leventhal's features disappeared completely. He turned and walked back to his office leaving them to close the door behind them.

Sitting at his desk, Leventhal asked. "What's this all about?"

Investigating the owner of a warehouse in East Orange, North Walnut Street. County Hall of Records states you pay the taxes and are responsible for any repairs and maintenance. Do you own this place?"

"No. Of course not. If you're asking me to divulge who does, I'm afraid this is attorney-client privileged information."

"That's bullshit, and you know it. We're homicide detectives.

Several murders have allegedly been committed in the warehouse in question."

"Doesn't implicate my client in any misdeed. The warehouse is empty—for now. Could have been used by anyone."

"Well," Matt continued. "Since you are responsible for paying the taxes the upkeep of maintenance and repairs, perhaps you are the one who used it?"

Leventhal rose from his full made-to-measure chair and eyed them sternly. "I think you should leave before I sue you for slander."

Well, he has balls Hank thought. Leventhal's posture struck a familiar chord with Hank. "I have one more question," Hank added.

The lawyer raised his chin a few inches.

"May I make a quick phone call before I leave?" Leventhal tilted his head to the side, a victory smirk slicing his flabby cheeks.

Hank turned and walked out of earshot. He dialed Ken's cell phone number. "It's Hank," he whispered. "We're in the office of an attorney by the name of Leventhal. Matt and I are trying to obtain information on the owners of the property on North Walnut."

"Morgan Leventhal?"

"Yeah. Sounds familiar to me somehow."

"Let me at the bastard. Bar revoked his license four years ago in a similar case."

Hank bit his bottom lip not to smile outright and walked back to face the attorney's smug expression.

"Someone on the phone would like to talk to you," Hank mentioned with as much nonchalance as he could muster. He indicated his cell phone.

When Leventhal did not move a muscle in his direction—the only sign he had heard Hank's request in the haughty raise of his eyebrows—Hank walked over to the desk and waved the handset in his face.

Leventhal grabbed the phone beads of sweat forming on his forehead and top lip causing Hank to hope he would not soak his cell phone.

The man turned toward the window with his back to them.

Before the lawyer had time to utter a word, Hank realized Ken had started in on him. He could not make out Ken's words, but he could hear him yelling from where he stood. Hank stared at Matt's round eyes loaded with questions and winked at him.

The one-sided conversation went on for a few minutes, the only pauses apparently Ken's while all the lawyer did was grunt at each and every break.

Finally, Leventhal must have been left hanging on the line as he stared at the phone having become silent.

His hand fell to his side still holding the handset as he stared out the window, speechless.

When he gave the phone to Hank, he said, "Certainly don't want a repeat of what happened four years ago," he mumbled to himself. Then he added louder as an explanation, "Swindled by a crooked tax evasion scam—two very respectable businessmen laundering money." With a sigh, he sat down his eyes on Hank stowing his phone. "Kenneth Riley helped me get my license back."

"Did you investigate this buyer?"

"I did. Of course, I did."

When Leventhal stared at him, Hank could see how tired and

drawn he appeared to be. "Found nothing out of the usual—A bright kid searching for extra storage for his inventory. Only reason buyer wanted to stay anonymous was he didn't want the seller finding out who he was."

"Why not?"

"Buyer's related to Karl Schmidt and Sons."

Statement knocked the wind out of Hank. He glanced at Matt, who merely shrugged. He flopped into the nearest chair. "What kind of relation?"

"His son, youngest of three."

Hank spotted Matt taking the other chair and giving three swipes to his bald head.

"So buyer is a Schmidt."

Leventhal nodded. "Yes. He is a Schmidt. Only, he doesn't go by that name. Old man Schmidt disinherited him. Not sure why. Goes by his mother's name."

"Where's old man Schmidt now?"

Leventhal got up to retrieve a folder from one of his cabinets. "Died in a warehouse fire, 1998." He slid the file on the desk in Hank's direction.

Hank picked up the folder, and Matt drew his chair closer. "Arson?"

"Nothing left to pick through. Deemed accidental."

Matt read the one-page report, then asked, "Where are the other two sons?"

"Germany. Put all their assets in the hands of one of my associates at the time, packed up and left, one week after the warehouse fire."

Hank eyed Matt. "Think something spooked them?" Matt

raised a shoulder his frustration evident as Hank watched him chew the corner of his mouth. Matt directed his rising anger toward Leventhal. "I can't believe you dug up all this shit, and you don't have the buyer's name. Makes no sense."

"Well, first of all, Detective," Hank caught arrogance in Leventhal's tone. "Schmidt is one of my oldest clients." He extended his arms to represent the room around them. "This storefront is a mere shadow of the practice I used to manage."

Sitting back in his chair, he savored the moment a few more seconds and Hank hated the cat and mouse game he played.

"Second of all, I do know the buyer's name. How could I not? This whole argument has been about me revealing the buyer's name hasn't it?"

Hank observed Matt rubbing his knuckles a sign he needed to step in. "What's his name? Where can we find him," Hank said with barely contained impatience.

Leventhal was up again rummaging in his folders. "I always forget his name," he mumbled to himself, and Hank wondered why he didn't have all this information on computer files. "Not Lillian Gersten's son," Leventhal continued, "Had a different mother," he said as he picked up a couple of folders.

"You must have seen him."

"Of course. Skinny kid, long hair."

"Crooked nose?" Hank wanted to know.

Leventhal hesitated his forehead scrunched in recall. Met him once eleven years ago. Come to think of it, yes. Prominent nose only he's not a kid. Should be forty-five or so by now."

Leventhal opened three folders. From the middle one, he produced a picture. "Here is a picture I snapped when he purchased the warehouse."

Hank took the photo lawyer handed him. "He let you photograph him?"

"Nah. Secret little camera—to protect my interests, you understand." Then he pulled another piece of paper. "Maurice Boleslaw. That's his name."

Hank smiled as he glanced at Matt, who nearly fell off his chair. He showed him the photo while giving him a my-hunch-was-right nod.

"You know him?" Leventhal's eyebrows rose abruptly giving him a worried expression.

Let's just say we've come across him lately," Hank answered.

Hank and Matt both rose. Hank bent closer to the lawyer sitting behind his desk and spoke in hushed tones "If you value your life, Leventhal I wouldn't repeat anything that went on here especially not to our friend, Maurice Boleslaw. This man has a foul temper— extremely dangerous."

"You must think I'm crazy," Leventhal uttered with a frozen smile resembling a rictus of death on his face.

"No. Boleslaw is. You have no idea how much he is," Matt spat at him.

Hank turned his back and walked toward the door followed by Matt.

Leventhal rose staying where he stood. "Now I'll be able to count the number of clients I have on the one hand."

Hank stopped in his tracks. Why would the lawyer attempt to draw pity from them? What sort of manipulation was in progress?

He walked back to where the lawyer stood and went behind his desk, pushed him back enough to have him vacillate and lose his footing so that he took a few steps back to regain his balance. "What are you doing?" He brushed off his suit and coughed his frustration in Hank's face.

"I swear, Leventhal. You breathe one word of this to anyone, and I will personally be back to make your life a living hell."

"Take it easy. I said I wasn't going to say anything."

"If you do, you will be an accessory to the recent murder of three little girls. Believe it." Hank waited to gauge a better read of Leventhal's expression and witnessed him cave, floundering as though he was rethinking an earlier position. "Boleslaw is not walking away from these charges, and any attempt to secure Boleslaw's loyalty in exchange for money will only get his lawyer in jail right next to him—or dead," he threw the last word.

Hank backed away and scowled at him. "After all, Leventhal. A meager living is better than no living at all. Make sure you get your priorities straight."

Thirty-Seven

Hank Consolidates His Plan

att drove to Abigail's house, and when he reached Englewood Cliffs, he complained about how all the lanes and croissants and dead-end streets looked identical. Hank, on the phone with Ken, redirected him a couple of times shortening the distance indicated on the GPS.

Two gates later after swiping the card given to them, through yet another sensor, they arrived in front of the central lawns.

Hank put his cell phone away and poked his head out the window. "Abigail wasn't exaggerating when she said they'd tightened security."

"What did Ken have to say?" Matt's curiosity stemmed from chewing on bits and pieces of Hank and Ken's conversation the whole time he drove.

Hank hated repeating. "Yeah, I should have put him on speaker phone." How communications got lost sometimes. "In a nutshell, he's having the report on the warehouse updated, and the blood from forensic checked more closely—to profile who would need to pack all those drugs."

"And."

"He's glad we're making leeway, but like you, he believes

what we found still doesn't tie our man to any crime—all circumstantial. He's already checked out Boleslaw thoroughly. Never encountered a parking ticket. Says if we get a search warrant and find blood from the victims in the warehouse, still doesn't tie him. All this would accomplish might be to give him enough notoriety to open his trap against Emma." Hank rubbed his forehead with a grimace.

"You sure you're all right? Personally, I think you're overdoing it. Doctor didn't even want to release you this morning."

"I'm all right." Hank lied.

Emma sat at her computer when Abigail opened her door. "Emma, sweetie Hank Apple and his partner are here to talk to you."

As soon as they crossed the threshold, Emma got up, grabbed a teddy bear amongst a vast collection of stuffed animals surrounding her work area, and curled up on a divan in shades of gold and saffron next to the French doors.

Hank hesitated. She somehow seemed so much younger than her age today, holding on tightly to the large bear sitting in her lap as though he could shield her from the outside world. "Hey, Emma."

"Hi," she said in a small voice.

Hank spotted the oudjat hanging from her neck. With the responsibility this fragile and gentle child was made to bear, the piece of jewelry dangling on a chain around her neck took the shape of a large wooden cross.

"I guess you and your grandma have been shoved around these past few days."

She pinched her lips as she nodded, her eyes as round as saucers.

"Listen, Emma." Hank looked around and realized he needed to sit. He opted for a small stool which he brought closer to face her. "I wondered if you remembered anything about the house or the area where I picked you up in Belleville. Any little detail you might recall anything to help us build a case against this man?" He got up and traded the stool for a place on the divan. "The reason we need to make a case against him, even though we are convinced he is the killer we need to apprehend, is we don't want to involve you by using your testimony. Do you understand?"

"I do. And thank you." She took a deep breath, and he had the impression she fought tears. "I'm sorry you were hurt. I hope you get better soon."

Hank rubbed her hand and sensed how deeply her fingers dug into the stuffed animal. "Thank you. Can you describe his house a little?"

"Just as I told you the other night, small like a doll house. The room was dirty, smelled dirty. A dresser stood against one wall." She stopped talking and putting her teddy bear aside, she got up and went to her table beside the bed. "I was shocked when I found I'd fully materialized in a stranger's room. I made sure by touching things around me." She walked back to Hank. "I grabbed this little locket by mistake. I forgot to put the chain back. I'm sorry," she said as she handed the chain and pendant to Hank.

Hank opened the locket, and though the picture was small, he recognized Anne Ripley, Boleslaw's third victim. He handed the pendant to Matt his eyebrows arched, and his whole being itched to tear the man apart.

Once he'd checked the locket, Matt began to pace. "Son of a bitch he is the killer." Turning toward Hank, he added. "How do we prove his guilt? Can't get a warrant on the grounds of—well, we can't," Matt glanced at Emma instead of finishing his sentence.

Emma sat down at her computer swiveling the chair to face them. "I could go back and search the house for you?" Hank caught her using the back of her hand to swipe at a tear.

Hank got up slowly. "Thank you, Emma, but finding evidence like this would be inadmissible in court." He walked over to where she sat and gave her a hug, planting a kiss on top of her head. "You're incredibly brave to suggest this," he said as he flicked her chin to stare better into her face. "Don't worry. It's our job to get him and we will."

Just before leaving, Hank turned toward her. "Do you think you would be able to recognize him if he wore another disguise?"

Matt had continued going and was already down the round staircase. Hank waited for Emma's answer. He dreaded her hesitation—the indecision signaling her old trust issue rearing its pointy head. "I will not divulge your answer to anyone, Emma. Matt and I will be the only ones who know. You have my word."

She rose from the chair and curled up on the sofa. Emma bent her head against the bear. "Without wearing the oudjat, I would be able to recognize him anywhere—under any disguise."

"Thank you. "

"Oh, and Hank?"

He waited while holding his breath.

"You don't have to be afraid of him hiding, or disappearing. I can find him wherever he is." A pale smile brought color back to her face.

Hank felt the lump in his throat, a lump of gratitude and admiration for the courage of this slight ten-year-old girl.

"That is," Hank took a few seconds to compose himself. "Extremely good to hear. Thank you."

***

Hank was quiet on his way to Boleslaw's place of business, trying to rehearse how he would play the game.

As they approached the air conditioning store, Matt asked him. "Ready for your academy performance?"

"Park a block away. Need to talk to you first."

Matt squeezed in between two cars, a few feet away from a fire hydrant the store insignia still in view. "What's going on?"

"For the last few hours, ever since I left the hospital, I've been thinking about what Ken said: how the maniac might dig a hole and bury himself in it until we lose track of him completely."

"So? With what Emma just told you. Doesn't matter anymore."

"Exactly. My gut tells me we should let the bastard know we're on to him. Screw the performance. Let's just nail him. What do you think?"

"That's the way to go."

"The only person I'm worried about is Emma. She's clueless when she wears her pendant. The creep ever sneaks up on her one day without any of us being the wiser I have no idea what she'd be able to do."

"Why not just play it by ear?"

Hank opened the car door and took a deep breath wishing he could pull on something to get out instead of using his neck muscles. With a grimace, he began walking toward Con-Air, Matt right behind him.

"Excuse me, Miss. My partner and I are here to talk to Mr. Boleslaw. Is he here?"

As the receptionist readied an answer, Hank spotted Boleslaw walking out of one of the offices into the showroom. Working hard to keep revulsion from stamping his features, Hank added, "Never mind. I see him."

"Mr. Boleslaw," he called out. "I'd like a few words." As Hank neared, he flashed his badge.

The man stared at him with such a blank expression Hank wondered if the man in cotton overalls was the creep they were seeking. "Of course," the man said.

When he surveyed Boleslaw's eyes narrow, and took into account the wicked smile, the hawkish tone, recognition seized Hank. "What can I do for you, Officer?"

"Detective Apple." *As if you don't already know*. "Matt Logan, my partner."

"Is this going to take long? I have appointments to get to."

"A few questions."

"Sure." Boleslaw walked toward where he'd come from, Hank thinking he expected them to follow. On his way to his office, Hank caught Matt casing the place. Racks of wall-mounted air conditioning machines hung on the display racks, along with parts of ventilation equipment. Brand name compressors were presented in a living-like environment, smartly furnished. Matt whistled to show the size of the operation impressed him.

Once inside the office, Hank closed the door. "We'd like a little information on the young man you reported stalking a house we were surveilling."

He smiled—a knowing little smirk. "This was a while ago. Why the sudden curiosity?"

"We're trying to find neighborhood punks responsible for a rash of thefts. We thought he might be one of them."

"I told police. I spotted a kid on a bike casing a house some of your officers had just left, so I called it in."

"Did you take a closer look, approach him? Try to follow him?" Hank asked.

"I may have yelled at him. No way was I going to catch him. He was on a bike."

"Well, should you think of anything else, here is my card." Hank slipped him his business card, and as he did, he was careful to allow the little chain Emma had given him to fall on the floor.

"You dropped your jewelry," Boleslaw said with a mocking tone as he reached to pick it up. He lost his smile when he examined the little locket Hank had deliberately left open.

"Anything wrong?" Hank asked when Boleslaw's frown indicated surprise to find the locket.

"No." He shrugged as he handed Hank the chain. "You have weird taste in jewelry," he enunciated slowly his eyes not leaving Hank's face.

Hank remembered those eyes, the ones who had stared at him, laughed at him the day before. The eyes who'd snickered at Franka's blows.

He pretended not to notice the subtle meaning of crossed swords Boleslaw imparted, not prepared to come right out and accuse him just yet. He chuckled instead. "It's not mine. Part of the heists I mentioned. Chain was recovered from the stash of a kid we arrested. Just west of here, near Joralemon Street? Hank dropped the chain back in his pocket.

"Yeah," Matt chimed in. "Ring of thieves is getting bigger and bolder. One punk tried to steal a poor woman's wallet a couple of days ago in Soho. Broad daylight. Shot a couple of people. Created quite a raucous."

Boleslaw rubbed his forehead vigorously. "I got to go. You fellas can find your way out."

"By the way, are you the owner?" Matt asked. Boleslaw gave him a crooked smile. "Yea. I'm the owner." He ran out of the store barely slowing to salute the woman behind the counter.

Outside on the sidewalk, Matt watched the truck pull out and barrel down the street. "Man, I came within inches of punching him in the face," Matt said.

Did you check his reaction when he picked up the chain?" Hank kept pumping both his hands into fists. Rage consumed him.

"Yeah. I caught that. Come on. I'll drop you off at the hospital."

Before getting into the passenger seat, Hank asked. "By the way, where's my car? I lost track of it yesterday when they shipped me off in the EMS."

"A police officer drove it to the precinct. Want me to wait while you have your bandage changed and take you back?"

"No. I'll grab a cab to the office. Pick it up there."

"What do I tell Ken about this chain?"

"Tell him we went to talk to Boleslaw. Went to his house, walked around and found the chain on the ground, out in his yard."

"He'll say finding an object outside is not incriminating. Anyone could have planted it there." Matt hesitated, then mentioned, "Here's where using Emma's testimony would come in handy, my man."

"Don't even go there, Matt."

"I'll think of something. After all, there are probably more of these in the house."

"I'm sure there are. Let me know what you tell Ken, and I'll corroborate whatever you say when I get there later," Hank said.

"We might enlist Meredith Ripley's help—to put pressure on the DA. Once she identifies this chain, I'm sure she'll be more than willing to do this," Matt suggested.

"I'd use Meredith as a last resort," Hank said. "No telling what her depressed husband might do. Liable to take a shotgun to someone."

<u>*Thirty-Eight*</u>

Hank Talks To Christina

At the hospital, Hank went to the emergency ward to get his wound checked, and his bandage changed. One of the nurses recognized him and pulled him aside. "No need to wait, Detective. I'll change your dressing."

"Thanks," he voiced tiredly. He followed the nurse down a Laurel green corridor to a room painted Russian Green. Hank knew the colors as he had asked, forced to stare at the dull dreariness of his four walls the night before.

She asked him to remove his sweater, and he stretched the collar over his head much wider than he needed to.

"Still that sore"? The nurse asked a frown marring her calm features.

"Let's just say the neck became more painful as the day wore on."

"Well, you weren't supposed to run around and chase bad guys today. Doctor had prescribed rest."

In other circumstances, Hank would have chuckled. Faced with the likes of a monster he hated as much as he feared, all he did was count down to six—six days left in Ken's ultimatum.

"I'll get the doctor," she said. Seems to be a little seepage around the stitches."

"Is that bad?"

"Normal. I merely want a medic's blessing."

***

An hour later, a prescription for antibiotics in his pocket, Hank took the elevators to pay a long overdue call.

He didn't have to knock. The door was open. Franka sat up in bed eating from the tray a nurse had just left.

"Hey, Franka. How are you doing?"

"Would love a little home cooking about now," she stated with a smile brushing away a tear. "I'm sorry, Hank. I heard how you got caught in the crossfire."

"Only a scratch. You were the brave one. No, no you were," Hank emphasized when she shook her head from side to side. "Most people would have caved in your situation." Hank smiled as he came closer to the bed. "I'm not surprised Emma is so fond of you."

She lowered her head to overcome shyness Hank figured, and she was still too close to tears to hold a conversation. "Of course, your captain, Ken I believe his name is, said the fact I didn't say anything most likely saved my life. He said he would have killed me for sure had I divulged Emma's whereabouts."

"Well, as it turned out he never had the time."

"Because you and Jimmy stepped in. I'm grateful."

"Mostly Jimmy. In fact, had it not been for Jimmy well, let's say my training taught me never to barge in uninvited in the middle of a hostage situation."

"Guess he was acting on instinct," Franka said looking down at her food.

"A lover's instinct. An instinct people say is all powerful. Good thing Jimmy did." He turned and walked toward the door. "I'll let you enjoy your meal. Someone mentioned they're letting you out tomorrow."

She nodded her smile broad and genuine. "Finally. I'll be staying with my mom and Emma for a while."

Hank hesitated. He didn't want to bring up the baby she'd lost. "Take care, Franka. Something tells me you and Jimmy will have a wonderful life."

"We're getting married this summer, and you're invited." She seemed to hesitate before she added, "You and Christina."

He winked and gave her a head salute.

***

On his way home, driving from the precinct, Hank encountered a lot of traffic. Dinner hour and traffic jammed the roadways, but he didn't notice, not with the same frustration he usually manifested. He'd discussed with Ken some drastic steps he intended to take with regards to his career, measures he was certain Christina would approve wholeheartedly.

Even so, no matter how much he attempted to instill order in his mind, replays of the masked man's eyes in yesterday's confrontation, and Boleslaw's bulging crazy eyes he'd encountered this afternoon spread chaos throughout his thoughts, the overlapping images making him woozy.

Stopped at a light, he realized he would have to be more present if he didn't want to create an accident. He also appreciated no new mask this man would wear would fool him anymore. Val had said it. No matter what the changes, people were unable to hide their eyes especially when they'd shown you the extent of vile emotions pouring out from them.

He also began to understand what Emma had to live through—although he suspected his throbbing premonitions measured a mere fraction of what she was made to bear.

The light had turned green, and the driver in the back sat on his horn. Hank jumped and yelled at him his eyes on the rear view mirror as though his anger could be better communicated.

Hank revved up to leave the corner, then slammed on the brakes causing the narrow miss of a collision with the motorist in the back who came out of his car cursing like a madman.

Hank lowered his arm from blocking his eyes. He thought he'd crushed Emma, unable to avoid her at the last minute. She stood in front of his car a little higher than street level, so he wondered if he was hallucinating or if she'd come looking for him again.

After he had heard her whisper an apology and a plea to talk to him, he scanned the area for a quick place to park. When the man approached his car looking for a fight, Hank lowered his window and showed him his badge.

"Sorry, I thought you'd hit the brakes as payback for the horn," the young man mumbled quickly walking back to his car.

Hank maneuvered to the right lane and putting the siren on the top of his vehicle he double parked momentarily the red cherry flashing on his roof. "Emma, is that you?"

Still outside his car as though affixed to the front bumper, she nodded. "Don't' worry. I'm still at my grandmother's house."

A couple of people crossed in front of Hank's car, and he observed them walking right through her.

Emma continued, "I worried about what the man might do, Hank. So I thought I'd keep an eye on him. He just got to his house, and he is rounding up other little chains and tokens lying around—putting them in a metal box."

"How many trinkets are we talking about?" Hank worried about the size of that metal box.

Emma seemed to hesitate. "More than three," she answered as though she understood why Hank was asking. Another hesitation. "A dozen—that I could make out, maybe more. Not all the items are jewelry. There is a little teddy, a yo-yo, a pack of gum, even spotted a key chain with a key on it."

Hank's sudden rise of blood pressure squeezed the wound at the back of his neck as though clamped in a pair of vice grips, and the pain threatened to have him heave. They had only found evidence of three murders.

He tried not to reason that Boleslaw had purchased the warehouse as far back as 2002. He couldn't wrap his mind around the horrible possibility. Plus, had there been more than three murders, they would have had more reports of missing children. "Any chance he saw you?"

Emma smiled. "No. I've learned how to project myself a little better."

"Thanks, Emma. Can you keep me informed?"

"I will."

"Please be careful. And please don't fall asleep without your amulet, sweetie." Hank removed the siren and prepared to pull out. "Oh, Emma, can you please find a way to give me a warning before you appear? Your unexpected presence could prove difficult now and then."

"I'll call out before I show myself next time, wait for your permission." She smiled and gave him a little wave. She was gone.

***

Twenty minutes later, in front of his building, Hank instinctively glanced at his window before taking the rear entrance to park in the underground garage. He did a double take spotting a vague shadow walking back and forth in his apartment. A second glance and the shadow disappeared.

In the elevator, he made sure his gun was cocked and ready. He wondered if crazy Boleslaw might be planning to ambush him. He'd called him by name. Chances were he knew where he lived. While unlocking his door, he remembered Emma's words that Boleslaw had just arrived home and was gathering the loot he'd stashed from his victims, probably with the intention of hiding any incriminating evidence. Little did the creep realize one of the little girls he failed to harm had her eye on him?

But the handle turned, and he didn't have to unlock the door. He entered cautiously as noise from the kitchen alerted him to an intruder. Cleaning person didn't come on Fridays. "Hello? Who's there?"

"Me." Christina laughed. She entered the living room and froze. "Guess I should have warned you," she added eyeing the gun he'd pulled. "I thought I'd surprise you not the other way around."

Hank holstered his weapon and smiled. "Not a good idea to

surprise a detective investigating a maniac. The crazy bastard who knows who I am and wants my head as a trophy."

"Sorry, Hank." She walked toward him and stopped a few inches away as though gauging his mood.

"Hey," he added scooping her up in his arms. "This is a great surprise." He kissed her slowly and deliberately.

"Oh," Christina moaned. "Keep this up and I'll send you to your room without dinner."

Hank smiled and kissed her on the temple. "How'd you get in?"

"Your doorman recognized me and said you wouldn't mind."

He smiled and walked toward the room to remove his gun and jacket—to hide and regroup. About to rub his neck, he stopped just in time. Suddenly, he felt uncomfortable ridiculously shy for no reason at all—well, for no reason he was fond of admitting to Christina.

"Hank, are you all right? If this is about me barging in without permission. I can take a hint. You can tell me. No need for the cold shoulder."

Hank cringed when Christina said those words. He came to her as she stood in the doorway seemingly unwilling to come into the room. He encircled her waist leading her to the living room. "I did that to you too many times—the cold shoulder."

He put up a hand to prevent an argument. He had a boulder the size of the Grand Canyon to get rid of, and he'd barely summed up the courage to recognize the void let alone remove the damn thing. "I'd get so angry when you wouldn't understand my job commitments. I remember thinking how selfish you were not getting any of my ambitions or how precious my time was."

"Hank, don't you think these old wounds should remain in the past?"

"That's just it. For me those wounds are still there, bigger than life—at least they were."

"I'm sorry I can't go back in time and make them disappear."

"There's nothing you need to do, Christina." He turned to face her spanning her waist with both hands. "You're not responsible for my self-inflicted wounds."

He urged her to sit on the settee with him. "I lay in the hospital thinking I'd been a hell of a coward while we lived together, a stupid, ignorant coward. No fault of yours." He toyed with her fingers. "I'm not sure why at some point we start to believe that what we become is more important than who we are. All my life I was told to focus, work hard, and make sacrifices to become the best at whatever I was aiming to do."

A long sigh escaped him, and he was grateful she listened wholeheartedly. "My mother spent her life commending my father for his bravery." He nodded. "Brave she would say, for being a conscientious, untiring worker. He managed to put a roof over our heads and food on the table. Don't ask me how this translates to me becoming the best detective there is. It's not about the money or even about earning a living. Somewhere along the way, I forgot how to be brave."

"You're one of the most courageous persons I've met," she said in a small voice while sleeking back his hair.

"Not brave. Audacity, I have. Yes. I would say my bravery is much more bravado." He smiled. "I'm talking about the courage we need to lead a simple life, recognize the precious moments that bless our existence every day—bravery to be present—in the here and now which I usually don't even grace with a thought." He stroked her cheek. "A loved one's smile, a gentle presence, so quickly dismissed. He caught her trembling sigh as she nestled in the crook of his arm. "I've made a decision. Rather, I want to run my idea by you first."

She pushed away so she could stare into his eyes.

"I'm going to take Ken up on his offer." He couldn't help notice the shock in her round eyes and little frown lines on her brow.

"Hank!" Christina whispered.

Confounded, Hank couldn't help thinking her exclamation sounded more like reproach than relief. "I thought you'd be pleased," he told her his tone slightly deflated.

"I am, but only if you're taking the position because this is something you want to do, not if you're making this move strictly for me. Hank, you'd only end up resenting me."

Hank ran his thumb and index finger over his eyes drumming up the courage to admit what truly troubled him. He twisted to face her, his knee touching her thigh, and he grabbed both her hands without having the courage to look her in the eye. He focused on the window to his right. "When the creep hit me, I couldn't see, heard nothing but a lousy buzzing in my ears. All I could think— hope was to get back to you."

Christina twisted his face to stare into his eyes. "You were scared. It's normal."

He nodded slowly. "Scared, more like terrified I'd never see you—be with you again. During the time I applied pressure on Jimmy's wound, crazy thoughts emerged. The years we lived together how I mistreated you and my goddamn stupid pride. I prayed to have a second chance promised I'd do a lot better this time."

He felt her wipe a tear rolling down his cheek. "I love you, Christina. I don't want to go chasing bad guys anymore. I want to be with you, have a family with you."

"Hum," he moaned when Christina knocked the wind out of him by wrapping her arms tightly around his torso and squeezing as hard as she could. Any doubts he had about her excitement with his plan melted away when he caught her whisper against his chest. "Love you so much, Hank."

He didn't know how long their embrace lasted, but he kissed the top of her head as he rubbed her back to calm her shivers. "I took my cue from Emma. Goes about the business of helping everyone around her, staying focused on Amelia's next visit, Tommy's next phone call. She remains anchored in the present more conscious about who she is than who she will become. Even Matt, sweet yet cynical Matt is bowled over by her courage."

Christina sat up gazing into Hank's eyes. "She is special. I love her, plain and simple. Oh, and speaking of Matt, he called earlier maybe ten minutes before you got here. Wanted to remind you. Tomorrow is Val's funeral."

"You going?" Hank asked flicking the tip of her nose.

"Of course. The Willis' are planning to go too."

"I'm not sure it's a good idea—Emma in a public place."

"I think she'll be all right. Can we go together?"

"You bet."

Hank bent and kissed her hard and long. "Want to skip dinner?" he whispered.

"I made your favorite—lasagna with meatballs."

"Hum. You know how I love my lasagna, right?"

"Reheated?" She laughed rising and leading him by the hand toward the bedroom.

Instinctively he patted the bandage at the back of his neck.

"Don't worry," Christina told him unbuttoning his shirt. "Leave everything to me," she told him sensuously. "And," she added unbuckling his belt, "Hospital supplied me with extra bandages should the need arise for me to play nurse."

He grabbed her hands and groaned as he nestled her against him. "Love you so much."

Thirty-Nine

I Can See You

*E*mma sat in bed, in the throes of battling sleep. With drooping eyelids, she eyed the amulet on her night table about to grab the pendant should she lose the tug of war Morpheus waged on her. Mercilessly his imagery slowly drained her will to stay awake.

She'd promised Hank she would keep an eye on the vile man. Only Amelia had arrived around dinner time, and the two had spent the evening chatting and playing computer games.

The little clock on her desk had just hit midnight, and the guilt of breaking her promise to Hank had her rise. She would walk to shake off this overwhelming need to sleep.

She paused in front of the window and stared at the grounds below. They brimmed with color during the daytime and the beautiful landscape never failed to entice her to enjoy the many activities. Now the pool, the tennis area, the garden paths and picnic tables were merely different shades of gray under the moonlight.

Emma leaned against the French doors to the patio and closed her eyes to project only an essence of herself, one that would not alert Boleslaw to her presence. She spotted him opening his garage door and furtively searching the area to make sure no one spotted him.

His truck's motor was idling, and he carried under his arm the metal box she'd seen him handle. He did not wear a disguise, so she figured he was headed somewhere to bury this box. She needed to alert Hank and let him know what the man prepared to do.

She concentrated on Hank while mouthing the little phrase, and sensing she neared him she called out to respect her promise. "Hank, Hank."

She had to do so several times before she got an answer while she anxiously kept an eye on the door to the adjoining room.

"Emma?" Hank sat up in bed and rubbed his face with both hands to remove the impression he was still dreaming. "Emma, is that you?"

"Yes. I can't speak any louder. Amelia is in the next room."

"What's going on?"

"Hank?" Christina asked in a sleepy voice. "Are you all right?"

"Yes. I'm talking to Emma."

"He's leaving with the box. He's going to dump the contents somewhere. Then we'll never be able to find the proof we need."

"Can you follow him without being seen?"

"I can, but I have to go now. I will give you directions later."

Still not sure he hadn't been dreaming Hank got up quickly while the painful reminder of the wound in the back of his head finished rousting him from sleep.

He slipped on a pair of pants, and a sweater over his head with a little more caution.

"Where are you going? It's past midnight."

"Call Matt, sweetheart. You'll probably have to ring him a couple of times before he picks up." He grabbed a pen and paper.

"But where are you going?"

"Boleslaw is on the move. He's trying to hide the evidence he dumped into a strongbox." Hank holstered his gun and checked he had enough bullets around his belt.

"Hank, you can't go out without backup. The man is crazy."

"This is why you're going to call Matt. Here's his cell number." He handed her the piece of paper as he kissed her lips.

"How will he know where you are?"

"Tell him to call my cell and I will give him directions," Hank shouted his last words from the front door. Every second counted.

Racing toward Belleville, Hank figured this had to be the craziest ride he had ever experienced. He found himself speeding through the streets unsure of where he needed to go. He had no idea when more instructions would arrive from Emma—an out of body expert who possessed more talent for getting to the truth and catching the bad guy than did all those working their tail off at the Second precinct—hell probably able to best all detectives in Newark.

Those acquainted with her gifts went through hell and high water to protect her as though she might be carved of glass. The comparison made him chuckle. He realized he needed coffee, a strong one. He had left in a hurry, and his brain still ran dream-like scenarios in his mind.

About to take Boleslaw's street, he swung first in an all-night drive-through to get coffee to go. He figured Emma had to give him directions from the man's house, and he hoped she would do so soon.

He grabbed the coffee from the teller, but the cup had no lid. "Can I have a lid please?" The boy practically threw the plastic top in his car, and he had a mind to step out and teach him an etiquette lesson.

As he was trying to secure the lid on the cup, his phone rang, and he jumped, spilling coffee on his trousers. He quickly yanked the pant leg away from his skin to avoid the burn. Bad wardrobe month!

"Hank," he yelled in his Bluetooth. "Where are you and what's this all about?"

"Emma contacted me. She spotted Boleslaw in his house gathering all the keepsakes he fleeced from his victims into a strongbox. He has now left the house and is preparing to dump them somewhere. She's been following him from a distance."

"Geez, all mighty. Wait a minute. What do you mean all the keepsakes?"

"Enough to fill a metal box," he added while blotting the stain on his pants with a tissue. "Emma lost track of how many. Let's just say, more than three."

"Son of a bitch."

Hank took a satisfying gulp of his coffee and sat the cup in the coaster.

"Hank, I'm here." He caught Emma's soft voice.

"Wow!" He overheard Matt enthuse in the background. "We've finally got a plan. And I think this is a bloody good idea. We'll catch him with his hand in the till.

Grateful to hear Emma's voice he listened while ignoring Matt for the moment.

"Go to the end of his street, to the corner where you picked me up and turn left. Then three streets later, there's a gas station on the corner, turn right and keep going until you come to a fenced park. It's more a grassy abandoned lot full of weeds and skinny trees than a park. He's on the farthest side along the outskirts of a clump of bushes."

"Got you, Emma." Hank repeated the instructions to Matt also giving him Boleslaw's address.

"Hank, I'm still twenty minutes away. Don't do anything stupid. Wait for me when you get there."

"Hurry, Hank," Emma added. "He's already started to dig. Once he leaves the park, you might not be able to have people believe the box belongs to him."

"I understand, Emma." *Bright girl. Catches on fast.* He closed his cell wanting to drown out Matt's cautious reminders nagging him in the background.

He stepped on the gas and barreled down to the location Emma had given him. At this late hour, streets held little traffic and no pedestrians. In fact, he paid no attention to signals merely watching out for other vehicles.

Emma worried the man might finish before Hank arrived. She thought perhaps if she talked to him she might be able to slow him down. Emma eyed his ponytail dangling down his back, the aquiline profile of his nose and somehow, even though she knew he was the murderer she feared, in this shape and clothing, he didn't scare her as much as his masked counterpart did. The wayward thought of a wolf in sheep's clothing crossed her mind as she gathered all the courage she could muster.

"I can see you." Emma told him to get his attention.

He raised his head and leaned on his shovel while he searched the area trying to catch whatever surprise might be lurking in the dark. He gave up and began digging again.

Emma worked hard to concentrate and make herself visible. "I can see you." She spoke in a louder voice. "I know you're digging to hide all the tokens you stole from those poor little girls."

This time, he turned and stared right at her with a wicked smile. "Oh, the big bad witch returns." He took a swing at her with the shovel. "Here only in her evil spirit."

"I am not evil. And neither are you."

"How dare you talk about me? You don't know me."

"I was there this afternoon when you tied your costume to a hook and began beating on it with a stick until it fell to the ground. You did this once before too, in your warehouse."

"You wretched, stinking witch. I forbid you to spy on me. Forbid it," Boleslaw yelled. His tone sounded mean and deliberately brittle. She suspected this was not his real voice.

"You hate what you've become. You can get help. It's not too late. This person is not who you are, who you were meant to be."

"Shut up, you prissy little sissy. Why can't you be more like your brothers?"

Emma saw him grab his head and fall to his knees, moaning and unable to dig or do anything else. Then she spotted a car pull up. She figured this was Hank, so she remained available but invisible not wanting to create any security risk for him.

Hank had caught Boleslaw's screams echo in the calm night air while he searched for the best place to park. He proceeded cautiously to where the sound had come from, gun in hand and trying to avoid snapping any of the fallen tree branches in his path.

The spot by the bushes Emma had mentioned was empty. He worried Boleslaw might have left already, but as he approached he spotted a shovel upright and planted in the ground as though his digging had been interrupted.

He swiveled to get a better view of his surroundings and came face to face with the man he was seeking. He also had a gun cocked and ready.

"I might have known." Boleslaw chuckled. "Where there's a wuss, there's Hank Apple not far behind which means you're an even bigger wuss. You don't scare me, tough guy. And, unless you drop your gun immediately, I will shoot you where you stand."

Hank had witnessed the pleasure Boleslaw derived from shooting Jimmy. He would without a doubt take the same pleasure killing him if he didn't comply.

He bent and dropped the gun on the ground.

"Good. Now, go to the shovel and start digging—move," he yelled when Hank took his time to do so.

Grabbing the shovel, Hank wondered about the odds of throwing the damn thing at the creep and knocking him out. But Boleslaw kept his distance. He'd picked up Hank's gun to throw the weapon in the bushes.

As Hank began to dig, Boleslaw started to laugh. "Ain't life grand? As always, the law of the jungle prevails. The strong ones survive. The weak and fragile wusses get their heads bashed in, their nose broken, their whole body tortured until they get confused." He laughed. "Until they're assigned to dig their own grave."

"Is that how it was growing up? With an abusive father and two older brothers?"

"You're never going to find out, are you? Of course, we're going to have to make this hole a little bigger than I'd planned. Got to bury you somewhere."

Digging with a square shovel while trying to get through solid, hard earth caused Hank enormous pain. He worried about his wound splitting open and him bleeding again.

The sound of a gunshot made Hank drop to the ground.

He got up and checked his arms, his legs. He appeared fine. "What's the big idea?" Then he spotted Emma standing between them in spirit only. Boleslaw had tried to shoot her, and the bullet had gone through her and barely missed him.

In the still of the night he overheard Emma's whispers, something about 'Heaven's eye to life beyond,' he couldn't make out all the words. Magically, the gun flew from Boleslaw's hand to his. Instinct made him grab onto it and point the weapon at Boleslaw to keep him from running.

Only Boleslaw wasn't going anywhere. He stood his ground, stunned and staring at his hand no doubt wondering—no less than Hank did—how Emma had accomplished this.

Emma was gone.

Boleslaw yelled at the top of his lungs the way a wounded wolf might howl. "I will not be defeated," he vociferated as loud as he could. He pulled out a small gun from his sleeve. "Thought you had me beaten, didn't you?"

"Don't be a fool, Boleslaw. My bullet can do much more damage."

"I got this little beauty in Germany. Weapon looks like a kid's toy. Fits in my hand, but at close range as my loving brother found out you can aim for the heart and kill a man in seconds."

"What happened to your other brother?"

He shrugged. "Who knows? Never did find the chicken shit. The beauty of this situation," he continued as though Hank's comments were unimportant. "I will shoot you down like a dog, whereas you will not. Duty demands you bring me in alive, right?" He laughed and laughed, and another shot echoed through the park.

Boleslaw looked down at the blood trickling out of his chest and lost the smile. "It's over." Hank caught his whisper. "Finally over," he added before he slumped to the ground.

Looking at Matt walking out of the shadows, Hank asked him. "What made you do this?"

"Man had a gun pointed at you, and unlike you, he was about to use it. Easy math—beating him to the punch."

Hank walked over to Boleslaw and bent down to take his pulse. "He's gone. So much we didn't know about him."

"Does it matter? He lived in pain, and knowing why or how won't bring back those little girls."

"You're right. Still, studying the man might have made us understand more about abuse, one more glimpse into how or why this sort of violence happens in the first place. Many books are written on the subject, yet we have uncovered little."

"I'm with ya. Obviously, when the family abused this little boy, they were signing death sentences for many others."

"I'll call Ken, ask him what he wants us to do." Hank walked over to the box Boleslaw had been trying to bury. "Let's not forget this. Especially that we'll have to try and match the belongings to the missing children."

Matt took the box from him. "Good luck with that." He couldn't resist opening the metal container. "Jerk didn't even lock this." Without touching anything, Matt scanned the content. "We only found three little girls. The haul demonstrates we need to add a lot more victims to the tally." Matt took a pen out of his pocket to pick at something in the box. "Where's your keychain?" he asked Hank.

Hank unhooked the chain from the side of his belt. "What do you want with it?"

"The little flashlight you have attached." Matt darted the light on something he spotted. "This is a subway token. Trying to read the date on this."

Hold the light still. I'll manage," Hank said. "Smudged, but I can read, Metro Green Line Mariposa. Valid all day, $5.00. Date reads, Sat, Jul 18, 09. Could be June. I'm not sure."

Hank and Matt stared at each other, and Hank read recognition on Matt's expression. "What?"

"Maria's family is from Modesto, California. Mariposa is a little town some sixty miles east."

"Your Maria, the Maria you just dumped?"

Matt nodded.

"There might be pieces here from across the country which means the man traveled." Hank padded the injury at the back of his neck to make sure he wasn't bleeding.

"Why do I feel putting this puzzle together will be the worst?" Matt shook his head defeat on his expression.

"Dredging up the pain again for so many people. Let's hope finding the killer brings the victims' families a little closure."

"Any idea on how we're going to do this?" Matt asked. Hank realized his partner had become too overwhelmed to think straight.

"We'll have to coordinate our efforts with The National Center for Missing Children—the only way we'll ever be able to match all these trinkets."

Hank vacillated a little, hooking the keychain back to his belt. Uncertain of the main reason he felt woozy, he took a moment to get his bearings.

"About now, you've got to be feeling like shit, man." Matt dropped the box and held on to Hank's arm.

"I've been better."

"Get some rest, Hank. "I'll call Ken. And now that the worst is over, take the bloody painkillers and time off."

"You need me here for anything?" Hank knew what a big softy Matt could be. Plus, he'd just shot a man, an action that happened to be a painful occurrence for him.

Matt squeezed his shoulder. "I'm good. Are you okay to drive?"

"Don't worry. Won't be driving back at the same speed."

Hank walked away but gave Matt one last hand wave. "By the way, thanks for stepping in when you did. Right call to make."

Forty

Rest In Peace

On his way up the elevator to his apartment, Hank looked forward to collapsing into bed. However, Christina was up taking a sip from a coffee mug. She sat in the corner staring down at the street and biting her nails, something he hadn't seen her do in a long time, and she never heard him coming through the door.

"What are you still doing up?"

"Hank!" She ran to him and wrapped her arms around him. "I was so worried about you taking on that madman."

He hugged her as he would a lifeline, and they spent most of the night talking about abuse, lost children, inattentive parents while Christina mourned the death of a man who'd never had the chance at a normal life. Of course, they discussed how bright their future was bound to become.

***

Next day mid afternoon, Hank rushed to the church to honor Val, a dear departed colleague. Christina had left without him, most likely tiptoeing through the room not to make noise so he might get an hour more of sleep.

The grounds were packed with cars when Hank got to the church. He found many vehicles double-parked although police officers would not likely disturb anyone with tickets today. Attended by colleagues, family, people whose lives Val had touched, all wanted to express their gratitude and say goodbye. He complimented his choice of taking a cab. "Right here is fine," Hank told the driver.

"Quite a gathering," the cabbie said. "Celebrity or something?"

Hank took out money to pay the man. "Guess you can say that."

The Grand Basilica in Brooklyn Heights had most likely not seen as many people at one sitting in a long time. He climbed the stone steps and smiled at passersby pointing at the crowds overflowing from the church's doors and taking a guess at which famous person they were burying today.

News vibrated with the huge catch Newark detectives had scored.

"The deep, dark threat overshadowing Newark has lifted." Ken had expressed his gratitude to the media a few hours ago while highlights of his press conference, as well as the pride in his department, were broadcasted every half hour. Televised information was all over the Internet already. "Thanks to our informant, Valenciana Mezzo a police profiler and psychic clairvoyant, two of our finest detectives, Hank Apple and Matthew Logan, who worked tirelessly and at the peril of their lives, have apprehended a dangerous child killer last night. Parents, as well as childcare givers all over New Jersey, can breathe again."

He'd also taken the opportunity to mourn Val's death which

most likely had something to do with the number of people at this afternoon's funeral.

In the same breath, Ken had wasted no time announcing his retirement along with Hank's new promotion. He sure wasn't giving Hank any time to change his mind. Hank had mentioned this to Ken the day before, a mere hour before going home.

Soon, Matt would demand an explanation, and he wasn't looking forward to more arguments on the subject. Of course, Matt would suspect the reason behind his decision was that he, at last, wanted a life. Matt would hate having to break in a new partner.

Casket sprays of red roses and easels of white chrysanthemums filled every corner inside the impressive Cathedral, the colorful displays no rival for celestial hues from stained glass rosettes as their color busted inward, crawling and dancing all over the congregation.

The sweet scent of innumerable bouquets overtook Hank's senses as he entered the nave unnoticed by the throng of people goose necking to catch a glimpse of the altar decked in its finest.

Hank prodded his way gently through rows of onlookers flashing his badge to the officers who kept late arrivals at bay. He proceeded down the aisle as rows upon rows of pews unfolded before him making him wonder where Christina sat.

Emma stood between her parents holding each one by the hand as the whole congregation rose to the entrance of officiating priests signaling the beginning of mass. Surrounded by all the people she loved, Emma murmured a prayer of gratitude for the blessings she'd received. The amulet dangling around her neck provided the tranquility and peace she needed to recover from the hardships she'd encountered.

She stared at her grandmother standing tall in her new heels beside her aunt Franka who smiled at Jimmy as he delicately draped his arm around her waist. Tommy in the pew across from hers sat slumped beside his dad and shook his head now and then to remove the tuff of hair falling in his eyes. Amelia and her twin sister, sandwiched by their mother and father, gazed wide-eyed at the intricacies of the altar never having attended this grand old church.

Of course, Christina Tyler in the pew right in front of her, the kind soul of her teacher forevermore entwined with hers, figured prominently amongst her loved ones. After all, she'd become the angel who had helped her come out of her shell and find the courage to admit to her parents the dilemma she'd been made to bear.

As mourners sat down, Emma spotted an empty seat beside Christina—where was Hank? These few front rows were reserved for them with their names on little cards posted at the ends of the rows. She spotted Matt, Captain Ken she'd just met, and Cindy she already knew. But where was Hank?

Letting go of her parents' hands she reached for her prayer book and delicately removed the amulet she dropped in the middle of the little prayer book's pages. Emma then closed her eyes. She searched for him.

She found Hank tiptoeing up one of the aisles as he scanned the area for a familiar face.

She whispered his name to warn him she was nearby. When she caught him nodding, she showed herself. Emma smiled as she spotted him taking a few steps back still unaccustomed to seeing her pop up out of thin air.

"Hank, Christina is in the third seat from the front, middle aisle next to Cindy and Captain Ken."

Hank smiled and thanked her. She could sense how relieved he was Boleslaw was out of her life for good. Hank Apple was another kind soul she would be eternally grateful to call a friend.

She eyed Hank as he made his way inside the pew excusing his intrusion while he straddled the kneelers to reach Christina's side. They gazed into each other's eyes, and Emma caught the love free flowing between them as Christina latched onto Hank's hand.

Other sounds soon filtered to Emma, some more urgent than others and gratefully, none of them from Boleslaw. Biting her corner lip, she hurried to replace the pendant around her neck. There existed a method of creating an island of silence around her without the use of the oudjat. She'd read about such a passage in one chapter of her grandmother's diary. Only, she had not yet mastered the technique. Someday she would.

As the priest called on the congregation to pray, Emma thought of all the people she loved, of Val who had so bravely taken upon herself to fill in where she could not. She prayed for the victims who had suffered and fallen at the hands of a sick man so that they may find peace. Lastly, Emma murmured a fervent plea for Maurice Boleslaw, for the young child who had lived through an onslaught of abuse so terrible, he had found it necessary to inflict his pain on others. Wherever he was, she asked the Heavens to provide him with the love he needed to heal.

If you enjoyed this book, please be so kind as to provide a review, Reviews are most important to authors and they appreciate the time you, the reader, will take to do this.

Other books by the same author:

Mirror Deep, a Romantic Suspense
Exhale and Reboot, A Novel, a Suspense Mystery
Ava Moss a Romantic Cozy Mystery coming out soon.
And Emma Willis Book II (I Can Find You) to follow.

To reach Joss Landry, simply google her name and you will be In touch with all her social information.

Keep in touch with Emma Willis. She will be available come March 2017 for another adventure. At fifteen years old, Emma encounters new friends, frays with old ones and discovers the world is bigger than the planet displays ...

Au revoir!